DANA LECHEMINANT

Crossing THE BROOKLYN Briggs

a sweet romantic comedy

Author's Note

The Love in Sun City series can be read in any order, as standalones or together. Writing this series has been such a fun experience for me because the four stories all overlap and share scenes over the course of a month. Not only did I get to discover the stories, but I also got to discover them *at the same time.* It was a cool experiment to see how this type of project would work, and hopefully it gets you excited for the other stories as you read this one. I've added dates to each book to help you keep track of shared events, if you so desire. :)

Enjoy your time with the Briggs siblings as they simultaneously (and quickly) fall madly in love!

– Dana

Chapter One

Brooklyn

October 10

THERE'S SOMETHING ABOUT GRADING tests that is just so peaceful. At least, that's what I tell myself, but month after month I go through my students' work and wonder if I'm really that bad of a teacher or if they're somehow messing with me. As if failing a midterm is a great way to prank their teacher.

In the quiet after-school stillness of a Thursday afternoon, I hum along to the song playing on my phone—I can't remember the last time I was able to connect to the Bluetooth speaker I bought specifically for moments like this—and remind myself that three failed tests out of forty-eight isn't bad. I'm not an awful teacher. Most of my students are right where they should be. There's no need to panic.

"Hey, Briggs."

I scream, sending a few tests flying toward the door, and it takes me a second to recognize the figure looming in my doorway. "Mark! Hi. You scared me."

He chuckles, folding his arms as he leans against the frame of my office door and looks far too attractive for a high school math teacher. They're supposed to be old, balding, sporting walrus mustaches. (I kid you not I had three different math teachers growing up who looked nearly identical. I'm not making this up.) But no. Mark DeNiro is like a mix between Milo Thatch from the cartoon movie *Atlantis* and Matt Damon, wrapped up in stylish sweaters and cardigans that always make me a little itchy when I look at them. But he wears them well and often, even though the weather here in Sun City rarely warrants the need for a sweater.

"I'm easily spooked," I add when he still looks like he might laugh. I sound breathless—I *am* breathless—but not because he scared me. I'm over that already. No, I can't breathe right now because in the few years we've been working at Sky View High School together, he's never once been in my chemistry classroom. I would know, considering I've been drooling over this man throughout each of those years, simping like a fool for a man who has never given me the time of day and always has a woman on his arm. (That's what social media says, anyway.)

Okay, did I really just think the word *simp*? Gag me. I am way too old to be using student lingo, especially a word that will go out of style more quickly than it took me to learn it in the first place.

Let me start over. I have had a *crush* on Mark DeNiro since the first time he introduced himself in our weekly staff meeting. Mark DeNiro has never once acknowledged he knows my name.

Until today, apparently.

"So, Briggs," he says, bending down to pick up a couple of stray tests. He looks at one and chuckles, probably catching the terrible math my student used to get to the wrong answer. "I just heard you're up for STEM Teacher of the Year."

How does he know about that? I just got the email earlier today. Tucking some hair behind my ear, I hope I don't come across as completely flustered. "Oh. Yeah, it's pretty crazy. I don't know why anyone would nominate me." Not that I'm mad about it. Each school in the district nominates a teacher from the STEM division. The district chooses one of those nominees to send to the state level, and then the state chooses their official "STEM Teacher of the Year" and awards them with a grant or some other high-level prize, which varies from year to year. This year, the University of Sun City is giving the winner a summer fellowship in whichever field they choose.

I am *desperate* to win that fellowship.

Mark leans back against the doorframe, taking in my office with his hazel eyes. "I think you'd be a great candidate," he says eventually.

I laugh. I can't help it. Put me in an awkward situation, and I'm going to make it more awkward. And of course Mark frowns, probably regretting coming in here because I am the weirdest person he's ever met.

"Well, I need to head out," he says, his eyebrows pulled together as he backs up. "Good luck, Briggs."

"Thank." Did I seriously just say *thank*?

Mark chuckles. "May the best of us win."

Wait, what?

The instant he's gone, I scramble to turn on my computer and pull up the email Principal Cheng sent me this morning. I accidentally delete it at first, search Google to figure out how to bring back deleted emails, and then scan through the body again until I find the phrase 'one of our nominees.'

"Oh," I breathe, feeling the excitement leave my body along with my breath. I thought for sure I had a chance, but clearly it's not as much of a done deal as I thought. "That's okay, though. Right?" I cringe at my own sad attempt at positivity. I'll probably need my sister, Micah, to convince me that this isn't as lame as it feels.

Luckily for me, I don't have much time to wallow because it suddenly hits me: Mark DeNiro just spoke to me. *To me.* For pretty much the first time since the day I met him years ago.

And I was a total dunce.

I groan and drop my head onto my test-strewn desk. Apparently the years of conversations I've had with the man in my head were nothing like the real thing. He didn't grin at me and praise my intellect. He didn't brush hair from my face. He didn't even call me by the cute little nickname he gave me after he realized we both like combining brownies with cookie dough. No *Brookie* for me.

Nope. In real life, Mark looked at me like he made a mistake in coming all the way down the hall to tell me I would be a great candidate even though he's clearly going to beat me.

When I'm sure Mark has left his classroom for the day, I scurry to the biology lab next door and am so glad when I find Jaydin in her classroom. "Jay!"

She barely has time to hold out her arms before I'm in her lap, fake-sobbing as I mourn the days I might have been normal and cool. (Not sure they ever actually existed, but I'm good at pretending.)

"Okay, what's happened?"

"Mark just came into my room."

Her scream is almost as loud as mine was. "What? When? Just now? Tell me *everything*."

We spend the next ten minutes hashing out every detail of my pitiful conversation with Mark, from his words to his intonation to his body language (which, coincidentally, I am *terrible* at reading). Jaydin is good at peopling, unlike me, but I'm pretty sure she's struggling to find the positives in my interaction.

"Maybe he was just as nervous as you were," Jay says with a shrug.

"Ha! I don't think Mark DeNiro knows what nervous is," I grumble. "There's no way he would ever be intimidated by me." Which is why he's going to get the final nomination and I'm never going to get the chance to get back into research like I want to.

"He doesn't have to be intimidated to be nervous. Maybe he was scared because he's really into you!"

I love that she's trying, but Mark is always dating someone. If he was interested in me, he wouldn't be out dating everyone *except* me. Our school doesn't have any policies against coworkers dating, so the only reason he would have to not ask me out is because he is decidedly *not* interested.

As if she can read my thoughts, Jay shakes her head and points to my phone. "Look up his social," she says. "See the last time he posted a picture with a hottie."

Though I really don't like that she calls all of Mark's girlfriends *hotties*—I'm sure they have lovely names and personalities—I do as she suggests and pull up the app that I pretty much only keep for the purpose of stalking my coworker. I type in his name in the search bar and wait for it to pull up the all-too-familiar photos, but instead it shows my own feed with his name front and center.

"Cookies and cream!" I curse, fumbling to delete my post before anyone— "How does it already have three likes?"

Jay takes my phone from me with a roll of her eyes and taps away, hopefully saving me from complete humiliation. I wish I could say that wasn't the first time I confused the post box for the search bar. "How does someone so smart have such a hard time with technology?" she mumbles. Then her eyes go wide. "Brook, he's *single*."

"What?" I snatch my phone back and stare at the post that he put up only a couple of days ago.

Soloing once again. Let's hope life brings new opportunities.

"That doesn't mean he's single," I say, even if my heart has latched on to the idea.

Jay levels me with a look that even I can interpret. She's spent the last few years listening to me pine over this man, and she can't believe I'm not jumping at this rare chance when Mark is the kind of guy who has his next fling lined up right after he ends the current one. "Brooklyn Briggs, what else could that possibly mean? It's not like he sings at clubs on the weekends and just lost his duet partner."

"We don't know that."

"We really do. We would have heard about it. This man is nothing if not co...proud...of himself."

I know that isn't what she originally wanted to say, but I appreciate her attempt at being nice. She doesn't understand what I see in Mark, but she hasn't been watching him as closely as I have. (For the record, no one should do what I've done. I'm borderline stalkerish at this point. I'm not proud of it.) She doesn't see his subtly good qualities, like the way he wishes his students good morning as they come into class or the smiles he gets whenever he tells the other math teacher that his kids aced their tests.

"Okay, let's say, for the sake of argument, Mark is single." Jay straightens her glasses as she fixes her gaze on me. "Let's say he came into your classroom today because he's interested in you and wants to ask you out but is a bit nervous. What are you going to do about it?"

What am I going to do about it? That answer is easy. "Absolutely nothing."

She blinks, caught off guard by that response. "What?"

I stand by what I said, even if it makes me look pathetic. "I couldn't even talk to him, Jay. How am I supposed to do anything beyond that? I'm awful when it comes to dating and guys and things."

"So you say," she mutters.

"It's true!"

"You look like a Disney princess, Brook, and you've got a brain to rival Neil deGrasse Tyson. If you can't get a guy, what hope do the rest of us have?"

She's used that argument before, and I've learned not to refute her claims. (For the record, I am not that smart.) But I'm not like my brother,

Houston, who has overflowing confidence, or my half-sister, Micah, who sees the world through the prettiest rose-colored glasses. I spend my days trying to look cool in front of teenagers who think I'm ancient, and then I go home to my empty basement apartment and grade tests and lab procedures. Men aren't exactly dropping out of the sky to talk to me.

Jay grabs my hand. "Don't sabotage something that hasn't even happened yet. Pretend this is a game of chess. He's made his move, and now it's your turn. It doesn't have to be anything big; you're just starting the game."

Okay, chess is something I do understand. "What if I make a mistake and do something like a fool's mate?"

"I have no idea what that is, Brook." She shrugs. "Just...if you like the guy, take your chance while you've got it. This isn't rocket science."

"Unfortunately."

She groans. "Go home, Miss Briggs. Sleep on it. You'll know what to do in the morning. And luckily for you, no kids tomorrow!"

Thank goodness for teacher work days.

October 11

When I wake up the next morning, I know without opening my eyes that I'm not going to be functional today, let alone able to make any sort of moves in Mark's chess game. This migraine must have crept in during the night, and one small movement of my head sends my stomach churning. Yay. I won't be making it into school today, but at least I don't have kids to worry about. It just means my Saturday will be spent doing all the work I should be doing today.

Who really needs a weekend, anyway?

I send a text to Principal Cheng to let her know I won't make it in, all the while rejoicing in the fact that I don't have to figure out a sub. I can just go back to sleep and hopefully wake to a world that isn't blurred at the edges. It's not the worst migraine I've ever had, but it's definitely up there.

Several hours later, I can open my eyes without wanting to puke, which is a nice improvement. Though still a little dizzy, I slowly sit up and take a moment to decide if I can function enough to make some food. It's a bit iffy. I should at least drink some water, though, so I inch out of bed and shuffle to the kitchen as smoothly as I can, eyes pinched shut until I need to see in the cupboard. I don't like that I've had enough migraines that I'm able to walk around with my eyes closed, but unfortunately that's my reality.

Once I've had a little to drink, I shuffle back to my room and pause at the window to peek up at the painfully bright sky. One of these days I won't live in a basement, and I won't have to practically press myself against the window just to get a glimpse of the weather. I feel like a prisoner down here, begging for a peek at the sun even though it's only going to make the headache worse.

I don't know why I bother checking. This is Sun City, where it is always pleasant and rains twice a month to keep the desert somewhat green. The sky is blue as ever and taunting me because there's no way I'm going out into the blinding sunshine when I can barely stand to open my eyes enough to look in the first place.

A melodic whistle fills the air half a second before an entire human man drops into the window well from out of nowhere. I scream and stumble back. My foot catches on something, and I go crashing to the ground, my head hitting a bookcase on the way down.

Chapter Two

Brooklyn

I HATE VIVID DREAMS, especially ones where I end up in crisis. Like, who needs a dream where an attack is coming in from the window? Not me. No, thank you. I'll deal with my stress the normal way—eating cereal for every other meal and pretending I'll use the yoga mat sitting in the corner, all the while knowing I am too wound up to do yoga despite knowing full well that that is what yoga is designed to fix. It's a vicious cycle.

I groan, surprised by the way I can almost feel a lump forming on the back of my head. I've never been more grateful to wake up from a—

"You're awake!"

I sit straight up and promptly tip over sideways, but a hand grabs my arm. A huge hand. Warm. Callused. Skin dark and smooth against my pale shoulder.

"Easy," a gentle voice says. "Don't move too quickly."

Why am I staring at a hand when I need to be getting a good look at the man who apparently *isn't* from a dream and is likely going to murder me and hide my body in a field where no one but vultures will find me for days? I look up, squinting but ready to memorize his face so I can come back as a ghost and inspire a sketch artist to lead my family to my killer.

Okay, well, a murderer should not have a face like *that*.

He smiles, white teeth gleaming in the dimness of my bedroom. I don't know where to focus first—on his straight nose? Striking jawline? Warm brown eyes? There's something familiar about him, but I can't place what it is. Maybe he's been stalking the house for a while... My stomach rolls, and I swallow back the building nausea.

"Are you going to murder me?" I ask stupidly. A murderer wouldn't answer that question honestly!

He pulls his hand away, holding both up to show me he's unarmed. That only goes so far when strangling is a pretty common form of murder. "No killing for me today," he says. "Seriously, Brooklyn, are you okay?"

He knows my name! Does that make this premeditated? Where did I leave my phone? Maybe I can sneak a call to my brother Chad and he'll have one of his police buddies here in no time. Or I guess I could just call the police myself and save a step...

Clearing his throat, the man sits back on his knees and grimaces a little. "I feel so bad about scaring you, but I didn't expect you to be home."

"So, you were planning to burgle me before it turned into a robbery?"

He cocks his head. "Aren't those the same thing?"

"You can't rob a house. You can only rob a person." And why am I explaining this to a thief/murderer/creep who knows my name and my schedule? I am way too dizzy to be dealing with this right now.

"Seems like you didn't hit your head too hard," he mutters, and his fingers rise toward me before stopping as soon as I flinch. "I want to make sure you're not bleeding," he says, concern wrinkling the skin between his eyebrows. "May I?"

Absolutely not.

"Would you relax?" he says with a chuckle. "I'm not going to hurt you, Queens."

I freeze. Only one person in the world has ever called me Queens, and I was under the impression—happily so, I might add—that I would never see him again. Suddenly, all of the familiarity about him makes sense, though it in no way makes me feel better.

"Why are you in my house, Jordan?"

His mouth stretches into a wide grin, so similar to the one that seemed to haunt me for years before he finally melted into a distant memory. "You remember me?"

"Hard to forget someone as annoying as you," I grumble, closing my eyes against the light coming in through the window. "Answer the question."

"Houston asked me to take care of the yard, and I didn't mean to scare you. When you fell, I came through the window—it was un-locked, by the way—to make sure you didn't get seriously hurt."

There's no way any of that is true. I open my eyes again because the room starts swaying with them closed. "Houston doesn't own this house. My landlord does. You don't look like a landscaper anyway."

He's way too attractive. And clean. And attractive. Oh goodness, I did *not* just think about my nemesis being *attractive*.

Jordan smirks. "You think I'm attractive?"

Sweet peanut butter cup, did I say that out loud?

Chuckling, he points to the logo on his t-shirt, which says 'No Mow Problems' and has a picture of a man on a lawn chair next to a lawn mower. "I've got my truck and trailer outside, if you need more convincing, but I think my attractiveness speaks for itself."

I groan, partially because this is the most ridiculous conversation I've ever had but mostly because my head is pounding, both from my lingering migraine and from the fall. Plus, little aches and pains are starting to make an appearance now that I'm no longer freaking out. I probably should be freaking out still, but now that I know this isn't some strange dream, I'm more frustrated than anything.

"You came in through the window?" I ask, squinting at it. It's still partially open, though he had the decency to close it most of the way. "I'm not sure I believe you were really landscaping."

Jordan folds his arms. "Are you sure about that? Because I've been doing the yard for the last six months."

"I don't believe you."

"You're usually at school."

"Not during the summer."

"If I remember correctly, you sleep like the dead in the summer."

First of all, rude. I don't need him bringing up certain bad memories of being woken by a bucket of cold water splashing over my head. Second of all, he has no right to pretend he knows me. I haven't seen this guy since high school graduation, and a lot can change in ten years. I don't care if he's my twin brother's best friend because he was never *my* friend.

"Why would Houston be hiring landscapers for my house?" I ask, rubbing my temple.

Shaking his head, Jordan shifts his weight into a crouch rather than kneeling. He holds up his phone. "You can ask him yourself. I was about to call him before you woke up." Then he frowns. "Actually, no, that's a bad idea because he's going to kill me for letting you get hurt."

I scoff. "Letting me." As if he wasn't the whole cause. I grab his phone—I have no idea where mine is—and try several times to unlock it, with no success. Not sure why I thought that would work. I'm being dramatic, but I glare at Jordan as if it's his fault I don't know his passcode.

He lets out a deep sigh and uses his fingerprint to unlock it. "You sure you want to sign my death warrant?"

"Yup." I type in Houston's number and fumble for the speaker button right before the line connects.

"Harry's Pizza, how may I help you?"

Eyes going wide, I look down at the phone and realize I typed one of the numbers wrong. "Oh! Sorry! I called the wrong number." I hang up, glad that it's too dim in my room for Jordan to see just how red I turn, and type the number again, this time with a two in place of the three.

It nearly goes to Houston's voicemail before he answers. "Hey man, game's about to start. Can I call you back?"

I instantly breathe easier at the sound of my brother's voice, even though he's hard to hear with all the voices and music in the background. "Houston." I forgot he had a game today, which is stupid considering his baseball team is in the *World Series*. That should be hard to forget.

"Brook? Why do you have Jordan's phone?"

"Because I accidentally scared her and she hit her head," Jordan says before I can find some other, nonthreatening reason for him to be inside my basement apartment.

"What?!" There's some shuffling on the phone, and everything goes quiet. "What do you mean, she hit her head? Scared her how?"

"I'm fine," I say at the same time Jordan says, "She might have a concussion."

I look up with wide eyes. Is he serious? But Jordan is focused on the phone, as if Houston can see him from here even though he's all the way over in Oklahoma for the Series.

"Details," Houston growls.

"I was cleaning out the window well," Jordan says, his eyebrows pulling together. "I didn't realize she wasn't at work, and I scared the crap out of her." He glances at me, his lips twitching. "Not literally."

I consider smacking him, but since I'm a grown adult, that feels like an overreactive response. "I told you, I'm fine," I say right before my stomach twists and nearly makes me throw up. That feels a little concussiony. It feels different from my usual migraine nausea.

Jordan puts a hand on my shoulder to steady me. "I'll take her to urgent care," he says.

"No!" I say at the same time Houston grumbles, "Good luck with that."

Jordan glances between me and the phone.

"I can't afford emergency care," I mutter.

"I'll pay for it," Houston replies, though he knows as well as I do that my excuse isn't the real reason.

"I'm fine," I say again.

"Not if you have a concussion."

"Don't you have a game to play?"

"Jordan, will you stay with her over the weekend?"

Jordan and I both choke, me dropping the phone and him shooting up to his feet.

"That's definitely not happening, Hou," I snap.

"I have work to do," Jordan mumbles.

"It's that or I'm calling an ambulance to your place right now and you can deal with the paramedics," Houston says calmly.

He'll follow through with that threat too. My twin has always been overprotective, and it's gotten worse since he was drafted by the Sun City Red-tails and spends so much time traveling. It's like he forgets that I'm technically older than him—six whole minutes—and have been taking care of myself for most of my life. I love him, but he's a pain in my neck sometimes.

"I don't need a babysitter," I say and hop up to my feet as if to prove it. Unfortunately, the dull ache I've been ignoring in my ankle since waking up is no longer dull or an ache at all, and my foot gives out beneath me, sending me toppling into Jordan's arm with a cry.

Holy cannoli, he's strong. I guess a landscaper would be, but Jordan literally lifts most of my weight with one arm as he attempts to help me avoid standing on my apparently injured ankle.

"Brook? Are you okay?" Houston sounds a little desperate.

"Fine," I gasp, though tears are sprouting in my eyes from the pain.

"You don't sound fine. Jordan?"

"She must have sprained her ankle when she fell."

My brother groans, the sound filling the room. "Blondie, just go to the hospital."

This isn't helping the tear situation. Nor is the realization that one of my hands is pressed up against Jordan's stomach and he's got muscles for days. And my head is still pounding, but the thought of being anywhere near a hospital has me borderline hyperventilating.

Groaning again, Houston starts muttering something, and I can imagine him pacing wherever he is. "I really have to go, so if you're not going to go to a doctor, Brook, then Jordan is going to stay with you until Monday. This isn't a request."

Jordan tightens his hold on my waist, though he's too focused on the phone to notice the way my breath catches from his touch. "You know I've got jobs this weekend, Briggs."

"I also know you have a team who can handle it. I'll pull funding if you don't stay with her."

"That's low."

"I'm not kidding."

"I know."

"Brook, I know you don't like him, but let him help. I gotta go win this game really quick." Houston hangs up, leaving a heavy silence in my room as Jordan and I refuse to look at each other.

This is so Houston. Acting like he can order me around just because he's a famous pitcher or whatever. Except, he's never ordered me around, not really, and he technically didn't tell me to do anything. He told Jordan, who looks like he might throw up as he glares at his phone.

"You don't have to stay," I tell him, though I don't want him to move right now because I'll definitely fall over if he does.

He exhales sharply through his nose, shaking his head. "Pretty sure I do."

"What did Houston mean about funding?"

"He was my main investor when I started my landscaping company."

"You own it?"

Finally he moves, looking down at me with a smirk on his lips. "I'm not sure how I feel about your tone of surprise, Queens."

"That isn't what I—"

"I know. I'm kidding. Houston and I own it together, technically."

Huh. I knew Houston invested in our stepsister's bookstore last year, but I didn't know there were any other companies. He certainly has the money—my brother gets paid an obscene amount to pitch because he's, well, obscenely good at it—but I never took him for being business-minded.

"How's your foot?" Jordan asks.

We glance down in unison, and even in the dim light I can tell it's pretty swollen. A thick purple bruise has begun spreading across my skin. "Not great," I admit.

"Can I check your head?"

I nod, preparing to feel him touch the tender spot on the back of my head. What I was not prepared for is the gentle way his fingers move through my hair and make me want to curl up against him while he caresses my scalp.

It's been a hot minute since my last relationship, and clearly I am feeling a little touch-starved if even Jordan Torres makes me feel something. He was the bane of my existence once upon a time.

"You don't seem to be bleeding, so that's good." I'm not sure why Jordan keeps brushing his hands through my hair while he says this, but I don't really care. It feels so nice. "I do think you have a concussion, though. Do you feel dizzy? Nauseous? Confused?"

Very confused, but I don't think that's from hitting my head. "Can I sit down?" I ask instead of answering his questions.

I expect him to let go of me so I can hobble to my bed, but instead he scoops me up into his arms. "Bed or couch?"

"Um, bed?"

"Better make a confident decision unless you want me to pick you up again when you change your mind," he says with a wink.

I didn't think anyone could wink without it looking creepy, but Jordan manages it. Maybe it's because he's always been solidly attractive so he is able to cross the unfortunate line that separates cute from creepy, but I think it's more because something about him feels incredibly genuine. He's always been that way, and as much as I disliked him in high school, he's always been entirely himself. I used to be a bit jealous of him for that, which generally fueled my dislike.

The things that come easily for Jordan—interacting with people, mainly—have never come easily for me.

I realize I've been staring at him, so I clear my throat and nod toward the door. "Actually, the couch would be great."

"Couch it is."

As he gently places me on the couch out in the living room and then crouches down to be at my level, we seem to search each other for something, though I have no idea what I'm looking for. Maybe I just want to figure out why I woke up this morning with a migraine and now find myself with the most handsome babysitter I've ever had.

It's too bad he's also the guy who made my high school years a lot more difficult than they ever needed to be.

Chapter Three

Jordan

One thing I learned quickly about Houston Briggs: if he wants something, he gets it. It's not a bad thing most of the time—I don't think there's a bad bone in that man's body—but it causes problems for the rest of us when we can't say no to him.

And I really want to say no.

Nothing against Brooklyn—literally nothing—but spending my weekend in this basement apartment sounds like the acutest torture of all time. I don't even know if *acutest* is a word, but torture certainly is, and I don't think anything could be more accurate about this situation than that.

I know what Houston's doing. Yeah, he's worried about his sister, but he could have easily followed through with his threat and called an ambulance. I almost did that myself when she got knocked out, but she wasn't out very long. No, Houston's order to stay with Brooklyn has more to do with me than it does with his twin, and I want to punch him for it.

"You really don't have to stay," Brooklyn says once she's situated on the couch.

I grunt as I head into the kitchen to find some ice for her swollen ankle. That will probably bother her more than the concussion, though neither injury is great. "I really do," I argue. How many times are we going to go through this? Brooklyn is just as stubborn as her brother, so I don't think this will be the last time.

I search her horrifyingly bare cupboards quickly until I find a Ziploc bag, and then I load it up with ice.

"We can just tell him that you did," she suggests.

"Nope. I won't lie to my best friend." I pause when I say that, considering the million and a half things I haven't told him. I won't outright lie to him, but there's plenty I keep from him. Always have. For being my best friend since we were fourteen, you'd think he'd be the guy I tell everything to.

He still doesn't know the real reason I left California, and I don't know if I'll ever be brave enough to tell him.

"I didn't know you were back in Sun City," Brooklyn says. "When did you come back?"

I grab a bottle of ibuprofen from above the sink and a glass of water before heading back to the couch and sitting on the edge of the coffee table. I'm surprised she even noticed I was gone, though I guess she probably would have felt relieved when Houston and I went off to college in California and she stayed in New Mexico. I didn't make her life easy. "About a year ago."

"Why has Houston never said anything?"

I chuckle, handing over the bottle of meds and holding the glass within reach. "Probably because you hate me, Queens." Almost as much as she hates that nickname.

Brooklyn frowns. "I don't hate you." She says it so slowly that I'm not sure she believes herself. I know I don't.

Not when the last words she ever said to me were basically along those lines. It's not like I can blame her for disliking me. I wasn't exactly nice to her back in high school. I wasn't cruel either—one, it's not in my nature and two, Houston would have beaten me to a pulp—but emotions and I didn't get along. I had a lot of feelings back then, none of which I knew what to do with. Houston was as emotionally stunted as I was, so his sister often got the brunt of our misplaced bravado and overall stupidity.

And pranks. She was on the receiving end of so many pranks that it's a miracle she's trusting me now. In my defense, she dished them out just as vehemently, but that's not exactly a good basis for a friendship now that we're civil adults. I hope we can be friends now that there's a full decade between us and our younger selves.

Brooklyn slowly untwists the cap on the ibuprofen, taking her time and keeping her focus on the bottle. It gives me a chance to really look at her without getting glared at, something I will absolutely make the most of.

She looks so much like I remember her—the same blonde waves, the same soft blue eyes. She's like if someone took a warm spring day and put it into a person with a sprinkle of sugar and cream. Everything about her is warm and gentle. But she has absolutely grown up in the last decade, all of the changes subtle but significant when combined. She lost any last traces of baby fat, her cheekbones becoming more pronounced and her jawline growing sharp. Though she's in loose pajamas, she's clearly shifted in other ways, though I'm trying not to catalog those changes. Just holding her earlier—something I don't think she would have allowed if she hadn't been concussed—gave me a pretty good idea of how her curves might look in something more form-fitting. I'm doing my best not to let my imagination run with that one. Brooklyn has always been beautiful, but this grown-up version makes high school Brook pale in comparison.

"Are you done staring at me?" she asks as she takes the water out of my hands.

"Almost," I reply, even if my stomach lurches from being caught. "Just trying to get over the shock of seeing you after all this time."

"You and me both," she says on a sigh. "You really don't have to stay, Jordan."

There it is. I knew she wouldn't leave it alone. "You and I both know that I do. If Houston finds out I don't stick around the whole weekend, I'm a dead man." Although, I'm honestly surprised he trusts me to be here alone with his sister. He must have been too focused on his game and the fact that Brooklyn is hurt to realize what he was saying.

I'm not going to argue. Not if I can take this chance to make up for some of the things I did in high school. Besides, I caused her pain this morning, which means I have to fix it as much as I can.

"I can hang out in the corner like a disobedient dog if that would make you more comfortable," I tell her, "but I don't feel great about leaving you alone with these injuries." I hand her the bag of ice, which I've wrapped in a towel. "Did I say I'm sorry for scaring you?"

"It's not your fault. I'm easy to scare."

"Oh, I know." I used that to my advantage more than once back in the day. "I also know you can dish it right back, so I'll be on my guard."

Brooklyn flashes a smile, the mischievous kind that temporarily leaves me breathless. Always has. "You'd better be."

"Are you hungry?" Oh good, I don't sound as dumbstruck as I feel. *Win.* "I can make you some lunch."

She narrows her eyes, as expressive as always. Since the day I met her—one of the better days of my life—Brooklyn Briggs has always been the most easy-to-read person I've ever known. It's strange to think she's twins with Houston, who can hide pretty much anything, because unless she's gotten better at it over the years, Brooklyn broadcasts every single emotion on her face. Every thought.

Right now, she's thinking I'm full of it by offering to make her food. "You cook?"

"Always the tone of surprise," I say, sighing deeply. "Are you hungry, or not?"

"I'm fine," she says right as her stomach growls so loudly that I practically feel the rumble.

I have to try really hard not to laugh as I jump to my feet. "Uh huh."

She looks around for a second, pressing a couple of fingers to her temple, before she says, "Oh, I left my phone in my room. If you go grab it, I can order us some food."

"Ha!" My laugh makes her jump, and instead of going to her room, I head back into the kitchen. "I'll make something if you say it's okay that I raid your kitchen."

"You want to cook for me?" She sounds completely incredulous. "Okay, Gordon Ramsay." Hopefully it's not because the idea of someone like me cooking is ridiculous. Although, I'm not sure it would be any better if she's surprised by the idea of *anyone* cooking for her. She's had boyfriends before. I know she has. Have none of them ever made her lunch?

Have I always been this interested in someone else's business?

Pretty sure I've never been this nosy in my life, thank you very much, though I'm not sure what it says about me now when I'm itching to do some more exploring of her nearly empty cupboards. I guess I've always had a weakness for Brooklyn, one that hasn't grown tougher by a decade apart.

That could be a problem.

Nope. I won't let it become a problem. That's old news.

"I really will sit quietly in the corner if that's what you want," I remind Brooklyn, looking over at her and fighting my smile when she stares back with utter bewilderment on her face. "But if you're hungry, I will happily make you something to eat. Say the word."

She blinks once. Twice. For being Houston's twin, she's far warier than her brother, who wouldn't have thought twice about it if I'd offered to make him food. Okay, so he may have found it a little strange the first time I did it, but the minute he tasted my risotto, he changed his tune. Maybe it'll be the same with Brooklyn. We just have to get over the initial awkward stage. At some point, she has to realize that I'm not an eighteen-year-old kid anymore.

Though her eyes jump toward her bedroom, probably in search of her phone, she seems to be considering the idea until she says, "You really don't have to cook. I can eat some cereal or something."

Oh, she did not. I saw the kinds of cereal she has in her cupboard when I searched for the bag, and it barely classifies as food. The first ingredient in every single one of them is sugar. "I'm going to pretend you didn't just say that."

"I'm pretty sure I don't have anything you can use. I don't do a lot of cooking."

"Oh, ye of little faith. You and your brother have that in common, and I've cooked for him plenty of times." At least Houston has an excuse, being on the road all the time. "What do you say?"

She shrugs, which I take to be a sign of agreement. Good enough for me!

As I dive into her tiny pantry, Brooklyn watches me but pretends she's fully focused on icing her ankle. I let her watch without interruption, knowing she probably needs some time to get comfortable with the idea of me being around as her temporary roommate. A weekend isn't very long, but if she's anything like she used to be, she likes her own space. It's probably why she lives in this dank basement instead of living with her half-sister, Micah. Then again, Micah even makes *me* feel moody. She's like putting a million fireflies into a sparkly balloon that catches every little breeze. She was only in school with us for a year before we went off to college, the twins and I, but I remember well how much energy that girl has.

"So..." Brooklyn almost doesn't speak loudly enough for me to hear her, like she's hoping I won't respond. "How did you and Hou become business partners?"

Though I have my arms full of ingredients, I pause and consider that question. There are a whole lot of things I could tell her, but what do I actually want her to know? The truth, obviously, and I'm really trying to get better about not holding on to things I should share. But telling Brooklyn anything is also telling the rest of her siblings, which is...daunting.

I've always wanted to be a part of the Briggs clan, but they're so close and connected that it has always felt like an impossible club to get into. Plus, I've never had an interaction with Chad that made me feel good about myself. The oldest Briggs is both terrifying and intimidating, and he knows it.

"When I moved back to New Mexico, I needed a job," I say slowly. "Houston got me on the maintenance team at the stadium, but I realized pretty quickly that I could start my own company and be a lot better off. And since your brother is loaded, he offered to help."

By *help*, I mean he tried to give me the startup money as a gift, and it was a back-and-forth battle for weeks before he finally agreed to call it an investment. He still gets mad every time I share the profits, small though they may be, but a deal is a deal.

I'm not especially fond of talking about myself—not with Brooklyn—so I change the subject before she can ask any more questions. "How do you feel about crab cakes?"

I don't think I could have confused her more if I tried. Okay, maybe I did try. "You're...you're making crab cakes?" She lifts up her head, trying to see over the counter.

"Would you be impressed if I said yes?"

"I would," she admits. "But only because I know for a fact that I don't have any crab so I would actually think you're full of it."

I chuckle. She thinks she knows me so well. "You would be right. I'm making alfredo. Just wanted to make sure your brain was still functioning right."

Well, the girl can still roll her eyes like a pro. "I don't have a concussion, Jordan. You don't have to stay with me."

Number three. She *really* doesn't want me here. Or, at least, she's really *pretending* she doesn't.

"While I accept your authority in your home and will listen to you if you tell me to do something, I respect Houston more than I'm afraid of you." Easy to do, considering her overall sweetness. Though, there is that feisty Briggs stubbornness that I know better than to underestimate. I can't let myself forget some of the pranks she pulled to get back at me. I'm pretty sure I still find glitter on my person from one of them. "I'm going to proceed unless you tell me otherwise."

"So, if I told you to go home and leave me here on my own because I don't need any help?"

"Then you would be lying." I pause, narrowing my eyes as I wait for her to argue with me. She's barely touching the ice to her ankle—I'll probably need to force that one if she wants to get the swelling down—and hasn't once made an attempt to move from the couch. Plus, she keeps rubbing her temples, so I know her head's bothering her.

I hate that I caused that, even unintentionally. Note to self: don't jump into unfamiliar window wells without full reconnaissance first.

"I guess you can stay," she says eventually.

I duck my head into the fridge so she doesn't see my grin.

Chapter Four

Brooklyn

THERE'S SOMETHING ABOUT THE way Jordan moves that has me fascinated. It's more than just the shift and flex of his muscles, which are many. There's a confidence about him that I've never seen before, and I wish I knew what it was so I could try to emulate it. Don't get me wrong; I've seen plenty of confidence in my life. My brother Chad has never once questioned who he is, and Houston is basically the king of confidence to the point of almost being arrogant sometimes. But with Jordan, it's a very...calm confidence. Self-assurance might be a better word for it. It's so much better than the cocky kid who was always hanging around my stepdad's house and driving me crazy.

Though I'm still getting high school flashbacks, I can't help but wonder what he's been up to over the last decade. I was so glad to be rid of him that I never put a lot of effort into thinking about what happened to him. I know he and Houston went to the same college together, but Houston got drafted two years in. What about Jordan? Did he keep playing baseball? Did he stay in California? Has he been single this whole time?

That last one I can probably answer on my own: definitely not single. Jordan was the biggest flirt I knew back in the day, always with a girl on his arm. I'm pretty sure he worked his way through the entire cheerleader squad at one point. It's a trait he shares with Houston, who hasn't been without a girlfriend since the day he turned fifteen.

Except now, I guess. My brother has been single for two months at this point, which is weird for him.

"Why aren't you at work today, anyway?" Jordan asks after a while.

He's been humming or singing to himself for the last little while, which has weirdly made my little basement apartment feel less gloomy. Hearing him talk to me returns the claustrophobia that has been creeping in since the moment we came out into my living room, though. I'm so used to being alone down here that sharing the space feels a bit overwhelming. Plus, I'm in my pajamas with a purple foot and a head that won't stop throbbing, so I'm feeling a bit self-conscious.

Unlike Jordan, who isn't self-conscious in the least. He doesn't seem to care that I can definitely hear everything he's been singing. He doesn't have a bad voice, but neither is it going to win him any votes on American Idol.

"I had a migraine this morning," I say. As always, I feel pathetic for admitting that a headache was enough to incapacitate me.

Jordan winces as he picks up two plates and brings them over. "And then I went and made it worse," he says, handing me a plate. "Sorry again. I've added it to my mental list of things to tell my guys; look before leaping."

"You have some employees who work for you too?" I take a reluctant bite of food and nearly groan because it tastes so good. This might be the best alfredo I've ever tasted, and I have no idea how he could have made this from ingredients in my kitchen. I'm almost convinced he somehow conjured it like some sort of wizard.

Jordan twists up his mouth and nods toward my plate. "You like it? And yes, I have four guys under me. I'm hoping to get a few more if—when—business picks up in the spring."

"It's a good thing you don't have to worry about snow getting in your way," I say without mentioning how hard it is to not devour this entire plate of pasta in one bite. I would like to have *some* dignity left over, and shoveling noodles into my mouth like a starving raccoon is not going to do me any favors.

I don't know why I care. Jordan has seen me at my worst, taking part in all my awkward teenage years. But adult Jordan looks a whole lot different from adolescent Jordan. He acts differently too, almost to the point where he feels like a different person, and that makes me nervous. I don't do well with strangers.

As he settles on the other side of my couch by my feet since I don't have any other seating in here, Jordan smiles and takes a bite of his own food. "What got you into teaching?" he asks. "I thought you wanted to go into research or something."

"You remember that?" My heart throbs in my chest.

He shrugs, like it's no big deal.

I think it's a big deal, considering he and I never really had a civil conversation. Especially not about the future. But I'm not sure I want Jordan to know about the complete one-eighty turn my career took a few years ago, so I give him the watered-down version. The version that feels like a lie.

"Um, yeah," I say. "Teaching felt like a safe option. And I really like it."

"I never understood how anyone could like something complicated like chemistry," he replies with a chuckle. "You are inspiring."

My face heating, I move my focus to the food in my hands, even though I've already eaten most of it. If only he knew how wrong he was about my skills. Or lack thereof... "Chemistry is a lot easier than real life," I mutter, which is true. I'm apparently not good at either. "It has rules. Predictable reactions. There's precision and order, which is essential to the world functioning how it should."

He makes a weird face, and I have no idea what it's supposed to mean. He must sense my confusion because he grins and looks up at me. "The chaos is what makes life interesting," he says, as if that should be obvious. "The most magical moments are unplanned and unexpected."

"Maybe for you." I don't think I would ever be able to embrace chaos even if I tried. I've lived without stability, back when my mom died and my brothers and I were left with a father who couldn't take care of himself let alone us. Chad was only fifteen, and he did his best to step up, but there were some days when Houston and I weren't sure what we would have for dinner, if anything. Chaos means hunger and fear and loneliness.

I don't expect Jordan to understand something like that.

He watches me for a moment before looking at his watch and standing up. "I should probably grab some things from home if I'm going to be here all weekend. Are you going to be okay if I'm gone for an hour?"

I scoff as he disappears into the hallway. "I'll be fine. I'd be fine even if you didn't come back."

But then my ankle throbs, and a wave of dizziness reminds me that I might be concussed, even if I argued that I'm not. The house suddenly feels empty, which makes no sense at all because Jordan has only gone into my room, returning a moment later with my phone. If Houston was in town, I would probably be begging him to come over anyway.

"So, you'll be back?" I ask, hating how desperate I sound.

Pausing at the door, Jordan looks back and gives me a wide grin that is both familiar and completely new, which makes as much sense as me wanting him to stay. "Sure, Queens."

Chapter Five
Jordan

WHEN I STEP INTO my parents' house, I'm hit with a wall of shrieks and giggles that makes me smile. Brooklyn's basement was so quiet, to the point where I started singing to fill the space before I went a little crazy, and this feels a lot more normal. Honestly, anything is better than what I dealt with in California, even if my nieces and nephew can be a bit deafening at times. That silence still haunts me.

"Danny!" When they see me, all three kids abandon the board game they were playing on the living room floor and tackle my legs with repeated shouts of the name only my family calls me.

I make a show of struggling against them, even if the oldest is only six and stick-thin, before collapsing to the ground with an exaggerated groan. "You got me!" Then Mia starts tickling me, and nothing is exaggerated when I burst into laughter and curl into a ball, trying to protect myself from her attack.

I have no idea how she's so good at finding the sweet spot, but the four-year-old is a tickling fiend.

"Okay!" I gasp, grabbing a kid under each arm and holding them tight. Thankfully, two-year-old Joshua can't do much yet, or I'd be in trouble because I only have two arms. "Okay, you win! Let me breathe, if you please." Once I've decided I'm safe, I release the girls and hop back up to my feet, my grin fully in place as I head deeper into the living room and lean down to kiss my mom's cheek. "How are you feeling?"

She smiles, and her brown eyes are brighter than usual today. "Today is a good day," she says, confirming my suspicions. It's always a gamble with her chemo treatments. "You're home early."

"Not for long." I crouch in front of her armchair to be at eye level. "I need to help a friend out with something over the weekend. Do you think you'll be okay if I'm out for a couple of days?"

She pats my cheek with a little more force than necessary. "I don't need you taking care of me, Danny. You know that."

"Won't stop me from doing it." Especially because she has been looking after my little brother Alejandro's three kids for the last year while he's been deployed and his wife is at work. With the cancer on top of things, she's doing way too much considering the minimal energy she has, and I hate seeing her so tired and rundown. When I only have myself to look after, it makes sense for me to do what I can.

"I see Houston is playing today," she says, pointing to her phone even though it's currently locked.

I nod, my grin growing. She's always been so good about paying attention to my friends and things in my life even when they aren't directly related to me. "You're a good mom, you know that?"

"Danny, come play with us!" Hannah puts a hand on her hip and points forcefully at the game, turning her request into a full-on order.

Mom laughs softly. "She's gotten feistier over the last few months, don't you think?"

"Too much of Alex in her," I agree. My brother has always been strong-willed, and the older Alejandro's kids get, the more I see him in them. Especially Hannah. Standing up, I ruffle Hannah's hair. "Sorry, kiddo, but I've got to go pack a few things."

"But Joshua doesn't understand the rules!"

Even now, the toddler is playing with the pieces like they're people, making them hop around the board with no rhyme or reason. I wish I could stay, but I'm already nervous about leaving Brooklyn alone for an hour. She'll probably try hopping around the apartment on her own and end up getting even more injured than she already is. She's too stubborn for her own good. Always has been.

"Maybe you can try playing a game that Josh does understand," I suggest before heading up to my room and digging an old duffel out of the closet.

You would think, considering I hadn't lived in this house for almost a decade until I moved back last fall, something would have changed in my room, but my mom is too sentimental. Even when Alejandro and I both moved out, she kept everything exactly as it was, which means my walls are plastered with baseball posters and team trophies, all things I cared about more than I should and couldn't care less about now. The only baseball I bother with is Houston's team, and even then it's mostly Houston that I care about.

As I toss clothes at random into my duffel, I grab my phone and pull up the Red-tails game, though I don't have time to watch much of it. Houston's pitching today, and so far in the two innings he hasn't allowed any runs. That doesn't surprise me. My best friend is easily the most consistent pitcher in the MLB right now. It doesn't matter if it's a practice game or the World Series, like now; he plays his hardest.

The fact that he remained on the phone long enough to order me to stay with Brooklyn over the weekend is a testament to how much he cares about his sister. The only thing Houston loves more than playing baseball is his family. Especially his twin. He's always looked out for her, even though she's technically older. And I know he'll rethink his order as soon as he's no longer focused on his game.

That means I have to convince *Brooklyn* to want me to stay, or I'll be sick with guilt for the next few days. Houston won't argue against his sister, no matter what his own opinions are.

It's not like he ever forbade me from dating his sister, but he made enough comments over the years for me to infer how much he didn't like the idea. So I never really thought about it.

Much.

Houston doesn't have a lot of people in his life despite his fame and fortune, and I would never make him choose between me or his sister if things ever got awkward. I would lose that battle, no question.

"Why am I even thinking about this?" I mutter out loud, only just now realizing that I've packed more nice clothes than comfortable ones. Am I trying to impress Brooklyn? Because if she sees me in slacks and a button up, she's going to look at me like I've lost my mind. There's little chance she'll be able to go anywhere this weekend with her sprained ankle, so I might as well plan to chill.

I laugh at that. I'm not sure I even know what chill looks like anymore, though I've been trying to figure out that whole leisure thing. Maybe Houston is right by forcing me to stay away from my work for a few days. Relax a bit.

I keep one nice outfit in my bag, just in case. In case of what, I have no clue, but I'm going with my gut here.

I also pack my laptop because—let's face it—I have way too much to do to actually take the whole weekend off.

Tucking my phone away with a mental reminder to check in later in the game, I step out into the hall right as my youngest brother, Mateo, reaches his own room. We both freeze, which is pretty par for the course with us, and I know I have maybe thirty seconds before he disappears into his room. I've been back home for a year now, and I've probably had only a dozen conversations with my seventeen-year-old brother.

It doesn't help that when I went off to college, he was seven. I pretty much have no idea who this kid is other than knowing he doesn't like me much. His scowl makes that pretty clear any time he sees me. If he would give me a chance to get to know him, I could change that, but he avoids me like the plague.

His eyes flick to the duffel on my shoulder. "Finally moving out?"

"Helping a friend for the weekend. Hey."

He pauses halfway through opening his door.

I swallow. I rarely feel awkward around people, if ever, so every interaction with my brother is the worst. "What do you say you and I grab some lunch or something next week?" I do a quick mental search of my calendar to make sure that's even possible. Dinner would be easier, but Mateo never seems to get home until late most nights.

As if he knows exactly how much I'm struggling to find a time to make it work, he rolls his eyes. "Not necessary. I get lunch at school."

"There are so many places that are better than the cafeteria," I say, wrinkling my nose. "I could pick you up and—"

"Don't bother." He slips into his room and shuts the door, and it takes everything in me not to barge in after him and demand he tell me why he dislikes me so much. I haven't even been around for the last decade! And, arrogant as it makes me sound, I'm incredibly likable. I can count on two fingers the number of people who haven't liked me after spending some time with me, and I still haven't figured out the reason for either. Yeah, there were all the pranks with Brooklyn, but she *started out* disliking me, and I never managed to change her mind.

Maybe I can change Brooklyn's opinion of me this weekend and cut that number in half. Mateo will have to wait.

By the time I get back downstairs, my head is swimming with thoughts of how to win over Brooklyn Briggs, and I almost don't notice my mom watching me head for the door until she clears her throat.

I stop in my tracks, wincing before dropping my bag and hustling to her side. The kids have vanished elsewhere, hopefully not getting into trouble. "Got sidetracked," I mutter as I kiss her cheek. "Are you sure you don't need anything?"

"I need you to remember that you're human," she says, raising a non-existent eyebrow at me. "And don't take Matty's surliness personally."

I have been convinced since I was a kid that my mom can read minds, and yet it always freaks me out when she does. I may be nearing thirty, but I will always and forever be slightly terrified of my sweet-as-pie mother. Disappointing her is one of my biggest fears. Sighing, I crouch down and take one of her hands between mine. "Hard not to take it personal when he barely looks at me."

"He barely looks at anyone," Mom admits with a frown. "I don't know what's going on with him. He disappears for hours at a time, doesn't talk when he's here, pretends he's busy with homework when I know he isn't."

I don't like the sound of that. "He just started at the new school, right? Is he failing his classes or anything?" That would be a sure sign of going down a path he shouldn't. I may not know much about Mateo, but I know he's always been smart. He got into some fights at his last school, and my parents decided it would be best for him to be in a new environment. Beyond that, I have no idea why he might be getting into trouble.

Mom shakes her head. "The opposite, actually. But I'm worried about him. Worried that he's getting himself into something he shouldn't. He always has a sort of guilty look in his eyes, and your father doesn't know what to do with him."

That's probably because my dad is home even less than Mateo. I love my dad, and he's a good man. But he's always been married to his job as much as he's married to my mom. At least I know where I get it…

My phone buzzes in my pocket, reminding me that I should probably get back to Brooklyn before she trips on her coffee table and cracks her head open. "I'll talk to Matty," I say, though I have no idea when. This weekend is putting enough of a strain on my team as it is without me doing my share of the work. "Call me if you need anything. I'm only twenty minutes away."

"Human," Mom reminds me, though I'm not sure what she means by that.

I know I'm only human. It's a source of frustration every day of my life, and I don't exactly need the reminder that I can only do so much when I know I need to do more.

As I climb into my truck and toss my bag into the back seat, I pull my phone out of my pocket and smile as soon as I read the stream of texts from an unknown number. I get texts from strange numbers all the time, but never do they get this kind of reaction out of me. I'm probably a little too excited, but I can't help but call this a win in my blossoming plan.

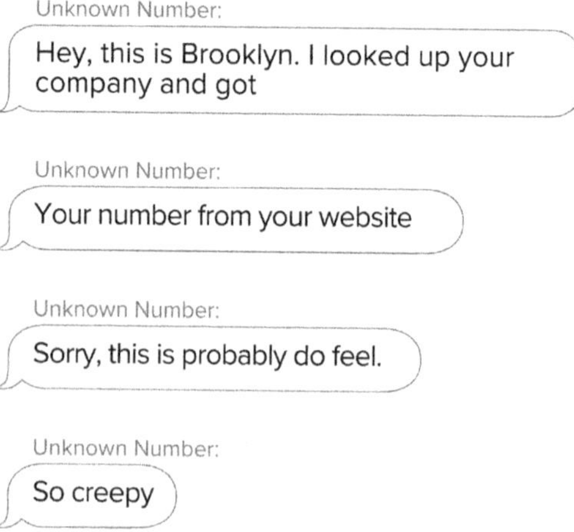

A part of me wishes I had been at texting levels with Brooklyn back in the day. After her failure to call Houston the first time, I have to wonder if she's always this bad with a phone or if I just make her nervous. I save her number in my contacts, choosing to ignore the strange sense of pride I feel for being able to say I have Brooklyn's phone number now.

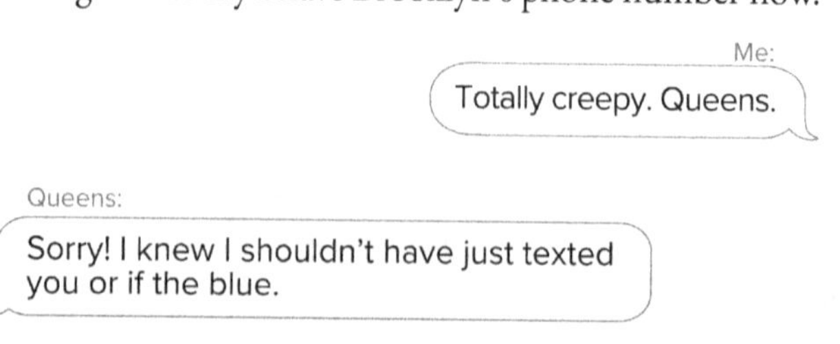

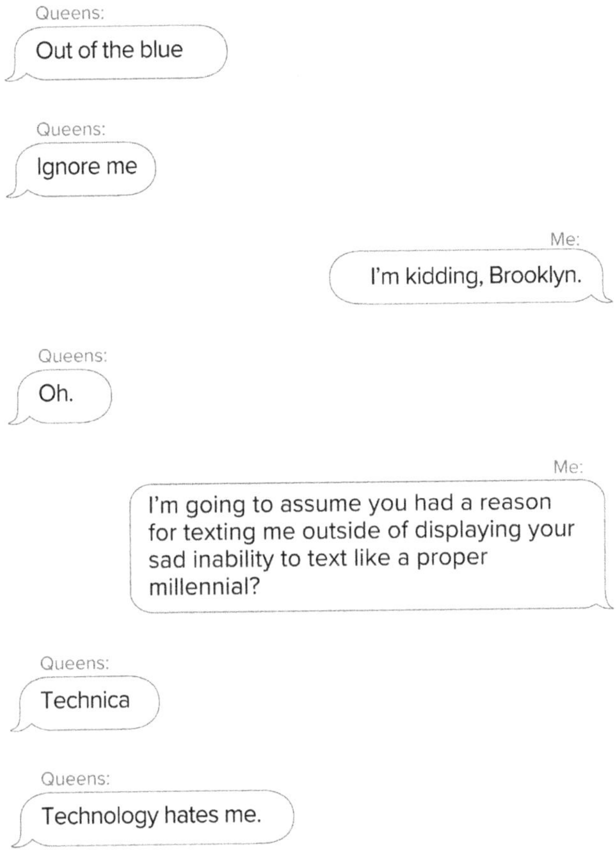

When she doesn't say anything else, I take a chance and hit the call button, wondering if she's the sort of person who stares at the screen and waits for it to stop ringing so she can send a text, or if she—

"Double mint chip!" Brooklyn's voice sounds distant and muffled, and there's a whole lot of rustling before she says, "Sorry! I dropped my phone."

I press my lips together before I start laughing, mostly because I just realized she was using an ice cream flavor as a curse word. Unlike her brother, who has picked up some choice vocabulary words over the years, she seems to be just as sweet and innocent as she always has been.

When I'm sure I won't bust up laughing, I switch my phone to my other hand. "I don't remember you being clumsy, Queens. Is this the concussion talking?"

She lets out a quick sigh. "I told you. Technology hates me. I'm convinced my phone is out to get me."

"Interesting theory. So, why did you stalk my number?"

"I didn't stalk—"

"You looked me up on the internet so you could send me cryptic messages. Pretty sure that counts as stalking."

"Forget it."

Okay, maybe I'm pushing the teasing a bit too far. I must still be on edge from my interaction with Mateo. "Brooklyn. I'm sorry. Do you need something?"

She's quiet for a moment, and I can imagine her debating whether to ask for help. It's that Briggs stubbornness that makes her so much like her brothers. "Could...could you pick me up a soda on your way back? It helps with the migraines."

I relax in my seat. A soda I can do. "Of course. What do you—"

"I'll pay you back. I could even send you some money right now if you have one of those apps. Oh, except the last time I did that, I accidentally sent Micah half my bank account. So maybe I could—"

"Brooklyn?"

"Yeah?"

"Just tell me what you want. I'll get it for you."

"I'll pay you—"

I groan. Is this what the whole weekend is going to be like? I can only argue for so long before I start forcing kindness, and I can't see that ending well for me. She may not be a nationally ranked superathlete, but Brooklyn can hold her own. "You're killing me, Queens."

She matches my groan with one of her own, reminding me of how easily I used to get on her nerves. That groan made up a significant portion of my high school soundtrack. "Fine. Dr. Pepper with raspberry and coconut. Please."

"Was that so hard?"

She mumbles something unintelligible, making me chuckle.

"I'll be back to your house soon, Queens. Don't get too bored without me."

When I let myself into her basement apartment half an hour later—I'm almost surprised she didn't lock me out—I find Brooklyn exactly where I left her on the couch, though she has procured a blanket at some point and turned on the TV. She turns to greet me, probably with some snarky remark, but she only gives me a smile.

And while I'm not in the market for someone to hang on to my heart, that's the kind of smile that makes a guy want to hand over his dignity and pledge fealty to his fair lady.

Hmm. That could make things interesting.

Chapter Six

Brooklyn

I MIGHT BE A little too excited to see Jordan walking through my door, and though I pretend it's because he comes bearing my favorite soda, I know better than to lie to myself. I'm excited to see him because I really, really have to pee.

It turns out hopping on one foot with a possible concussion is incredibly painful, and I quickly discovered I landed funny on my wrist as well because crawling was an immediate non-option. And I may not have a lot of dignity left, but army crawling to the toilet felt like too much.

"Oh, thank goodness you're here," I say breathlessly. I've been bouncing on the couch for the last ten minutes, doing everything I can to distract myself.

Jordan lifts a dark eyebrow. "You must really like this soda."

I hold out an arm. "Pick me up." He did it so easily the last time that I'm sure he can do it again.

"Um."

I have very little bladder room for patience, as much as I wish I did. "Daniel Jordan Torres, pick me up and carry me to the bathroom before I explode. Please!"

Though he does as he's told, he gets an odd look on his face as he slides one arm behind my back and the other under my legs. Sure enough, he lifts me easily and crosses the room to the little hall leading to my bedroom.

"The door on the left," I tell him and click the light on as soon as I can reach it.

"I forgot how tiny your bladder is. I'm going to assume you don't need help beyond this point." He smirks as he places me on my feet. Well, foot.

I give him a shove. "Absolutely not. At least, not until I'm done."

He salutes—a man this annoying should not look that handsome—and then shuts the door on his way out.

Ah, sweet relief.

"By the way," he says, and I'm so glad I don't have a shy bladder or I would be ready to murder him for standing right outside the door. "How do you know my full name?"

I wait until I'm finished with my business and washing my hands before I respond. I almost expected him to make this whole thing awkward, but he acts as if using the bathroom is a basic human function. Which it is, obviously, but I expected him to tease me about it or something. Had we still been in high school, he probably would have made me do the army crawl or found a way to make me pee my pants.

"I don't know," I say with a shrug he can't see. "Houston must have told me at some point."

"I'm not sure Houston even knows. I've always been Jordan to him."

When I open the door, I find Jordan waiting for me with one dark eyebrow raised. Still waiting for an explanation, I suppose. It's too bad I don't have one to give, but I distinctly remember thinking about calling him Daniel at one point to see if it would bother him. I never did—*thanks, cowardice*—and I wish I could read his expression right now. He's either confused or angry. Maybe just curious?

"I guess I picked it up at school or something," I say.

He smiles. "And you never used it against me?"

"Would it have worked? Daniel isn't a weird name."

"No," he agrees, "but it's my dad's name, so I'm Jordan to everyone except my family." He holds out his arms, and I hope he's asking if I want him to carry me again because I lean right into his hold until he picks me up. "Couch or bed?" he asks.

Now that I know I have a soda waiting for me, I'm far less inclined to take a nap than I was after he left. Or maybe it's just because I feel weird sleeping when he's in my house. "Couch," I say as definitively as I can. I have a feeling he would question me again if I didn't sound confident.

"Couch it is."

For the next five minutes, we both get ourselves settled on either end of the couch, me with the TV and him with a laptop. It makes me glad that I didn't skimp on my thrift store buy and get a loveseat instead of a full couch, even if it would have fit better in my small space. This way, I can keep some distance between us until I can process how weird it is that I'm hanging out with my brother's annoying best friend after ten years of knowing nothing about where he is or what he's doing. Not that I ever really thought about him. Though he was always around, it wasn't like I devoted a lot of brain power to thinking about Jordan Torres outside of sometimes watching him play as catcher on the high school team or wondering what girls saw in him when they swooned over him in the hallways. (Okay, that's a lie. I thought about him a lot, but not because I was interested. Because we were at war. It's a long story.) Jordan was always that guy who was friends with everyone and constantly going out with all the girls, and I never knew how everyone could overlook his sheer extra-ness.

Jordan never did anything small.

As he busies himself with whatever he's doing on his computer, I grab my phone and resume my outline of what I'm going to do the next time I see Mark. Jay texted me soon after Jordan left, asking if I was still interested in Mark—obviously—and then demanding a game plan, and I know better than to ignore her. She's heard enough of my moaning and swooning to let this go now that Mark has made the first move. I think she's mostly just hoping something will happen so I'll stop complaining to her that nothing has happened.

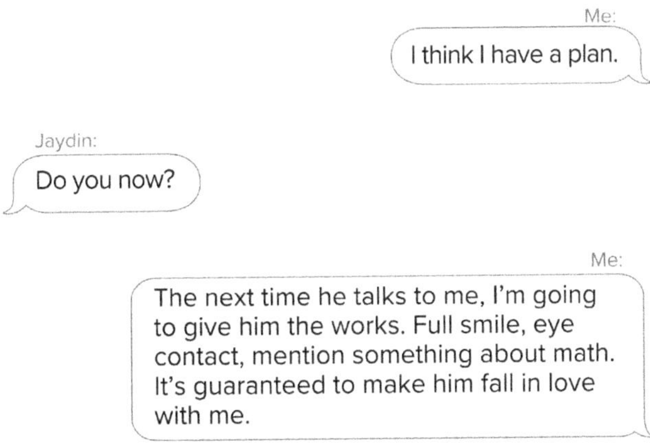

"You're going to make me fall in love with you?"

I jump at the sound of Jordan's voice and throw my phone at him out of reflex. Thankfully he catches it before it hits him in the face, though a part of me wishes it *had* hit him in the face because then I wouldn't have to see his amused grin.

Feeling my own face light on fire, I swallow and almost don't want to ask. "Did I just text *you*?"

He purses his lips, which does nothing to hold back his smile. "Sure did, Queens. I'm guessing I was not the intended recipient."

"That was supposed to go to my coworker!"

"So, you're going to make your coworker fall in love with you?"

"No!" I groan. "I mean, yes. Not the one I was trying to text, but the male one. The math one. The..." I should probably just curl up in a ball and die now. "The Mark one," I finish lamely. It can't get much worse than it already is. I'm just glad I don't have Mark's phone number for some reason, or my phone probably would have decided to send that text to him instead of Jordan.

I can't imagine the torture of Mark learning about my ridiculous crush in the worst possible way.

Jordan closes his laptop, brown eyes bright with interest. "Math teacher?" he guesses.

"We really don't have to have this conversation," I reply. "I'm positive this is not how you want to spend your Friday afternoon."

"That's a pretty bold assertion, Queens. Though, now I'm curious." He moves his computer to the floor and turns to face me. "How do *you* usually spend your Friday afternoons? Have I deprived you of a thrilling evening spent cutting coupons and knitting scarves?"

I roll my eyes. "No, I usually go clubbing."

Of course he only laughs at that, not for a second considering I might be telling the truth. I probably haven't changed much since high school, and he's going to use that to his advantage. It isn't fair, considering there seems to be quite a bit about him that is unfamiliar after our time apart. He may still have that mischief in his eyes, but he's already proven more than once that he isn't the same obnoxious teenage boy I knew. Not all the time, anyway.

"I bet you're always the first and last on the dance floor," he says, "showing off your moves all night."

Has Jordan ever seen me dance? I hope not. Yeah, okay, we had to slow dance together once, but that doesn't count. Anyone can sway back and forth. But other dancing? I'll don paintball gear every summer or go to a shooting range with my brother Chad each Valentine's day, but ask me to be graceful and lithe...good luck. I was raised by manly men, and it shows. My stepsisters always cluck their tongues behind my back, not-so-secretly discussing what a shame it is that I'm so beautiful but so not in touch with my femininity.

"You dance, right?" For a second, I wonder who said that until my concussed brain catches up to itself and I realize the question came from my own mouth. But where in the world did it come from? It's not even an actual question.

Jordan cocks his head, eyebrows twisting together as he watches me. "Why do you say that?"

That's a real question, but it's one without a current answer. This is why I shouldn't have conversations I haven't prepared for. Especially why I shouldn't have conversations with boys who have become men in the blink of an eye and are way too attractive to want to spend a weekend with me.

And yet my mouth keeps talking without permission. "I've seen you."

"When?"

"At, like, dances and stuff."

His eyebrows shoot up. "Are you telling me that you were watching me instead of focusing on your fancy football star boyfriend? Actually, that doesn't surprise me. Butler was such a squeaky grocery cart."

I fold my arms. "Why'd you have to bring Garrett into this?"

Jordan mimics me, only he smirks instead of scowling as he crosses his arms over his chest. "Still defending the wet sock, huh?"

"I'm not defending—"

"You are! Heaven knows why."

I groan. It was bad enough dealing with this antagonism toward my boyfriend senior year while I was still in high school, and I don't need it now. Not while my head is still throbbing. "You're seriously going to tell me you're *still* jealous of him?"

"Never was, never will be," he argues calmly. "He played an inferior sport and was the greasiest tool I've ever met. His popularity was overrated."

"He was Student Body President for a reason. You just hated that the football team got more attention."

"Of course I did. They got all the budget, and we had to keep our equipment in that broken down shed."

"That wasn't Garrett's fault." I groan again, realizing too late that now I *am* defending him, and Jordan is not about to let that go.

Sure enough, he leans one arm on the back of the couch and fixes me with a judgmental look that even I couldn't misinterpret. "How about when he cheated on you? Was that not his fault either?"

I still remember vividly the night I found out, when I saw the flirty texts from one of the girls on the student council asking when he was going to ditch me to go spend the night with her. *When*, not *if*. He'd responded too, telling her that he would get away as soon as he could. Instead of confronting Garrett, I pretended to be sick so he would leave (which he did happily), and then I found Houston and started sobbing. Unfortunately for me, Jordan was over that night, though that did come in handy when he and I had to physically restrain my brother from hunting Garrett down in his initial rage.

I found out the next morning that Garrett mysteriously had all of his tires removed and placed in his trunk that night, while his jack seemed to go missing, leaving him stranded at the girl's house and getting her in major trouble when her parents got home. I gained a lot of respect for Houston and Jordan after that. No violence, no damage of property. Just a whole lot of inconvenience and righteous justice.

I sigh, curling my uninjured leg up to my chest. "I never said thank you for what you guys did," I mutter. Partly because I wished I had had the guts to do it myself.

Jordan smirks. "I don't know what you're talking about. Kinda made me wonder if I should have gotten a job on a pit crew at some point, though. So." He hops to his feet and heads for the broom closet near the door, like he's on a mission. "Hopefully this Mark guy is less of a bad hair day than Garrett the Skunk."

"You have strange insults," I say, frowning at him as he pulls out my broom and dustpan. "What are you doing?"

As he begins sweeping the linoleum, he lifts an eyebrow without looking up at me. "What does it look like I'm doing?"

"It looks like you're sweeping my floor."

"Ding ding ding!"

I narrow my eyes at him. "*Why* are you sweeping my floor, Jordan?"

"Because it's dirty. And I need something to do."

And the something he picked is *sweeping*? Sweeping is the worst chore in the world! Which, now that I think about it, is probably the reason he's doing it. I can't actually remember the last time I swept.

I groan. "Jordan. I'm not going to let you—"

"I'd like to see you stop me, Miss Cripple. Besides, we're not done talking about your little crush."

"I don't *want* to talk about him. You'll just find all the things wrong with him like you did with all the other guys." No matter who I went out with in high school, Jordan always had a snarky comment pointing out the guy's flaws. He was always right, but that's beside the point.

Jordan shrugs as he moves closer with his broom, like he's taunting me. "Does he have red flags I should know about?"

"No. You don't need to know anything about him."

"So he does have red flags?"

"Jordan!"

Lifting one hand in surrender, he purses his lips again, giving me that ridiculous, poorly concealed grin that makes me want to smack him with a pillow. "You don't have to tell me about him if you don't want to, Queens. But can I say one thing?"

I narrow my eyes at him, knowing full well I have never been intimidating in my life. Plus, he's started shoving the broom underneath the couch, and I'm a little worried about what he's going to find down there. "I'm afraid to say yes, but okay."

"If your big plan is to say something about *math*, I'm not sure you're going to get the results you want."

What would he know? "But he loves math. He teaches it every day."

"Would you fall in love with me if I said something about chemistry?"

I fell right into that one, though I try my best to deflect. "Depends on what you said."

"So you're saying I have a chance?"

I swing my pillow onto his head, though I keep my attack gentle. He doesn't deserve my full pillow smackdown, especially because he is cleaning my house for me. "Yeah, I'm not going to fall in love with you, Jordan."

"We'll see about that." Maybe it's just me, but the way his mouth curves up as he looks at me has my temperature rising by a few degrees.

He's an incorrigible flirt and always has been, but I'm starting to see how he managed to get so many girls to fall in love with him. All he has to do is smile with that mouth of his, and they probably come running. Swarming. Flocking. Whatever it is girls do with good-looking guys.

There is absolutely no way I would ever fall for *Jordan Torres* when I know what he is, and that realization brings a sudden sense of peace, one that relaxes my shoulders so much that I'm surprised I didn't recognize I was so tense.

Jordan is just here to help. Under my brother's orders. I don't have to make this weekend awkward because there is no sense of expectation. He knows enough about me already that I doubt I could lessen his opinion of me by being myself. Even if I did, it wouldn't matter because I would never date this guy.

"Brook?" Jordan reaches down, and then he crouches and rests his arms on the back of the couch. In his fingers, partially obscured by a big, nasty dust bunny, is one of the earbuds Houston bought for me last Christmas. "How long has this been under there?"

I cringe. "I don't know."

"You lost this within a week of getting them, didn't you?"

I should probably hate how well he knows me. It's not even my technology curse that snatched this bud; it was just me. I've always had a bad habit of losing things—never anything important—and Houston often found stuff in his room back in high school. No idea how it ever ended up in there, but it happened more often than I'd care to admit.

I wrinkle my nose and hold out my hand for the bud, flinching when Jordan laughs as soon as he hands it to me.

"Maybe I should come over and clean more often," he says as he hops back up to keep sweeping. "I know it's not your favorite, and I find it relaxing."

"There is nothing relaxing about cleaning, Jordan."

"Tomato, tomahto. We've all got our strengths, Queens."

I can't believe I'm even thinking this, but he's right. And when it comes to Jordan's strengths... Maybe he can help me with the whole Mark situation. I am *not* a flirt, and I'm definitely out of dating practice. I could use an expert in the field.

"I've been interested in Mark for years," I say, tensing a little when Jordan's eyes focus on me from over by the kitchen. I forgot how much of an eye contact guy he is, never afraid to be seen as much as he sees. "This is the first time he's been single since I met him."

"I'm sensing some anxiety about the idea," he says slowly, his sweeping matching the pace of his words.

I laugh. "You could say that. We had our first real conversation yesterday, and it was awful."

"Awful how?"

"Awful in that I had no idea what to say and basically made a fool of myself."

He cocks his head to one side as he does one long sweep without looking down, and it feels like he forgot what he was doing for a second. "I don't think that's possible, Queens."

"You weren't there."

"Tell me this guy isn't another Garrett Butler." My frustration rises from his comment, which he must pick up on because he turns his focus back to the broom. "Not my place. Got it. As long as you think he's a good guy, you can date whoever you want. I'm assuming you want to date him, not just win him over?"

Why else would I want him to fall in love with me? "But I'm out of practice," I mutter, not sure I like admitting as much to someone like him. "It's been a while."

Jordan shakes his head. "Sometimes I can't fathom how you and your brother came out so different."

"You can say that again."

As much as I love Houston, he has always had a bad habit of dating anything that moves, and I genuinely don't remember the last time he didn't have a girlfriend hanging on his arm. Except for now, of course.

"Speaking of..." Jordan grabs his phone, typing for a second until I hear the sounds of a baseball game.

I lean a little closer, though it's not like I can see anything from my new permanent spot on the couch. "Is the game still happening?" I must have really hit my head because I totally forgot he was about to start his game when I called him earlier. I could put it on, but I never understand the rules when I try to watch so I always end up frustrated.

Jordan shrugs. "Yeah. It's almost over, though. Red-tails are winning—no surprise there."

If I remember right, the World Series is seven games, and this is only the third, which means the next week is going to have me feeling sympathetic stress for my brother. I don't know why, but I've been more and more nervous every time he plays, like I know there's something wrong but I don't know what it is.

"Would you tell me if you knew something about Houston that I didn't?" I ask, wincing as soon as those words are out of my mouth. Did I really just ask my brother's best friend to spy on him? He's been acting strange the last little bit, though, and if anyone would know why, Jordan would.

Jordan locks his phone before he meets my gaze, dark eyes fixed on mine as he studies me. He's been doing that a lot since this morning, which isn't exactly out of the norm for him, but it's out of the norm for me. No matter what Jay says about me being irresistible, it's been a long time since I really let myself be seen. It's not exactly easy to be open and vulnerable when the last guy you dated somehow managed to ruin both your career and your confidence.

"I guess it depends," Jordan says, pulling his eyebrows together. "There are things Houston has made me promise to keep to myself, and I don't plan on breaking that trust."

"Even if it would help him?"

His smile returns in a slow stretch of happiness. I wish I could see life through his eyes so I could know how he smiles so easily. "Now I'm starting to wonder if there's something you know that I don't."

"No." I sigh. "I guess I just feel like I haven't been around my brother much lately, and I miss him. I was curious if you get his attention more than I do."

"Only because I demand his attention whenever I get the chance. Especially lately." His expression has changed again, and whatever he sees in my face seems to confuse him. Or worry him? I wish I was better at reading people, like he is. "Do you wish he was around more?"

"No. I mean, yeah, of course I do, but I know he loves baseball too much to give that up until he has to." I could never ask my brother to make more time for me when he's worked so hard to get to where he is, even if I would love to see him more than once or twice a month when his team is at home.

He's always been my best friend, but being adults makes that friendship difficult. Who'd have thought adulthood would be this lonely?

"I'm just going to have to be patient and be on my own until his season is over," I say, hoping it doesn't make me sound too pathetic.

Jordan hums, as if thinking about something as he looks down at his phone once more. He laughs at whatever he reads, and then he gives me a grin that makes me nervous. He pulls the dustpan off the broom and starts scooping up the honestly horrifying amount of dirt that he's collected over the last few minutes. "Unless you get yourself a man in the meantime," he says, like it's a perfectly normal thing to say over household chores. "What's this coworker like? The one you're trying to seduce with math?"

Okay, well, when he puts it like that, it sounds pretty stupid. "One," I say, holding up a finger, "I'm not trying to *seduce* him. I'm not you." He scrunches up his face as he dumps the dust in the trash, but I ignore whatever that is supposed to mean. "And two, I'm obviously going to do more than talk about math."

"Like what?"

I can hear the challenge in his voice, and I hate that he knows how to push my buttons so well. Rising to the challenge is a little too tempting, but I'm not going to play his game. "I don't have to tell you," I say.

"Meaning you don't have even a little bit of a plan," he guesses, rolling his eyes. He comes back over to the couch and plops down next to me. "Brooklyn Briggs, the woman who *always* has a plan, is going to take a years-long crush and turn it into a relationship by winging it?"

Oh goodness, that sounds like a nightmare. Now I understand why Jay was so interested in me telling her my plan. "Okay, well, I have all weekend to think of something." It'll have to be when I'm not still mildly hungover from my migraine. And who knows how much I'll be able to concentrate when I've got Jordan "God's Gift to Women" Torres chilling on my couch and looking at me with that signature look that, back in the day, generally signaled something about to go wrong for me.

I might not have a plan, but I'm starting to think *he* does. And that's dangerous.

"You could ask for my help, you know," he says, wiggling his eyebrows. How does he even do that?

I scoff. "I definitely don't need your help."

"Pretty sure you do."

"If anyone is going to help me, it's Micah. She goes on dates, like, every night."

I've never really understood that part of her. One, I don't get how my little sister manages to get asked out so many times—and it's never her doing the asking—and two, how does she not get tired of being out with people all the time? It's going to be hard enough for me to share my space with Jordan for the next two and a half days (though he's a special sort of frustration all on his own), and I can't imagine having to be that social all the time. Then again, Micah is the most outgoing of my siblings, and she seems to love being the center of strangers' attention.

"Look," Jordan says, bringing my attention back to him. "You can tell me to keep my nose out of your business, but I promise this guy would be an idiot to not fall in love with you the moment he spends any amount of time with you outside of work. But he's also a guy, so it wouldn't be a bad idea to help him out a bit."

While I appreciate the surprising but vague compliment, I'm not sure I like where he's going with this. "Help him out how?"

He grins. "I think it's time I gave you some lessons in flirting, Queens."

Chapter Seven

Jordan

I MIGHT BE AN idiot. Okay, no, there's no *might* in this. I'm just an idiot, plain and simple. While this isn't exactly news to me, it doesn't mean I'm cool with the idea, especially because I've just dug myself a massive hole that I'm not going to enjoy scrambling out of.

The text I got from Houston a few minutes ago tells me this isn't going to end well.

He's literally in a World Series game and texting me from the dugout. He may not have told me anything like this in high school, but it seems Houston is not above being direct. I know it's just his protective side making an appearance, and no one cares about Brooklyn more than he does. But I have to wonder why he decided that now was the moment to tell me something like this, fourteen years after the day I first met her.

Outside of showing her that I'm not the same guy she knew in high school, I had no intentions of doing anything with Brooklyn beyond hanging out and being her mode of transportation, but for some reason Houston thinks I might do otherwise. I'm pretty sure if I tried to make a move, Brooklyn would punch me, and I'm too pretty for a broken nose.

I snort a laugh at my own comment because calling myself pretty is as ridiculous as imagining Brooklyn punching someone. I only realize my mistake when I remember I was in the middle of a conversation with Brooklyn.

And I just offered to teach her to flirt.

Probably shouldn't make her think I'm laughing at that, but it's clearly too late.

She scowls at me, a maelstrom forming in her expression. "What's so funny, *Daniel*? You think I can't flirt?"

"Oh, I know you can flirt. You had half the baseball team in love with you." And it drove Houston crazy. The number of guys he threatened when he caught wind of their interest was astounding. Don't get me wrong—Houston isn't some macho control-freak who scared away all of Brooklyn's prospects. He—we—scared away the ones we knew were jerks, who only went after Brooklyn because she was Houston's sister. Guys like her boyfriend, Garrett Butler, who ignored all of Houston's warnings and dated her anyway.

At least until he got bored and wanted to have a makeout session or worse with his vice president.

I clear my throat before Brooklyn can argue my claim about the team being into her, like I know she will. "Your problem is—"

"My *problem*?"

"You have no idea how to flirt *on purpose*. Remember when you were into the new kid? TJ?"

She swallows, as if the memory leaves a bad taste in her mouth. "I have vague recollections," she admits slowly, which means she absolutely remembers that disaster. "His eyebrows eventually grew back."

I laugh. "You forgot you were holding a *lit* propane torch and tried to smooth his hair back at the Fourth of July barbecue. How do you even forget something like that?"

"I was nervous!"

"And you should probably remember the many Bunsen burners you have in your classroom when you prepare yourself for a conversation with Matt."

"Mark."

"Isn't that what I said?" See, this is why I'm an idiot. It is way too easy to fall back into old patterns of driving her absolutely crazy. I tease people by nature, but with Brooklyn's vindictive side, she makes it all too fun. And teaching her to flirt? That's like giving myself a veritable buffet of teasing fodder, especially if this Mark guy is as much of a pre-chewed piece of gum as I fear he is.

For all the attention Brooklyn gets, she only ever goes for the jerks. I never asked Houston for details about the guys she's dated over the last decade, but knowing she's been single for the last few years after a consistent stream of relationships, I'd guess she has probably taken some emotional hits in her dating life. Houston didn't like any of her boyfriends, which is telling enough. He likes most people.

Let's hope this math teacher is up to snuff. I may be the least qualified person to give her dating advice, considering what I did to my last relationship, but Brooklyn deserves the best. If I can help even a little, I'm going to do it.

"What are these flirting lessons going to look like, exactly?" Brooklyn asks, narrowing her eyes at me as she sips her soda. The fact that she hasn't shut me down makes me wonder how out of practice she really is.

A sense of unease settles in my stomach now that I'm starting to have a chance to really think about this, so I get to my feet to put some distance between us. Heading into the kitchen, I grab some more ice for her ankle as I talk.

"We'll start with the basics and go from there," I say. "What kind of conversations do you and Morgan have?"

"We don't," she replies, surprising me by not correcting his name again. "We've said a few things to each other at, like, staff meetings and things, but we've never really had a conversation until yesterday. And I got all flustered like I always do around guys."

When I return to the couch, she's gone bright red, her eyes locked on the throw pillow she holds.

I gently place the bag of ice on her foot. "You don't get flustered around me."

I say that as an indication of her ability to have a normal conversation with someone, but she must take it a different way because she rolls her eyes.

"Yeah, well, that's because you don't intimidate me."

That's a good thing. But in a weird way, it hurts that she doesn't see me as someone intimidating. Maybe if she'd seen the Jordan Torres who was in California, the one who worked PR for some of the richest people in the state, she would change her tune.

A shudder runs through me. I hope Brooklyn *never* sees that side of me. I hope *no one* does. And yet my eyes jump to my laptop sitting on the floor nearby, and the urge to grab it is only curbed by the ice in my hands, which I still hold because Brooklyn is letting me help her with her injury in a rare show of vulnerability. I miraculously forgot about work for a moment there, and I need to keep my focus on Brooklyn so I don't end up pulling up my website and spending the rest of the night deep diving into market research to find new clients. I should do that at some point this weekend, but I have a feeling Houston would somehow know it if I took my focus off of looking after his sister.

"Why is Mario intimidating?" I ask to distract myself.

Brooklyn barely resists an eye roll, though it threatens to make an appearance if I keep misnaming her crush. "He's crazy smart," she says.

"Ouch. Is that why I don't intimidate you?"

"That's not what I meant."

"I'm kidding, Queens." Mostly.

"I just mean he's basically a math genius, and his kids always get really good test scores which means he's an excellent teacher too."

That's something. I'm pretty sure most of her past boyfriends have been way beneath her, so it's nice to know the guy at least has some decent qualities. Teaching isn't an easy profession, and teaching well takes some skill.

"He's totally cultured and classy, and he has really great tastes in fashion and music. He travels all the time and probably knows a million languages based on where he's gone. And he reads things like *Moby Dick* and Jack Kerouac."

I adjust my hold on the ice before my fingers go numb; I've been gripping the bag too tight. "What does this guy look like?" I ask. Right now, the image in my head is along the lines of a white Steve Urkel, complete with oversized glasses and suspenders. Not someone I can picture with the ever-gorgeous Brooklyn Briggs.

Brooklyn frowns at me. "Why does it matter?"

It doesn't, but her hesitation has my curiosity piqued. "Just answer the question."

"He looks like a thinner Matt Damon with, like, sharper angles." She gets a dreamy look in her eyes that has my stomach twisting in knots. From the sound of things, he's very much not like me, and I hate that more than I should. Brooklyn and I are never going to be an item, but my ego would like to know if she finds me attractive. It's been a question in the back of my mind for years, even if I've never spoken it out loud.

Oh wait. *She told me I'm attractive.* This morning, though I'm not sure I can count it if she's concussed.

Whatever. I'm counting it. Let it be known that Brooklyn Briggs finds me attractive.

"Here's the thing," I say, both to pull her away from her little Mark fantasy and because I'm feeling way more confident now that I've remembered the things she said this morning. "Conversation is crucial to any good relationship. Without it, things fall apart." Something I know a little too well. "Try finding a common interest with Miguel and running with it as long as he seems into the topic."

"That makes sense..." she says slowly, and her hesitation comes out clear. I'm pretty sure she grasps the concept, but she finds the execution a bit more difficult.

"Let's practice," I tell her, moving her legs onto my lap so I can also put my legs on the couch and face her. "Even if you're not intimidated by a lowly landscaper, I'm sure we can at least find something in common and have a conversation. Baseball?"

Her deadpan stare makes me laugh. "Seriously?"

"You never know. It's been a long time since I saw you last. Are there any sports you like?"

She shakes her head. "Do you listen to any podcasts?"

"Nope." I should, though. Houston has recommended a few self-help books that he says have been changing his life one chapter at a time. His favorite stepsister recently got married, and apparently her husband suggested he read them. According to Houston, that guy is *#goals*. Houston practically idolizes him. "I already know you're not big into cooking."

"I *can* cook," she argues. "I just don't like to. Pets?"

I wrinkle my nose. "I'm allergic to cats and haven't ever been into dogs. They're too needy. Do you like running?"

She looks at her swollen ankle, as if that's answer enough. "This clearly isn't working, Jordan. What am I supposed to do if I have nothing in common with Mark?"

Rejoice? Because I may know nothing about the guy, but I already don't like him. He sounds pretentious. Besides, Brooklyn and I have never struggled with conversation. Not even back in the day. I remember some evenings where Houston would give up on trying to keep up with us and play a video game or something while we went at it. Brooklyn always acted like she suffered through our long winded back-and-forths, but she was more often than not the one who started them.

"We can find something," I tell her. Honestly, I don't care what we talk about; I just want her to see that she can do it. "What do you most love doing on the weekends?"

Shrugging, she gestures to the TV. "I don't know. I like watching period pieces. But I doubt you—"

"That's awesome!" And while I may not have seen many—if any—period films, her eyes lit up when she mentioned them, and I am nothing if not good on my feet. I can't have my first flirting lesson fail because I apparently have nothing in common with my best friend's twin anymore. "What's your favorite?"

Though she raises a skeptical eyebrow, she thinks about that for a second and then says, "It depends on my mood. But you can never go wrong with Jane Austen."

"Are you a *Pride and Prejudice* purist? Six-hour version only?" Thank goodness Natalie watched that one all the time when we were together, though I never joined her. At least I know who Jane Austen is, and she mentioned once that the ridiculously long version was way better than any other.

Brooklyn stares at me like I just spoke nonsense, and her voice comes out slightly breathless. "I don't really care. I love them all."

"What do you like about period pieces?" I ask.

She shrugs. "I guess the past seems simpler. There's more structure, and everyone follows the rules. Everyone knows their place and no one has to wonder what kind of life they might live unless they get lucky enough to move up. It all sounds so easy."

I disagree with that—expectations can seriously limit choice—but I keep my thoughts to myself. Brooklyn is smiling now, her gaze going distant as if she's imagining herself living in a different time. I wonder if she's picturing her childhood and envisioning a better life for herself, one where she didn't have a father who cared more about getting his fix than looking after his three kids. I didn't know her and Houston then, and Houston pretty much never talks about his deadbeat dad, who has been in prison for the last decade and a half. But I've inferred a lot over the years, and I know their younger life was pretty rough before they moved in with their wealthy stepdad.

"You and your rules," I mutter, hoping to bring her back to the moment.

She looks at me and scoffs. "Why does it not surprise me that you don't like rules?"

"Rules are great," I argue. "In certain situations. I've already told you that great things can come from chaos. Chaos is the reason Houston and I became friends, isn't it?"

She rolls her eyes. "What's your favorite period film?"

I chuckle, shifting the ice on her ankle again. "I haven't actually seen one," I admit. "Feel free to judge me."

"Oh, I am," she replies. "But I'm also thinking I need to educate you. My house, my movies."

That sounds like the most boring thing in the world—give me mystery and adventure instead—but she's right. I'm already invading her space for the weekend, so I should let her dictate what her weekend is going to look like. "Teach away," I tell her. "Start with one of your favorites."

She narrows her eyes. "*Pride and Prejudice?*"

I don't think I can sit still for that long, but I nod anyway. "If that's what you think will sell me, go for it. I want to see why they're so fascinating so I can better understand you. It will help with tomorrow's flirting lessons." It won't, but I'm going to pretend it will.

She pulls it up, and I nearly breathe a sigh of relief when I see that it's the newer version, the one with the girl from that pirate movie I never saw. Even back in high school, I didn't have much time to sit and watch a movie, and I definitely haven't in the last decade. This is going to be a test of my patience.

"Are you sure you can handle this?" Brooklyn asks, smirking at me in a way that almost feels like a challenge.

"Oh, I can handle it," I growl back.

I just hope I'm right. My computer is still sitting there, calling my name, but I refuse to let work get in the way of building a relationship. Even if that relationship is only a friendship. Someone like Brooklyn is too valuable to toss aside, and I know Houston would kill me if I neglected her when she's injured like this.

And my friendship with Houston is something I can't ruin. I won't. He needs me as much as I need him.

Chapter Eight
Brooklyn

Five minutes into the movie, during which I've barely been able to focus on the Bennett sisters because I'm too busy chiding myself for getting too excited about historical films, Jordan picks up my foot. He was already holding my legs in his lap to ice my ankle, but his cold fingers wrap around my uninjured foot and start kneading. I'm not even sure he realizes he's doing it because his eyes are fixed on the TV, but *I* realize.

I can't think about anything else.

And while it feels amazing, my face burns from his careful touch. "Um."

He freezes, glancing down at his fingers curled around my foot before meeting my gaze. "Sorry," he says with a wince. "I'm not really a 'sit still' kind of person. I can stop if you don't like it."

"No, you can...keep going, I guess." I grimace because that sounded pathetic. "I mean, it feels really nice. I just don't want you to feel obligated."

He trails his cold fingers across the skin of my swollen ankle now without looking down, and that touch sends a shiver through me that doesn't mix well with the heat in my face. "It might be the only way I make it through this movie," he admits with a chuckle. "But it's up to you. I know you have your personal bubble."

I honestly forgot he was in my bubble in the first place, even though I can't remember the last time I sat this close to anyone. The last guy I dated was years ago, and he wasn't really a touchy-feely kind of guy. He didn't even kiss me until we'd known each other for months. Jordan, on the other hand, has never had a concept of personal space, and he was always touching everyone back in high school. High fives, arms around shoulders, holding girls' hands in the halls. He's so similar to Micah in a lot of ways, so if I remind myself that none of these touches mean anything, I might be able to make it through this weekend.

"I would hate for you to get bored," I say and wiggle my toes.

He grins wide, which isn't exactly helping the heat situation. That's the kind of smile that gets women to fall in love with him. It shines so bright against his dark skin, and he's always been quick to smile so it looks full and natural no matter the circumstances. Jordan is generally just happy, and I wish I knew how he did it.

He digs his thumbs into the arch of my good foot, nearly pulling a satisfied groan out of me. "So, you want me to keep going?"

Anyone else, and I might get frustrated by his constant questions, but Jordan remembers my people-pleasing tendencies too well. I kind of love that he gives me every opportunity to tell him what I actually want. And I remember *him* well enough to know that he isn't afraid to do what *he* wants, so this isn't him being unsure of his own actions. He's deferring to me on purpose, something that doesn't happen to me often.

I'm not sure how I feel about Jordan being so grown up and mature. It's messing with my notions of who he is.

"Keep going," I tell him as decisively as I can. "But be careful with—"

He strokes my swollen ankle again, cutting me off with his featherlight touch. "I'll be gentle," he assures me. "I like to leave things better than when I found them."

I'm not sure what that means for me, but whatever worry I might feel from his strange declaration, I quickly forget it as his massage continues. I turn my focus to the movie, as much as I can anyway, and get lost in the story and the sweeping soundtrack, all the while growing more and more comfortable as his hands work across my skin.

Then Jordan switches both hands to my injured foot, and somehow he manages to massage that one too without it hurting. In fact, he makes it feel so good that I almost cry, and I hug a pillow up by my face so he doesn't see. Maybe it's the concussion or the lingering migraine or just the fact that someone is caring for me for the first time in years, but all of this is overwhelming. In a good way. And before Mr. Darcy can smile at Elizabeth when she comes to Pemberley, my eyes droop and I fall asleep.

I wake to a pretty dark room, and it takes me a few seconds to realize where I am. There's a blanket over me that wasn't there before, and the TV is at such a low volume that I can barely hear it. Subtitles flash across the screen as an episode plays from the first season of *Downton Abbey*. How long have I been asleep? And why didn't Jordan turn it off?

Blinking sleep out of my eyes, I look over at him. He's still holding on to my feet, but his hands sit still, one stretched out across my shin as if he'd started moving his massage up along my leg before going motionless. At first, I think maybe he fell asleep like me, but then I realize he's fixated on the TV, nodding along to something Sibyl is saying.

My leg twitches, pulling his attention down to me. "Hey," he says, moving his hands and leaving my leg feeling cold. Who knew hands could be so warm? "Have a nice nap?"

"Why didn't you change it to something else?"

He purses his lips as he pauses the show. "Turns out I really like history. *Pride and Prejudice* sucked me in, and then I wanted more. Don't tell Houston." His smile turns a little more mischievous, which worries me until he says, "Are you hungry? I'll make you some food." He's on his feet before I can say anything, carefully putting my bad foot on a pillow and then heading into the kitchen.

I barely hold back my laughter and reach for my phone before he sees me. Though tempted to tell Houston all of that, I figure I shouldn't alienate the guy who is willing to make me dinner.

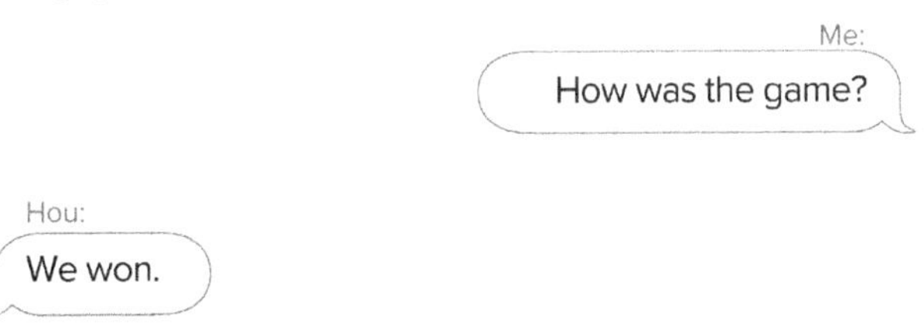

I'm surprised he texted me back so quickly. Usually, on game days, he takes a day or two to respond because he's busy doing interviews or working with the physical therapist to get his arm ready for the next game.

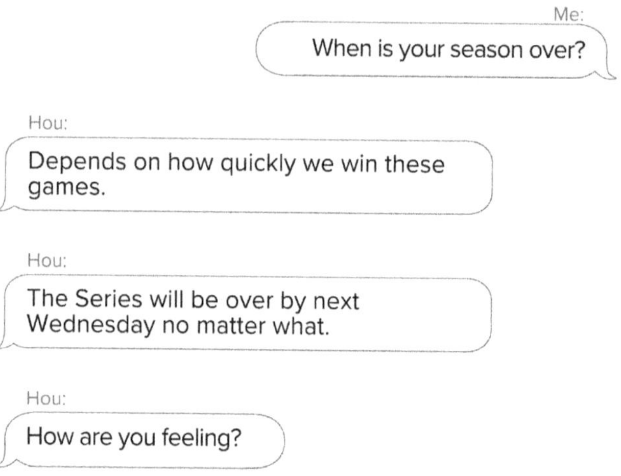

I scowl at my phone, even if my brother can't see me. I *do* proofread, but that means nothing when my phone is determined to make a fool out of me. Who puts the delete button right next to the send button anyway?

I glance over at Jordan, who hums something as he rummages through my cupboards, as if he might have the answer to that question. If I had been on my own, I probably would have lied and told Houston I was fine, but I have a feeling Jordan is going to be giving my brother updates just as much as I am.

Sighing, I tell him that I still have a bit of a headache and probably won't be able to walk for a day or two. He's not going to like that, and I wait for him to tell me that I need to get myself to a hospital so I can get my foot checked out.

"Why is Houston telling me to take you to the hospital, Queens?" Jordan asks. He's frowning down at his phone, but when he meets my eyes, a shiver runs through me because he looks fiercely worried. I didn't even know that was a thing.

"Because he's overreacting," I say, doing my best to sound confident. "I'm fine."

"Would you tell me if you weren't?"

I don't feel like I can say yes to that, so I keep my mouth shut.

He narrows his eyes. "Should I be taking you to a hospital?" he asks, his voice low and dangerous. I appreciate that he's asking, rather than making the decision for me, though I don't know how long that will last.

While I try to match his expression, I feel like I'm squinting more than glaring. "I'm fine," I say as sharply as I can. Being forceful isn't usually in my wheelhouse, but I do my best.

Jordan folds his arms. "Prove it."

How in the world am I supposed to do that? I'm pretty much stuck on this couch until my ankle shrinks back to its usual size. Still, I push myself up off the couch and balance on one foot, glad that my remaining headache is duller than my migraines tend to be.

"Is this proof enough for you?"

It might have been if I'd been able to keep my balance, but my attempt at standing confidently tips me sideways, and I let out a shriek as I go tumbling toward the coffee table.

A pair of arms wrap around me, tugging me into Jordan's strong chest only a moment before disaster. Thank goodness my apartment is so tiny, or he might not have made it to me in time.

"Sorry," he says, the word more of a breath than anything. "I shouldn't have challenged you. You okay, Queens?"

Nope. Mostly because this is the second time he's held me like this, and I'm enjoying it even more than the first time. The way Jordan holds me feels like he's holding my whole life together, which makes absolutely no sense. He's supposed to be the guy who unravels all of my strings because that's what he does. He pokes and pulls until something comes loose.

We were nothing but reluctant acquaintances for all of high school, forced together by our mutual love of Houston, and now we're basically strangers. I have no reason to feel like this man could be good for me somehow. Especially when Mark has finally started talking to me.

"Baseball!" I blurt. *Nice one.* Clearing my throat, I peel myself out of his hold and slump back onto the couch. "Will you tell me how the World Series works? I want to practice having a conversation about something I don't know much about."

Though he stands there looking mildly lost, he recovers quickly and heads back to the kitchen, returning a moment later with two sandwiches that I'm convinced he materialized out of nowhere because they look way too good to have come from my kitchen. "Does Mike like sports?"

"I don't know. Thank you, by the way." I hold up the sandwich, but I also mean thank you for saving me from further injury. I never would have considered myself clumsy before this weekend. "Where did you learn to cook?"

He snickers. "Are we talking about sports or cooking? Because those are two very different things and one has nothing to do with me."

"You used to play baseball," I argue. "So you're not completely unfamiliar with that topic."

"I haven't played since Houston got drafted."

"You played catcher, right?"

His lips twist to one side, as if he can't decide if he likes the direction I'm taking this conversation. Honestly, none of this will be helpful when it comes to Mark, but I feel like I need to know more about Jordan if I'm going to let him teach me to flirt. I never paid enough attention in high school to really get to know him—in fact, I actively avoided him as much as I could—but he seems to know so much about me. Either I haven't changed much since high school (probably true) or Houston talks about me more than I realize (also likely true).

"Yeah, I played catcher," he says eventually. "It's part of the reason Hou and I became friends since we had to work together so much at practice. But I quit the team after he left UCSB to join the Red-tails so I could focus on school."

"What did you study?"

"I thought we were talking about sports."

I narrow my eyes. Hopefully it's less squinty this time. "Is it a difficult question?"

"Just trying to figure out how this information is relevant to the conversation."

"Pretend this is a date," I say and immediately turn bright red, my face so hot that I'm tempted to press my cold fingers to my cheeks. "I mean for me. Pretend you're Mark, and we're on a date, and answer the question."

"Am I answering as if I'm Mickey or myself? Because I don't really know your math textbook crush, so I'm not sure I can—"

I groan. This is why I never bothered to get to know him. He's way too good at pushing my buttons. "Will you stop making this so difficult?"

Chuckling, he holds up his hands in surrender. "Public relations. I got recruited to a firm in Newport Beach right after graduating and worked there up until a year ago."

"Why did you come back?"

"A lot of reasons," he says with a shrug, and I get the weird feeling that he's hiding something in that response. "It's been nice being home while my mom goes through another round of chemo."

My heart sinks, aching for him as I imagine what he's going through. I was so young when my mom got sick, but I have enough vague memories of those days that I know how hard it is to watch someone go through something like that.

As if he sees my shared pain, Jordan reaches out and grabs my hand. "She's doing really well, all things considered. And the doctors are hopeful she'll be in full remission."

"Thank you," I choke as my body relaxes. I hadn't even realized how tense I had gotten. "I mean, thanks for telling me. I'll be sending good vibes her way."

"Thanks." He swallows, studying my face, and then he looks down at our clasped hands before pulling his fingers back. "Uh, you wanted to know about the World Series? What sort of stuff?"

I'm not sure why the room feels slightly different than it did a minute ago, but it does. Like things have shifted ever so slightly. And I have no idea what to do about that. "How does it work? Houston said something about how quickly they win."

Jordan's smile looks less real than it usually does, which makes me wonder if he feels the shift too. "Well, it's best out of seven, so if they win the first four games, the Series only lasts four games. But they lost the first game, so they'll play at least five."

"They won tonight," I say, even if that's hardly contributing to the conversation. I'm sure Jordan already knows that part. "And they won the last game too."

His smile growing wider—more natural—he nods. "They did. They won today because Houston rarely loses. If his team plays well tomorrow, he might not even have to pitch again since he won't pitch until Game Six." For some reason, he seems relieved about that.

"Who decides which teams get to play?" I ask, though I'm tempted to ask why Jordan doesn't seem to want Houston to pitch again this season.

My brother only has a year left on his contract, so wouldn't he want Houston to play as much as he can? Whatever the reason, it feels like something Jordan or even Houston would tell me if it was important, so I'm going to let it go for now.

Instead, I let Jordan walk me through the ins and outs (literally) of baseball because I like the way he relaxes the longer he talks. And, it turns out, I like talking to him. He never makes me feel stupid for not knowing something, and he explains things in a way that's so easy to understand.

And maybe there's a small part of me that wonders if he's always been this easy to talk to and I was just too annoyed to see the real guy underneath the teasing. That's as intriguing as it is slightly terrifying, and I don't let myself dwell on the idea of forming an actual friendship with my brother's best friend.

Or anything beyond.

Chapter Nine

Jordan

THERE IS NOTHING CUTER than a sleepy Brooklyn Briggs. While she's cute no matter how awake she is, I discover pretty quickly that she loses all inhibitions when she gets tired. I don't mean she starts saying weird things or spilling random truths. No, when Brooklyn gets tired, she goes into sweetness overload.

After telling her about how my mom taught me to cook, especially over the last year, our conversation shifts to the types of food we like, and Brooklyn goes off about this Chinese place nearby that is run by a cute lady who barely speaks English but always gives her an extra fortune cookie, which means Brooklyn always tips extra.

Then we talk about how fortune cookies aren't even Chinese, and she says she loves them anyway and keeps all of her fortunes. Apparently she has a stockpile of them somewhere in this basement, though she won't tell me where. When I mention never paying attention to my fortunes, Brooklyn offers to share hers because everyone needs some extra luck in their lives.

After several more random topics, she starts getting extra tired, and we turn on *Downton Abbey* again, which leads to Brooklyn saying everything she loves about each of the characters and crying during the more emotional scenes. She makes it seem like the characters are her friends. No matter how interested I am in the show, I'm way more fascinated by the girl on the other side of the couch who feels so much.

Maybe a little too fascinated. I've always wanted to know her, but now that she's actually giving me a chance to see beyond the beautiful exterior, I'm learning she's even more beautiful inside. Houston talks all the time about his twin's kindness and empathy, but I'm starting to think he has grossly underestimated her pure heart. It has me wondering again why she has only ever dated jerks and guys who think watching paint dry is interesting.

Does she not realize that she deserves someone who will adore every facet of her? I know there are good guys out there, but somehow she always picks the bad ones.

Who Brooklyn dates is definitely none of my business, but I have put myself in a unique position with this flirt coaching idea I came up with. For however long she lets this last, I have the chance to build her up and make sure she stops settling.

When she eventually falls asleep beside me, I pause the show so we can pick back up tomorrow. Even if I'd like to keep going, I don't know if watching it on my own will compare to appreciating the characters the way Brooklyn does. I wonder if she sees everything with such love and fascination, and then I come to the conclusion that I'm doing way too much wondering when it comes to Brooklyn.

"Hey, Queens," I say, nudging her shoulder. She doesn't budge, which is surprising with how much she's already slept today. "Brooklyn, I'm going to take you to your bed, okay?" I probably shouldn't just pick her up and take her to her room, as easy as it would be. I've taken a lot of liberties as it is.

Slipping off the couch, I crouch in front of her and give in to the temptation to tuck some hair behind her ear to get it out of her face. It's as soft as it looks. "You gotta give me something, sleepyhead, or I'll be trading you for your bed if you stay here. I'm not sleeping on the floor."

Her eyes snap open. "You're going to sleep here?"

I laugh. "Who else will help you to the bathroom in the middle of the night?"

She shakes her head at the same time she turns bright red. "I wasn't planning on asking you to—"

"You have the bladder of a child," I say with a laugh. "Pretty sure that hasn't changed since we were kids." And maybe me knowing that is creepy, but there were plenty of nights when I didn't want to go home and instead spent the night on the couch in Houston's room. Most of the time, I couldn't sleep—a problem I still face years later because my brain never shuts off—and without fail I would hear Brooklyn creep into the bathroom she shared with her brother in the middle of the night.

It was nice, knowing someone else in the world was awake. Even if it was just for a few minutes.

"I don't want to wake you up," she says, biting her lip as she studies me. "I feel bad enough that I only have a couch to offer. And that you're stuck here in the first place."

At this point, I've lost count of the number of times she's tried to get rid of me. Grinning, I make a bold move and push even more hair back away from her face. "Will you just let me take care of you?" I ask with mock frustration. "It's my favorite thing to do."

"Really?"

"I'm not sure how I feel about your tone of surprise yet again, Queens. Come on. Bedtime."

Though I can see the reluctance in her eyes, she reaches up and wraps her arms around my neck. "Have I told you how much I hate this?" she says as I pull her into my arms. "I feel so lame."

"You are anything but lame." I glance at her swollen foot as we make our way to the bathroom. "Okay, technically you *are* lame. But not in the figurative sense."

She snorts. "You're still such a dork."

"Always."

Once I'm sure she's good on her own in the bathroom, I borrow her bedroom to change into sweats and a t-shirt since I have no desire for her to somehow appear in the living room while I'm in the middle of changing. Coming in here, though, might have been a bad idea. Now all I want to do is explore and see what I can learn about Brooklyn Briggs. She's so similar to the girl I knew in high school, but that doesn't mean she hasn't changed. I wonder if I can figure out why she seems to have closed in on herself more than normal.

She's always been on the quiet side, but I know there's a wild girl in there somewhere. She can't be Houston's twin without having some backbone and adventure underneath the calm. She once locked Houston and me in the laundry room all night because I called her boyfriend a flat tire filled with sewage, and she was never afraid to call me out when I was acting obnoxious, which happened often. Plus, there were all the pranks...

Where did that girl go?

"What have you become, Queens?" I murmur as I begin my perusal of her room.

Everything is pretty straightforward and, frankly, boring. She has a couple of plants that look like they're barely hanging on because they're not getting enough light in this basement—I make a note to get her something sturdier. Textbooks line the little bookshelf that is the cause of her concussion, but she also has a few different versions of all of the Jane Austen books—isn't one copy enough? Beyond that, everything else in her room is generic, mismatched, and, from the looks of it, thrifted, which fits Brooklyn so well but also gives me nothing when it comes to learning something new about her.

She always puts herself second. Secondhand furniture, pictures of her siblings but none with her in them, a closet full of skirts and dresses even though I know she hates wearing dresses. Or she used to. But I'm going to guess that's the sort of thing she wears to work because it's more professional.

I shift some dresses to the side, hoping to find a secret stash of emo-punk band t-shirts somewhere. There's no way she didn't keep them when I have fond memories of listening to her belt along to her favorites in the car anytime the three of us drove somewhere together.

"Are you going through my closet?" Brooklyn calls, her voice higher in pitch than normal.

I grin, glad she can't see me. "How else am I supposed to learn all your secrets?"

"I'm ready for bed, if you care to be useful."

Chuckling, I abandon my search and head over to the bathroom, scooping her up as if I've been doing this our whole lives. She may have said she hates that I have to carry her everywhere, but she also leans right into me. I still have her phantom hand pressing against my abs like she did this morning and making me glad that I've been getting up early in the mornings to hit the gym. Dating is the last thing on my mind right now, but at least I know I can jump back in with confidence if I ever get brave enough to try again.

After what happened with Natalie, who knows when that will be?

"You are taking too much pleasure in being my dashing hero," she mumbles as I place her on top of her bed.

"Thank you."

"I wasn't trying to give you a compliment."

Stepping back, I fold my arms and raise an eyebrow at her. "You called me dashing. That sounds like a compliment to me."

There's the eye roll I know and love. How many times am I going to get that out of her this weekend? I should probably warn her that one day her eyes might get stuck in the back of her head.

"Has anyone ever told you that you think too highly of yourself?"

"I'm pretty sure *you* have."

She lets out a deep sigh. "Can I go to bed now?"

Still grinning, I nod and head for the door, though I pause before I reach the hallway and look back at her, tucking my amusement away so she knows I'm no longer joking. "I'm serious about helping you in the middle of the night if you need it, Queens. I'm a light sleeper anyway, so I'll probably wake up regardless."

She cringes, but to my surprise she nods. "I'll let you know. Thanks, Jordan. For all of this."

I can't help but smirk. Something about Brooklyn Briggs just brings out my annoying side. "How painful was it for you to say that?"

She groans. "Close the door on your way out."

I do, chuckling to myself as I make my way to the couch that is going to be my home for the next two nights. It's late, and I am strangely tired from having spent most of the day looking at the TV. But instead of settling down to try to get a few hours of sleep, I grab my computer and pull up my schedule now that there's nothing to distract me.

This weekend is pretty sparse in terms of jobs, which is why I'm mostly okay with letting my team handle the rest of the jobs we have lined up. But it's *too* sparse. Granted, No Mow Problems has only been up and running for about six months, but even with Houston putting in all of the startup money, I'm barely breaking even right now.

"Not enough," I mutter as I send an email to my website guy with a few tweaks I want him to make.

My dad brings in a pretty decent paycheck with the contract work he does with the military, and I know Alejandro and his wife, Paige, are paying for the kids' care even though my mom tried to refuse them because they're in a lot of debt. But my mom's medical expenses aren't small, and I need to start bringing in more money so I can actually help more than making meals a few times a week when I have the time. I haven't even let myself think about what it would cost to get myself a house so I don't have to crowd my family, even if I'm dying being a twenty-eight-year-old living with his parents after being on my own for almost a decade. My mom is already stressed enough with whatever is going on with Mateo, my niece Madi is showing signs of needing extra tutoring because of a potential learning disability, and there's basically nothing I can do to help. And it's killing me.

I used to work with the biggest names in California, making more money in five years than my parents have seen in a lifetime. I don't regret giving everything to Natalie after what went down, but sometimes I wish I had thought to give more to my parents when I could.

There were a lot of things I neglected back then.

Needing a distraction, I pull up another Jane Austen movie—this one called *Emma*—and turn my focus back to my work while it plays in the background. I need to find a way to get my client list to a sustainable level and start bringing in some better money.

It's the only way I'm going to get back to a real life.

October 12

When I wake, my computer slides from my lap, and I barely catch it before it crashes to the floor. Nice way to get my heart rate going, I suppose. I'm not sure what woke me up—could have been anything—but the room is a lot lighter than I expected.

"Hi."

I should have taken out my contacts, but I wouldn't have been able to see my computer. Fine time to forget to bring my glasses with me. I have to blink a few times before I realize Brooklyn is sitting on the ottoman with a bowl of cereal in her hand as she watches me. How did she get there?

"Hi," I say, rubbing my face. Did I sleep through the night? I don't remember the last time that happened. (Though, can I really call it *through the night* if I fell asleep around three? Not that the semantics really matter...)

Brooklyn smiles, and it's the kind of smile that usually precedes a prank. "Did you know that you talk in your sleep?"

It takes everything in me not to cringe. I thought I'd made it through life unscathed when she didn't figure this out about me in high school, but now that secret's out. That could be dangerous. "I did know this," I say warily, eyeing her phone where it sits beside her. "What did I say?"

Her grin grows wider. "You were complaining about the price of eggs being atrocious. I didn't know you were such a cheapskate, Jordan."

I mean, eggs really have gotten expensive, but I have no idea why I would be dreaming about it.

"Don't worry," she says, as if I actually had a response. "When I tried to record you, I only ended up with about a thousand pictures of my forehead, so you're safe."

I'm not sure I like knowing that the only reason the whole internet doesn't now know my stance on egg commerce is because Brooklyn is technologically challenged.

I need to change the subject. "What are you eating?" I ask, putting as much disgust into the question as I can.

The face she makes at me reminds me of seventeen-year-old Brooklyn, the one who somehow figured out that I was making out with my girlfriend under the bleachers during a football pep rally and sent one of the assistant principals to put me in detention, all because I *accidentally* spilled ketchup on her quarterback boyfriend's jersey at lunch. She's trouble.

The best kind of trouble.

"I'm eating breakfast," she says lightly. It's like a switch got flipped overnight, and I'm not sure if it's because she no longer has a migraine or because that concussion knocked some sense back into her. The quiet and subdued Brooklyn I saw yesterday was fine, but this morning she seems more like the girl I knew.

I wrinkle my nose. "That is not breakfast. That's diabetes in a bowl."

"I can get you some if you're jealous." She glances down at her foot, which is still swollen. "Okay, you can get yourself some. I may have spilled half my bowl trying to get over here to sit down."

Glancing toward the kitchen, I spot the puddle of milk and cereal, my whole body growing tense. Something tells me she left it there just to see what I'll do, and I'm torn between cleaning it up for her like the gentleman that I am and being more unpredictable to keep her on her toes.

Why not do both?

"Give me that," I say, grabbing the bowl from her before she can fight me on it. I take a bite, just to mess with her, and then I shudder. "New flirting lesson. If this Mochi guy is as sophisticated as you say, he's not going to appreciate your love of Captain Crunch. I'm taking you to breakfast." I say that last part as I head to the kitchen, stepping over her mess and dumping the rest of her food in the sink.

"Why?" Brooklyn folds her arms in indignation. "I've already eaten."

I grab a few paper towels to clean up her spill. "You're going to be hungry again in twenty minutes. Have you showered yet?" I glance up. "You're going to shower, and then we're going out. I'm taking you on a fancy brunch date."

I don't miss the way she turns bright red, though I have no idea what to do with that. This is uncharted territory, and I'm going to take things one minute at a time. Wherever we end up, I just have to hope we're both better off for it.

Chapter Ten

Brooklyn

THIS MIGHT BE THE most humiliating moment of my life. Which is a shame because the morning started off so well.

It's a good thing my foot can take a little weight today, or I would have had to shower while sitting on the floor. It's weird enough showering with Jordan in my house, and I don't need to feel like I'm not capable of my usual routine.

Routine might be the only thing that keeps me from losing my mind this weekend.

For about twenty seconds after I woke up, I forgot about the events of Friday. It was just a normal Saturday morning, full of silence and nothing to do. But as soon as I tried to get out of bed, my sprained ankle reminded me of the man sleeping just down the hall, and I praised the heavens that my bladder decided to hold its peace during the night. I managed to crawl to the bathroom on my own, but once I reached the living room where Jordan clearly fell asleep while working, I knew I had reached the end of my independence.

Today doesn't feel as awkward as yesterday did though, which is nice. I'm fully functional again—mentally, anyway—and seeing Jordan when he's asleep sparked something inside me. I don't think I realized how much expression he really has until I saw him without it. When he was sleeping, he looked so much more at peace. For someone who doesn't read body language super well, I feel like it means something for me to notice how *not* tense he is while he sleeps.

There's a lot more to this man than I was giving him credit for yesterday, and I feel like I need to make myself forget how things were back in high school. I can't dwell on how often he teased me or my boyfriends—especially them—even if he's still very much a teasing kind of guy. He's different enough that I almost want to pretend I don't know him at all so I can really get to know the man he is now.

I just don't want to know him *this* well.

Holding my towel firmly in place, I crack open the door and peek my face through. "Jordan?"

It only takes him two seconds to appear from the living room. "You ready to…" Yep. Only took him two more seconds to realize I'm in nothing but a towel. "Oh."

I sigh. "My room isn't that far. I can…" But I can't hop. I'm barely managing to stand as it is after my mostly one-footed shower, and I don't trust my towel to do its job if I have to hop to my room. "Just carry me quickly."

"Nope." Jordan stuffs his hands into the pockets of his sweats, which look way too good on him. Sweatpants are not supposed to look that good on anyone. He may not have played baseball since his college days, but that doesn't mean he's lost the physique.

Have you ever seen a guy in baseball pants? I don't especially like sports, but I can appreciate a guy in uniform.

Jordan clears his throat, pulling my gaze back to his face. "Sorry, Queens, but I'm drawing a line. Too much skin."

I suppose I should be insulted that he doesn't want to touch my skin, but I know Jordan. He's always been a hands-on kind of guy with everything he does. He probably has a point.

"Can you grab me some clothes, then?"

He looks towards my bedroom and then keeps his eyes directed away from me. "What do you want?"

"Anything." Anything to get me away from standing here almost naked in front of my brother's best friend.

A smile twitches on his lips. "I'm going to have to open your underwear drawer," he warns, and I want to smack him.

"It's not like you haven't seen women's underwear before," I snap.

He doesn't argue, which sends my stomach tumbling. *Oh*. I guess I was hoping my comment wouldn't be true, though I don't know what I expected. Just because I'm waiting for marriage, doesn't mean everyone else has the same viewpoints. How many women has he… Nope. I don't need to know.

"Just grab whatever," I say, my words stuttering. "Anything hanging in my closet is fine, and just whatever, uh, underwear is on top." Really, I should have just put my pajamas back on once I realized I forgot to grab a change of clothes. It wouldn't have mattered that much.

"I'll be right back," Jordan says, and he glances back at me for half a second before disappearing into my room.

He takes way longer than I'd like to come back with a pile of clothes, complete with a bra and panty neatly folded on top. Honestly, I expected him to rummage through my drawer and find the sexiest thing I own—a black lace set that I only have because one of my stepsisters gave it to me years ago—but he picked out my comfiest bra even though it's plain and beige and does nothing but hold everything in place.

I must be making a face because he chuckles. "Don't think I wasn't tempted," he says, which could mean anything.

Jordan picked out a pair of black leggings and an oversized long-sleeved shirt—again a surprise—so when I finally open the door, fully dressed in one of my comfiest outfits, I have no idea what to expect from this guy. It's like he was designed to know exactly what women really want. There's no way he's this perfect.

Then again, Jordan has always operated by the mantra that life is meant to be lived. He has never hidden who he is or what he wants, which has always been both inspiring and irritating. He makes it look so easy, like being known isn't the most terrifying thing in the world. So unless that part of him has changed, this thoughtfulness is just who he is.

When he hears the door squeak open, Jordan gingerly pokes his head around the corner and then smiles when he sees me fully clothed. "How did I do?" he asks as he lifts me into his arms.

"I hope you're not planning on taking me somewhere fancy dressed like this."

He laughs. "Oh, it'll be fancy. You need proper tutoring. But I figured you might as well be comfortable while you're still in training wheels."

Confirmed. Jordan is too good to be true.

"I'm going to take a quick shower," he says as he sets me on the couch and hands me a bag of ice. "Make sure you keep the ice on your ankle until I get back, or we're never going to get you walking again."

Though I roll my eyes, he's probably right. Even if it hurts, I dutifully press the ice to my ankle and raise my eyebrows at him. "Are you going to shower, or what? I'm not going anywhere with you if you smell like that."

He laughs. "Nice to see you coming back into your old self, Queens." And then he's gone.

I frown. What does he mean by that? I know I was fairly quiet (and embarrassing) yesterday, but I don't feel like I'm acting all that different today. I'm still just me, the same boring Brooklyn Briggs who can't use a smartphone to save her life.

Speaking of phones, I notice Jordan has moved mine from my room to the coffee table, where he plugged it in to a charging cord that is definitely not mine. The man is even charging my phone for me? I doubt he knows how often I accidentally let it die because I don't pay attention to the battery until it's too late. But the fact that he even thought to check has my heart swelling in my chest all Grinch-like.

I should be nicer to him. He may be good at teasing, but he's also been incredibly helpful to me and is giving up his whole weekend just because my brother asked him to. I'm looking for a catch to his do-gooder routine, but I can't seem to find one.

What is he hoping to get out of this weekend?

He showers quickly and returns to my living room in jeans and a Henley, looking way too comfortable in my space as he tucks his sweats into his duffel bag and slips on a pair of canvas sneakers. I've been good and kept the ice on my ankle the whole time, but I am more than happy to hand it over to him and let him dump the bag out in the sink.

When he comes back to my side and holds out his arms, I cringe.

He laughs at the look on my face. "Hey, don't look at me like that. You're the one who refused to go to the hospital."

A shudder runs through me. Yeah, I refused, and unless I'm bleeding, missing a limb, or about to have a baby, I'll probably keep avoiding the hospital. It doesn't matter how many times I tell myself that doctors are good and important; they're always going to remind me of my mom.

Shaking away the gloom that starts to settle over me from thinking about the day she died, I fold my arms. There's no reason for me to be stubborn, but I can't help it. Jordan makes me want to be stubborn. Always has. "It's humiliating enough letting you carry me around the house where no one can see me. I don't think I'll survive you carrying me around town."

He lifts an eyebrow. "You know I'm not going to give you a choice, right? You can't spend your Saturday locked up in this dungeon and expect Matthew to think you're interesting."

I know he's saying Mark's name wrong on purpose, and I know I should just ignore him. But that's easier said than done. Especially today when I'm fully lucid. "His name is Mark," I snap.

"And you know I'm right," he argues back. "You gotta get out there and live a little."

He may be right—I hate how much he's right—but that doesn't make this easier. "I don't want you carrying me around in your arms, Jordan."

"How about piggy back?" He spins, crouching down and showing off his backside. Of course I find Mark attractive, but I have never once admired Mark's body. He's slim and trim, probably spending more time indoors with books and documentaries than physical movement. It's one of the reasons I like him. But Jordan?

Jordan is the definition of fit and strong. And hot fudge, does he look good.

"I'm waiting," he says, looking over his shoulder at me.

I sigh. He's really not going to let me fight him on this. "Fine," I grumble, and then I hop forward and awkwardly climb onto his back with my arms wrapped over his collarbone.

He straightens and heads for the door with the haste of someone who knows I'm likely to change my mind. "Was that so hard?" he asks.

"Yes. Yes, it was." Only, I'm just now realizing how good this man smells, and suddenly it's all I can think about. I know for a fact that I don't have this scent in my bathroom, so he must have brought some body wash from home. I will be investigating immediately upon returning home because I need to know what this is so I can buy out the whole stock and have it forever. It's taking everything in me not to nuzzle my face into his neck and breathe in deeply.

When we reach his large truck, he opens the passenger door and then spins around, letting me slide off his back onto the seat. Then he gives me a smirk. "You can keep smelling me as we drive."

Kill me now. It's a good thing there's no chance of Jordan ever wanting to date me because I am clearly way too awkward to act like a normal human around men. I'm great with teenagers and other women, but I'm even more hopeless than I thought when it comes to interacting with the opposite sex.

It's possible I spend my life focusing on the wrong kind of chemistry. It's no wonder Mark hasn't talked to me before now.

He quickly works to unhook the large trailer that holds a bunch of yard equipment, and then he hops into his seat and starts up the truck. There must be something written on my face, though, because he doesn't pull away immediately. Instead, he softens his smile. "Don't worry, Queens. I'll get you in tip top shape for your buddy Miles. When I'm through with you this weekend, he'll be all over you." He winces at the same time I do. "Not... You know what I mean."

"I'll be lucky if Mark even talks to me again," I mumble.

"Luck has nothing to do with it. It's all about confidence."

I huff. "Easy for you to say."

Though he shakes his head, he's quiet for a while as he heads downtown. Whatever he's thinking about, I'm not sure I want to know what it is. Most likely it means something nerve-wracking for me. That's usually the case when Jordan gets contemplative.

When we hit a stop light, he glances at me and then laughs, which doesn't exactly make me feel any better. "Would you relax? You're looking at me like I'm driving you to your doom."

"Knowing you, that's more likely than you seem to think."

"I'm just trying to help you. And remember, you agreed to this."

I fold my arms, nodding at the light when it turns green. "I was concussed. I can't be held responsible for anything I may or may not have agreed to yesterday. Besides, your notion of 'helping' has never been very helpful."

He can't stop smiling, which is making all of this worse. "Name one time I helped but didn't help."

Where do I even start? "Prom."

"Which one?"

"The one where you 'helped' me get voted prom queen and then cheated to get yourself picked as king over Garrett."

His argument comes so quickly that he must have been thinking of our senior year already. "First of all, I didn't do a single thing to get you voted in. That was all you. Second, I'm insulted that you think I couldn't win prom king all on my own. Third—"

"Preferably in a quieter section of the restaurant," Jordan replies. "My date got a concussion yesterday."

He must give her one of his potent smiles because she turns a pretty pink and smiles right back. "I'll see what I can do. Wait here."

Jordan adjusts his hold on me, though he could easily put me down while we wait. "I agree you know how to capture a man's interest," he says, continuing our conversation, "but that doesn't mean you know how to invoke *desire*. There's a difference between catching notice and capturing attention. Unless you want Mr. Math to be like every other guy and leave you when he gets bored, you need to learn the art of finesse. Reel him in until he's good and hooked and can't picture life without you."

I understand what he's saying, and I know he's trying to help. But my mind latches on to one word in particular, leaving me feeling dizzy and nauseous. *Bored.* Is that why no guys have stuck around? I'm boring? I don't actually need an answer to that question because I already know. I watch old movies and study textbooks, and I spend more time in my dark little basement by myself than I should. Houston took all the interesting genes, leaving me with nothing to *keep* a man's interest.

That must be why Mark hasn't shown any interest before now. He's seen enough over the last few years to know I'm not worth his time. Despite chemistry being my best subject, I'm not skilled enough to make it in the research world on my own, so what do I really have to offer a man?

"Right this way," the hostess says when she returns with another bright smile for Jordan and more of a smirk for me. Not sure what I did to earn her dislike, but I'm going to blame the outfit Jordan picked out. Just to make myself feel a little better.

Jordan helps me into my chair and then settles in his own seat looking right at home in a fancy restaurant. The only time I ever go out to eat is when my siblings do something together, but I can picture Jordan spending a lot of his time out on the town. Then again, he's pretty skilled in the kitchen, so maybe not?

"Why are you looking at me like that?" he asks as the hostess leaves to get our waitress.

I wish I knew what my face was doing. "Like what?"

He chuckles. "Like you're mad at me for calling this a date? Or maybe like you're trying to decide if it's worth crawling out of here and leaving me behind. You're hard to read right now, which is why I asked."

"Neither of those things," I admit. "Though, this is not a date." I can't even imagine what Houston would think if the two of us actually went on a date. My brother knows how much we annoyed each other back in high school, so he generally tried to keep us apart. Besides, Jordan is Hou's best friend. His *only* friend. I would never want to make things awkward for him by changing the status quo.

"What if it were, though?" Jordan asks.

My stomach does a flip. "What?"

Throwing his head back, Jordan laughs like I just said the world's funniest joke. "Okay, wow, I guess I didn't need my ego. It's fine if you think being on a date with me is that horrific. Relax, Queens. I just meant you should pretend you're on a date with Michael."

"Oh."

"Hi, welcome to La Bella, can I get any drinks started for—oh hey, aren't you Micah's sister?"

Still off kilter from momentarily thinking Jordan might want to be on a date with me, I can barely process what the waitress just said. "Huh?"

She's similar in age to Micah, and the name on her name tag—Kinley—sounds familiar, so Micah has probably talked about her. Micah talks about a lot of people though, mostly because she has a new date every other night, so at this point all the names I've heard have blurred together.

"Sorry," she says with a broad smile. "That's probably weird 'cause we haven't met. I'm Micah's best friend, Kinley."

Suddenly I feel like a terrible sister for not knowing the name of her best friend. "Oh, right. Hi."

"We were just talking about you, actually," Jordan throws in. "Thought maybe you would be working this morning."

I give him a look that I hope says he's full of it, but then Kinley turns a pretty pink color and smiles even wider. She seems sweet, exactly the kind of person Micah would like, and apparently being talked about is a pretty big confidence boost for her.

"I don't usually waitress," she says brightly, "but I'm covering some-one else's shift. What are the odds of running into you guys, huh?" Her eyes go wide as she looks at me, then at Jordan, and then back to me.

I know she's trying to tell me something, but I have no idea what it is. The one thing I do know is Micah is going to hear about this "date" as soon as Kinley goes into the back, and I'm not looking forward to that.

More than anyone, Micah pushes me to get myself out there and find my true love, and she's going to take me sitting here with Jordan as a sign that the universe has finally brought us together. She was just a middle schooler most of the time Jordan was around at our house, but she knows him almost as well as I do.

Which, at the moment, feels like not at all.

"I'll just have water," Jordan says, thankfully pulling Kinley's atten-tion away from me. "Brook, what do you want?"

I haven't even looked at the menu, but if this were a date with Mark, who is cultured and mature, I wouldn't order hot chocolate like I want to. Sun City may never drop below seventy degrees most of the time, but hot chocolate is good no matter the temperature outside.

"Water with lemon?" I say, though it comes out like a question.

Kinley flashes another wide smile. "You got it! Be right back with those waters."

She's barely out of earshot before Jordan sits forward, leaning his elbows on the table like he's about to spill the tea. "Don't go giving me dirty looks for saving your bacon," he says with narrowed eyes. "And no, you probably shouldn't order bacon. Bacon is a layman's breakfast, and probably not something your fancy mop bucket of a crush would approve of."

Mark probably wouldn't approve of ordering pancakes at a fancy restaurant either.

"Thanks," I mutter. "I'm pretty sure I've heard Micah talk about her before, but I guess I don't pay that much attention."

"Hey." He reaches across the table, like he might put a hand on mine, but instead picks up his napkin-wrapped cutlery and opens it. "I've barely even talked to my youngest brother since coming back from California. It's hard to stay connected sometimes."

That doesn't really make me feel better, but I appreciate the solidarity. "I guess this is my sign to try a little harder to be a part of Micah's life."

Jordan twists his lips, his eyebrows dipping low as he looks at me. Whatever that means, he's really laying into the expression.

"Here's that water for you!" Kinley is back, still full of smiles. "It's so fun to finally get another Briggs sib in here! I love Micah, but she's here so often that I've gotten used to seeing her around."

"She must really like the food," Jordan says.

"She really likes the familiarity," Kinley counters with a laugh. "Plus, I've gotten good at chasing away her dates when they're duds. It's always fun to see the kinds of guys she brings in here."

I frown. "Micah brings all of her dates here? Really?"

"That's how we met. I started recognizing her and realizing she had a different guy every time, so I asked her about it. And here we are! It's too bad you didn't come tonight instead of this morning so you could watch the date she has with her mailman."

I'm sorry, with her *what*?

This time Jordan *does* grab my hand, probably to stop me from freaking out about my little sister going out with random men who shouldn't be asking her out in the first place. "I think we're probably ready to order," he says, even though I still haven't opened my menu.

I glance down, scanning the brunch items for anything that sounds like something Mark would like even though the waffles sound amazing right now. "Uh, I'll have the salmon omelet," I say warily.

"Biscuits and gravy." Jordan doesn't hesitate at all with his choice, and it sounds a million times better than whatever I just said. But if I'm going to pretend to be on a date with Mark and practice this whole fish reeling nonsense, I have to play the game right. Not that fishing is a game. Or dating. Games are supposed to be fun.

Only when Kinley heads back to the kitchen does Jordan free my hand, sitting back in his chair and giving me an easy smile. "So," he says. "Logarithms, am I right?"

If this is him trying to pretend to be Mark, this is going to be an epic failure. "Do you even know what a logarithm is?"

"Something mathy. PR doesn't really require algebra or trigonometry, so…"

"Did you know chemistry has a ton of math to it?"

He laughs. "I knew there was a reason I didn't like it."

"Hey, don't be hating on chemistry."

"Oh, I'm a huge fan of chemistry. It's the most important ingredient in a budding relationship, so I hope you and Mushu have it in ample supply."

I wouldn't know, considering our one and only conversation started with me screaming. "What kind of PR work did you do, anyway?"

"Deflection. I see how it is. I worked mainly with high profile celebrities and business tycoons. The big fish."

"What is with you and fish metaphors?"

"What is with you ordering salmon for breakfast?"

I scowl at him, even if his comment is perfectly valid. "You don't know my tastes, Jordan. I've grown up a lot since you saw me last."

"I'll say," he mutters, though I'm not sure he meant for me to hear it. "We're getting off the topic of your flirting training, but I'll allow a slight detour if you really want to know about my work. I was pretty important once upon a time."

That should come across as bragging, but it doesn't. Jordan has this way of saying things that always sound easy and carefree, and I've always been jealous of his confidence. I once heard him tell someone at one of the baseball team's afterparties that he had a knack for saying all the right things to girls, and I found myself nodding along with him even though I had only snuck downstairs to grab a snack and hated the way he so easily charmed girls.

Jordan Torres could tell a guy that he had the emotional range of a cowbell, and the guy would probably thank him for the compliment.

"What is your craziest client story?" I ask, too curious not to.

He spends the next ten minutes regaling me with ridiculous shenanigans that I can't believe he managed to sweep under the rug, like when a popular music artist got caught climbing the rafters of a Costco warehouse and Jordan convinced the company that the singer songwriter was actually promoting the product on the shelves. Apparently sales of that product tripled after a video of the incident went viral.

When our food arrives, I catch a whiff of Jordan's biscuits and gravy first, and it smells heavenly. My omelet...not so much. I don't especially like fish to begin with, and it's so early in the day that my brain is fixated on breakfast food. Salmon is not that. Still, if I were here with Mark, I couldn't just not eat my breakfast and then ask him to stop at McDonald's on the way home. That would do the opposite of impressing him.

So I cut into the omelet and take a bite, telling myself over and over that this is going to be delicious.

It's not. It's not even close to delicious.

Right as I consider flagging Kinley down and ordering something else, Jordan grabs my plate and pulls it toward him, simultaneously pushing his own food in my direction.

My heart beats hard in my chest when he doesn't even look up before taking a bite of the omelet and nodding like it's the best thing he's ever tasted. Though I should suck it up and deal with my own choice, I take a tiny bite of the biscuits and gravy, nearly moaning with pleasure because it's so good.

"You really don't have to do that," I murmur, desperately hoping he argues.

He grins at me before taking another bite. "I like salmon," he says, as if switching meals is totally normal. "Besides, I do this all the time with my wife."

His face falls at the same time I choke on a piece of sausage, and then we stare at each other in the most awkward silence of my life.

Chapter Eleven

Jordan

"Ex-wife." I say that so quickly that it comes out in a breath, but it doesn't really change the way Brooklyn stares at me like I'm suddenly a stranger.

I hadn't meant to bring up Natalie. She's the kind of thing you bring up on an actual date, but, like, the third or fourth date. Not on a mock date after a decade apart, in which you're trying to build her up for some other guy who probably doesn't deserve her. I don't often get angry, but I'm angry with myself for letting that slip because whatever casual energy Brooklyn and I had between us is now gone.

Swallowing, I stab my fork into my food a few times as I search for the best explanation about Natalie. Brooklyn won't ask—she's too good of a person to be nosy—but I know she wants to. "We got divorced about a year ago," I mutter. Will she let me leave it at that?

Brooklyn tilts her head and takes another bite of my biscuits, and though her eyes nearly roll into the back of her head with pleasure, she keeps her focus on me. She's full of unasked questions, most of which I would prefer not to answer.

"Natalie would come with me to client meetings sometimes," I say, sitting back. Suddenly I'm not all that hungry, even if the salmon omelet is good. "She liked to order whatever sounded fanciest to help impress the clients, but most of the time she didn't enjoy whatever she got. So I got in the habit of ordering something she would eat and swapping with her because I'm not as picky."

I know she is probably dying with curiosity, but Brooklyn slowly takes a sip of water and seems to be telling herself not to ask me anything. Her lips pucker, and she sends a glare to her glass.

Guess she doesn't like lemon either. Sighing, I swap our glasses too.

"We got married two years after I graduated UCSB," I tell her because I know she wants to know. "Married for three years. No kids or anything."

We would have had to have time together in order to have kids, and that was not something we had in abundance. It's probably for the best, all things considered. Kids would have made our divorce messy, and I wouldn't have been able to come back to Sun City if we had shared custody. Natalie will never leave California and the lifestyle she has there.

The lifestyle I drove her to.

Brooklyn takes a long drink this time, clearly happier with her plain water. Her eyes never leave my face. If she'd been anyone else, the eye contact would have been unnerving, but Brooklyn has a way of putting people at ease because she's so calm. People can't help but be calm right with her.

"Was it hard to leave?" That's it. That's the only question she's going to ask, of all the things she could ask.

I'm not even sure how to answer it. A whole lot of varying emotions swim in my chest, colliding into each other and making breathing painful. "Yes," I say. And it's true. There's still a part of me that will always love Natalie, and it's not like our marriage was ever bad. "And no," I add because I am so much happier now than I was then, but that has nothing to do with my marriage.

And now that things are good and awkward, I stuff half the omelet into my mouth because I'm classy like that.

We pretty much eat in silence after that, which means we eat quickly, and I'm more than ready to pay the check when Kinley comes back to see how things are going. We need a distraction, and I know just the thing.

"Come on," I say as soon as I get my credit card back. "Time for our next stop."

Brooklyn's eyes go wide. "Next stop?"

She sure knows how to make a guy feel unwanted. I can't help but laugh as I crouch down to get her on my back again. "This was only stage one of your training. You still have a lot to learn about romance, Queens." And if I could stop calling it that, that would be great. Flirting is one thing. Romance is another. Until I actually meet this guy, which will probably never happen, I'm not all that cool with thinking about him in a relationship with Brooklyn. He could be better than any of the last guys she dated, but I'm not holding my breath.

For how smart she is, Brooklyn has terrible taste in guys.

"Where are we going?" she asks when we get back to the truck.

I get her in her seat and have the truck started up before I answer. I'm not sure if I'm stalling or worried she'll try to escape. "I'm taking you to The Glendale."

"The art gallery?" Her eyebrows dip low, though she's smart enough to figure out why. Based on her completely bare basement, I don't really see her as an art connoisseur, but it absolutely sounds like a thing her teacher crush would be into. "Jordan, I have to work today."

I glance at her, ignoring the alarm bell in my head that tells me *I* should be working today too, especially because I didn't get anything done yesterday. But the team is fine. Rick said so when I told him I had an emergency come up this weekend. Why is it so hard to believe it? Rick wouldn't lie to me.

"It's Saturday," I say, forcing myself to stay in the conversation.

"Yeah, well, I didn't do any of my stuff yesterday because of my migraine. It's fine."

I grip the steering wheel a little tighter. Natalie used to get migraines, and it was a sore spot for both of us. She complained endlessly that I didn't take them seriously, and I honestly never knew if she really had a headache or if she was just trying to get my attention. If she hadn't admitted to faking it sometimes, I never would have questioned it.

I shift in my seat, forcing myself to stop thinking about my marriage. It's not going to help anybody. "Do you get migraines often?" I don't know how that question is supposed to help me stop thinking about Natalie, but whatever. At least I can count on Brooklyn telling the truth.

Brooklyn shrugs, watching the car in the lane next to us. "A couple of bad ones every month, and some little ones here and there. I've learned to deal with it."

"That sucks. Have you been to a doctor?" As soon as that question leaves my mouth, I know it was the wrong one. With the way she fought so hard against getting her ankle looked at, I don't think she's a fan of doctors. I can relate. Every time I take my mom to get her treatments or scans, a part of me crumbles.

Still, Brooklyn shrugs again. "A couple, but no one can really figure out the cause. It's fine."

It's not fine, but Natalie went through the same thing. She learned a couple of her triggers but never really got a solution, and that was after going to some of the best doctors money could pay for. I didn't do a lot for her, but at least I did that.

I pull into the parking lot of the gallery and turn off the truck, leaving us in silence. I miss the easy casualness we had between us before I brought up Natalie, and I need to find a way to bring it back. Brooklyn is already too serious for her own good.

"We don't have to stay long," I tell her. "But this lesson is going to be important."

She looks at me out of the corner of her eyes. "What's the lesson?"

"Temptation," I whisper.

Reaching out, I brush the back of my finger along her cheek and get a little thrill from the color that rises in her fair skin. *Don't get any wild ideas*, I tell myself. That's not my blush to earn. Is that going to stop me?

Probably not.

I try not to think too highly of myself, but this is one of my more brilliant ideas. And by brilliant I mean stupid. For me. It is absolutely going to help Brooklyn if she pays attention, but I know before I've even started that I'm setting myself up for disaster.

Admitting this means also admitting something I'm not ready to admit, so as I carry Brooklyn on my back into the gallery, I pretend there's absolutely no danger lurking ahead of me. I'm good at that, pretending I can't see something staring me in the face.

I probably shouldn't count that as a skill I want to have when that's the very thing that ended my marriage.

"Are you ever going to explain yourself," Brooklyn asks, "or do I just have to interpret?"

Okay, I *need* to admit it, at least to myself, or I'm never going to make it through this morning.

I am attracted to Brooklyn Briggs.

There. I acknowledged the truth, and I can put it behind me because nothing is going to come of it. Brooklyn and I are never going to be more than friends, if we even manage that, and that's okay. I can be attracted to her without acting on that attraction and therefore putting my friendship with Houston in danger. I'm not ready for a new relationship after Natalie, and Brooklyn deserves someone who can show her how valuable she is.

That isn't me.

"Would you relax?" I tell her and stop in front of the first painting I come across. It's a rather gruesome battle scene, not exactly helpful to my lesson. I grimace. "You need to ease into this one."

Otherwise known as I need to make sure my plan isn't going to bite me in the butt.

"Tell me about what you see in this painting, Queens."

Brooklyn adjusts her hold around my collar bone as she looks at it. I can feel each of her breaths, and my hands are tucked around her thighs to hold her up, only a thin layer of fabric between my fingers and her skin. I got rather familiar with these legs of hers yesterday, and I have to resist the urge to try to find the mole behind her knee that I discovered while she was asleep and my hands were exploring her leg as I massaged. Her skin is so soft, and at one point I forgot I was touching her because it felt so natural to have my hands on her.

Okay, wow, that sounds creepy. And I am so not doing a good job of moving on from the whole attraction thing.

I probably should have asked the front desk if they had a wheelchair or something, but it feels too late for that now.

"I see a lot of blood," she says finally, and her voice mimics the roll of her eyes. "Jordan, if you're trying to teach me how to like art because Mark likes art, you're going to have to actually teach me. I'm a science girl. Art has never been my thing."

I move deeper into the gallery, trying to find the best place for my demonstration. "You're telling me there's not a sort of beauty in a chemical reaction?"

"I guess there is."

"What is your favorite lesson to teach your kids?"

She thinks for a second. "Stoichiometry."

Yep, I have no idea what that is. "Why is that your favorite?"

"Because it's a really difficult concept, but when it finally clicks in their heads and they see the way it ties a lot of things together, I feel like I've done something good."

I gently set her down in front of a bench that coincidentally sits in front of a painting that depicts a man and woman in the middle of a dance without touching each other. Perfect. "Art is about finding beauty and emotion in whatever is in front of you," I tell her. "Some people see it in stoik-whatever. Some people see it in architecture. Some people see it in other people. You don't have to know anything about paint strokes or history for something to make you feel."

When I turn to face her, she's gaping at me, like she had no idea I could ever say something like that. I honestly can't tell if she's impressed or confused, but she's something.

Then she snaps out of it, shaking her head and turning to the painting in front of us. "I guess that's a pretty good lesson, though I have no idea what it has to do with temptation."

"Oh, art appreciation isn't why we are here. That was a bonus lesson."

She literally gulps. "So what's the real lesson?"

"I already told you."

One delicate eyebrow rises. She didn't put on any makeup today, but that doesn't make her any less beautiful. "Temptation?"

She has no idea how much she embodies that word.

Mark, I remind myself. *You're doing this to help another guy.*

Gesturing for her to sit, I settle myself on the edge of the bench, leaving plenty of room for her to sit nowhere near me. Just as I hoped, she takes the other end.

I smirk at her. "Today's lesson is about the hand flex."

Her face immediately turns red, though she tries to hide it by shaking her hair over her shoulders and keeping her gaze straight ahead. "What hand flex?"

She knows exactly what I'm talking about. I inch a little closer. "You know. Mr. Darcy helps Elizabeth Bennett into the carriage and touches her hand."

Though she sits stiffly, she does her best to sound aloof. (She fails.) "I recall the scene."

I scoot closer. "Then you'll recall the moment right after that." It really is fortunate that I saw the movie just yesterday, and there were moments in the other things I watched that reinforced my point. Long glances, almost-touches, brief moments of contact that would be insignificant or ignored today.

I hold my hand out in front of her, waiting until she looks at it, and then I stretch my fingers out wide.

"Funny," I murmur, "how much a little touch can feel so big."

Her breath catches, which means she is fully understanding where I'm going with this. I fight a grin and turn my hand over so my palm is up, like I'm waiting for her to take my hand.

"When you think about it, physical contact is something so important when it comes to relationships. We hug people we care about. Shake hands when we meet someone new. We show affection with a kiss." I let those words linger for a moment, enjoying her blush as I lean in closer. "And when we want to be close to someone, we hold their hand."

Just as she reaches for my hand, I pull it back and tuck both my hands between my knees. "So here's your assignment," I say at a normal volume, fixing my eyes on the painting.

Brooklyn sounds a little breathless when she says, "Assignment? You're giving me homework?"

"More like a pop quiz." I look at her and almost burst into laughter because she's scowling at me like I just gave her legitimate homework. "Okay, calm down. I promise this will help you. Do you want to learn to flirt or not?"

She seems to genuinely consider that for a moment. "Fine. You are the master, after all."

I shift once more in my seat so we're only a few inches apart now. "Yes, I am," I agree, but only because flirting is too much fun not to do it. Being honest and complimentary has always brought a lot of joy to my life and to the people around me. "Now, listen carefully."

I already know I'm going to regret this, but I proceed anyway.

"Catching a man's interest is easy. You're beautiful and kind, and you bring light into any room you enter. Keeping a man's interest requires subtlety. Intention."

She folds her arms, though she is redder than ever after my quick assessment of her. "Meaning?"

I rest my hand on the bench between us, not quite close enough to touch her. "Meaning you need to learn to tease, Queens. To make a man desperate for your touch because he knows it isn't easily earned. You need to drive him mad with desire."

"How am I supposed to do that?"

I nod toward my hand. "If you wanted to hold my hand right now, what would you do?"

Rolling her eyes, she keeps her own hands safely tucked away. "I don't want to hold your hand, Jordan." Her lips twitch, pulling inward in the way they always do when she lies.

My heart kicks up a little faster, but I ignore it. "Pretend."

She sighs. "I guess I would make sure my hand is easily available." She sits back, leaning her hands behind her and resting her right hand just an inch from mine.

"Good. That's a great start. Now, say I was focused on this painting and not paying attention to your signs. What then?" I turn to the painting, though I keep as much of my focus on her as I can.

She considers my question, looking down at our hands and back up to my face, and then she puts her hand over the top of mine.

I glance down. "Oh, sorry." Then I sit up straighter and put my hand on my thigh instead, returning my gaze to the painting.

Brooklyn groans. "What did I do wrong?"

"Subtlety," I repeat. "Isn't this painting such a visceral depiction of desire? The way the artist captured the longing..." I lift my fingers to my lips and do a chef's kiss, and then I put my hand back down on the bench. Waiting.

"You know you could just tell me what to do," she says, definitely irritated by my teaching skills.

"I learn better by doing," I reply. "Maybe you will too."

Sighing, she looks at the painting again and seems to study it for real this time. The couple in the painting are in the middle of an intricate dance, each with a hand raised in the air and nearly pressed against the other's. But there's still that space between them, however small, and most of the tension is in their expressions.

"I guess I can see what you mean," Brooklyn says, and she leans a little closer as if to look at it from my angle. "It's like they want to touch but can't because the social rules at the time prevented them from touching in public. If they did, they would be forced into something they might not be ready for."

Her pinky suddenly brushes against mine, and my whole body reacts, like she just lit a fuse. It's a fuse I need to stamp out—immediately—but instead I turn to look at her right as she looks at me. My heart jumps into my throat at the wary look in her eyes. It's almost as if she's asking...

She looks down at our touching fingers. "How was that?"

Maybe a little too good. A pinky brush shouldn't be enough to send a raging fire through me, especially because I already know she doesn't want to hold my hand. Except...she lied about that. Maybe there is some truth in her words, but there's still a part of her that feels some sort of attraction. What am I supposed to do with that?

I swallow. "I think with a little practice you could have every man in Sun City falling in love with you."

Including me, which absolutely cannot happen.

Chapter Twelve

Brooklyn

I HAVE NO IDEA what I'm doing, but I know Jordan's wife is entirely to blame. Ex-wife. Whatever she is, the instant I realized she existed, the sickening burning of jealousy started bubbling up in my gut, and I am smart enough to know I can't just ignore that.

Insane as it sounds, I'm attracted to Jordan Torres. The guy who relentlessly teased me throughout high school until I learned to retaliate and start playing pranks on him and my brother to try to get him to leave me alone. It never worked.

I'm supposed to hate him, but here I am, aching for him to let me hold his hand while we sit on my couch, each of us with a laptop while *Poldark* plays in the background.

We didn't spend a lot of time in the gallery after I touched his hand, and Jordan didn't give me a chance to touch him again until he lifted me onto his back and carried me out to his truck to take me home. I can't decide if he doesn't like touching me or if he likes it a little too much, and I badly wish I was better at reading body language. He's been acting pretty normal since we got back a couple of hours ago, so he probably wasn't affected by my touch as much as I was.

Still, I've been watching him since we sat down, and he definitely seems stiffer than usual. Every once in a while his hand moves, like he's going to reach out to me, but he quickly turns it into a stretch or grabs his water bottle. He's kept himself pressed against the arm of the couch so there's as much space between us as possible. And fool that I am, I'm probably reading way too much into this.

The only way to find out is to run an experiment.

Observation: Jordan is maintaining a distance between us that wasn't there before his flirting lesson.

Hypothesis: Jordan is attracted to me like I am to him but doesn't want to cross any boundaries.

Prediction: If I tease him with tiny touches like I did at the gallery, he will react accordingly.

Now I just need to run the experiment and see what happens, but I can't make it obvious. Jordan is too smart not to notice my attempts if I forget the *subtle* part of his lesson, so I need to make sure any points of contact come across as accidental. Can I do that? I don't know. Is this a bad idea? Probably.

I hold back a groan as I try to psych myself up for this. It shouldn't be that hard. I've had plenty of boyfriends, so I can't be totally helpless, but I'm also never the one to initiate things. I usually just have to fall in with whatever the guy is doing. I've never had to question if he liked me, though, so I've never had to conduct an experiment in the first place. *Just get on with it, Brooklyn!*

Here goes nothing.

I stretch my arms out and yawn, first leaning to my right, away from Jordan, and then leaning toward him until my shaking fingers brush his hair. "Oops! Sorry." I stretch a little more and then settle deeper into my seat. We're sharing the ottoman between us, but my bad ankle is the one next to his foot, so I probably won't be able to do anything there. We'll see.

After a few more minutes, I look around me and then put my hand on his arm. He tenses up, causing me to tense up too. "Hey, could you get me a glass of water? I don't have a fancy water bottle like you."

"Sure." Setting his laptop on the cushion between us, he hops up. "Ice?"

Does he want me to freeze? "No th—" I stop myself. I could potentially use that, snuggling closer because I'm cold. Ha! Like I'll ever do that. Still, I'd better set myself up for success. "Actually, yeah, that would be great. And I could probably use some for my ankle, while you're up."

He chuckles, relaxing the farther he gets from me. "You're actually asking me for help now? Should I be worried?"

"I know when to admit defeat."

When he returns, I take the water with both hands and nod toward my ankle. "Do you mind? I have the hardest time bringing myself to hold it there because it's so cold."

He goes stiff again, and he seems to be weighing his options as he looks from the bag of ice to my foot. He didn't have a problem with this before, so something has definitely changed. "Sure," he says eventually. He shifts in his seat, which pulls him farther away from me, and maneuvers his computer so he can keep working while holding the ice for me.

I notice he is careful to only touch the ice instead of my skin.

That adds evidence to my theory but doesn't help me figure out whether he wants to touch me or not. I'll have to try something else in a few minutes.

I think I last maybe five minutes before I give up on trying to concentrate on grading these assignments. I am not at all focused, and I'm more likely to mess up on grades right now than I would like. Can't have my students suffering just because Jordan is distracting me.

He seems engrossed enough in whatever he's working on that I can probably examine him a little more closely than normal without him noticing. See if I can try to read him better.

He changed out of his nice shirt and jeans as soon as we got back to my house, which probably means he isn't planning on going anywhere else today, which is fine by me. Now that he wears sweats and a t-shirt, I've got a great view of his upper arm muscles and the way they have a fluid motion to them every time he moves. Houston and Chad are both plenty strong—Houston's pitching arm is frankly a little ridiculous—but Jordan has a leanness to him that intrigues me. He's like a jungle cat, built for speed and agility more than for power. It fits his quick and light personality, just like his near-constant smile. My resting face is a little more moody, or so I've been told, but Jordan's showcases his general cheerfulness.

How does he do it? Sure, he has his own company right now, which is cool, but I didn't get the feeling that it's a raging success. His mom is dealing with cancer, and he is only a year or so off of a divorce, so it's not like his life is super great. Maybe it is. Maybe he's like Micah and only sees the good in things. Either way, I wish I could share his *joie de vivre* and be more confident that my life is how I want it to be.

Maybe if I win STEM Teacher of the Year, it will be. This is my only chance to do the one thing I've wanted to do with my life.

"How is that feeling?" Jordan asks, lifting the ice. Has it already been fifteen minutes?

I shrug. "Numb?"

That gets a smile out of him, which I am quite proud of. "I guess that's better than in pain." He hops up to dump out the ice, and when he returns, he seems to forget his goal to keep space between us. He's definitely closer than he was before, even if he's still on the other side of the couch.

I should get back to my experiment.

I pick up the remote and then pretend to lost control of it, sending it flying in Jordan's direction.

He snorts a laugh and holds it out to me. "Does your war with technology extend to TV remotes too?"

My face heats. It adds to the illusion that it was an accident, so I only sort of care that I'm turning red. "All technology," I confirm. As I take the remote, I make sure my fingers brush his. There's definitely a spark of connection when we touch, but Jordan barely reacts. Hmm. "Actually, do you want to pick what we watch? I'm not really feeling *Poldark*, and we don't have to keep watching period dramas."

He eyes the remote, which I'm holding in an awkward way that will make it impossible for him not to touch me. It's probably a little too obvious, but whatever. A crease forms between his eyebrows, but he takes the remote anyway. This time when our fingers brush, he grimaces.

Not exactly the reaction I was hoping for.

He switches the TV to *Downton Abbey* of all things and goes back to his computer.

"Are you sure you want to watch this?" I reach over and touch his arm for half a second.

He looks down at the place I touched, closes his eyes, and then looks back up at me. "I like watching this with you. But I can pick something else if you want. I still need to finish the first season of *Bridgerton*."

My reaction surprises even me when I take his arm in a death grip. "What do you mean, *finish*? When did you start watching *Bridgerton*?" And why would Jordan watch something like that?

He actually looks embarrassed, wrinkling up his nose and looking around the room as if looking for an escape. "I meant to keep that one as a guilty pleasure," he mumbles. "I started it last night and got sucked into the story. Skipped most of the steamy scenes, though. According to the internet, the second season is better, but I didn't get that far."

I tried watching that show, but when I'm used to the "no touching each other" aspect of Jane Austen stories, the physical intimacy between the characters was too much for me. It surprises me that Jordan would be more interested in the story than in the other aspects, not that I've ever thought him to be that kind of guy.

"What?" Jordan says, and I realize I'm still gripping his arm.

I let go. "Sorry. You just keep surprising me. We can keep watching *Downton*."

I've ended up closer to him during this conversation, which means I can see his computer better. I'm not trying to pry, but I'm curious what a landscaper would work on online. "Is that your website?"

He turns his screen so I can see, but I scoot myself closer, both because I'm interested and because I'm still conducting my experiment. He tenses up yet again when my shoulder brushes his.

"What do you think?" he asks, his voice a little strained.

I think there's something going on between us that I don't understand, and I wish I did. "It looks really good! Though, being technically challenged, I wouldn't know how to schedule you to work on my yard."

He frowns, shifting the screen back to face him. "Huh. I never thought about that. There's a contact form here, but otherwise you have to go to this screen over here to schedule a quote." He shows me what he means. "I still need to take care of your yard, by the way. I'll do that tomorrow."

That is something I need to see, but I should probably stay focused. I point to the form he showed me. "I definitely wouldn't have found that form. The fewer clicks I have to make, the less likely I am to mess something up."

After a little shudder, he switches to his email and starts typing in a half-drafted email, outlining the need for a quote request on the home page. I have to lean closer to read what he's typing, which means my shoulder presses against his more firmly. He clenches his jaw, his breathing becoming a little more measured. I may not be good at reading people, but even I know my nearness is affecting him. I just don't know if it's good or bad.

"Has it been hard, starting your own company?"

He shrugs, rubbing his shoulder along mine with the movement. He has the space to move away, but he doesn't. "Depends on which day you ask me. I started off a lot more excited than I am now, so it was more fun than it was work back then."

"Why aren't you excited now?"

"I am. Some days. Other days I get focused on how I don't have enough clients to make much of a profit, so I feel like I'm letting a lot of people down."

"Like Houston?" I doubt my brother could ever be disappointed by his best friend. They've stuck together even though they barely ever saw each other for years.

"Yeah. And other people."

I wonder if he still gives money to his ex-wife, but I'm too much of a coward to ask. Just thinking that brings back the jealous feelings I got this morning, which is really starting to bug me. I shouldn't like Jordan. I *can't* like Jordan. Even if we didn't have a rocky history, our relationships with Houston are too important to make things complicated.

I don't have enough luck with men and dating to risk ruining one of the few good relationships my brother has in his life. Even if I wanted to date Jordan, there's no way it would last. He's way too good for me.

Suddenly realizing how close we are, I clear my throat and scoot back to my side of the couch. I expect Jordan to relax, but instead his shoulders rise a little higher and his fingers curl into a fist. What does *that* mean?

"Hey, Jordan?"

He doesn't look at me. "Hmm?"

"I hate to ask, but..." I shouldn't do this, knowing it will probably torture us both, but I need more facts if I'm going to have a decent conclusion to my experiment. "Would you mind massaging my foot again? It felt so good the last time."

His eyes jump to my feet, but not before a look of panic crosses his face. That could either mean he really doesn't want to, or it could mean he wants to but knows that proximity is dangerous. Which it is. Maybe not for him, but it's certainly dangerous for me.

Setting his computer on the floor, Jordan holds out his hand and mumbles something I don't quite catch, though it sounds a lot like, "I taught you too well." The instant my feet are in his lap, he relaxes, and his hands start working their magic.

Conclusion: Jordan wants to be close to me.

Now I just have to figure out what that means.

Chapter Thirteen

Jordan

"But it doesn't make any sense!"

The only thing stopping me from dying of laughter is an enormous sense of self-control. Brooklyn looks ready to fall apart as she sits on her countertop and scowls at the ingredients I've laid out for dinner. I'm still working with limited ingredients because I got too caught up with work to remember I wanted to hit up the grocery store today and get her some proper food, so I've had to get creative with tonight's meal.

Brooklyn doesn't seem to appreciate my creativity. "You can't tell me to 'chop some onion' but not how much. 'Some' isn't a measurement, Jordan."

I fold my arms, leaning against the stove. I've already peeled and chopped the sad, wrinkly potatoes she had in her pantry and put them in the oven, and the frying pan is hot, oiled, and ready to go as soon as she gets the onions diced.

"We just need a handful," I tell her.

She points her knife at me. "Do you have any idea how imprecise that is? Your handful is way different from my handful. Have you even measured what a handful should be?"

"No, because there's no point in measuring."

"Jordan!" She looks ready to cry, and I hope it's because she started slicing the onion before asking how much we needed.

"Like I said when we started," I say, trying to sound soothing, "I never measure things when I cook. It's fine."

Groaning, she sets the knife on the counter—I appreciate that so much after the way she was waving it around—and pulls her hair up off of her neck as if this argument has her overheating. "What about when you're following a recipe?"

I shake my head.

"How do you know it will taste good if you're not measuring everything?"

I shrug, still fighting a smirk. I knew she was a rule-follower, but I didn't realize it was this ingrained in her. "I don't know. That's what makes it fun. Are you going to chop *some* onion or not?"

Her eyes are wide with panic, but I think she realizes I'm not going to give her any sort of guidelines beyond what I already have. I could tell her that a quarter cup would work great, but with how much this bothers her, I've decided she needs more chaos in her life.

"You know," she says as she resumes her chopping. "If I didn't measure everything at work, I would probably blow up the school. Precision is important." She scoops up what she has, shakes it around in her fist as if weighing it, and then goes back to chopping.

I peek inside the oven at the potatoes. "I'm not saying precision isn't valuable in certain places. But in cooking? Cooking should be done with the heart. Matters of the heart can't be planned or measured. They're too important for that."

Deciding she has a proper handful of onion, Brooklyn scoops it all up and holds it out to me. "Are you telling me that all this practice and planning that we're doing for Mark is impractical?"

When our hands touch as I take her offering, I do my best not to react. I don't need her knowing how much I'm affected by her since my stupid teasing lesson at the gallery. Even if I expected it, I don't know why things have changed. Why didn't I feel this zing yesterday? We touched plenty of times then, and my heart didn't start racing with every contact.

"Is that enough?"

I blink, realizing that my attempts at not reacting left me frozen. I don't even look at what's in my hands; I toss it into the pan, focusing on the sizzle as I remind myself that this is only an attraction. It doesn't mean anything. She has always been attractive, and this is just a delayed reminder after our decade apart.

Maybe being around her is simply reminding me of the way things used to be. The way *I* used to be.

I miss carefree Jordan. He was fun.

"It's not like we're going to plan out your whole conversation with Malcolm," I say, stirring the onions so they're all coated in oil. "I'm just giving you some tools so you're better equipped to charm him off his feet."

Though, if the guy hasn't realized by now that he can't do better than Brooklyn Briggs, he's an idiot. He's probably an idiot anyway. It would fit her MO.

Why am I so fixated on who she dates? That can't be good for me.

"What if I completely blow it? He'll never talk to me again."

The question catches me off guard because she sounds so defeated already. She looks it too, staring down at the floor with her head hanging low. Once upon a time, this girl snuck out of class early and hid in my locker so she could jump out and shower me with glitter right before baseball practice. She had most of the guys at school in love with her because she shone so bright just by being her fun and confident self.

Where did that girl go? Who cut her down so thoroughly that she doesn't think she can even have a conversation with a guy who doesn't deserve her?

Though I need to say something, and soon, I grab my phone and quickly shoot off a text.

Me:

> When was the last time Brooklyn had a boyfriend?

I clear my throat. "As long as you don't light the guy's eyebrows on fire, you've already improved. I think you'll be fine. You don't have a lot of technology in your classroom, do you?"

She peeks up at me, her smile making it easier for me to breathe. "They tried to install a smart board last year, but I begged them to leave the white board."

My phone buzzes, and I turn to stir the onions while I glance at the screen. I probably shouldn't hide things from Brooklyn, but I doubt she would appreciate this text conversation.

Houston:

> A few years ago, I think. Why?

I stifle a laugh. It's not Brooklyn he needs to worry about when she spent all afternoon sending my nerves spasming with each accidental touch. If anyone's going crazy, I am.

"Are you going to tell me what you're making?" Brooklyn asks.

I slip my phone back into my pocket, though I know I can't ignore Houston's questions for long. If I don't reply soon, he'll start overthinking and jumping to conclusions. Probably some right ones, and I don't need Houston Briggs jumping anywhere.

"Why do you want to know?" I ask.

Brooklyn frowns. "Why wouldn't I want to know?"

"If I tell you, will it change whether you eat it?"

Looking at the ingredients I've laid out, she shakes her head. "Probably not. But—"

"It doesn't matter what you call something; it doesn't change what's inside. Sometimes it's better not to put a label on something so you don't invite any biases."

"Okay, yeah, you definitely worked in PR. Though, I don't know what it has to do with dinner."

I smirk and point to the cutting board. "We need some ham."

"How much—"

"Have you learned nothing? However much you want, Queens."

She groans but starts slicing the deli meat I found in her fridge. "You're definitely making it a lot easier to remember how frustrating you are," she mumbles as she slices.

I laugh. "This coming from the girl who constantly made me look like an idiot in front of the whole school?"

She gasps and points her knife at me again. "I did not!"

"Did too."

My phone buzzes once, twice, three times in rapid succession, which means Houston is getting paranoid. Gritting my teeth, I pull it out of my pocket and try not to let my reaction show on my face as I read my friend's texts.

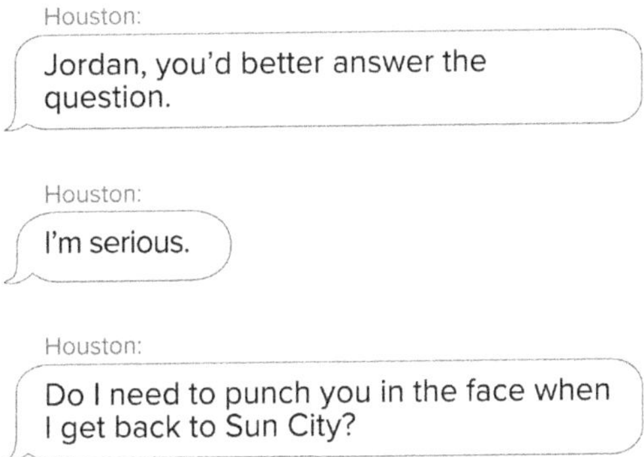

I roll my eyes. Houston makes a lot of threats, but he would never actually punch anyone in the face. He's too interested in being liked, and he likes me too much to threaten our friendship. Knowing that reminds me that I need to be careful with Brooklyn. If I end up hurting her by openly flirting when I'm in no position to date her, Houston will not hesitate to cut me out of his life.

"Who are you texting?" Brooklyn asks with clear curiosity in her eyes, but then her phone buzzes on the coffee table in the living room, pulling both our attention that way. "Uh, could you...?"

Though I'm tempted to sneak a peek at the text Houston sent her, I force myself to keep the screen of Brooklyn's phone facing the floor as I grab it and bring it back to the kitchen for her. I immediately regret that decision when she groans and starts typing furiously. At this point, we should probably just start up a group chat between the three of us and let everything be out in the open.

I'm less likely to pry where I shouldn't if I tell myself that I can't say anything to Houston unless I also say it to his sister.

"Why does Houston want to punch you in the nose?" Brooklyn asks.

I snort. "Did he say that?"

"Apparently you're bothering me." She says this with a look of such long-suffering that I'm a little worried for Houston's health when he gets home. His twin might strangle him for being overbearing.

The onions are looking good, so I hold the pan out toward Brooklyn so she can add the ham. She does so, watching me carefully to make sure she doesn't add too much, and then I return the pan to the heat.

"Aren't I bothering you, though?" I say, folding my arms. "You did call me frustrating just now."

She seems to think about that, which makes me wonder if she actually is bothered by me. I know I can be annoying if I tease too hard, and I've invaded her space here in her basement to spend the unplanned weekend with her. But I like to think I read social cues well enough to know when I should back off. Part of winning over a new client is being able to anticipate their needs.

Not that Brooklyn is a client. In fact, even if she needed a PR guy for some reason, I would have to decline because there's too much history between us. That history might be cloaked in pranks and frustration, but it's there.

"I guess I just don't know what to do with you," Brooklyn says.

"Huh. My mom says that to me all the time."

She scoffs and kicks her foot toward me, and I catch it on instinct. That was a bad idea. The instant my hands wrap around her ankle—the good one—I don't want to let go. I don't know what it is about running my fingers along her feet, but it settles my mind. Even now, just standing here in her tiny kitchen and holding her toes against my abdomen, I can practically feel my breathing grow steadier.

It doesn't make any sense, but this woman simultaneously calms me down and freaks me out. My heart is beating like crazy while the rest of me relaxes.

"Can I have my foot back?" she asks, color rising in her cheeks.

My fingers refuse to listen to reason telling me to let go. Instead, I dig my thumbs into her arch and revel in the shudder that runs through her. I can only imagine how much she would enjoy a foot massage after being on her feet teaching all day. I can picture her coming back to her little basement and flopping on the couch, turning on a love story and sipping her favorite soda while I work out the tightness in her calves...

I need to stop. That's not a future I should be imagining if I want to keep my sanity and stay focused on building my business into something sustainable.

"That depends," I tell her.

Her eyes snap up to meet mine. She and Houston have the same eyes, a bright crystal blue, but hers have always been softer. They're the sky on a warm day, a breath of fresh air, a…a good reason for me to get punched in the face if I keep going on like this.

"Depends on what?" she asks.

I…don't have an answer. I just don't want to let go. With her eyes on me, I scramble for a response that doesn't sound completely stupid. "If you want me to let go, you have to promise me you're not going to choke when you talk to Mark on Monday."

She narrows her eyes. "I can't promise that. I don't even know if I'll see him on Monday. Even if I do, I'll most likely trip over my own—"

I tighten my hold around her ankle, cutting off her words. I'm not actually gripping that tight, but she locks her eyes on my fingers like she's worried they will become a permanent fixture. "Brooklyn Briggs, I don't know why you're so nervous to talk to a guy who would be a fool not to love you, but I need you to stop. Start channeling that confidence I always admired about you."

To my surprise, her expression falls, leaving nothing but misery on her face. "What if I can't?" she asks quietly. Desperately.

Slowly releasing her foot, I step closer, moving in until my hip brushes her knee. Then I tuck a stray lock of hair behind her ear. I've got her attention, which hopefully means she'll know I'm completely serious when I ask, "Why?" Why has it been a few years since her last relationship? Why has she lost all her vibrancy?

Why doesn't Houston know how muted she is?

When she doesn't answer, I rephrase my question because I know there's something I'm missing and I'm desperate to know what it is. "What happened?"

As her eyes fill up with tears, she gently pushes me away and slides to the floor. "It doesn't matter." She starts limping away, using the countertop to hold up her weight instead of her bad ankle.

I shift the pan off of the hot burner and grab her arm. "It does matter," I argue. "Especially if it's making you cry. You only cry when you're truly hurt, Brooklyn."

I don't know if it's the fact that I used her real name or if it's because she can't hold things in anymore, but she spins and tucks herself into my hold. Chest aching, I fold my arms around her and pull her in tight as my mind jumps into every scenario possible. Someone attacked her. She's dying of cancer like her mom. A man broke her heart.

"Please talk to me," I beg, tightening my hold because none of those scenarios make me feel any better. "Brook."

"I'm fine," she mumbles into my t-shirt. "It happened a long time ago."

"You say that like it makes me any less nervous. *What* happened?"

Brooklyn was never much of a sharer, and she's always kept personal things to herself. Honestly, when she told Houston about her limp celery stalk of a boyfriend cheating on her back in high school, I thought for sure it was another one of her pranks, designed to rile us up. But then she started crying, and Houston stared at her like he hadn't realized she knew how to cry.

She's crying tonight, and I don't like it. It can only mean whatever it was was terrible.

Sniffling, she slowly shifts her hands so they're no longer tucked in between us, and she slides her arms around my waist and pulls herself in even closer. "I'm sorry. I shouldn't have brought it up. But it's just been so hard to…"

I'm not a violent person, but I want to punch something. "You have to give me something, Brooklyn. Anything. I'm jumping to all the conclusions, and you know I'm going to ask Houston if you don't tell me—"

"He doesn't know." She takes a shuddering breath. "He thinks James and I broke up because he moved to Cincinnati."

"Did he move to Cincinnati?" Whoever this James guy is, I already don't like him.

"No."

"When was this?"

"About three years ago."

Three years ago was when my job started to take off, leaving me feeling like I was on top of the world. It's hard to imagine Brooklyn going through whatever this is when everything was golden in my world. Golden until it wasn't…

It was only a year after that upturn+ that Natalie started spending more weekends at her friend Sally's, claiming she wanted to let me have the house to myself to decompress after my stressful weeks. She only told me after a month's worth of weekends away because I happened to come home right as she was leaving one Friday afternoon. Before that, I hadn't noticed she wasn't around because I had hardly come home to begin with.

It's terrifying how long it took me to realize the other side of the king-size bed was empty, but that's what happens when you crash at one in the morning and are up again at five every day. There's no time to realize your wife isn't there.

"We worked together in a research lab downtown," Brooklyn says, pulling me back to the moment. "James was my boss."

I am not letting her have this conversation while she's standing on one foot in the middle of her kitchen. Flipping off the stove and the oven, I scoop her up into my arms and head to the couch. I get her settled on one end, take a seat on the other, and then I gesture for her to give me her injured foot.

"I didn't know you worked in research," I tell her to keep her going.

She nods and grabs a pillow to hug. "It was a facility here in Sun City that focuses on cancer treatment research," she says quietly.

"I didn't know that either."

That gets a little smile out of her. "I really liked it. I felt like I was making a difference, you know?"

I shift my gaze to her foot while I ask this next part, guessing she would rather not have me staring at her while she tells me all about her half-cooked noodle of a boss. "You started dating your boss?"

She sniffs and takes a few seconds to reply. "Yeah. We had a lot of late nights. The other researchers on our team had families, so they didn't often stay late. I liked having something to do, so I tended to stay after hours when it was quieter. James started staying with me and bringing in dinner. He said..."

I look up. "What?"

"He said I was the most dedicated employee he'd ever had, and he admired my conviction. He was always full of praise and very professional...in the beginning." She hisses when I accidentally squeeze her swollen foot.

"Sorry," I mutter and take hold of her other foot. I need to keep myself moving, and that one will be harder to accidentally injure. "What happened?"

She shrugs. "One night we were working late, and he kissed me. He told me he'd wanted to do it for a long time but didn't want to cross any boundaries. He said he'd been holding back because he was pushing for me to get a promotion and a raise because I'd been working so hard."

I stop rubbing her foot, instead letting my fingers curl into fists. I really don't like where this is going. "Did you ever get the promotion?"

She shakes her head. There's so much more to this story—somehow she ended up teaching instead of doing research—but she clearly doesn't want to tell me. Can I keep pushing, or will that just make her clam up and pretend this conversation never happened?

I'm going to risk it. "Why did you break up with James?"

She opens her mouth. Looks at me. Closes it again. Then she says, "We hit a dead end in the research, and I lost my job instead. I was too humiliated to… I tried getting a job at another facility, but no one even called me for an interview. So I took up teaching and got alternative licensing. Those who can't do, teach."

There's something she's not telling me. I know there is. I have my suspicions, but without hearing it from her own mouth, I'm going to be left speculating and hating a guy who may or may not have been just as much of a jerk as the rest of her boyfriends have been.

I take up her hands in mine, every part of me aching to fix this for her. But there's nothing I can fix, and I hate that. I hate that her confidence crumbled with one setback—okay, it was probably multiple setbacks if she applied with other companies—and I hate that she isn't trusting me with the rest of this story. She doesn't owe me anything, but I wish she *wanted* to tell me.

Swallowing, I ask my next question gently. "Do your siblings know that's why you left research?"

Brooklyn doesn't answer.

I swear under my breath. She's been keeping this to herself for years? "Not even Micah?" But I know that answer too. I may not have spent a lot of time with the littlest Briggs—she was only fifteen when we graduated—but I remember Micah being the brightest ray of sunshine. The kind of person who can see the light in any situation, no matter how dark things seem. She would have fixed this already. "Why didn't you tell anyone?"

"And have them do what, exactly? Tell me it's okay that I lost my dream job and only have one chance to try to get back into it? They can't fix this, Jordan. No one can."

I tilt my head. "What chance?"

Shrugging, she plays with the fringe on the nearest blanket. "I just found out I was nominated to be STEM Teacher of the Year at my school. If I get that and make it all the way to the state level and win, I can get a fellowship with the University of Sun City and get back into research that way. Hopefully learn a little more so I'm qualified for something."

"That's amazing, Queens."

"I'm not going to get it."

Those words hit me straight in the chest, and I have to resist the urge to rub my fingers along my sternum. She sounds so sure of that fact. "Of course you'll get it," I argue.

She scoffs. "There are four high schools in our district. Thirteen districts in the state. There are over eighty teachers trying to get this award, and that's assuming I beat out Mark for our school's pick in the first place."

Stiffening, I grab a pillow so I can clench my fingers around it before I strangle something else. Why do I get so violent around this woman? "Mark was nominated too?"

"He's a really great teacher, Jordan."

"So are you."

"You don't know that."

"But I know you."

Her eyebrows pull low, which makes me wonder what she's thinking. Of course I know her. I spent so much time around her back when we were teens—albeit it was reluctantly on her part—and I've seen enough signs of high school Brooklyn to know she's still in there somewhere. I know her, and I've admired her since the day I met her.

"We should finish making dinner," she mumbles, refusing to look at me now.

As much as I want to keep having this conversation, I get to my feet and accept it when she doesn't give any signs of coming with me to the kitchen. "I'm going to help you, Queens," I say as I flip the stove back on. "I'm going to help you build up your confidence again and show you that you're worth more than you feel right now."

She takes a long time to answer, though I don't let my eyes stray in her direction. I need her to really process what I'm telling her so she knows exactly what I'm saying. This is more than helping her get a date with her crush. More than silly lessons in art galleries.

"How are you going to do that?" she asks eventually.

I finally look over, watching her expression shift from irritation to interest to fear and back again. I wish I could read her thoughts as well as I can read her face. I wish I could go all in with this and help her the way I want to help her, but there are too many risk factors. I need to make sure the chances of casualties are as small as possible. "I'm going to help you get yourself a man who actually deserves you. If that's Mark, then great."

"You're already teaching me how to flirt," she says slowly.

I let my lips curl up in a smile I don't feel. "Flirting is important. But let me teach you how to be *loved*."

Her blush starts at her collarbone and works its way up until her whole face is bright red. To her credit, she doesn't break eye contact, but I know she's terrified. Terrified and intrigued.

This might be the worst idea I've ever had, and that's saying something.

Chapter Fourteen

Brooklyn

October 13

WELL, LAST NIGHT TOOK a dark turn. What was supposed to be a fun and flirty dinner prep started with an argument about onions and ended with me spilling my guts about a guy I've been doing my best to forget. I have no idea what Jordan is thinking about all of it, but he's been quiet ever since. Thank goodness I didn't give him the full story, or he might have gone all John Wick on James.

Jordan finished making the breakfast tacos, which were delicious, and then he sat with me and watched *North and South*. It's the stillest and quietest I've ever seen Jordan in all the years I've known him, which probably means there's a lot going on in his head. Most likely about me.

Not sure how I feel about that.

When I started falling asleep, Jordan picked up on it immediately and offered to carry me to my bed before I could ask for his help. Part of me wanted to try to fall asleep on the couch with him, just to see what he would do, but I couldn't stop thinking about what he said.

Let me teach you how to be loved.

I've had boyfriends tell me they love me, and I believed them. But seeing the way Jordan looked at me, I couldn't help but wonder if I've been wrong all this time about what love actually looks like. It's not like I'm thinking Jordan loves me by any means, but I do think he understands what love is.

I wish I knew what that means for me.

I've spent too long in my bed this morning, but I haven't been brave enough to get up and face Jordan after my confession last night. He was so quiet about it after his offer, but I don't know if he will still be that way today.

The sound of a leaf blower or something similar finally perks me up, and I sit up quickly, gaze jumping to the window. I can't see much from here, but a shadow crosses the window as someone passes by.

Suddenly I remember that Jordan said he was going to work on the yard today—that's why he was here in the first place—and I have never wanted to see anything more in my life.

Grabbing my phone, I scramble out of bed and remember too late that my ankle is currently a ball of fluid. By some miracle—that miracle's name is Jordan Torres—it almost holds my weight, which makes it possible for me to hobble to the bathroom and make myself presentable. Do I put on a little makeup? Yes. Has Jordan been around me for the last two days when I've looked completely awful? Also yes. But that doesn't stop me from putting in a little effort.

Logic tells me there's no point in trying with Jordan. He's the guy who drove me crazy in high school, my brother's used-to-be-a-player best friend, a compulsive flirt who knows all the moves to make a girl fall in love with him and has successfully used them to get himself a *wife*. These are all things I know.

But there's a part of me that longs for him to be more than that. To be the guy who looks after me when I'm hurt. Who sees when I'm feeling down and tries to fix it. Who doesn't waste his breath on useless compliments but makes me feel special and important anyway. That part of me wants to think that when he told me last night that he was going to show me how to be loved, he meant it.

I'm still not sure why he reacts so much to my touch, but after the weekend I've had so far, I don't want to be logical. I want to think he senses some sort of connection between us just like I do and is brave enough to see what that might mean.

I want to think that when he looks at me like I'm the most amazing woman he's ever known, it's not just for show.

Once I'm washed, beautified, and changed into a cute pair of shorts and a t-shirt from my favorite band from the 2000s, I limp out the door and slowly make my way up the steps and peek out at the lawn.

Jordan has moved on to the lawn mower. He makes his way around the little yard, and the sight is just as delicious as I was hoping. He wears a pair of basketball shorts—hello, calf muscles—and a loose tank top that shows off every curve of his arms. He was always strong from the baseball team workouts, and though I never said it out loud, I always admired him in those baseball pants.

But adult Jordan? He is all things smooth and ridged, each line of his body showcasing the strength beneath his skin.

He pauses, lifting up the bottom of his tank to wipe the sweat from his face, and I scramble to take a picture. I know it's creepy, and I hate myself a little for it, but the man's abs deserve to be immortalized.

After a moment of admiring the picture, I send it off to Jaydin with a stupid caption: *I think I understand women's obsession with their gardeners*. It takes a couple of tries to get it to send, but I manage it eventually and am proud of myself when my friend replies immediately.

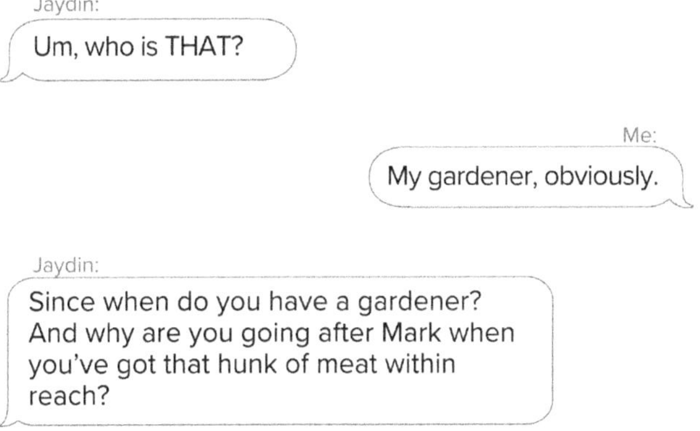

Jordan brings the lawn mower closer to where I'm sitting and shuts it off. Guess I wasn't hiding all that well. Grinning, he plops down at the top of the steps next to me and stretches his arms over his head.

I'm probably drooling. I almost don't care.

"Obsessed with me, huh?" he says.

My heart skips a beat, and I scramble to turn my screen back on to check my texts. Sure enough, my first attempt at sending the picture to Jaydin ended up sending to *Jordan*. I drop my face into my hands. "What are the chances the earth might swallow me whole so I can die of embarrassment?"

"Slim to none, probably."

"I promise I don't usually objectify men," I mutter, peeking at him.

He's grinning as always. "Just me, then?"

"How did you even see that text? You were mowing."

He holds out his watch, which is of the smart variety that I have never considered buying. I can't even imagine the nightmare that would be my life with technology attached to my wrist. "Honestly, I'm impressed you managed to get a clear picture so quickly. I'm more proud than anything."

I groan. "How are you so good at letting nothing bother you?"

Shrugging, he settles his hands behind him and leans back, showing off that lean torso of his. "I've learned that life is so much better if you let things roll off you. I shouldn't change who I am or how I live because of someone else's opinion, but they're welcome to think what they want." He gestures toward me. "You can think I'm super attractive, but—"

"Whoa, no one said *super* attractive." I certainly thought it, though.

Jordan chuckles. "Fine. You can think I'm *incredibly* attractive, but that's just your opinion. It doesn't change who I am."

I cock my head. "Why do I feel like this is turning into a life lesson?"

"Because it is. Yeah, your old company was the equivalent of an overdraft bank fee, but no matter what they decided about you, you can't let it affect you. Your value comes from you and you alone."

I understand what he's saying, and I badly want to believe it. But if I had value, surely someone would have seen it by now. I wouldn't be spending my weekends alone in a dark basement, grading labs while watching movies about eras long past and wishing for my own Mr. Knightley to come along. I would be finding a cure to cancer so I could save people from the heartache I went through, and then I would come home to a guy who makes me smile more than he makes me hurt.

I should probably change the conversation before I get sucked into one of Jordan's lessons again. I don't need to be confessing all of my past regrets to him. "Where do you come up with these insults of yours?" I ask.

He narrows his eyes, like he knows exactly why I'm deflecting, but then he shakes his head. "I don't like being mean to people, but sometimes they deserve my ire. I thought maybe getting creative would be a middle ground between taking the high road and calling them what I really think they are."

That shouldn't make me more attracted to him, but it does. Okay, let's be real. At this point, everything is attractive, and that makes me all sorts of concerned. What am I supposed to do with this attraction if not channel it into something that will only lead to disaster?

Time to change the subject again. "Houston's pitching again tonight, isn't he?"

"Tomorrow." Jordan watches me for a moment, then sighs. "The Red-tails only have three in their starting rotation, which is pretty small, but they like to play him as often as they can."

"Is he really that good?" And am I really such a bad sister that I didn't already know this? That feels like the kind of thing I should know, but every time Houston tries to explain sports to me, my mind wanders. I know he's good enough to be in the pro league and make millions of dollars, but beyond that? I don't know where he compares with other pitchers because he has always just claimed to be the best.

Laughing, Jordan hops to his feet and pulls me up with him. "He really is. I kind of hate how good he is, but it's not like he hasn't put in the work."

That's true. From the day he discovered baseball, Houston has dedicated his life to the sport. It would be inspiring if I understood any of it

"What about his contract?" I ask. "He has a year left, right? Can he keep playing in Sun City after that's up?"

I definitely don't expect the frown that appears on Jordan's face when I ask that question. He tries to hide it by looking around the yard, but he isn't fast enough. "He'll be a free agent, so he can choose whatever team he wants."

"But?"

Jordan glances at me. "But he's getting up there in years."

"He's only twenty-eight. And are you calling me old? Because *I'm* twenty-eight."

"You're older than me, which makes you ancient."

"By three months."

He cocks his head, laughter in his smile as he gazes at me. "You remember that?"

Apparently I do, though I have no idea how I know when Jordan's birthday is. It's not like I ever celebrated with him and Houston. Jordan was usually around for my birthday, but never the other way around. "Don't read too much into it," I mumble right as I realize Jordan hasn't let go of my hand since helping me up.

He follows my eyes down to our fingers laced together and seems to contemplate the meaning of life while he stares at them. His thumb rubs over mine, making my breath catch, and he leans closer as if that might make this any less weird.

"Fun fact about Jordan," he murmurs. "My whole job used to be reading between the lines. I'm really good at it."

I'm not sure it's actually October because with the way I'm sweating, it feels like the middle of July. "What does that mean?" I ask, apparently feeling brave.

His lips quirk up. "That's a good question. I..." He sighs. "I should really finish the job before your landlord thinks I'm slacking and complains to Houston. Need to keep up good relations with my clients, few as they are."

I reluctantly let go of his hand, feeling as if letting go of him is going to get harder and harder each time he touches me. That can't be good for my emotional health. "Can I make you breakfast?"

His eyebrows shoot up. "Why?"

"As a thank you for taking care of me this weekend. And an apology for sending a picture to my friend without your permission."

"You sent it to someone else?"

I cringe. "Maybe."

"Did they agree with your assessment?"

Smacking him, I bend down and pick up my phone from where I left it by my feet. "She might have, yes. But don't let it get to your head."

"Were you listening to nothing I said earlier? I'll be fine, Queens. And you're not making breakfast."

"Why?" Does he really have such little faith in my cooking abilities?

He laughs. "Because I want to make you French toast. This could be my last chance to make you breakfast."

Oh, I really don't like that. Does he think I won't let him hang around after this Houston-mandated weekend? Maybe he doesn't *want* to hang around. "We can be friends, right?"

I ask that right as he turns to head back to the lawn mower, but he freezes when he hears my question. Looking over his shoulder, he eyes me from head to toe. "Is that what you want?"

Do I want to be friends with Jordan Torres? Of course. I'm starting to wonder if I might want to be more than that, but a friendship is far less risky. "What if I do?"

"Then I'd have to wonder if you really mean it. We tried that once."

"We've never been friends before."

He wrinkles his nose. "Speak for yourself. I considered you a great friend back in the day."

"*Houston* was your friend."

"A guy can have more than one friend, you know."

That's true, but that doesn't change what things were like back then. Unless he really thought I was his friend? It would explain why he never left me alone, but it would also make me feel like a terrible person for trying to drive him away. "We drove each other crazy, Jordan."

"The mark of a true friendship." He folds his arms, giving me the kind of pinched smile that always makes me a little nervous because it looks like he's planning something. "You really want to be friends?"

I do my best to look unconcerned. "We can be adults about this."

"I know I can. I'm not so sure about you when you're over there taking stalker pictures of your landscaper."

Heat blossoms in my cheeks, but I ignore it. He's trying to goad me into reacting, and it's working, but I can't let him know that. He's always been like this, picking up on tiny little responses and poking where he knows I'll feel it the most. I need to poke back before he realizes he's hit a nerve.

"I did not take *stalker* pictures. I only took one. And I was thinking of setting you up with my coworker and wanted her to see what she would be getting into."

His whole expression drops in a way I've never seen before, like he forgot that he's supposed to always look a little mischievous. "You were?"

No, I wasn't, and already I'm feeling jealous of Jaydin even though I hadn't even considered setting her up with Jordan until the lie slipped off my tongue. Still, I have to stand my ground so he doesn't call my bluff. "Yeah. I think you'd be great together."

I didn't know it was possible, but I've rendered him speechless. He stands there with his mouth slightly open and seems to be digging into my soul with his eyes on me. But the moment passes quickly, and he's back to smiling. "I'm flattered, Queens, but I'm not looking to date right now."

"Oh." Why am I so disappointed by that? It's not like I was actually considering dating my brother's best friend. "Okay. I guess I'll leave you to finish up the yard?"

He tilts his head. "Was that a question?"

"No." It was, but he doesn't seem to like it. "I'll leave you to the yard."

"Better. And after, do you want me to make you French toast?"

I absolutely want that. "Only if you want—"

"I'm asking *you*, Queens. Do you want French toast?"

"I'm good with whatever."

Folding his arms yet again, he moves in closer until he's almost nose to nose with me. I'm frozen to the spot, barely breathing. "You're not," he says. "What if I change my mind and decide to make salmon omelets? You'd be good with that?"

This feels like a test, but one I don't have the answers to. What does he want me to say? "If that's what you want to make, I would be fine with—"

"Brooklyn."

I swallow, a shiver running through me from the way he said my name. "What?"

He puts his hands on my shoulders, which basically makes him impossible to ignore. Not that I was trying. "You need to stop being a sheep and act like the lion you are. Starting now."

What is that supposed to mean?

"You're in charge for the rest of the day. I won't do anything unless you tell me to, and if I get the sense that you're just trying to do what you think I want you to do, I'll ignore you."

"This doesn't sound like a good way to spend a Sunday," I mumble. It sounds like a nightmare, and I know I'm going to annoy him or make him think I have no idea how to be an adult.

"See, you're already failing," he says and presses his thumb between my eyebrows, smoothing out my frown. "Relax. I'm going to finish the yard and take a shower, and then you're going to tell me what you want for breakfast. If you don't tell me with confidence, I won't make anything."

"I can have cereal."

He groans. "That's the one place I'll put my foot down. You need to take care of yourself and eat better than that sugar crap for every meal."

This take-charge attitude isn't helping the weird attraction I've developed toward this man over the last couple of days, but I remind myself that he doesn't want to date me. Or anyone. No matter how he reacts to me touching him, there's no chance of things moving from a tentative friendship to anything beyond.

Which is good. Dating Jordan Torres would only complicate my already complicated life, and with Houston coming back at the end of the week and spending a couple of months at home before spring training, I can't make things weird for him. I can't risk ruining his relationship with his best friend when something goes wrong, as it always does.

But I can do what Jordan says. I'll take command of the day if that's what he wants.

"French toast would be great," I say, though I'm not sure I hit the level of confidence he's hoping for. "And then I have to finish grading."

He smiles his devastating smile. "Great. Do you need help getting back inside?"

Though I haven't been putting much weight on it, my ankle throbs as if it's reminding me that I twisted it. "Oh, I can—"

Jordan clears his throat. I don't know how he can read my thoughts, but he can.

I sigh. "Yes, please."

And when he scoops me up and I get up close and personal with his slightly sweaty face, my own face burns with heat. I never thought sweat could be attractive, but Jordan tends to defy all expectations with whatever he does.

"Thanks," I breathe as he heads down the stairs.

"Anytime, Queens."

I'm pretty sure he means it.

Chapter Fifteen

Jordan

October 14

BORING AS IT WAS, I let Brooklyn decide to spend all of Sunday inside. She did have plenty of work to do, which she apparently couldn't concentrate well enough to do on Saturday, so I couldn't argue against her choice. Besides, I meant it when I told her I would follow her lead, even if I could see how difficult it was for her to make decisions that involved me. At least she's trying, if only to appease me.

I'm still reeling from what she told me about her last boyfriend, even though it's Monday morning and I'm in the middle of taking a hedge trimmer to a dinosaur-shaped topiary and should probably be concentrating so I don't accidentally take off its head or something. Though we didn't once bring up the subject again, I've been stuck on one little detail she didn't tell me.

She didn't say who broke up with whom, which has me pretty convinced that it was him. If James broke up with her when she lost her job, that makes him just as horrible as the company that fired her because that would have done nothing to help her self-esteem. She would have taken his rejection as a statement that she wasn't worth keeping around.

What kind of guy could date Brooklyn Briggs and not know she's the best thing to ever happen to him? This James guy sounds like a turd dipped in hot sauce and I want to sit him down and revisit every failure he's had in his life, starting with how he treated Brooklyn by letting her go. It's no wonder she's lost the spunk I've always loved about her when her life has been nothing but jerks tearing her down, whether or not they did it intentionally.

I would do anything to see her spark return. I can only imagine how great a weekend would be with that version of Brooklyn. The one who always made me slightly nervous because she was so out of my league.

"Yo, Torres!"

I freeze right as my trimmer digs into the dino's belly. *Skewered.* Cursing, I turn off the trimmer and take a step back before I do any more visible damage.

Behind me, Rick laughs and folds his arms. He's my top guy, a landscaper I stole from the Red-tails stadium when I started my company, which makes his laughter extra frustrating. He trusted me enough to leave a stable job to work with me, and now I'm over here murdering leafy dinosaurs.

"Something on your mind?" he says when I take off my hearing protection. He nods to the slice in the topiary.

Everything. Everything's on my mind. It's not just Brooklyn, who agreed to talk to Mark today and be assertive in their conversation.

I sigh, fluffing the belly branches to try to hide my mistake. "Mom's having a down day." My dad even took the day off to take her in to see her doctor, which means it's more serious than Mom wants me to know. He rarely leaves work.

Grimacing, Rick pats me on the shoulder. "Sorry, man. That's hard."

He would know. He lost his wife to cancer five years ago, so he knows exactly how hard it is to watch someone go through the treatments.

And if that was the real reason I was distracted, I could move on from this conversation. But it isn't. And I can't.

Groaning, I rub the back of my neck and shut my eyes tight. "I did something I shouldn't have."

"That sounds ominous. Should I be keeping an eye out for the cops in case you need to run?"

His joke eases some of the tension in my shoulders. "What kind of a guy do you take me for?"

Rick shrugs. "Not the kind who breaks laws. So, what did you do that's got you disemboweling the velociraptor?"

I glance at the dino shrub, cocking my head to the side. "I thought it was a T. Rex."

"Nah. You made it more raptor." When I raise an eyebrow, he laughs. "My kid's into dinosaurs. Anyway, give me the details so we can get on with our lives. Those flamingos aren't going to power wash themselves."

Honestly, this client is probably the strangest one we've worked with so far, and the eclectic yard is my favorite. He pays well too, which is an added bonus, and I always make sure I am one of the guys shaping dinosaurs and clearing weeds from around the dozens of gnomes because it's too fun to give it to the other guys.

Rick clears his throat when I take too long to respond.

I roll my eyes. "I flirted with Houston's sister, okay?"

"Okay."

When he doesn't say anything else, I frown at him. "That's it?"

"I was waiting for the problem part."

"That was the problem."

"Flirting is a problem?"

"When it's my best friend's twin sister, yeah."

"Says who?"

Says every bro code ever, but I'm not sure if Rick is the kind of guy who has a bro code. He was entirely devoted to his wife—still is—and couldn't care less about what other people think he should or shouldn't do when he knows he's right. It's one of the reasons I hired him, knowing he would always do the best job regardless of my opinions.

But that's not helping me right now. I pinch my nose, grateful that the other guys are working on the backyard right now so they don't jump into this conversation. I need rational advice, and I can't trust the others to take this seriously.

"Here's the thing about Houston Briggs," I mutter. "He's the most loyal person I've ever known, and the only thing he loves more than baseball is his family. Especially Brooklyn."

Rick folds his arm. He's got the serious dad look down, which makes me want to listen to him. "If you're about to tell me you're not good enough for her, I'll slap you right here and now."

I put my hand on my cheek, preemptively feeling the sting. "Not where I was going, but thanks for the warning."

"Where were you going, then?"

"He may seem like the kind of guy who has a million friends, but Houston doesn't make attachments lightly. He doesn't trust people to stick around, so he doesn't let himself care." I point a finger at him. "And if you ever tell this to anyone, I'll turn Houston's lawyers on you before you can collect your tip money."

Rick doesn't even flinch. "Sounds like you dating his sister would be a good thing."

"It would be horrible." Even if I like the idea.

"Why?"

"Because if things went badly and we broke up, Houston would have to choose between us, and I would be out a best friend."

He rolls his eyes. "Then get a new best friend."

I could never do that. I owe everything I am to Houston, even if he doesn't know it. Every decision I made from the day I met him was influenced by him in some way or another, from which girls I did or didn't date in high school to the major I chose in college because he said I had a knack for making bad things sound good. Even some of my favorite foods are my favorites because Houston liked them first. I started this company because of him, and I never would have been able to do it without his support, both financially and emotionally.

"You're missing the point," I grumble.

"Which is?"

"Dating Brooklyn Briggs will only lead to disaster."

"Why?"

"Because I'm not good—"

That slap comes so quickly that I don't have time to dodge, nearly knocking me off my feet. I swear loudly and stare at Rick, who doesn't look even a little sorry. "What was that?"

He shrugs. "I warned you."

"I was going to say I'm not good at relationships!"

Pinking, he loses some of his serious expression to make way for a smile. "Oh. Sorry."

"I feel like this should go without saying, but it's not the brightest idea to slap your boss."

He shrugs again. "I told you on day one, Torres. I work with you, not for you."

"Can I be you when I grow up?"

Chuckling, he gestures to an intricate wrought-iron bench nearby, as if he knows this conversation is far from over. It's nice to sit in the shade for a minute, but I'm not looking forward to what Rick is going to tell me.

"Have you talked to Houston about this?"

I laugh. "The guy who is in the middle of winning the World Series for the second time? Oddly, I haven't had a chance to bring it up."

"Why do you think you're bad at relationships?"

I knew he wouldn't let that one go, though a part of me hoped the slap had made him forget the sentence I regretted as soon as it came out of my mouth. I should have just pretended I meant I wasn't good enough for Brooklyn (which is true) and accepted the slap.

Rick and I have worked together for a year now, which means we've done a lot of talking. About a lot of subjects. But the one subject I never touched was Natalie.

"I was a serial dater up until a few years ago." I grimace, hating how that makes me sound even if it's true. "Never went out more than a few times with any one person. Dating was more for fun than for settling down." I peek at him, expecting disapproval in his eyes. He's complained enough about a couple of the guys on the crew who only date casually that I know he's not a fan.

But Rick smiles at me and nods for me to continue.

"When I was in California, I met Natalie at the firm's Christmas party. She was friends with one of my coworkers, and we hit it off. Started seeing each other pretty regularly. It was the first time I thought about spending my life with someone, and we got married eighteen months later."

This is the part I hate, but if I'm going to get any actual advice from Rick, he needs to know the whole story.

"Things were good all around. Nat and I clicked, and I was moving up through the ranks at work and making a name for myself. I wanted to give her a good life, you know? The harder I worked, the more raises I got, and each bonus meant a better car for Natalie, a kitchen remodel, a trip to Cancun."

When I go quiet, Rick nudges my arm. "What went wrong?"

I laugh without humor. "Turns out when you spend your resort vacation in the hotel room working the whole time, your wife doesn't especially enjoy herself. Shopping sprees only fill that gap so much. And when you work so many late nights that you never see your wife, she starts to look for affection elsewhere."

Rick winces. "She cheated on you?"

"No. That might have been easier, honestly. But Natalie is too good for that. She let herself get more and more miserable until she couldn't handle the loneliness anymore and moved in with her friend. The day she asked for a divorce was the day I realized how deeply I had failed her as a husband, and it broke me seeing how much I had hurt her. I've never felt so low. As soon as the divorce was final, I quit my job and moved back here."

I drop my elbows to my knees and run my hands over my hair. "I can't be trusted with a relationship, Rick. Especially not with Brooklyn Briggs."

She deserves so much more than a recovering workaholic.

"Working hard to give your wife a good life doesn't make you a failure, Torres."

"I know." My dad is proof of that. He works all the time, but he still shares little moments with my mom whenever he can. He leaves her notes to tell her he loves her. He takes time off when his wife needs him because he's attentive enough to notice when she can't do something by herself.

I take a deep breath, holding it in my lungs for a few seconds. "But choosing to stay at the office until midnight and missing our anniversary dinner because of a client meeting I didn't need to go to aren't exactly winning traits. It stopped being about Natalie and turned into being more. *Doing* more. And I still find myself getting sucked into my job and forgetting there's more to life than work."

"I know," Rick says, laughter in his voice. "I nearly had a heart attack when you took the weekend off."

I shove him. "I'm a work in progress, okay? But that's why I shouldn't have flirted with Brooklyn. I'm in the middle of building a business, and there's no way I can give her the attention she deserves." The attention she *needs*. I meant it when I told her she needed someone to show her how to be loved, but it was stupid for me to think I could do that without losing my heart in the process. I can't afford to fall for Brooklyn any more than I can stomach risking her heart if I fall back into my toxic ways.

I refuse to be the next James. The next Garrett. The next bozo who can't see a good thing when he's got it. I have to hope this Mark guy is as good as she seems to think because right now he's the only thing standing between me and a bad decision.

As if she knows I'm thinking about her, Brooklyn texts me right then and makes my heart skip a beat when I see that it's her. That's a problem.

I know she means the last one of the Series, but I still wonder if she knows something she shouldn't. Does she know Houston's arm is giving out on him? Houston begged me not to tell anyone, so I'm guessing not. Apparently not sharing is a Briggs trait.

I chuckle.

Goodness, someone needs to teach this woman how to use voice-to-text, though she'd probably mess that up as well and end up sending a lot of ramblings to people she shouldn't.

Me:

> Fine. You get a pass. But I'm only coming to watch the game with you because I know you won't watch it otherwise.

Queens:

> *pukey face*

Queens:

> That was supposed to be a thumbs up...

"You're hopeless," I mutter.

"Nah, I think you're the hopeless one," Rick replies, making me jump. I forgot he was here. He grins at me, like a bunch of things suddenly make sense to him.

I point at him. "No. Don't look at me like you know something. There's nothing to know."

"Mm hmm." He gets to his feet, heading for my abandoned hedge trimmer. "You can lie to yourself all you want, Torres, but I'm pretty sure you more than flirted with Brooklyn."

My stomach does a weird sort of flip in my gut, leaving me nauseous as I hurry after him. "You can't make an accusation like that and walk away, old man."

"I've got fifteen years on you. I'm not old."

I jump onto his back like I'm thirteen and trying to prove to my brother Alejandro that I'm stronger even if he's bigger. Bad move. Rick immediately flips me over his shoulder and I land in the dirt hard, the air rushing out of my lungs on impact. *Ow.*

"Sorry," I grunt. "How did you do that?"

"My kid's a wrestler."

"The one who likes dinosaurs?"

It's a joke—I know he has four kids—but Rick chuckles and nods. "Yeah. Up you go." He grabs my wrist and helps me up, which I appreciate after that body slam. "Face it, kid. You're falling for Brooklyn Briggs, and you can't spend your whole life standing in the middle. You either have to go back the way you came, or you're going to have to cross to the other side and hope the grass is greener."

I rub my shoulder, which took the brunt of my fall, and shake my head at Rick. "Come up with that metaphor on your own, did you?"

He grins. "I thought it sounded pretty good. Plus her name is—"

"Brooklyn Briggs, I know." I also know she hates getting called Brooklyn Bridge more than she hates me calling her Queens, and she literally punched a guy after school when he took the taunting too far.

That's the woman I'm trying to bring back, but I know it won't be easy. Crossing the Brooklyn Briggs to a relationship isn't as simple as walking across an actual bridge. There are too many places to misstep. Too many loose boards and broken ropes. No one has bothered to care for her the way they should, and her boyfriends' negligence (and in some cases deliberate damage) has left its mark.

"So..." I wrinkle my nose as I examine his metaphor a little more closely. "You're saying I either need to go all in with Brooklyn or walk away?" I don't like either of those options, though one certainly sounds more appealing. I'm already missing her, which is ridiculous because I only left her house a few hours ago after spending three straight days with her. But I know pursuing anything romantic is a bad idea—at least until I can talk to Houston, and he won't be back in Sun City until the end of the week. Later, if they have to play a seventh game.

Let's hope Houston can keep his win streak going tonight.

Rick picks up the trimmer—apparently he doesn't trust me with the dinosaur right now—and gives me a grin. "I'm saying you might not have a choice. The heart wants what the heart wants, Torres. You can either fight it or embrace it, but I know which one will make you happy. Go clean some flamingos before the boys beat you to it, eh?"

As I head to the truck to grab the power washer, I think about what he said. I trust Rick enough to know that he wouldn't give me stupid advice, and when it comes to love, he knows what he's talking about. But what happens if I listen to him? What if I give into this attraction to Brooklyn and things go wrong?

My chest aches thinking about a life without Houston's friendship. It's not a new hurt, but the familiar fear isn't the only one sitting heavy in my soul. There's worry for my mom and the responsibility over my family that will come if she doesn't beat this cancer. There's concern over my brothers—Alejandro while he's in the Marines and who knows what's going on with Mateo. But there's a new fear working its way into my heart, and that's living without Brooklyn Briggs.

Rick is right. I'm in trouble.

Chapter Sixteen

Brooklyn

I shouldn't be relieved that Mark took a day off, but I've been breathing easier all day, since the moment I saw the sub setting up at his desk. I know Jordan won't be happy, but this gives me one more day to build up my courage. One more day to practice being brave. Honestly, I could use a whole week, but that wouldn't make a difference. Plus, a week with Jordan teasing and challenging me sounds like the worst kind of torture.

Now, though, that torture feels different. It's no longer frustration and annoyance I feel toward that man but something else. Something new. Something that pushed me to practically beg him to come back to my house tonight because I'm afraid to go back to the silence and loneliness that I've gotten used to over the last few years.

"Girl, learn how to answer your phone."

I glance up as Jaydin waltzes into my office and throws herself into the other chair with all the drama of a teenager. I didn't jump at the sound of her voice, which should worry me. Just how long have I been sitting here thinking about Jordan? "I don't know where my phone is," I admit with a grimace. After I sent the wrong emoji to Jordan, I hid the phone as if that might hide my embarrassment, and now I can't find it.

Sighing, Jay grabs her own phone and dials my number, sitting in silence until my ringtone blasts from the garbage can. She winces. "Why is your ringtone 'Hot in Herre'?"

I wondered why that song kept playing...

I scramble to grab my phone and deny the call before it keeps blaring at us. "Because every time I try to change it, it somehow becomes something worse than before."

Jay rolls her eyes. "Then just put it on vibrate." I hold it out to her, knowing whatever I try will end in disaster. "You're hopeless, Brook, you know that?"

"I know."

"So, are you going to tell me about this hunk of a landscaper, or what?" She flips my phone around to show me the picture I took of Jordan yesterday, as if I haven't snuck a peek multiple times throughout the day. "Don't try to tell me this is just a random guy and there's nothing going on between you two, because you just turned redder than a cherry tomato."

I press my palms to my cheeks, trying to cool them. "I don't know what's going on." Which is true. "But nothing is going to come of it."

"Why not?" She pinches the picture to zoom in, probably on his abs. "I'd be hitting this so hard."

"Don't be gross."

"I'm just saying, he's way hotter than Mark, whoever he is."

"He's Houston's best friend." I slide my fingers up to cover my whole face, as if that might make this less awkward to talk about. "I've known him for years, and I'm not going there. I can't."

"Why not?"

"I just told you. He's Houston's best friend."

Clicking her tongue, she hands my phone back to me. "And has your brother forbidden you from dating his friend? Which would be stupid, by the way."

"No, but—"

"Then there's no problem."

But there *is* a problem, and it comes in the form of my curse when it comes to men. "Jay, I am a magnet for terrible relationships. I'm not going to ruin Jordan just because he's flirty."

"And mega hot," she adds, as if I've forgotten that part.

I groan. "You're really not helping things, and this is why I avoided you at lunch. You're just going to try to push us together. Besides, he told me yesterday that he's not looking to date right now, so there wouldn't be a point."

"But you *do* want to date him?" She looks at me with a wide-eyed expression that probably means I'm doing a terrible job at hiding my feelings. Ha! As if I've ever been good at hiding my feelings. "Girl, I know you think you're cursed, but you're not. There's no such thing."

I haven't told her about most of my relationships, even though she's basically my best friend. She was so nice to me on my first day of teaching and welcomed me to Sky View with open arms, and my luck with friends has been about as good as my luck with boyfriends. That's probably because my dating life usually took up most of my free time before I gave up on men, so no one had a reason to try to keep me around. I wasn't around in the first place.

I don't want Jay to think this friendship has an expiration date as soon as I start dating someone. *If* I start dating someone. There's no telling how things will go with Mark.

To my utter relief, Principle Cheng knocks on my door, stopping Jaydin from continuing her argument. She gives us a wide smile, probably the happiest administrator in existence. "Sorry to interrupt, ladies. Brooklyn, I just wanted to give you a heads up that you'll be getting a new transfer student for your third period. I hope that doesn't throw anything off."

"No, of course not." I'll have to figure out what to do about lab partners, since that class is already even numbers, but I can make it work. Besides, I refuse to say no to Cheng until she makes her decision about the Teacher of the Year thing. "I'll be happy to take anyone who needs a place."

She smiles even wider. "Excellent. I'll warn you, he's had some trouble in the past, but his parents assure us that he will be on his best behavior here at Sky View."

I scramble to grab a pen. "What's his name?" I could look it up on our online portal, but that's always a dangerous place for me to go unless absolutely necessary. It's a miracle I haven't messed up any grades yet, and I don't want to know what might happen if I were to go into a student's profile unnecessarily.

"Mateo Torres."

My pen stills. Torres? It's not like that isn't a fairly common name, but there's a part of me that is pretty sure Jordan's youngest brother's name is Mateo. It's something with an M at least, and I know he's a lot younger than Jordan. Is he young enough to still be in high school, though?

"I'll leave you ladies to it," Cheng says, and she leaves with a wave.

Jaydin doesn't even wait until she's through the classroom door. "Why do you look like you've seen a ghost?"

It's not a big deal. It's probably not even his brother. But what if it is? Isn't there some sort of conflict of interest?

No. Maybe if Jordan and I were dating, but even then I don't think the school would care. They've always been pretty loose, and Mrs. Buehler in the English department had her own daughter as a student last year. Besides, what am I supposed to say to Cheng? *Sorry, but I won't take on this troubled student and show you I can handle more because I'm worried it will make things weird with the guy I'm not dating.* Ha!

"Brooklyn!" Jay snaps in front of my face.

"It's the concussion," I mumble, which honestly is a pretty good excuse now that I think about it. I don't think I *actually* got a concussion on Friday, but I can pretend. "Sorry."

She narrows her eyes. "That excuse will only work for a few days, hon, so cash in on that while you can. But if you're still dreamy-eyed by Thursday, just know that you'll need to expect a hearty 'I told you so'."

"About what?"

"About you and that bronze god you have showing off in your yard."

I snort. "God? And bronze isn't the color I would use."

"What would you call him, then? Because he's all-around yummy, and you know it."

She's not wrong. Jordan's mom is African American, and his dad is Mexican, leaving him blessed in so many ways. Where I'm pale, he's dark, and my skin goes straight from white to red with the smallest bit of sun, while he always looked better after a baseball season in the sunshine. Despite his muscle, he's generally lean, all angles and ridges and strong features. Though he keeps his hair short, it has the most incredible curl to it, unlike my barely-holds-a-curl blonde locks. And his eyes! Don't get me started on his eyes. I've never seen eyes like his, so warm and deep, like I could dive into them and disappear.

Yeah... All-around yummy sums him up pretty well.

"Oh, you've got it bad, girl."

I blink. "What?"

"Mark who? Hunky Landscaper is in town and taking center stage."

"No."

"Your drooling says otherwise."

I wish I had a pillow right now; she deserves a good whack. "This conversation is over and I'm going home." I gather up my purse and hope I don't limp too badly as I head for the door.

"Is Jordan going to be there? He is! Your face says it all."

Curse my inability to control my expressions! I wonder if Jordan could teach me that like he taught me how to flirt. "Bye, Jaydin."

"Have fun with your sexy gardener!" Her words echo in the empty hall as I head to my car.

As much as I'm looking forward to seeing Jordan again, which is a strange feeling, I doubt tonight is going to be *fun*. I'm going to be on edge, trying not to continue my experiment because Jordan made it clear that he won't be pursuing romance with me anytime soon. Or ever. We've known each other since we were fourteen, so you'd think he would have done something by now if he was ever interested.

And okay, yeah, there were those ten years after high school where we didn't interact at all, but it still feels like I've known him forever. And unlike the rest of the baseball team, Jordan never tried to ask me out. He had plenty of opportunities, but our interactions almost always involved some sort of prank or pushing all my buttons.

That's what I keep telling myself the whole drive home, but it doesn't do anything to make me less nervous as I stress-clean the basement in anticipation of Jordan coming over. I know it's ridiculous—he just spent three days in this basement with me and cleaned a lot of it already—but I want to make a good impression. Why? It's not like a clean toilet is going to change his mind about dating me.

When I pull back the shower curtain to give the tub a scrub, I freeze when I see the dark bottle of body wash that isn't mine. Jordan must have forgotten to grab it this morning when he packed up his stuff and headed back to his parents' house.

I have no idea what time it is—my phone disappeared soon after I got home—and Jordan will probably be here soon, so I should get to scrubbing. Instead, I open the bottle of body wash and inhale deeply. Yep, this is my new favorite scent, and I will absolutely be keeping this bottle. It's basically empty, so he'll need to get more anyway. I'll just tuck it away in the cabinet and—

"Pilfering my stuff, Queens?"

I scream and squeeze the bottle, which sends a stream of luscious body wash straight into my nose. Guess it wasn't as empty as I thought...

Jordan bites his knuckle, which is probably the only reason he's not dying of laughter right now. He really needs to stop because that combined with his grin is not doing me any favors.

"Towel," I demand, holding out my hand. Thank goodness none of it got in my eyes or mouth. A small miracle, I suppose.

He tosses the hand towel at me and then leans against the door frame, arms folded. Yep. That's worse. My little bathroom is suddenly a million degrees. "I promise I didn't mean to scare you." He purses his lips and tilts his head. "Okay, maybe a little."

Once the bulk of the soap is off my face, I stand to wash off the rest in the sink. "How did you get in here?"

"Door was unlocked."

"So you just let yourself in?"

"I knocked. And tried calling you."

"Ah, right, I don't know where my phone is."

As if he knew the conversation would go here, he holds up my phone. "Sitting on the welcome mat outside."

Well, that's embarrassing. "I think it was trying to run away from me," I grumble. Clicking it on, I find two missed calls from Jordan, as well as a text, and it looks like Micah just sent a text to our sibling group chat.

Micah:

> Good luck with your game tonight, Houston! Break a leg!

"I'm surprised Micah remembered Houston is playing tonight," I mutter and start limping my way to the living room right as Houston replies. I only make it two steps before Jordan slips my arm around his shoulders and basically carries me to the couch.

"How's that foot today?"

I hadn't realized how much it was throbbing until Jordan elevates it on a pillow. "It's mostly better," I tell him, "but I did a lot of walking and standing today. Do you think you could...never mind."

He rolls his eyes and heads for the kitchen, going straight for the ice. "I'll rub it out for you, and then you'll ice it."

I turn my attention back to my phone and focus on sending a fully correct text so I don't start thinking too hard about Jordan's hands on my skin.

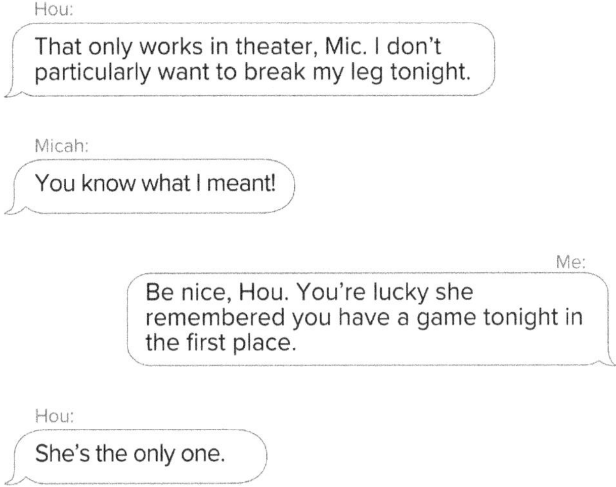

I don't like that he doesn't think I'll be watching tonight. And okay, I probably wouldn't have if I hadn't spent the weekend with Jordan, but still. Am I really that bad of a sister that my twin brother doesn't expect my support on one of the biggest nights of his life?

"There's a face," Jordan says as he lifts my foot to sit beneath it.

I should keep my fears to myself, but something about Jordan's expression drags it out of me. "Do you think I'm a bad sister for not watching all of Houston's games?"

His eyebrows shoot up, and he glances at my phone as if he knows there's something there that sparked this fear. "Of course not. Houston knows you don't like baseball."

"Houston doesn't like science, but he still helped me proof my papers in college before he signed with the Red-tails."

I feel like the text conversation is waiting on me, so I send the only thing I can think of that has nothing to do with me.

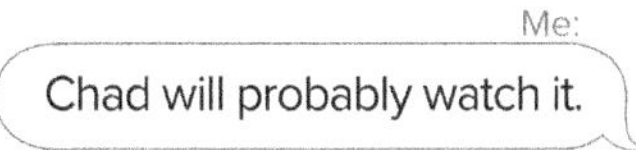

"Want to talk about it?" Jordan asks.

Not really. Besides, my siblings keep texting.

What in the world is that supposed to mean? Chad mentioned the other day that he was heading to Laketown, but I'm pretty sure it wasn't to get himself a girlfriend. He only broke up with Mercedes six months ago after dating her for several years, and my oldest brother isn't one to jump into something quickly. He takes things slowly, and he wouldn't settle in a tiny town like Laketown, which is where Micah's dad does our annual family reunions.

Unless Micah knows something I don't?

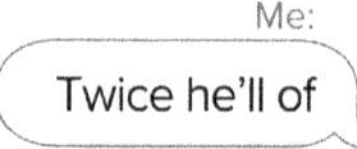

Well that's just ridiculous, and I curse autocorrect and go for the delete button. Only, my thumb hits the send button instead, and I groan at my stupid phone. "Stupid send button," I growl, taking extra care with my next couple of texts.

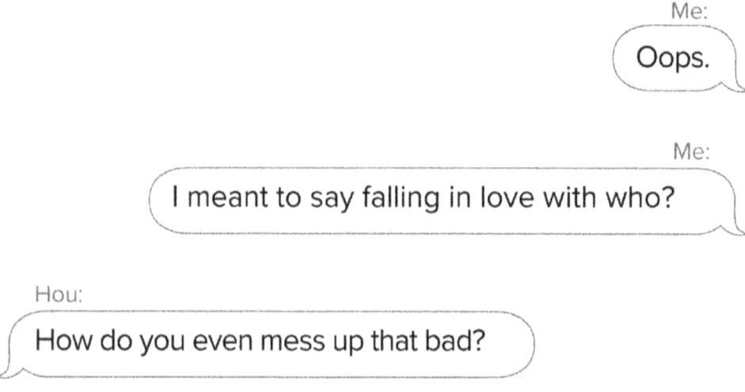

I can practically see his face, looking at me like he can't believe we came from the womb at the same time.

I glance at the time. If the game isn't for an hour, why did Jordan show up so early? And then I remember that Jordan is sitting there waiting for me to respond to him because I never actually said anything when he asked if I wanted to talk about it.

"Why are you here?" I clap a hand to my face. "That's not what I meant. I meant why are you here so early?"

Jordan raises an eyebrow. "What was your plan for dinner?"

"Um." I glance at my closed pantry, which is just as stocked as it was yesterday. Jordan and I went grocery shopping last night, but that doesn't mean I was ever planning to cook any of it because I don't know how. And maybe he spoiled me by cooking for me all weekend. "Probably a frozen pizza or something?"

He smirks. "That's why I'm here early. But first." His warm hands wrap around my ankle, and instantly half the pain goes away. He hasn't even started his massage yet. It's like my body knows what's coming so it's relaxing preemptively.

I glance down at my phone as Micah texts again.

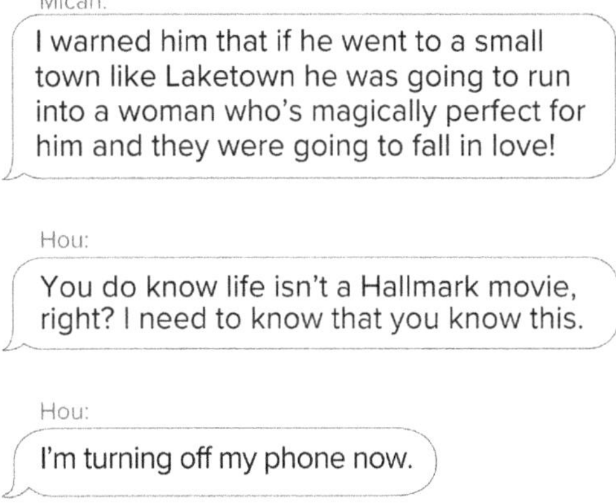

Poor Houston. He and I are similar in that neither of us has been in a serious relationship. At least not a good one. And that makes it hard for us to believe in love. Not exactly a trait I want to share with anyone.

He's probably turned off his phone already, but I send him a text anyway.

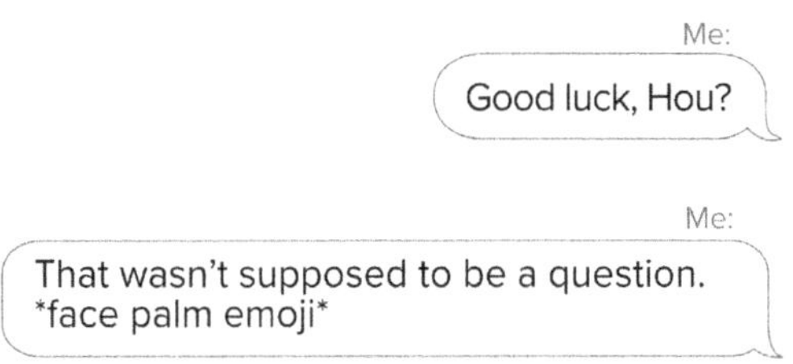

"Why is texting so hard?"

Jordan chuckles, his focus on my ankle as he slowly works his magic. "Most people our age find it pretty easy, Queens. I think it's just a 'you' problem."

"Why did someone think it was a good idea to put the send button right next to the delete button? I can't be the only one who accidentally sends things when she's trying to backspace and fix her mistakes, can I?"

He holds out his hand. "Let me see your phone."

"What? Why?" And why am I cradling it to my chest like I have something to hide? He already knows about my stalker photo of him.

"Just trust me, Queens."

It probably means something that I do trust him, which is not something I ever thought would happen. Handing over my phone, I hold my breath as he does whatever he's doing, which seems to be a whole lot of nothing in between a couple of taps.

"What are you—"

"Here." He hands it back and then hops up, resting the bag of ice on my ankle before heading to the kitchen.

I glance through my phone, but everything looks the same. He didn't send any texts or delete any photos. I'm too afraid to ask, so I ask a different question.

"Hey, what's your brother's name?"

Jordan looks over as he chops something. "Which one?"

"The youngest one."

"Mateo."

My heart stutters, though I don't know why. "Did he just transfer to Sky View?"

Pausing, he loses his smile as he looks over at me again. "Uh, I think so. But how did you know—"

"I think he just got put in one of my classes."

"Really?" For some reason, he suddenly seems incredibly excited about this topic. "If that's true, you can..." Then he frowns. "Okay, no, I shouldn't ask that."

Now I have to know what he was about to say. "What?"

He folds his arms, hunching his shoulders and giving me a smile that isn't really a smile at all. "I was going to ask if you could look out for him for me. He's going through something."

"What something?"

"I have no idea." And that seems to bother him as he resumes chopping with a little more vigor. "He won't talk to anyone lately, and then there were all the fights, and..." I don't think I've ever seen him with such a deep look of worry on his face, and I can practically feel his tension from here as he keeps talking. "If he would just let someone in, maybe he wouldn't get into trouble, and it's not doing anything to help my mom's recovery when she's stressing over him like she is. And with Alex overseas, she has enough to worry about already, you know?"

Despite my now-frozen foot, I get to my feet and hobble over to him, though he doesn't even notice me until I'm right next to him and nudge him with my shoulder. "I'll check up on him as much as I can, Jordan."

His eyes light up in a way I've never seen before, sending a shiver through me. "You are amazing," he whispers, and then he presses his lips to my cheek.

We both freeze, neither of us breathing as we stand there. I have no idea what he's thinking, but my thoughts are a convoluted mixture of warning bells and fireworks. My cheek is on fire, and I am all too aware of the way he puts his hand on my arm just above my elbow, like he's holding me steady.

"Uh." He seems to be working several different things across his tongue as he stares at me. "Sorry. That was..."

"Weird," I finish for him. Which it was. But that doesn't mean I hated it. Nope.

A wrinkle forms between his eyebrows. "Sure."

"I'm..." I look around for something to say that might make my pounding heart calm down. "I'm going to go sit back down. Let me know if you need any help?"

His lips twitch in the briefest of smiles. "Yeah."

He doesn't ask for help.

Houston's team wins the game, which doesn't surprise me. According to Jordan, this means they've won the World Series for the second time since my brother signed on with the team several years ago, which is incredibly impressive.

Houston wins more often than he loses—he hates losing more than anything—but as the TV turns to post-game interviews and commentary, Jordan relaxes, as if he's just glad the game is over. I'm more convinced than ever that he knows something I don't about my brother, though I have no idea what that might be.

I had way more fun than I thought I would watching this game. Jordan explained all the rules as things were happening, so they made sense for the first time in my life, and we did a lot of cheering and high-fiving, each contact sending an electric shock through me. I can almost imagine us doing this for all of Houston's games, and the idea definitely doesn't suck.

Not long after the game ends, an interview starts up with the most gorgeous sports reporter I've ever seen. She's thin and curvy, with electric blue eyes and dark brown waves, and I'm instantly jealous of the way she rocks her body-hugging dress. I would never be brave enough to wear something like that.

"I'm Tamlin Park with Enhance Media," she says brightly, "and I'm about to have the immense pleasure of being joined by none other than Houston Briggs."

"This should be interesting," Jordan mutters, though I don't get a chance to ask why because Tamlin keeps talking.

"After a whirlwind week of nail-biting competitions, the Sun City Red-tails have come out victorious against the Oklahoma Burrs. Tonight's Game Six win will no doubt be credited to the remarkable stamina of the Red-tails' favorite starting pitcher, the only man in the sport this year known for consistently pitching entire games without relying on subs to finish out what he's started. While some may question Red-tails manager Hiroshi Fujimura's choice to not send in relief pitchers for Briggs, who clearly has a bit of a control issue by refusing to leave the mound, no one can deny the southpaw pitcher has a knack for carrying his team to victory."

"I can't decide if I love her or hate her," I mutter.

Jordan chuckles and turns up the volume. "Tamlin has a talent for ambiguity," he agrees.

"And here is the man of the hour," Tamlin says as Houston steps up to her. "So, Houston, what's your take on how well the Red-tails played tonight?"

I may not read people well, but I know my brother. And I know he would rather be anywhere but standing there talking to this reporter. He looks like he's either going to throw up or start planning her murder.

Maybe both. He's still in his uniform, blond hair curling beneath his hat. (It never ceases to anger me that my brother's hair will curl while mine won't.) Though he stands relaxed, one hand is in a fist at his side, which means he's wildly uncomfortable right now.

"We won," he growls. I know for a fact he's gone through a million trainings on how to interact with people from the media, being team captain, but he's clearly not remembering any of that as he glares at the woman next to him.

Tamlin doesn't seem to mind, all smiles. "Barely," she replies in her husky voice. "Some might say you were looking pretty tired in the eighth inning."

"Are you forgetting that strikeout I threw?"

"Right before Dalton hit that home run and pulled the Burrs into the lead? That strikeout?"

Houston is definitely going to throw up.

"Okay, I'm leaning toward hate," I say right as Houston starts talking again.

"Luckily for me, I've got a good team behind me, and we regained the lead pretty—"

"So you admit the rest of the team had to make up for your subpar performance?"

I hiss, practically feeling the way Houston tenses up as he says, "That isn't what I—"

"What do you say to all the people who think you're losing your touch in your old age?"

This time Jordan hisses, though he's got a weird little smile on his face. It's like he knows this interview isn't going well for my brother, but he's almost glad about it? Though I can't imagine why. "Don't say it, Hou," he mumbles.

Houston looks right at the camera and smirks. "Old? I'm just getting started, baby."

"You said it," Jordan replies with a groan.

Houston winks and walks off camera, even though I'm pretty sure that wasn't supposed to be the end of the interview based on the way Tamlin looks ready to laugh. She watches him go for two seconds and then turns back to the camera.

"Well, if you ask me, Houston Briggs is on the wrong team. Something tells me he would make a good Dodger. There's no denying Briggs is good at what he does, but you heard the man. It takes a team to win the World Series, and Sun City knows how to pick champions. I'm Tamlin Park from Enhance Media, and stay tuned for more Red-tails excitement coming your way!"

The interview ends, and Jordan turns off the TV before setting the remote in between us. That leaves his hand resting right next to mine, though I try to ignore the burning sensation where our pinkies rest against one another. I could move my hand before the contact drives me crazy, but I don't.

Neither does Jordan.

"You were right," I tell him, trying to distract myself. "That interview was interesting."

Jordan chuckles. "She knew how to get right under his skin. I think I love her."

I whack his arm, regretting that decision immediately because I suddenly want to give that arm a squeeze and see if he really is all muscle, like he looks. "She called Houston old!"

"He *is* old."

"Hey!"

Snorting a laugh, Jordan turns and pats my head as if that might ease the sting of indirectly being called old by twin default. "For a baseball player, especially a pitcher, Houston is practically ancient. He's almost thirty. No matter how talented he is, he is well past his prime, and everyone knows it."

Huh. I guess I never thought about how there aren't many middle-aged pro athletes out there, but it makes sense. I was basically down and out for an entire weekend because my body didn't respond well to a little tumble, and Houston puts his body through a lot every time he plays a game.

I'm tired just thinking about how many balls he threw tonight. "Why doesn't Houston use relief pitchers?"

"Because he's a self-important idiot," Jordan mumbles. "But he somehow makes it work. I have no idea how."

"It's because he hates to lose. That interview with Tamlin is probably going to bug him for days."

For some reason, that makes Jordan grin. "Oh, I hope so. I hope he has to talk to her again because that was wildly entertaining. Can you imagine if Houston ended up dating someone like her?"

I can't help but laugh. "He would lose his mind. Houston would never date someone who isn't already in love with him because he's famous."

"I don't know. He's still single after breaking up with Bonnie, and he doesn't seem to be looking for the next temp."

I've noticed that too. I don't remember the last time my brother didn't have a girlfriend, so the last couple of months have been weird. Even if he's rarely home, I talk to him enough to know who he's dating, and there hasn't been anyone new since he broke up with his movie star girlfriend, Bonnie. I don't think he's even been on a date. Either he's hung up on Bonnie, or something has changed, and he was never that into Bonnie in the first place.

"Do you think he's ready to settle down?" I ask, though I have no idea if Houston and Jordan talk about stuff like that.

Jordan shrugs. "It's hard to know. I think he's restless, unsettled, and he isn't sure what he wants. With his contract being up soon, I think he's been thinking more about his future. But that doesn't mean he'll be brave enough to be vulnerable in a relationship. You saw the way he ran away from Tamlin just now, so I'm not holding my breath for him being brave enough to face something real."

He makes some good points, but that just makes me sad. Houston is such a good guy, and I want him to be happy. "Maybe he is already falling in love with Tamlin Park and he got spooked."

Snorting a laugh, Jordan turns his gorgeous smile on me and seems to study me for a second. Then he pats my leg and gets to his feet. "I should go. You're talking to Mark tomorrow, right?"

Mark. *Right.* "If he's there, I will try to—"

"No." He fixes a stern expression on his face. "No trying, Queens. You gotta do."

"Okay, Yoda."

I expect him to do the voice, something he did a lot when we were younger to bug me, but he just smiles and heads for the door. "Goodnight, Queens. And good luck."

With my track record with dating, and especially with Mark, I'm going to need it.

Chapter Seventeen

Jordan

October 15

BROOKLYN CALLS ME WHILE I'm driving between jobs on Tuesday, and I wish I could say I'm not wildly excited when I see her name on the screen in my truck. Watching the game with her last night was far too fun—way better than watching it by myself or with the kids screaming around the house—and it was a whole lot harder to leave than it should have been.

I force myself to let the phone ring a few times before I answer the call. "What's up, Queens?"

Silence.

"Brooklyn?"

"You okay, Briggs?" It's a male voice on the line, but in the distance. I almost can't hear him.

"Fine," Brooklyn says, though she sounds anything but. "Guess you just have a habit of scaring me."

Uh, what? I glance behind me and then pull my truck over to the curb outside the neighborhood I just left. I turn off the engine and let the radio stay on with residual power so I don't lose any of the call.

"We missed you on Friday," the man says.

"Why? I mean, uh, I was sick."

"That's too bad."

"Where were you yesterday?"

Hang on, is she talking to Mark? With me on the phone? While the chances are high she dialed me by accident, I can't help but wonder if she called me so I could make sure she doesn't mess this up. There's no way she's *that* hopeless, is there?

"An appointment downtown," Mark says. He doesn't sound quite as weasely as I was expecting, but it's not like I had much to go off of. Brooklyn spent too long talking about him with stars in her eyes for me to have any idea of what he's actually like. All I've got is her comparison to a movie star, which I don't love.

I've been around too many movie stars. The thought of Brooklyn crushing on someone that self-important has me feeling restless.

"Any word on the nomination?" Mark asks.

There's a shuffling of papers. "Oh. Um. Not really. I think Cheng wanted to make a decision soon, though."

"You'd be a great option."

"Thanks. You too."

"Thanks."

Silence again. This might be the most awkward conversation I've accidentally listened to. Yes, I know I could just hang up and pretend she never called, but there's still that chance that she called on purpose. I'll feign ignorance if this ends up being a butt dial, but I refuse to let her down if she wants me here.

I glance at my watch. These two had better start talking, or I'm going to be running behind the rest of the day.

"So, Briggs, are you busy tonight?"

I nearly swear, holding it back just in case Brooklyn can hear me. I lost track of the number of times she got after Houston and me for using bad language back in the day, and I doubt she's any fonder of it now than she was then.

Mark's not wasting any time, is he?

Brooklyn stumbles over several words before she finally lands on, "No."

"Dinner on me?"

"Say yes, Queens," I mutter.

Say no, another voice says in the back of my mind.

I remind that voice that Brooklyn has been pining after this guy for who knows how long and I just spent my weekend building her up to this moment.

"That..." Brooklyn probably swallows, and I would bet money that she's completely red right now. "That sounds good."

Good. Not great, lovely, fun, awesome, or anything else that packs a little more punch than *good*. Maybe her next lesson should be a revisit of how to stroke a man's ego.

Next lesson. As if we're going to keep hanging out and pretending there's no attraction between us. I should really give Brooklyn the benefit of the doubt and let her handle things from here. She's had enough boyfriends over the years that she can't be completely clueless when it comes to dating. I'm hoping this lapse in flirting skills is only a side effect of her jerk of a boss, James, not standing up for her. Jerky James should really be paying for damages when it comes to this woman, even if he wasn't directly involved with her losing her job.

Jury's still out on that.

After another painfully long pause, Mark finally seals the deal. "Can I pick you up?"

I freeze right as my truck turns off completely, cutting me off from Brooklyn's response. Scrambling, I dive into the backseat to grab my phone from my bag where I left it earlier. "What did she say?" I ask the silent cab.

My hand finally connects with my phone, and I lift it to my ear right as Brooklyn says, "Jordan? When did you call me?"

I have to fight to keep my breathlessness out of my voice. "You called me."

"I did?"

So this wasn't intentional. Suddenly I feel like I've just broken a level of trust, and I don't like it. "Just now, yeah. Everything okay?"

"Everything's good. Mark just asked me out."

My voice cracks as I say, "That's great." It's not great. It's not even *good*. I hate everything about the fact. "When's the big date?"

"Tonight. Um." She's quiet for a second. "Could you come over before? I'm kind of freaking out."

No! the little voice screams in my head. *That is a* terrible *idea.*

"Sure, Queens. I should be finished up around six."

"Thank you."

She shouldn't be thanking me when tonight is most likely going to be torturous for me. There's no saying how I might act, and that is very, very dangerous.

"I'm an idiot."

Rick doesn't look up from the sprinkler pipe he's cutting even though I've stepped into his sunlight and thrown his work into shadow. "Took you this long to figure that out?"

I consider tackling him but think better of the idea when I remember what he did to me yesterday when he flipped me. "See if I come to you the next time I need advice," I grumble.

"Why are you an idiot in this instance, Torres?"

"Brooklyn's going out tonight."

"That's great!"

"Not with me."

"Less great."

"She's going to dinner with her longtime crush, and I agreed to hang out with her until he shows up."

Rick finally looks up, and the expression he's giving me makes me feel like I just proposed that we change our company uniform to being completely in the buff to drum up more business. "Why would you do that?"

"Because I'm—"

"An idiot. Yes, I'm seeing the connection. Did you forget the part when I told you to either stop playing games or go all in?"

"Is that what you were saying with the bridge metaphor?" I rub my arms, feeling itchy. "I seem to recall telling you exactly why I can't *go all in*. Houston would—"

Rick laughs, cutting me off. "Oh, kid, if you let other people have a say in your love life, you're going to end up lonely and bitter, and nobody wants that."

He's right. He's always right. "What do I do? I can't tell her that I won't help her tonight." I'm too full of pent up energy to just stand here, so I crouch down and take over the pipe repair. Rick's already cut out the broken part, so it's halfway done.

"What, exactly, are you helping her with?" Rick asks.

That's an excellent question. "I have no idea. She just said she was freaking out and asked if I could come over before her date." Everything with Brooklyn is so complicated, unlike this pipe. To fix this, all I have to do is throw on a couple of clamps and attach a slip coupling between them, and then the water pressure will be back to the sprinkler head. Easy.

But with Brooklyn, I have no idea what to do. Does she need me to talk her out of the date? Talk her into it? Scare the guy away because he's a creep and she deserves better? The fact that Brooklyn asked me to come over means there's more to tonight than a simple date, but of course she didn't give me any details. Why would she? I'm just the guy who constantly teased her because she intimidated me and I didn't know what else to do with her. It wasn't flirting, but…

Wait.

Have I been flirting with Brooklyn all this time and I had no idea?

It's only when I've tightened the clamps and I'm back on my feet that I realize Rick has been standing there watching me instead of continuing the conversation. His smirk doesn't bode well.

"What?" I ask, tensing.

Rick chuckles. "Do you often talk to yourself?"

"Do I…what?" But based on the slight dizziness that washes over me—subconscious embarrassment—I think I understand. "I just said all of that out loud."

"Sure did."

I knew I was prone to sleep talking, but sprinkler ranting is a new one. Clearly this problem is bigger than I've admitted to myself.

"No," I say with a shrug. "No, I do not."

"This girl really has you hot and bothered, doesn't she?"

Denial sits on the tip of my tongue but rests there, tasting bitter. "I think I'm in way deeper than I realized even yesterday."

"And what are you going to do about it?"

Outside of confessing my growing feelings for her, there's nothing I *can* do, and that option sounds like the worst thing I could ever do. Especially right before she's about to go out with the guy she's been in love with for years.

"She's not in love with him," I mutter to myself, though it doesn't make me feel better. If the last four days have taught me anything, things can move pretty quickly when Brooklyn Briggs is involved. "Rick, you gotta help me, man. I don't know what to do."

He raises an eyebrow right as the rest of the guys come around the corner, apparently finished with the other side of the building. "Do you really want advice?"

"I wouldn't ask for it if I didn't."

To my horror, he waits until the guys are in earshot and then he says, "Torres is in love with his best friend's sister and doesn't know what to do about it."

Heat that has nothing to do with the sun overhead blasts through my face, and for a moment I consider giving Rick an official warning that he's in serious danger of losing his job. But I would never do that. He's the best thing to happen to No Mow Problems, and things would fall apart without him.

As the other three guys raise their eyebrows at me and shoot each other looks, I scramble for a way out of this conversation that is not going to go in my favor. "We don't have to talk about this. We should probably get going to—"

"I still have to finish this up," Rick says, pointing to the exposed sprinkler. "So you've got some time to kill."

I grit my teeth. "I was hoping for sage advice from the man who was happily married for twenty years," I grumble. "Not from a bunch of one night standers and commitment-phobes. No offense."

Emil and Chase laugh, while Seth rolls his eyes. "That doesn't mean we can't give advice," Seth says. "We date around because we're young and not ready to settle, not because we're jerks."

I fold my arms, feeling restless again. Unfortunately, Rick has the sprinkler under control, so I've got nothing to keep my hands busy. "Sorry. I didn't mean it like that. What do you got for me?"

"We need some context," Emil says. He's the youngest of my team, only twenty-two, but he works hard. "How long have you been in love with her?"

That's not an easy question to answer, and I should make one thing clear. "I'm not in love with her."

Rick huffs a laugh.

"I'm attracted to her," I correct. "And I've known her since we were teenagers, but dating has never been on the table."

"But it is now?" Chase asks.

This conversation is making me feel tense when I don't want to be. Rolling my shoulders, I try to find the best explanation. "It's not that simple. Neither one of us wants to make things weird for her brother."

Seth cocks his head. "So you've talked about it?"

"Not directly, no."

"So, how do you know what she wants?" Chase asks. "I never know what women want."

"Which is why you can't get a date to save your life," Emil says and then gives Seth a high five.

I groan right as my watch buzzes with a text, and since the guys start ribbing each other about their dating lives, I don't feel bad about looking to see who messaged me.

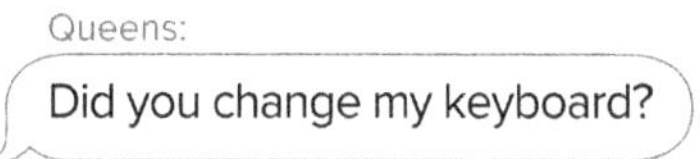

I grin. I can't help it. Wiping my hands clean on my pants, I grab my phone from my pocket and type back a response.

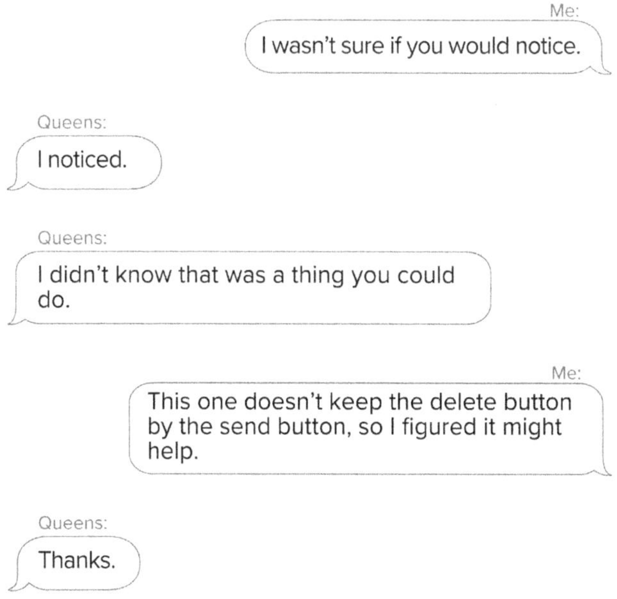

"You're texting her, aren't you?" Chase says. "You have the look."

I glance up. "What look?"

"The look a guy gets when he's texting a girl he's into," Seth says, rolling his eyes again. "Dude, you're clearly in denial."

"I thought you guys were going to give me advice. We should really get back to—"

In unison, all three of them fold their arms, like they're forming a wall against me.

"Nuh uh," Emil says. "I don't want to work with you if you're going to be all lovesick. Why haven't you talked about dating with her?"

Because she's going out with another man tonight, though I don't especially want to tell the guys that. "I'm too busy to give her the attention she deserves," I argue.

Chase frowns. "Why?"

I gesture my arm around the grounds we're working on.

Seth cocks his head. "I still haven't figured out why you're doing the work with us. I thought that's why you hired us."

"It is, but I like doing the work."

"Why?" Chase asks again. "No one wants to do manual labor if they can help it."

That comment catches me off guard. "Wait, then why do you work for me?"

"Because you pay better than most people," Emil says.

Seth whacks him. "Please don't pay us less. We like working for you. But that just goes back to the fact that you could honestly sit back and let us do our thing, and then you don't have to worry about being too busy to date this girl."

Before I can come up with some sort of argument, Rick stands up and fixes me with a stern look. "He's right. Just because you started this company, it doesn't mean it all falls on your shoulders. You've got a team for a reason, Torres, and we've got your back."

I didn't mention the other reasons I can't date Brooklyn—Houston and Mark—but weirdly I feel better about things. A little, anyway.

"Talk to her," Rick says. "Or step out of her life. You're never going to be able to have it both ways now that you feel something for her. Cross that bridge or go home."

"I'll talk to her," I agree, though I have no idea when. It's not the sort of thing I can throw at her right before she goes on a date with another guy, but if her date goes well...

I'll just have to show up tonight and hope for the best.

Chapter Eighteen

Brooklyn

"Queens?" Jordan's call makes me jump, even though it sounds like he's still at the front door and nowhere near my closet, where I'm on the floor buried in clothes.

"I'm in here." I sound breathless, like he scared the bejeebers out of me. Because he did. "Why didn't you tell me you were on your way?"

He appears at my bedroom door with my phone in his hand and one eyebrow raised high. "You should get a smart watch so you don't have to—"

"No way. I'm convinced one of those would try to eat me alive or something."

"What are you doing down there?"

I look at the floor around me, which is piled high with most of the contents of my closet. "Uh, I was trying to find something to wear."

"Most people keep things on the hangers as they search. Here." Reaching out his hand, he helps me up to my feet and makes sure I'm steady before letting go. "Are there any you're trying to choose between?"

No, because everything I own is lame. I didn't used to care much, but then I dated a guy who was all about appearances, and he took me shopping until my wardrobe was full of fashion-forward pieces that never felt comfortable. I had to replace it all when I became a teacher, buying most of my stuff at thrift stores because I couldn't afford much else. That left me with nothing but t-shirts and professional attire, which means I have absolutely *nothing* to wear on this date tonight.

Probably seeing my distress, Jordan sighs and looks at my mess of clothing. "What are you doing for your date tonight, anyway?"

"Dinner. And, uh, going to the art gallery." I smack him when he smirks. "Don't laugh! I told you he liked that kind of stuff."

"But do you like it?" He mumbles that to himself, picking up a pantsuit and making a scrunched up face. "Queens, when was the last time you updated your wardrobe?"

I fold my arms. "A few years ago. After..." Biting my lip, I pick up a maroon sweater that's kind of classy. "What about this?"

He barely looks at it before shaking his head. "Remember that lesson I gave you about temptation? That won't cut it. You want him to look twice when he first sees you."

"What, you want me to wear something revealing?" I shudder.

"No, not..." He clenches his jaw and picks up a light pink blouse. "You want something that makes him wonder. That tells him you're interested without giving him the wrong idea."

He speaks with such authority that I can't help but wonder how many people he dressed while he was working at that PR firm. How many clients did he give makeovers to? How many women did he coach through a date or a business deal?

What did his wife wear when he first saw her?

I tuck my arms a little tighter around myself. "I'm pretty sure I don't own anything that can do that, Jordan." More importantly, *I* can't do that. I may have learned to do the subtle touches, but one weekend of spontaneous lessons doesn't equate to natural allure. I'm still amazed Mark asked me out in the first place, but I can't be certain that he'll remain interested after he actually gets to know me a bit.

As soon as he gets beneath the surface, he'll no longer wonder. He'll know that I'm not worth pursuing.

Something catches Jordan's eye. He leans past me, reaching to the very back of my closet, and pulls out a navy blue cocktail dress that I wore to Kit and Skyler's wedding. My stepsister made me one of her bridesmaids, and thankfully she went with an understated design so I didn't feel ridiculous when I wore the dress. With a high neckline, the sleeveless dress falls just above my knees and hugs my curves without making me feel exposed, and I honestly forgot I had it even though I wore it only a few months ago.

"This one," Jordan says, though he gives no sign that he's going to hand it over to me. He's too busy staring at it with distant eyes, like he's imagining what it will look like.

My heart beats a little harder. "You think? It's pretty fancy."

My words break him from his little trance. He blinks, turning to me with a half-smile. "It's perfect. And if Mark doesn't trip over his own feet at the sight of you, something's wrong with him." It still takes him a second to hand me the dress, but then he disappears, closing the door behind him.

By the time I've changed, pulled my hair into a braided side bun, and spent way too long on perfecting my makeup, I've run out of time to get any last-minute advice from Jordan. Mark will be here any second, and my heart feels like it's going to beat right out of my ribcage. I've never been this nervous for a date, and I can't figure out why I'm so anxious now. It must be because I've been interested in Mark for so long, and he's so far above me that it doesn't make sense for him to want to date me in the first place.

It'll take a miracle for this date to lead anywhere.

Stepping out into the living room, I close my eyes as I say, "What do you think? Tempting enough for tonight to go well?"

I'm met with silence. Fearing Jordan left because I took so long, I open my eyes quickly, only to find him gaping at me.

Oh.

I may not know a lot about expressions, but I'm pretty sure I know what his is saying, and it has nothing to do with wishing me luck on my date. Jordan looks like he just received the giant hot fudge sundae he ordered on a hot summer day and doesn't know where to start.

I clasp a hand around one elbow, ducking my head as my face lights on fire. That's not what I expected from tonight, and I have no idea what to do with that reaction.

"Sorry," Jordan says, pulling my gaze back to him. He's closed off his expression, leaving nothing but a queasy-looking smile. "You caught me off guard. You look amazing, Queens."

"Really?" I feel stupid asking, given the way he stared at me just now, but my heart is having a hard time believing anyone would look at me that way. "I feel way overdressed."

"You're not. Really." He stands, his phone slipping from his lap to the floor. He doesn't notice. "You're going to blow him away tonight."

Maybe I look nice, but that won't change my inability to hold a conversation when we have nothing in common. It won't change the fact that I can barely speak at all when I'm around Mark. My stomach is already full of butterflies, which should make dinner interesting. "What do I do if we can't find anything to talk about?" My voice sounds so small.

Jordan slowly steps closer, cocking his head to one side as he goes. "You'll find something. Talk about work if you have to."

"What am I supposed to do while we're at the gallery?"

"Exactly what you did with me at the gallery. Talk about how the paintings make you feel. Touch him to subtly let him know you're there." He gets close enough that his hand brushes mine. It's barely a whisper of a touch, but I feel it everywhere. He smells so good, which must mean he showered before coming over. He put on a Henley again, a dark gray one that hugs his chest.

Gazing up at him, I can barely find my breath. "And if he wants to hold my hand?"

Jordan slides his fingers between mine. "If that's what you want, you let him."

"And..." I swallow. "What if, when he drops me off, he wants to walk me to the door? What do I do?"

Jordan's eyebrows tug together, almost like he's in pain. "That depends," he says, his voice strained.

"On what?"

"On where you want the night to end. If you want to leave him in the car, you say goodnight to him before you open your car door. If you want him to follow, don't say a word until he gets out first. And if you want..." His words fade, but he moves in closer. Too close. "You've been in this situation before. You don't need me to show you how to send the right signals."

He's sending signals. I'm almost convinced of it. But why? How? Why now? And why do I want to answer the call?

"What do I do if he wants to kiss me?" I whisper right as Jordan's nose touches mine.

He tenses, closing his eyes as he pulls back. "I'm not going to kiss you, Brook."

My heart sinks. "Why not?"

He opens his eyes, and I feel like I can see through them right into his heart. My question just changed something. "You know why."

A knock on the door makes me jump. Though Jordan tries to free his hand, I hold him tight. "Please don't leave," I beg him. "Will you be here when I get back?" That's a terrible thing for me to ask, but I'm too scared about tonight. If I don't know that he'll be here to pick up the pieces when everything falls apart, I'm not sure I can go through with this.

Jordan looks like he's desperate to say no, but he nods right as Mark knocks again. "I'll be here."

When I answer the door with shaking fingers, Mark smiles. Then his eyes slowly drift down my body, taking me all in, and his smile grows wider. "You look incredible, Briggs."

Thank you. That's what I'm supposed to say, but the words stick in my throat.

Mark falters in my silence, but he recovers quickly, holding out his arm. "Should we go?"

"Yes." Thankfully that word makes it out.

"Brooklyn?"

I turn to find Jordan standing in the middle of my living room with something heavy in his expression. Regret? "Yes?"

"Have fun tonight."

Chapter Nineteen

Brooklyn

MARK DOESN'T SAY ANYTHING about Jordan until he opens the passenger door of his car for me. "Who was that?"

For some reason, I don't want to tell him that Jordan is my twin brother's best friend, or even that he's *my* friend. Nor do I want to lie, so I find an awkward middle ground as I climb into the car. "Oh, uh, he works for my landlord. Landscaping."

Is that technically true if Houston is the one who hired him for the yard? I still haven't figured out exactly how my brother fits into the house where I live, but I'm going to guess he and my landlord are in business together or something along those lines. I had no idea Houston would be interested in real estate, but maybe I shouldn't be surprised. He invested in a bookstore as well as a landscaping company, so clearly he's got some breadth.

"Briggs?"

The way Mark says that tells me this isn't the first time he's said my name. We've already left my neighborhood, which means I was lost in thought for longer than the few seconds I thought it was. "Sorry, what did you say?" I feel like I should have some sort of explanation. "I got a concussion the other day, so I'm still a little fuzzy."

Mark smiles, though it feels a little condescending. "That's too bad. I was just curious if you had that new troublemaker student that transferred to Sky View this week."

Oh my goodness, I was supposed to tell Jordan that Mateo didn't show up for my class today! I didn't want to tell him over text, but then I got so distracted by finding something to wear that I completely forgot. "Uh, he's in my third period, but I haven't met him yet."

Mark clicks his tongue. "First week and he's already ditching? That's a bad sign. He barely paid attention in my Calculus class today, so I'm thinking he's a lost cause."

"I hope not." Jordan is already worried about his brother, and this isn't going to help anything.

"Oh?" Mark glances at me. "You think the delinquent has a chance?"

"I think everyone has the capacity to change," I say quietly.

"You're a better person than me. He clearly doesn't want to be at school, so I'm ready to give up on him."

"I'm sure he already feels like a lot of people have given up on him. I don't want to be another one."

"Huh. Interesting take."

We're quiet the rest of the drive to the restaurant, which is fine by me. It gives me a chance to process what just happened in my living room. Or almost happened, I guess. Despite what he said, Jordan nearly kissed me. *Jordan Torres* almost kissed me.

And I almost let him.

That's crazy, right?

"Ever been here?" Mark asks as he pulls into the parking lot of one of the fanciest restaurants in the city.

I gape at the stonework on the building's exterior and the large fountain by the entrance. Why on earth would a high school teacher choose a place like this for a date? I'm going to have to pay for my own food so the guilt doesn't eat me alive, and my bank account won't be thrilled by that.

"No," I squeak, "I haven't been here. Are you sure we should—"

He unbuckles his seatbelt and slips from the car, coming around to my side to let me out.

I guess I'm not as overdressed as I thought I would be.

The restaurant name is something French that I can't pronounce, which only makes me feel slightly stupid when we get inside and the hostess says it with ease. Mark does all the talking, saying something about a reservation he made weeks ago, which sets my face burning. How long has he been planning this date?

Once we're seated, Mark gestures to the menu that I'm too scared to pick up because then I'll see the prices. "I'm happy to give you some recommendations if you need."

If I let him do that and then order something else, he'll get offended, so I open up the menu and smile. "I'll let you know."

Pistachio pudding! There aren't any prices on the menu. I was going to order the cheapest thing that looked edible, but nothing on this menu has a number next to it because the people who regularly eat here are the people who don't bat an eye at spending a hundred dollars on a steak.

Squirming, I scan the menu for anything that looks like it has cheap ingredients, hoping that gets me a less expensive meal.

"Here is the wine list," our waiter says, handing it to Mark. "I recommend the Cabernet Sauvignon to go with the prime rib."

Mark looks at me. "What do you think?"

I think Mark and I probably should have gotten to know each other better before we went out on a ridiculously fancy date. This feels like the kind of place you're expected to know your wines.

"Oh, um, I don't drink."

Mark's eyebrows shoot up. "Really? Why not?"

Because I've seen the effects alcohol can have on a person and the way they lose control of their life. My dad's in prison because his drinking led to harder substances until he spiraled out of control, and I was always slightly terrified whenever I came home from school and he was drunk. He never showed signs of physical or verbal abuse, but Chad still never let him near me unless he was sober. I think my brother knew, even back then as a teenager, that someone under the influence had the potential of being dangerous.

I swallow. "It's not something I've ever wanted to try."

Mark orders a wine for himself and then settles against the back of his chair. He seems so comfortable here, even though he's on a teacher's salary. "So, Briggs, tell me about yourself."

My fingers are still shaking slightly, so I tuck them into my lap. "What do you want to know?"

"Anything. Everything. What did you do before you came to Sky View?"

Right to the one topic I don't want to discuss? I take a sip of water, knowing this night is going to be a long one. "It doesn't matter. What about you? How long have you been at Sky View?"

I'm more than ready to move on to the gallery when Mark finally finishes his food. He spent most of dinner talking about himself—by my design—so I ended up eating a ridiculous amount of healthy, wheaty bread to keep myself occupied after I finished my carbonara while he slowly worked his way through his prime rib.

He has a more impressive resume than I expected, with a lot of accolades and awards I've never heard of under his belt. He told me he teaches high school because seeing his students succeed makes him feel like he's done something well, and he takes a lot of pride in their knowledge by the end of the year.

He carries on his monologue as we head to the gallery, stopping only to pay for our entry tickets.

"Let me get them," I say, since he refused to let me pay for my half of dinner.

Mark waves me away and hands over his card. "Don't be ridiculous, Briggs. Tonight is on me."

Once we get inside, Mark takes hold of my hand and tugs me to the right like he's on a mission to find something specific. He doesn't stop until he reaches the modern art section, and then he launches into his opinion of the first piece as we come to stand in front of it.

Every other painting, according to Mark, is "evocative," though he can never expand beyond that. It makes sense, given he's a math and numbers guy, but the longer we wander the gallery, the more I start to wonder if he knows anything about art or if he's just trying to impress me. He's using a lot of words that sound artsy, but I'm pretty sure they don't actually mean anything.

It's kind of cute that he's trying. I guess.

He doesn't let go of my hand, which negates Jordan's lesson on temptation. I must have done better than I thought while at dinner, even though I barely said a word outside of asking Mark questions. I guess Jordan was right when he said I knew what I was doing, and a bubble of confidence grows in my chest.

I haven't felt that in years.

"What do you think of this one, Briggs?"

I look at the painting in question, which is just a bunch of crisscrossing lines of varying thicknesses and distances. They're all different shades of blue, and while the right angles where they intersect speak of rules and order, there's a sort of chaos to the painting. Like an underlying mischief waits beneath the mismatched patterns.

"It feels free," I say, unable to find another word to describe it. A shiver runs through me, and I fold my arms against the sudden gnawing sensation in my chest. "It reminds me of something I used to know."

"Fifth grade coloring projects, probably," Mark mutters. "Are you cold?"

He shrugs out of his corduroy jacket and drapes it around my shoulders, lingering near me in a way that I feel everywhere. Heat spots my cheeks while I wrap the fingers of one hand around the collar of his jacket to hold it in place.

"Thank you," I whisper.

"I failed to properly express how stunningly beautiful you are tonight, Briggs," he murmurs back.

I don't remember the last time a man ignited a swarm of butterflies in my belly, the kind that seem to be on fire and are as uncomfortable as they are pleasurable. Mark's looking at me in a way I can't misinterpret, his desire written all over his face.

I've wanted him to look at me this way for so long, which makes the next words out of my mouth the most pathetic thing I've ever said.

"It's a school night."

Mark blinks, clearly processing my words, and then he chuckles. "You're a more disciplined person than me, Briggs. I guess I'll take you home."

Was he not planning on doing that?

We reach my house far too quickly, which means I haven't decided what I want to happen next. Mark's already out of his seat and opening my door, so I take his offered hand and let him lead me down the stairs to my door.

He picks up my other hand, making it impossible to reach for my keys. "I'm glad we finally made this happen," he says.

"I." That's the only word that comes out.

Mark doesn't seem to mind. He leans in closer, eyes fixed on my lips. "You have no idea the temptation you present every day at work."

"I?" Apparently that's a question.

He grins. "You are both beautiful and intelligent, and no man stands a chance."

That's not true. Plenty of men have taken that chance and moved on, leaving me behind because I have something left to be desired.

But I can't tell Mark this because he presses his lips to mine, claiming my mouth in a kiss that speaks of a yearning I didn't expect from him. It's not frantic or greedy, but he kisses like he's hoping to find something.

And despite my reservations earlier, I melt into that kiss because it soothes some of the ache I've carried the last few years. He wants me, and I badly want to be wanted. I reach up, hand cupping his smooth jaw, and focus on the way his touch ignites something in me.

"Wow." Mark breaks away but presses his hand to the small of my back, holding me close. "That was better than I expected."

I don't know what to say to that, so I focus on slowing my rapid heartbeat before it breaks out of my chest. That kiss wasn't exactly how I imagined it over the last few years, but I felt it down to my toes.

"I know this complicates things with work," he continues, "but I like you, Briggs. I want to see where this goes."

"Me..." *Come on, Brooklyn, use your words.* "Me too. I've wanted that for years." Oh, sweet caramel sauce, did I just say that out loud?

Mark chuckles and kisses me again. "We'll have to figure out what to do about the Teacher of the Year nomination."

"You're right. We...wait, what?" I try to pull back. I'm too close to think rationally right now, but Mark holds fast. "What about the nomination?"

He pulls his eyebrows together and then presses his lips to my forehead. "I mean, you and me getting together puts Cheng in an impossible situation if she has to choose between us."

I guess that makes sense?

Running his hand over my hair, he seems to be cataloging everything about my face that he likes. "You and I both know that you'll get nominated next year, or the year after. You're too good at your job, and you make the rest of us look bad."

He's saying nice things. So why does my stomach twist more the longer he talks?

"What if, this year, you take your name out of the running? I guarantee you'll be a shoo-in next year, but I need this, Briggs."

"You need this," I repeat. The warmth of his kiss is gone, and suddenly all I can smell is his cologne. It's all over me, not just on his jacket but on *me*. Was it always this strong? Did it always cloud my head like this? "Why?"

Mark brushes my cheek with his finger. "I can't be a high school teacher forever. I was meant for more than this. Working with the university would help me climb the ranks so I can become a professor. Take over as dean of the math department so I'm not stuck dealing with students all day."

He presses his thumb below my lips, almost gripping my chin so I can't look away from him. "I know you'll let me have this one, Briggs. You're too good of a person to put my chances at risk."

I'm also smart enough to recognize when someone is trying to gaslight me because I've been down this road so many times before.

Why did it take me so long to see it? He's not interested in me. He's *threatened* by me. He's just like all the other guys who got scared off by my degree or decided I was doing so well that they thought I would surpass them and take what was theirs.

This is James all over again.

Tears pricking at my eyes, I force myself to hold everything in as I wriggle myself free and hand his jacket back. "Can we talk about this tomorrow?" I say, voice wavering. "I'm, uh, I got that concussion the other day, so I'm not really..."

Something flashes in Mark's eyes, but it's gone quickly. "Of course. You should get to bed. I'll see you tomorrow, and we can make a plan for what to tell Cheng."

I don't fight the final kiss he gives me, even though it's more demanding than I'd like. I don't have the energy to respond.

As soon as he starts up his car, I scramble for my key, but my fingers are shaking too badly for me to fit it into the lock. "You're so stupid," I tell myself as I fumble, tears blurring my vision. "Why do you always do this? Why do you always fall for their tricks? You're supposed to be smarter than this, but you're not. You're naive and foolish and gullible and—"

The door opens, blinding me with light. Not that I can see much through my tears. Jordan stands there for a few seconds, but then he spreads his arms out wide.

I fall into his hold right as the sobs break free.

Chapter Twenty

Jordan

I DON'T KNOW WHAT to do. One minute I'm doing everything I can to ignore the low murmur of voices on the other side of the door, and the next I'm holding an inconsolable Brooklyn and wondering who I need to call to make sure the murder I'm about to commit doesn't get solved.

I've never seen Brooklyn like this. Not even when her frozen blanket of a boyfriend cheated on her in high school. At least then she'd been calm enough to tell us what happened, but right now I am literally the only thing keeping her on her feet. My whole body feels stretched to its limits as I simultaneously hold her as tightly as I can and force myself to not crush her because I'm so tense.

Honestly, I thought maybe she was drunk when she struggled so much to unlock her door, but this is so much worse. Drunk can be fixed with some aspirin and a good night's sleep, but I have no idea what to do with the kind of tears that seem to come from deep in her chest.

"Can I take you to the couch?" I ask, trying to sound as non-threatening as I can.

She nods against my chest.

Lifting her into my arms, I don't miss the way she curls up into me, like she's too exhausted to do much else. It's only been a few seconds since I opened the door, but those seconds have felt like an eternity.

I sit with her on my lap so I don't have to let go of her, and then I start pulling out the pins from her hair as gently as I can. Once her hair is loose, I unlace the heels she's wearing—shoes she probably shouldn't have worn with her bad ankle, but I was too caught up in my own drama to think about that earlier. Removing her shoes takes a while, so by the time her feet are free, she has finally stopped sobbing. Tears and snot still drip into my shirt, but she's breathing again.

I rub my hand across her back, arms aching from the tension in my body, but I'm too scared to say anything. I don't want to make whatever this is worse, and I'm getting a little too much pleasure in imagining the black eye I want to give Mark right now.

"I'm so stupid."

I freeze, praying that I heard her wrong. "Brook?"

She sniffs. "What kind of idiot confuses manipulation for attraction?"

Oh, I don't like the sound of that. "The kind that sees the good in people. And you're not an idiot, Brooklyn. You're the smartest person I know."

"If I'm so smart, why do I always choose the men who hurt me?"

"*He hurt you?*"

Brooklyn presses her palm over my heart, holding me in place. "Please don't kill him. He didn't do anything to me." She sounds so empty, and I hate that she's using what little energy she has to defend the guy who made her cry.

I swallow. "Brooklyn, I know you don't want to, but you have to tell me what he did. Please."

She scoffs and starts tracing her fingers across my chest. Any other day, and that soft touch would be driving me crazy, but I can't even feel it right now. "He was never interested in me. He wants me to drop out of the running for STEM Teacher of the Year."

You've got to be kidding me. "An award? He seduced you to get a stupid award?"

"It's not stupid. It's a statewide thing, and the winner gets to do a fellowship with the University of Sun City, remember?"

"That's great and all, but I still don't see why—"

"It's my only chance to get back into research, and he wants me to drop out so he can climb the education ladder. But I need this. James made sure I can't get hired anywhere because I messed up his project, and I can't be a teacher forever. I don't love it. It's fine, but it's not..." She drops her head against my shoulder and sighs. "I want to make a difference. Save people from the heartache I went through. What you're going through right now. But I can't. I'm never going to be smart enough to—"

"I'm going to stop you right there." There's so much to process in what she just said, especially with the whole James bit, but I can't let her keep talking. She'll talk herself into a downward spiral, and she's already so much worse off than I realized. The years have not been kind to Brooklyn Briggs, and it's a miracle she's still standing in one piece.

I tuck her hair behind her ear so it doesn't hide her face, even though I can't really see her right now. It's the principle of the thing. "I want you to listen to me, Brooklyn Briggs, and listen closely. You're going to change the world one day, whether you're finding the cure to cancer or teaching the kid who figures it out down the road. Whether or not Mark is interested in you has nothing to do with who you are as a person and how much you're worth because nobody gets to decide your value except you. Do you understand me?"

She takes a shuddering breath but says nothing.

I lean back, tilting her chin up so I can look into her eyes. "Please, Queens. Please believe me."

She closes her eyes. "I don't know if I can."

"Then I'll find a way to help you believe." I pull her back in, wishing I could protect her from the world that hasn't been kind to her.

Honestly, I don't know how I'm supposed to do that. I've never struggled with confidence, and my failed marriage was my own fault. I've never had anyone tear me down the way Brooklyn has. How am I supposed to get her to see her worth when all she can see is the muted version of her others have turned her into? How do I get her back to the girl I used to know?

At this point, I'm not sure that version of Brooklyn still exists.

When her breathing grows deeper and more steady, I adjust my hold on her so I can carry her into her room to go to bed.

She grabs my arm. "Will you stay with me? I don't want to be alone."

Staying is a bad idea. With the intense jealousy that sprouted as soon as I saw Mark at the door, I can't pretend that what I feel for Brooklyn is only attraction. I'm falling for her, and falling fast, and spending another night in her basement isn't going to do me any favors.

"Please?" she whispers, and my heart breaks. Yeah, I'm not even falling at this point. I'm gone for her. Completely.

I pull her closer, wanting to never let go. "Of course I'll stay."

I'll stay forever if she lets me.

Chapter Twenty-One
Brooklyn

October 16

Look, I'm not proud of the way I reacted last night, and I'm becoming increasingly aware that my issues run deep enough that I should probably get some help in sorting out my ridiculous propensity for dating scumbags. I wouldn't be surprised if it had something to do with my dad, who was always pretty awful before he got clean. Still, I've always figured the problem was me, not them, when I looked at the common denominator.

Jordan, on the other hand...

My mind wanted to believe what Jordan was saying last night about my worth, even if my heart refused it. He said it with such conviction, and I can't imagine Jordan would ever lie to me. I do hate that he saw me fall apart after Mark revealed his true intentions, but...

But there's a part of me—a majority—that isn't mad about the results of last night's breakdown.

I've never fallen asleep in a man's arms before, and it might be my favorite place to sleep now. Jordan forced me to change into pajamas, even though the task felt impossible, and he made me a cup of chamomile tea and ordered me to drink every last drop. Then he took me up in his arms and settled on the couch with me until I fell asleep, and I slept more soundly than I have in months.

What does it say about me that I'm clearly dysfunctional without a man to hold me together?

Though my phone buzzes on the coffee table with an alarm—Jordan must have set it last night—he doesn't stir, which is surprising. I remember him being a light sleeper, just like he said over the weekend. If I ever had to get up in the middle of the night when he was at my stepdad's house, he was usually reading a book or playing a video game in Houston's room rather than sleeping. And with how much TV he managed to watch over the weekend, I don't think he slept much here either.

By some miracle, I turn off the alarm without jostling Jordan or causing my phone to do something disruptive. Then I take a deep breath.

I don't know how to face Mark today. He thinks I'm on his side, or at the very least considering his suggestion to take my name out of the running. Does he expect me to kiss him at school because suddenly we're a couple in his mind? I could play along, but I know it won't last. As soon as one of us gets picked for Teacher of the Year for our school, he won't have any use for me.

I refuse to let him humiliate me. I went through that with James, and my whole career fell apart because of him. This fellowship is my last chance to get back to the field I am truly passionate about, and I'm done letting people walk all over me.

First, I have to get myself out of Jordan's arms. Much as I would love to stay here all morning, I have to face today with my head held high. But I would rather avoid waking him if I can help it. With him being such a terrible sleeper, dealing with my nonsense last night can't have been good for him. He's always been protective, and I can imagine some of the things he wanted to do to Mark last night. If the way he held me was any indication, Jordan Torres is the kind of guy you don't want as an enemy.

Rolling slowly, I put one hand on the floor and the other on the coffee table and maneuver one foot down to hold up the rest of me. I wish it wasn't my bad ankle, but I deal with the pain until I'm completely free and Jordan is left breathing gently on the couch by himself.

He looks less peaceful than he did when I found him the other morning, like even in sleep he's worried about me. Frowning, I reach up and brush my fingers through the tight curls on his forehead, wishing I had spent more time over the last few days learning about his problems instead of burdening him with mine.

Why is he putting so much energy into comforting and helping me when his mom is going through chemo and his brother is ditching classes? I think his other brother might be in the military in some capacity, which is stressful on its own, and then he's got his business he's trying to build. I shouldn't be putting more on his shoulders.

I used to take care of myself, and it's high time I start doing that again.

Leaning up, I press a kiss to Jordan's forehead and then head to the shower, making a plan as I go. Mark DeNiro is going to regret crossing me.

I'm halfway to school when Jordan finally calls me, and he sounds half-asleep still.

"Why didn't you wake me up, Queens?"

I can't tell if he's worried or hurt, but I try not to dwell on either of those things as I drive. "You needed the sleep."

"But—"

"Don't try to deny it. You were exhausted."

He's quiet for a second. "I don't remember the last time I slept that long."

"Ha! I told you."

"How are..." He sighs, and I picture him running a hand down his face as he tries to wake up. "How are you doing?"

I'm fluctuating between vindictive and terrified, which, let me tell you, is not a great combination. "I'm dealing," I tell him. Maybe not in the best way, but I'm doing what I can.

Jordan grunts. "What are you going to do when you see Mark?"

"If," I correct. "I'm actually really good at avoiding him, which should have been my first sign that he wasn't the right guy for me."

Honestly, this morning I've felt so much clarity that it's almost laughable how long I was hung up on the stuffy math teacher who probably wears clip-on bow ties because he doesn't actually know how to tie a tie. What was I thinking?

"It probably isn't your best option," Jordan says through a yawn, "but I recommend punching the guy if you do have to interact with him."

I laugh, which is a miracle unto itself. A week ago, Mark would have broken me. Or maybe I still would have woken up and seen the light, but I'm not sure how I would have come out the other side if I didn't have Jordan to hold me together. "While I don't love my job, neither do I want to get fired, so I'll go with a different plan."

"You have a plan?" He sounds nervous about that.

He shouldn't be surprised. I used to be full of plans and backup plans and backups to my backups. Jordan and Houston never pulled a prank without me having one to throw right back at them.

I pull into my parking spot, and the nerves start to settle in more permanently as I look at the building in front of me. Mark's in there somewhere, and there are no rulebooks or guidelines for the situation I'm in right now. I have no way to prepare, and I hate that.

"Tell me I'm strong enough to get through this," I say, my voice breaking a little.

"Brooklyn. You don't need me to tell you anything."

"Tell me anyway."

"Of course you're strong enough. You're one of the strongest people I know."

"Thanks, Torres." I don't know why I call him by his last name. I've never done that before. But I smile at the way it rolls off my tongue, feeling a strange sense of camaraderie with him as if we're in this together.

Jordan's voice comes out a little strangled when he responds. "Anything for you, Queens."

By some miracle, my day passes without any sign of Mark. It's harder to avoid Jaydin, who doesn't know Mark even asked me out, but I know I'll fall apart if she asks me how my day was yesterday, so I eat lunch in my car and leave my classroom the instant my contract time is over. Yes, I have a plan for Mark, and yes, I'll tell Jaydin everything that happened, but I need some time to breathe.

As soon as I'm safely tucked away in my car after school, I text Jordan.

Me:

Made it through the day without incident

I am genuinely amazed at how much easier it is to text when I can delete typos without the risk of accidentally sending a message, though I know it won't rescue me from my curse entirely. Anything is an improvement, and I have Jordan to thank.

He texts back after a long minute of waiting.

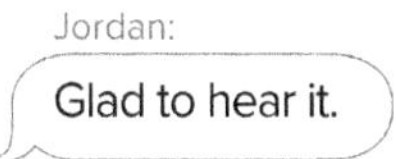

That's it? I expected more from him, like a tease or a comment on my luck. Maybe a part of me hoped he would offer to cook me dinner or watch a movie. No, not just a part of me. All of me. I've spent the last five nights with Jordan in my house, and the thought of going home to an empty basement makes it harder to be brave when it comes to dealing with Mark.

I type out three different texts to Jordan but delete them all. Mostly delete. I somehow manage to send a part of the last one, so he gets a text that says "Can" which hopefully means nothing to him. Knowing my luck, he'll infer the rest of the message and realize I almost asked him if we could talk about what happened last night before Mark showed up.

That should probably happen, but maybe not yet. Not until I get on top of the Mark debacle.

With nothing else to say to Jordan, I type out a text to Houston.

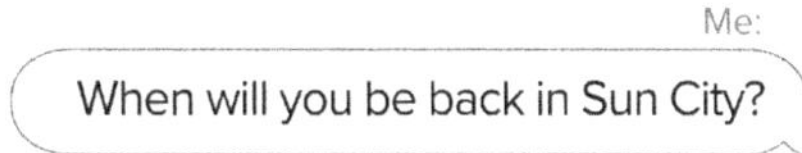

He doesn't respond until I'm home and in pajamas, even though it's only four in the afternoon.

Houston's agent, Alan Roundy, always likes to get Houston in front of as many cameras as possible, even though Houston doesn't like doing interviews. He used to like them more, when he was young and cocky, but the older we get, the more he likes to fly under the radar.

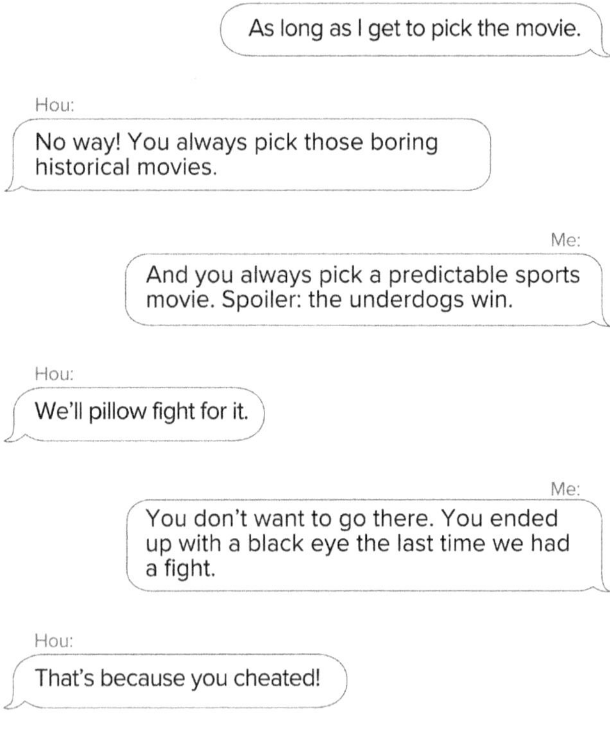

A warmth flickers to life in my chest. I hadn't fully realized how much I was missing my twin until he said that. Yeah, he can be annoying, and he's got an ego the size of a baseball stadium sometimes, but he's a good brother.

I snicker, though this would be more fun if he were here and I could threaten him with a pillow. Houston learned pretty quickly when we were kids that it was a bad idea to challenge me to a pillow fight unless he was prepared to lose. I may not be good at a lot of things, but I'm good at that. Houston made the mistake of turning his back on me before we'd called truce, and I ended up knocking him into a doorknob.

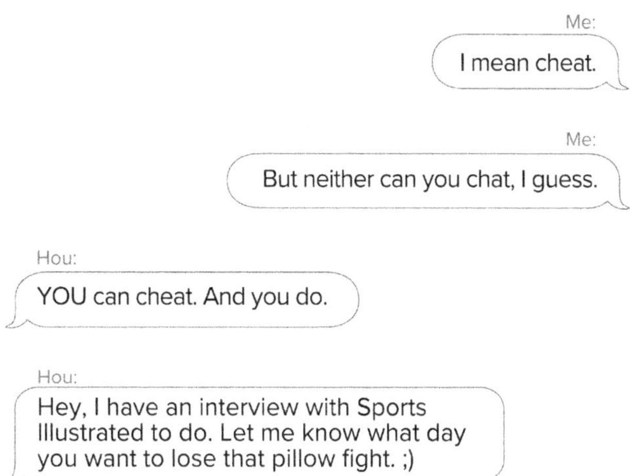

I roll my eyes, but this conversation, short as it was, has helped me relax for the first time since this morning.

That's when I notice the flowers in a vase on my coffee table. The daisies weren't there this morning, and my heart beats a little stronger at the sight of them. How did Jordan know they were my favorite?

Chapter Twenty-Two

Jordan

I'M EITHER READY TO toss my phone into the garbage or drop it by my feet and stomp on it until it doesn't work anymore. It's been ringing nonstop since late this morning, and the only reason it isn't ringing right now is because I put it on the "do not disturb" setting before I lost my mind. That's only a temporary fix, as my voicemail is full of messages I haven't had a chance to even listen to let alone respond to.

"Rethinking your decision to not have an office?" Rick takes a long swig of his milkshake as he watches me. He came and found me at the diner about twenty minutes ago, telling me he was worried I hadn't eaten yet today because I've been too busy trying to deal with the sudden influx of calls we've gotten about quotes.

He was right.

Though the young waitress who has been working the section where I'm sitting has dropped off lunch and dinner over the course of the day, both meals sit untouched.

I sigh, pinching the bridge of my nose. "I still haven't figured out what happened," I mutter. We get maybe one or two calls a day on a good day, but I've literally been on the phone for hours. Some of the calls I've taken have been people in Arizona and Texas, which makes absolutely no sense. "I made some tweaks to the website, but there's no way it would make this much of a difference."

Rick studies me for a moment and then steals one of my cold fries. "You should go home, Torres. You'll have a clearer mind in the morning."

"I'm fine. I can work for a few more hours after I take a quick breather."

"It's eight o'clock."

My stomach drops. "It's what?" I glance out the window, finding the street way darker than the last time I looked out there. I could have sworn it was only four or five.

That means I've been sitting at this booth for ten hours. Since ten this morning. Suddenly my back aches, though some of that is probably because I slept on Brooklyn's couch again.

Brooklyn! I curse, scrambling to grab my phone and sort through the millions of texts I've gotten, but the only one from her since earlier this afternoon looks like one she sent accidentally.

My heart rate slows a little, though I'm still not thrilled with the idea that I basically ignored her all day because of work. I slipped back into workaholism a little too quickly to be comfortable right now, and that's probably why Rick is staring at me while he polishes off his milkshake.

"Where are your kids?" I ask.

He shrugs. "My oldest is in charge. It's nice having him take on some of the responsibility, and he likes collecting his babysitter fees each month. Win win. What about you?"

I pick up a fry and chew it slowly, even though my stomach has decided to finally remind me that it exists and has started rumbling. "What about me? I don't have kids."

"Which is honestly a shame. Did you do anything about your bridge problem?"

I shake my head, even though that's not fully accurate. I got so close to telling her how I feel. And by telling her, I mean I got so close to kissing her instead of using my words. Then the whole Mark thing happened, and I fell asleep holding her, and my heart is all twisted up inside because I'm not sure I can go back to thinking of her as a friend but neither can I pursue a romantic relationship with her until Houston gets back.

Speaking of Houston, he texted me a few times today as well. Grateful for the distraction from Rick's piercing gaze, I pull up his texts, which started earlier this morning, when I was still asleep.

> **Houston:**
> If Roundy tries setting me up for another photo shoot, do you think I can refuse on account of being too old to be on a Wheaties box?

> **Houston:**
> That's a rhetorical question. I totally want to be on a Wheaties box. Do people even eat Wheaties anymore?

The next text came a couple of hours later. At that point, the calls had started flooding my phone.

> **Houston:**
> Heads up, you might get some more business popping up. An interviewer asked how I balance home life with baseball and I might have mentioned your company and how it takes care of my landscaping for me so I don't have to worry about that part.

> **Houston:**
> You're welcome. And stop stressing yourself out about getting more business.

I groan, even though Houston was trying to help. And it will help, but only once I sort through all the calls and emails that have come in. "It was Houston," I mutter and hand my phone to Rick so he can see for himself.

"No wonder you're getting so many calls. Who wouldn't want to hire the same guys that Houston Briggs uses at his house?"

My stomach is becoming relentless, so I pick up the hamburger that came later in the day—at least, I hope this was the later meal—and take a big bite. It probably would have tasted better when it was warm, but it's food. "Most of these people either can't afford us or they're nowhere near Sun City," I say with a mouthful of food. "It's going to take forever to find actual clients in all of this."

Not to mention one of us has to go to their locations to get an idea of the scope of the jobs and provide quotes. That will take forever. Usually

I fit in new prospective clients in between jobs, but I've got at least a week's worth of work in quotes alone, and that's just the people who are actually in Sun City.

Yes, I want—need—to expand the business, but taking on this many clients would triple the workload we've got. I don't have the bandwidth or the people for that. I really should capitalize on Houston's shout-out—his fame and influence won't last forever—but today was a pretty good indication of my inability to balance work with living life.

I thought I was getting better. Turns out I just didn't have enough to keep me busy.

"Okay, here's what's going to happen," Rick says, getting to his feet.

My burger is already gone, and I look up at him with a literal handful of fries poking out of my mouth.

He chuckles. "You're going to go home and go to bed. You're exhausted, Torres."

"Mmf."

"No. I don't care if people are still calling. There's a thing called business hours, and if they're calling outside of that, that's on them."

I finally finish chewing the fries and swallow, though I need a giant gulp of water to go with it so I don't choke on cold potato. "We need the business," I remind him.

"And that business will still be here tomorrow. You have to remember that you're human, and you need a break."

His words sound like what my mom told me the other day, and they hit hard. Is that what she was trying to say? Probably. Deep down, I know they're right, and I've already seen what happens when I let my job take over my life.

I don't know why it's so hard to let go, but it is.

I clasp my hand on Rick's shoulder and try to give him a look that tells him how grateful I am to have him. "Sorry," I say. "This is exactly why I got out of California, but I can't..."

He smiles. "We all have our demons, Torres. Turn off your phone, okay?"

I do it right now, where he can see. Otherwise, it probably wouldn't happen. "Thanks. Hopefully tomorrow isn't so chaotic."

"If it is, we'll deal. *We.*"

When I get back to the house, Mom is still awake, lightly sleeping in her armchair in front of the TV. Whatever she was watching on Netflix, the screen is asking if she's still watching, so she's probably been asleep for a while. Dad must not be home yet or he would have carried her up to bed.

I brush my finger across her cheek to wake her.

It takes her a second, but her eyelids flutter open and then she smiles. "Where have you been, Danny?"

I crouch beside her. "Houston sent some business my way, so I was trying to get that all organized." Trying and failing.

"He's such a good boy. Who's he dating now?"

"No one, at the moment."

"Hmm. And you're not dating anyone."

My heart throbs in my chest, and I have to resist the urge to rub my sternum to try to ease the tension. No, I'm not dating anyone, but I did fall asleep with Brooklyn last night. She probably moved to her bed sometime in the night, but I never noticed her leaving. I must have been dead asleep, which is new for me.

"I'm not ready to date yet," I tell Mom, even if that feels less true than it did a week ago. Still, today was a good test of how I handle the pressure of work, and I failed.

Smiling sadly, she pats my cheek. "Handsome man like you? I know things didn't work with Natalie, but you can't let fear hold you back. You're a good man, Danny, and anyone would be lucky to have your love."

I can't love anyone like they deserve if I can't stop myself from working without someone intervening.

Mom frowns. Whatever she sees in my face, she doesn't like it. "Mateo skipped some of his classes yesterday."

That's not what I expected her to say. "What?"

"Can you talk to him? He won't listen to me."

If he won't listen to his mom, a literal angel, there's no way he'll listen to me. But I nod and kiss her forehead. "I'll talk to him. You should go to bed."

"I'll wait for your father."

It's nearing nine. If he's not home yet, he probably won't be home for a while.

As I head up the stairs, my feet dragging beneath me, I can't help but imagine what a future with Brooklyn would look like if we moved forward with things as they are now. She's so broken, and she would absolutely wait up for me. What would happen if business continued to grow? What if I kept working late nights? She would lose sleep waiting for me and be exhausted in the morning when she got up for school, and her teaching would suffer. She would blame that on herself and get more and more miserable, and I would be too busy working to notice, and it would be Natalie all over again.

I can't do that to her.

I run into Mateo in the hallway between the stairs and the bathroom, and we both freeze. He looks ready to bolt, but he has nowhere to go except back to the bathroom where he just came from.

I pull my eyebrows together. I'm probably too tired to have this conversation right now, but when else am I going to see him? "You skipped classes?"

He rolls his eyes, his deer-in-the-headlights look shifting to a scowl. "What do you care?"

"What's going on with you?"

"I'm not having this conversation with Mr. Perfect."

His words hit me right in the gut. "What? I'm not perfect." I'm so far from perfect it's laughable.

"Sure you are." Since he can't run, he folds his arms and leans against the wall. "Star athlete, college graduate, bigshot job in California. Your only flaw is that you came back here because your wife got sick of you."

I take a step forward out of reflex, not really sure what I plan to do. Mateo flinches, his eyes dropping down to my fists as he turns slightly pale.

Nausea washes over me. Did he think I was going to hit him? "Matty."

He clenches his jaw. "Can I go to bed now? I have school in the morning."

"Are you actually going to go?"

"Do you actually care?"

Of course I care, but he doesn't give me a chance to answer. He pushes past me, knocking his shoulder into mine, and then slams his door shut behind him.

Well. That went about as well as I expected.

I stand there for a minute, debating if it's worth barging into his room to continue the conversation. But I know it won't make things any better, so I trudge the rest of the way to my room and collapse onto my bed, wishing it was a lumpy thrift store couch on the other side of town.

Chapter Twenty-Three

Brooklyn

October 17

I DON'T KNOW WHAT I expected when it came to Mateo, but it wasn't a miniature version of his brother. When he steps into my classroom, I have a sudden flashback to high school and the first time I met Jordan.

I was waiting for Houston under a tree in the quad after school and trying to ignore the kid who decided he should sit with me and talk my ear off about how he was so good at basketball. Part of me thought it might be a good idea to tell him I needed to use the restroom, but I didn't want to be rude. Still, I wasn't into sports at all, and whoever this kid was, he seemed to think I wanted to know all his stats even though the basketball season had just ended and our school had finished dead last in the district.

"And I scored the final three-pointer," he was saying, while I focused on my chemistry homework. Why was he still here? School ended hours ago, and the only reason *I* was still here was because Houston had base-ball tryouts. "It was awesome, and I totally killed it during that game."

"You mean the game we lost?" Houston said, appearing on the quad.

Sighing with relief, I gathered up all of my things and stuffed them into my bag. Houston could be annoying, but he certainly came in handy sometimes. My new buddy had gone mute after Houston's comment.

I only noticed the kid next to my brother when I was on my feet and suddenly face to face with him. "Oh. Uh, hi." I'd seen him before, but only ever in passing, so I had no idea who he was.

He grinned at me, and I couldn't decide if it was a friendly smile or a cocky one. It reminded me a lot of the way Houston smiled, and I couldn't decide if I liked that or not. It was hard enough to deal with one self-important ladies man.

"Brook, this is Jordan." Houston waved a hand toward the new guy, glancing between us. "We just tried out for the baseball team together. Jordan, my twin sister, Brooklyn."

Jordan's smile got wider as he held out his hand for me to shake. What kind of person greeted someone with a handshake? This wasn't a job interview. "That's a cool name. Brooklyn. It's like Manhattan or The Bronx." He chuckled at his own joke. "So you're both named after cities?"

Houston shrugged. "Our dad is from New York and our mom was from Texas." He turned when someone called his name, showing me for the first time a deep bruise on his temple.

I gasped and grabbed his arm. "What happened to you?"

Both boys cracked up, like there was some inside joke I was missing. Something told me Jordan had something to do with the bruise, though I hoped it wasn't a fight or something. They seemed to like each other well enough.

"Come on," Houston said without answering the question. "Sam's giving us a ride."

I groaned. Of all my stepsiblings—of which there were many—Sam was the most annoying.

Jordan punched Houston lightly before turning to me. "Don't worry, Queens. I'll protect you from your big bad brother."

I frowned. "That's not my name."

"I know." Then he winked at me, and I had a feeling he was going to be a thorn in my side for the rest of my life.

Mateo may not have Jordan's smirk, but he has the same spark of mischief in his eyes as he approaches me at the front of the room. I'm tempted to sneak a picture of him and compare it to one of Jordan from our junior year, just to see if my memory is accurate, but that would be illegal. Or at least frowned upon.

"You must be Mateo," I say with as warm a smile as I can manage. "I'm Miss Briggs."

He examines me for a second, hardly any expression in his face. "Where should I sit?"

He sounds like Jordan too, only there's an undercurrent of defiance in his words. He clearly doesn't want to be here but is smart enough to know he can't skip every class.

I keep my smile firmly in place. "We're doing a lab today. I'm going to pair you up with Meghan."

Right on cue, Meghan hops up and approaches us. She's on the student council and incredibly smart, so she'll be able to both make Mateo feel welcome in our class and help him settle in. "Hi! It's Mateo, right? We have US History together."

Mateo's eyebrows pull together as he looks at her, but he doesn't say anything.

"Were you taking chemistry at your last school?" I ask him.

He drops his eyes to his shoes. "No."

That's going to make this hard for him, but I can put in some extra time after school if he's willing to take some tutoring. I'll suggest that once I have a better idea of how much he needs to learn to get up to speed. "We're done with the first quarter, but hopefully you can catch up without too much trouble."

He lets out a deep sigh that sounds too weary for a seventeen-year-old. "Where's our table?" he asks Meghan.

She shows him to her station, where her partner is waiting with a leery expression that has me slightly worried about how Mateo will be received. Meghan will be nice to him, but that doesn't mean Ethan will take kindly to working with someone who doesn't know what he's doing. I'll have to keep an eye on them.

Halfway through the class period, Meghan comes up to me and hands me her finished lab report.

"Wait," I say, looking it over. "You finished already?" This was supposed to take two lab periods, and I haven't even taught one of the formulas they'll need to finish. I was hoping Meghan would take her time and explain everything to Mateo.

After glancing at the class behind her, Meghan leans in and mutters, "I don't think Mateo should be in this class."

To say I'm disappointed in her is an understatement. "I know he's new, but he can—"

"He did the whole thing, Miss Briggs." She points at the lab report. "All of it. We didn't even do half of the experiment because he'd already filled that part in."

I look over at Mateo, who is slouched on his stool and looking at his phone. Even I can see the boredom in his expression.

Turning back to the lab report, I check all the answers. Sure enough, everything is accurate, including a description of some of the reactions I know they wouldn't have done today.

Looks like Mateo Torres lied to me.

"Thanks, Meghan. Would you and Ethan mind helping out Sadie and Jess? They look like they're struggling a bit. And if you could ask Mateo to come over here, that would be awesome."

When Mateo comes over, he looks like I'm about to tell him he's in trouble. "What did I do?" he asks before I can get a word in.

I point to the lab report. "You said you weren't in chemistry at your old school."

"I wasn't."

"Then how did you know how to do all of this?"

Stuffing his hands into the pocket of his hoodie, he shrugs. "I took a college class last year."

That catches me off guard, and I'm sure my shock is all over my face. "As a sophomore?" And why isn't it in his file?

He shrugs again.

This time, I point to one of the final equations. He didn't actually use the formula I would have recommended, instead using a more complicated one that has better accuracy. "You're telling me you learned how to do this last year?"

"It's not that hard."

I barely hold back a laugh. Not that hard? "Mateo, you're clearly too smart to be in my class."

His head shoots up, eyes wide. It's as if he isn't sure if he should believe me. "I've always been pretty good at math and stuff."

A sudden idea sparks to life inside me. "You have Mr. DeNiro, right?"

"Yeah."

"Is he a good teacher?"

He scoffs. "If he's doing it right, sure."

Well, that's interesting. I tilt my head to one side. "Did he do something wrong?"

Mateo's eyes light up. "He did one of the equations completely wrong the other day. I had to tell the kid next to me how to do it because he wasn't getting the right answer."

Oh, I could use this. Though I'm surprised Mark would do anything wrong, I'm inclined to believe Mateo when he says he made a mistake. "Did you know that Mr. DeNiro loves when people call him out when he does something wrong?"

Mateo clearly doesn't believe me, but he pulls his hands out of his hoodie pocket and runs his fingers through his hair. It's such a Jordan move that I can't help but smile. "Really? He seems like he would hate that."

I'm pretty sure he would. "Oh yeah, he loves when students correct him because it makes him better at his job."

I fully expect him to remain skeptical, but then he smiles. "Okay. I guess I can let him know if he messes up next period. Thanks, Miss Briggs."

He turns to head back to his table, but I call him back. "Hey, do you think you could help those two in the back corner the rest of the period? They look like they could use your expertise."

There's something in his grin that makes me miss Jordan like crazy, which is a pretty good sign that I need to have that conversation with him. He hasn't texted me at all since yesterday, which could mean a lot of things, but I'm trying not to read into it. I can't trust myself when it comes to other people anymore.

If Jordan wants to talk to me, he will.

And I'll be waiting.

Chapter Twenty-Four

Jordan

Of all the things on my to-do list today, I did not expect going to the principal's office to be one of them. As I step into the school where Brooklyn teaches, I'm hit with a weird sense of déja vu, even if this high school looks nothing like mine. It smells the same, like body odor and the tears of over-emotional children.

I really wish I didn't have to be here, but when my mom asked me to step in, I agreed without hesitation. Even if I'm ready to strangle my brother for getting into trouble during his first week here.

I find him sitting in a chair just inside the administrative offices, and Mateo is as happy to see me as I am to see him. "What are *you* doing here?" he grumbles.

I can barely get the words out through my anger. "It's a treatment day."

"Oh." His tough guy demeanor drops, and he actually looks seventeen for a second. "I didn't think…"

Sighing, I drop into the chair next to him. I barely slept last night, and today has been full of more phone calls and emails. There's a part of me that's grateful for this distraction from work, even if I don't love the reason for it. I'd gotten trapped in the grind again, just like yesterday, and if it hadn't been my mom who called me…

The worst part is I almost didn't answer.

I run a hand through my hair, glancing around the office as memories of my own high school days come flooding back. I ended up in the office plenty of times, but I always felt justified in the reasons. At the very least, I'd gotten some good entertainment out of it, and I never did anything to harm someone else.

"What'd you do, anyway?" I ask.

The tension returns to his shoulders as he puts his hands in his hoodie and drops his head against the wall behind him. "I didn't do anything."

"So you got sent to the principal for your cheery disposition?"

"The teacher's an idiot."

"Hey."

He flinches. "He was doing it wrong, so I told him the right answer. That's it."

That's clearly not it, but I don't get a chance to ask because the principal's door opens and out steps Mr. Math himself. He immediately shoots a glare to Mateo, who glares right back, but then his eyes land on me. Recognition sets in quickly, turning his glare into a gloating smirk.

"The landscaper. He's your kid?" Laughter colors his words.

Okay, maybe I'm on Mateo's side this time. I stand, pleased to see I'm a few inches taller than Mark and fifty pounds of muscle heavier. "He's my kid brother."

He steps closer, dropping his voice so only I can hear him. "No wonder he's a troublemaker, if his parents can't bother to show up. Looks like he's bound for a dead-end job just like you."

He's lucky I have self-control or he would be flat on the ground right now, a bruise the shape of my fist on his face. Without speaking another word to him, I look past him to the older woman who must be the principal.

"Can we move forward?" I ask.

She gestures for me and Mateo to follow her into her office. To my dismay, Mark follows us in and stands behind the woman's desk like some security guard. He looks far too smug, and I hope it's not because he thinks he has Brooklyn under his thumb. I still don't know if the two of them have interacted since their date, and I hate that I haven't been there for her.

"Mr. Torres, thank you for coming. I'm Principal Cheng." She shakes my hand before settling in her chair. "I'm sorry to hear about your mother's condition."

"Thank you."

She glances between me and Mateo, clearly struggling to figure out how best to proceed. "Mr. Torres, Mateo is a bright student, and we are happy to welcome him to Sky View High School. But we do require a level of respect for our teachers, and—"

"I'll respect him if he respects me," Mateo mumbles.

I kick his foot. "You're not helping your case," I warn him.

"All I did was correct him on the equation on the board!" Mateo says this to Principal Cheng, ignoring me and Mark. "He was teaching it wrong."

Mark scoffs, and Principal Cheng purses her lips. "I am sure Mr. DeNiro was perfectly—"

"He was wrong!"

"What would you know?" Mark says with a sneer.

Principal Cheng holds up a hand. "Whether or not he was wrong, that does not give you the right to bad-mouth your teacher in front of the class, Mateo."

He slumps in his chair. "I didn't bad-mouth him, ma'am. I just corrected him."

"You humiliated me," Mark says.

"Doesn't seem hard to do." When all eyes turn to me, I realize I said that out loud. Cringing, I duck my head, but I don't miss the slight smile Mateo has. "Sorry. It's been a long day. What's going to happen, Mrs. Cheng?"

She glances between me and Mark, who looks furious. "Well, considering this is his first offense, I think—"

"It won't be the last," Mark growls.

"Mark, please. As this is Mateo's first offense here at Sky View, I will let him off with a warning. But he has already skipped a few classes, and we only tolerate so many absences, excused or otherwise. Mateo." She leans forward, clasping her hands on her desk. "What you do in your high school years will determine the start of your adult life. I know you have it in you to be something brilliant, but it requires effort. You can't sit on the sidelines of your life and expect to get somewhere."

Dang, she's good. Whenever I got stuck in the principal's office, he tended to yell about how I'd never amount to anything. She is legitimately inspiring.

Mateo still has anger and defiance in his expression, but there's something else lingering under the surface. Fear, or desperation. *Something.* I try to see this moment from his perspective.

Honestly, I didn't know he was smart enough to correct a teacher who's up for STEM Teacher of the Year. Mom said his grades were good, and if he's managing that while skipping classes, there's probably a lot more going on in my brother's head than he lets anyone see. If he really was trying to help make sure his fellow classmates learned the right thing, getting called out like this would be really frustrating.

I turn my gaze to Mark, who is too busy glaring at Mateo to notice me. "Was he right?"

Blinking, Mark looks at me. "What?"

"Was Mateo right about the math problem he corrected?"

Turning a deep red, he splutters something unintelligible, which is answer enough.

I stand and offer my hand to the principal. "Thank you for taking the time to help my brother, Mrs. Cheng. I'm sure Mateo will work on offering suggestions in a more respectful manner, but it sounds like this was just a misunderstanding." I give Mateo a pointed look.

He seems to consider going against me, but then he sighs. "I'm sorry. I'll work on it." He says it to Mrs. Cheng, not Mark, but I'm fine with that. I'm not sure Mark deserves an apology with the way he's still scowling.

How is this the guy Brooklyn has been admiring for so long?

Mrs. Cheng nods to me, gives Mateo a parting smile, and then I lead Mateo out into the hall beyond the administrative offices.

The instant we're on our own, Mateo turns to me. "You believe me, right? I wasn't trying to—"

"I know." I massage the back of my neck, wincing at the tension in my shoulders. "I think Mr. DeNiro is just a..." Probably shouldn't finish that sentence because I'm not coming up with a nicer way of putting it.

Mateo smirks. "Yeah, he is. I dunno, when Miss Briggs told me I should correct him in class, I thought—"

"She told you what?" I doubt there is more than one Briggs teaching here.

Mateo shrugs. "My chemistry teacher. She said Mr. DeNiro likes when his students call him out."

Oh, Brooklyn, you didn't.

Holding back a groan, I look around the hallway, trying to decide my best course of action. She's probably gone by now, and I haven't spoken to her since yesterday morning. But if this is the start of a revenge mission against Mark, I need to stop it before it gets even more out of hand.

I need to talk to her.

"Matty, I need you to go straight home."

He doesn't waste a breath before he starts protesting. "I can't. I need to—"

"Mom wants you at home." I grab his shoulder, begging him to listen to me for once. "Please don't make her worry about you today."

To my surprise, tears fill his eyes, and he nods once. "Okay. I'll go home. Jordan?"

It takes me a second to realize why that sounds strange, but then I realize he's never called me that before. To my family I've always been Danny, and I had no idea Mateo even knew that I prefer my middle name. "Yeah?"

He swallows, eyes on the ground. "Thanks. For defending me."

Something in my chest clicks into place, like a brick that was off center and affecting the rest of my soul, making my edges rough and uneven. Now it's smoother than before, if not perfect. It's like I can breathe more deeply as I stare at my little brother like I'm seeing him for the first time.

I smile. "That's what a big brother is for, right?"

Though he doesn't say anything, his answering smile is good enough for me.

Chapter Twenty-Five

Brooklyn

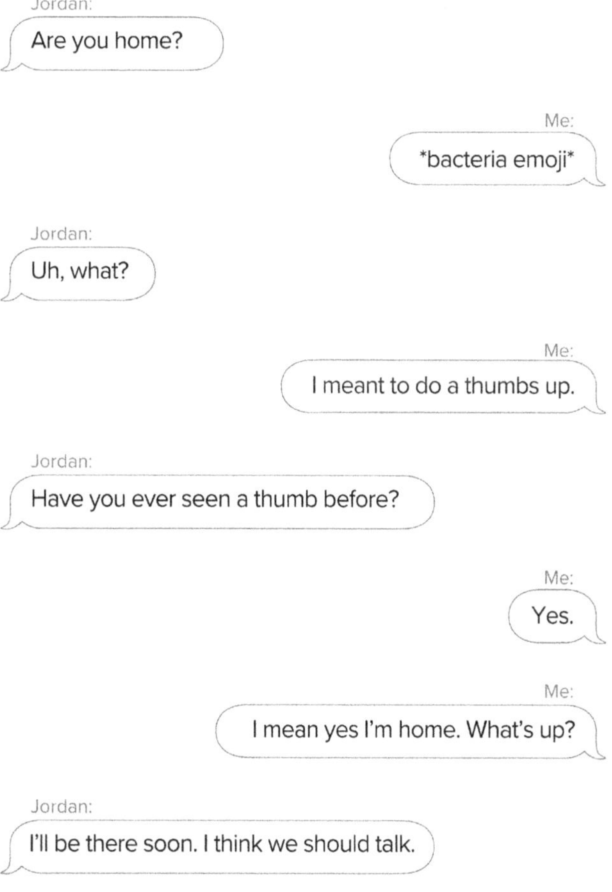

THAT'S ONLY THE MOST terrifying text someone can send a person, and I've been on edge for the last ten minutes, pacing around my living room because I can't sit still while I wait for Jordan to show up.

What does he want to talk about? About what happened with Mark? I said some things about James I shouldn't have said, so maybe he wants to talk about that. I would really rather not. Or maybe he wants to talk about that almost-kiss, which is the most terrifying option of all.

He said he wasn't going to kiss me, but what if that's changed now that Mark isn't an obstacle?

A knock on the door scares me out of my skin, even though I should have been expecting it. Struggling to breathe, I open the door with shaking fingers and do my best to smile at Jordan when he looks at me.

"Hey."

His eyebrows pull together. "Why did you tell Mateo to talk back to Mark?"

My stomach drops like I'm on the world's worst elevator. "What?"

He hasn't made any move to come inside, which might be the worst part of this conversation (which is likely only going to get worse). "You. Told my brother. To correct. A teacher." He says it slowly, like I might be too dumb to understand if he doesn't enunciate.

I've never seen Jordan angry before. And I'm not sure I can say he's angry now. But he's definitely feeling some strong emotions, all of them directed at me.

I don't know what to say to him, which is fine because he keeps talking.

"Mateo got sent to the principal's office, Brooklyn. They called my mom while she was in the middle of her chemo treatment, and I had to show up at the school because you thought it was a good idea to use a *kid* to get revenge on a guy who isn't worth your time. What is wrong with you?"

Clearly a lot of things. "Jordan."

He holds up a hand. "No. I know what Mark did was crappy, and he's a jerk. I'm not saying he isn't."

"Then what are you saying?" I wrap my arms around myself, wishing I had someone stronger to hold me.

Jordan groans and grabs the door frame, his eyes locked so thoroughly on me that I can't stand to look at him. I stare at my toes instead, wishing I had thought to put on socks because they're getting cold standing in the open doorway.

"I'm saying you're better than this, Queens. You've always been the bigger person, and I've always loved that about you."

My head snaps up, but he's not done.

"It didn't matter how much I teased you or made you miserable. You were only ever kind to me. Yeah, you had your comebacks, but they never hurt anyone. Where's the Brooklyn who switched Houston's soap out for a potato? Who threw water balloons at us when we were playing video games?" His expression falls, leaving him looking lost. "Where's the girl I had the biggest crush on but never knew it until you were gone?"

I can't speak. I can't *breathe*. He's saying so many things that mean so much, but I don't have any of the answers to his questions. Not ones he would like, anyway. Where's the old Brooklyn? She grew up. She got dumped time and time again because she wasn't enough for the men who decided she was their next shiny new toy. She lost her dream job—her passion—because she trusted the wrong man, but she can't tell her siblings because they only see the happy and content Brooklyn.

It's the only version of me I ever let them see because they all have their own problems to deal with.

Jordan groans again, and suddenly his hands are on my face, thumbs brushing the tears from my cheeks. "I'm sorry. I didn't want to make you cry. I'm just frustrated, and confused, and maybe a little angry with you."

"I deserve that," I mumble.

"Yes. But no, you don't. I shouldn't take out my problems on you."

"I caused your problems."

"*Problem*. Single." He scowls. "I won't let you take the blame for the rest."

I let out a single laugh. "Now you're mad at me for trying to say sorry?"

"Is that what you were going to do?"

He's standing so close, hands still tucked around my head in a gentle hold. At some point, I put my hands on his chest, which means I can feel his heart beating rapidly in his chest. When he started talking, this isn't where I expected the afternoon to go, but I can't say I'm mad about it.

"I'm sorry," I whisper. "As soon as Mateo left my class, I wanted to call him back and tell him not to do anything. But I didn't think Mark would take it so personally and try to get him in trouble."

Jordan snickers, brushing his thumbs along my cheeks again. "You really know how to pick 'em, Queens."

Meeting his gaze, I summon every ounce of courage I might possess, though I can still barely breathe. Time to send some signals and hope he reads them right. "I'd like to think I've gotten better at it."

His eyes drop to my mouth. "In less than twenty-four hours?"

I can barely concentrate anymore. He's so close, exactly where I want him to be. "I had an idea of what I wanted before Mark ever asked me out."

"That soon?"

"You don't think I can change?"

"I think you can do anything, Queens."

"Jordan, will you ki—"

"Sorry, hang on." Jordan steps back, his face scrunching up as he pulls his phone out of his pocket and answers a call.

I take this chance to breathe and seriously question what I was just about to say. Am I crazy? Yes. Asking him to kiss me is definitely crazy talk.

Jordan keeps talking, growing increasingly more agitated. "Rick, what... What do you mean, everything's been canceled? By who?" He walks up the stairs and starts pacing across the lawn. "But you and I are the only ones with access to the schedule."

The rest of his conversation doesn't last long before he hangs up and comes back down the stairs. He looks annoyed and frazzled, which is not a good look for him.

"Is everything okay?" I ask. It's a stupid question, but I don't know what else to say. I definitely can't say *kiss me*.

He shakes his head. "Someone canceled all of our appointments tomorrow. Fridays are our busiest days. I need to go figure this out before we lose a ton of business." Wrinkling his nose, he reaches out and tucks some hair behind my ear. "This conversation isn't over, okay? I'm still frustrated with you, but..." His eyes drop to my mouth again, making my breath catch.

Then he says the one thing I wish he wouldn't say. "Houston will be home tomorrow."

I sigh. Houston. Anything we do will affect him. "We need to make sure he'll be okay."

Jordan nods without a trace of a smile. Not that I expected him to smile, but I hoped he would be more optimistic than I am. "I'll talk to him. And you…" He taps my nose. "Let me know if you find the real Brooklyn again. I'd really like to see her, and I know she's in there somewhere."

He presses a quick kiss to my forehead, and then he's gone.

For the next hour, I wander my basement in a daze, simultaneously telling myself not to get my hopes up and talking myself into believing Jordan feels something for me. It's not a good use of my time and it's honestly making me dizzy, so I drop onto my couch and call the one person who will give me unbiased advice.

"Well, this is unexpected." My brother Chad sounds like he's on the verge of laughing, which is unusual for him. Especially lately. I'm pretty sure he's been in a funk ever since he and his girlfriend broke up last spring.

I sigh. "Yeah, I know. How's Laketown?" I wonder if he's actually falling in love with someone like Micah thinks, though that seems unlikely. Chad dated the same woman for six years and hasn't been on a date since their breakup six months ago. He's as bad at relationships as the rest of us right now.

"Laketown is…interesting," he says.

What is that supposed to mean? "Wait, don't tell me Micah is right about you falling in love."

"I'm not falling in love, Blondie. I have a neighbor of the female variety, and Micah is being Micah."

I stretch out my legs, gazing at my ankle. It hasn't bothered me at all today, and weirdly I'm a little bummed that I can't use it as an excuse to get Jordan to touch me anymore. "You know it's okay if you do fall in love, right? One of us should."

"Okay, what's up?"

I wince. Probably shouldn't have said that last part. "Oh. It's nothing."

"With you, it's never nothing. Talk."

Chad pretty much raised Houston and me, from the time we were seven up until we moved in with Lloyd when we were ten when our dad went to prison. Three years isn't objectively a long time, but for me it felt like my entire childhood. Chad's always been the one looking out for me, and he's always noticed when something is bothering me. The fact that

I've been able to keep so many things a secret from him lately makes me feel like a terrible sister.

"I finally talked to Mark. You know, that math teacher I like?"

Chad grunts, which probably means he's looked into Mark at some point over the last few years. His private investigator tendencies run deep, and I don't think I've ever had a boyfriend who didn't get a full background check.

I take a deep breath. This could be dangerous, but I need someone to understand. "We went out the other night, but it turns out he just wants me to take my name out of the running for STEM Teacher of the Year so he can win."

Chad swears, then immediately apologizes. "Sorry. I wondered if he was a tool. Now I know."

"Why didn't you warn me?"

"Because I don't like to interfere."

"You're my brother. You're supposed to interfere."

"Tell that to Houston."

I laugh. I've been on the receiving end of plenty of Houston's rants when it comes to Chad offering up unwanted information. Honestly, I think Chad has brought so much stuff up with my twin because he's trying to stay connected to Houston, but I'll never be brave enough to ask if I'm right. Chad is eight years older than us, but he's always tried his best to be a part of our lives. Houston doesn't make it easy for him.

"Why did you really call me, Blondie?"

I drop my phone. How does he do that? Scrambling to pick it up, I stammer through my response. "Oh, well, I guess I… It's just that… Jordan. And Houston. I messed up, and I'm just different. Do you think I'm different?"

Let's see what he makes of that nonsense.

Chad clears his throat. "Different from what?"

Oh good. I'm glad he focused on that part and not the Jordan part. I don't know how to explain the Jordan part. "From me. From how I used to be."

I probably don't need his confirmation. As soon as Jordan said I didn't respond to Mark's betrayal the way I should, I knew he was right. I guess I'm looking for a way to fix it. How do I get back to that person who knew exactly who she was and where her values lay?

"Is there something specific you're worried about being different?" Chad asks.

I shrug. Oh wait, he can't see me. "I don't know. I pulled a sort of prank on Mark that ended up getting someone else into trouble."

Humming, Chad lets a few seconds pass before he speaks. "You used to do that all the time, didn't you? When you were living with Lloyd."

"Yeah, because Jordan drove me crazy. It was the only way to keep him in check."

I gasp as a realization suddenly hits me. Jordan said he had a crush on me in high school. It sounded like he hadn't realized it, but he's acknowledging it now. Was that why he pushed all my buttons? Because he liked me?

Chad chuckles. "Sounds like you might be coming across some epiphanies."

Let me know if you find the real Brooklyn again, Jordan said. *I'd really like to see her.*

Is that what I need to do? Do I need to dig down to my roots and pull some harmless pranks in order to get in touch with my inner prankster? That's the girl Jordan knew. She was fun, and she didn't let anyone push her around. Does she even exist anymore?

"I don't know," I admit out loud. But maybe I do know. Even when I hide my sadness, I never feel more myself than I do with my family, and that's because there has never been a risk of rejection with them. Houston has been on the receiving end of too many pranks to believe I'm no longer like that, and Micah is the queen of optimism and friendliness so it's easy to be sweet right along with her. Chad has seen me at my worst and always looks beyond the surface.

I just need to find the courage to be me around everyone else.

Around Jordan.

As if reading my mind, Chad chuckles and says, "So, are we going to talk about your sudden interest in Houston's friend, or are we—" He cuts himself off and then swears again. "Sorry, Brook, I gotta go. Talk later."

Then he hangs up.

And while I hope everything is okay in the sleepy town of Laketown, I can't help but grin as I pull up the website for the nearest party store. I have the best idea.

Chapter Twenty-Six

Jordan

October 18

IT'S A GOOD THING Houston doesn't know I have his agent's phone number because Houston doesn't know that I know he's home now. Roundy likes me because I've helped him with PR issues with some of his other athletes, so he was more than happy to tell me when Houston's flight was landing.

I may have lied about wanting to pick Houston up from the airport this morning, but Roundy doesn't need to know that.

It's early enough as I pull up in front of Houston's house—just after eleven—that I know he probably went straight to bed and crashed. That's exactly where I want him.

Okay, that sounds weird. But it didn't take long yesterday for me to figure out that it was *Houston* who canceled all of our jobs today, and that deserves some retribution.

Grabbing the bag of Doritos I bought for just this moment, I creep up to the house in the unlikely event that he's awake. He's definitely going to regret giving me a key, but I can live with that.

Once inside, I pause as I always do and look around. Nothing about this house would make sense to someone who doesn't know Houston. For one, it's a duplex, twelve hundred square feet at most. The man is a multi-millionaire, but his house only has two bedrooms. For another, it's clean. Like, anally clean. The average person would think Houston pays someone to clean it for him, but he does it all himself during the rare moments he's actually home. Then there's the sterility of it all. It looks like a showroom because there's nothing personal except the small box of records he keeps by the record player and a few baseball books. Beyond that, this house could belong to anyone.

I really hope he's ready to start thinking of settling down because this house always makes me sad. It's the kind of place that would make a guy extra lonely. And if Houston is losing his arm as much as I think he is, he's about to spend a lot more time here at home.

I find him in his bedroom, dead asleep with the blackout curtains drawn. I don't blame him. After winning the Series on Monday, he's been in non-stop interviews and photoshoots, and it's probably been close to a month since he spent any significant time here at home. That would make anyone tired.

Plopping into the armchair he keeps by the window, I get myself settled in, nice and comfy. Then I tear the bag open as loudly as I can. If the guy made sure I didn't have any work to do today, he gets to deal with me and all my free time.

He doesn't stir despite my noise. Hmm.

I pop a chip in my mouth, chewing with my mouth wide open.

With a little moan, Houston moves. *Of course* that's what gets him. It still takes him a while to open his eyes and look around while I keep snacking. The instant he sees me, he panics, limbs flailing as he screams and tries to get out from under his sheets. All of his scrambling sends him tumbling to the floor in a heap, and I lose it, busting up in laughter and wishing I had thought to record the moment. That would have gotten me all sorts of views.

"Jordan?" He mumbles something that I know his sister wouldn't like, while I open his curtains so he can actually see me.

"Language," I say before popping another chip in my mouth.

Houston groans as he sits up and rubs the sleep lines from his face. Just how dead was he? "Not you too." Then he fixes a glare on me, a clear question in his eyes.

Though I know it's not what he's asking, I grin. "You gave me a key."

"I don't care how you're here. I want to know why." He disappears into his closet, hopefully to find some clothes. Currently, he's wearing nothing but his boxers.

"I'm here because I haven't seen my best friend in weeks, and he just helped the Red-tails win the World Series. By the way, I am so glad to learn you don't sleep in the nude now. That is not something I need to see." Even if I've seen plenty in locker rooms over the years. Still, I can't help but be a little jealous of the man's physique as he comes back into the room halfway through pulling on a t-shirt. High school and college Houston Briggs were tiny compared to MLB Houston. No wonder they want him on a Wheaties box.

"You would have deserved it," he mutters, and then he snatches the bag of chips out of my hands. "No eating in the bedroom. What are you, a caveman?"

"Your sister doesn't have the same aversion to food in the bedroom."

Okay, that might have been a little mean, and Houston looks like I punched him in the gut as he meets my gaze.

"How in the world do you know that?"

I hold up my hands. "Wow, would you relax? She ate some snacks in her bed after she got that concussion last weekend." It was one of her Sunday activities the day she was in charge.

I can practically see his thoughts churning in his head. He's confused, then worried, and then the guilt sets in, which probably means he completely forgot about her getting hurt. It's not his fault, when his week has been madness, but I know Houston. As much as he loves playing baseball, he loves his family more, but he doesn't have a good way to balance them both.

I know that feeling well.

"I'm the worst," he says, looking more exhausted than he should.

When he moves his hand to his shoulder—his pitching shoulder—I figure I should lighten the mood.

"You're fine. I've been keeping an eye on her."

"Still? It's been a week since—" He stops himself, eyebrows pulling low as he searches my face for something. I can't tell what he's thinking with this one, and I don't like that. I have a pretty good guess, though, and it has to do with the text he sent me from the dugout.

Keep your hands to yourself, Torres.

"I know what you're thinking," I tell him, which is too close to a lie for comfort. "But I've been trying to help her make a move on her teacher crush, so would you stop glaring at me?"

Ugh, that still feels like a lie, even if it's true. Or it *was* true, up until Tuesday night. A man doesn't sleep on a bad couch with a beautiful woman in his arms because he wants her to date someone else.

Under no circumstances can I let Houston find out about that couch.

"Thanks for looking out for her," Houston says eventually, though he still looks halfway murderous. I'm going to hope it's not just about me.

Taking a deep breath, he leads the way down to the kitchen and stuffs the chips into the garbage. That makes me chuckle. He hates the Salsa Verde flavor with a burning passion, and apparently he's not in the greatest mood this morning.

That's probably because I woke him up after he'd only been asleep for an hour or so, but I would hazard a guess that there's a lot more going on in that head of his.

He confirms it when he says, "I don't know why I'm so tense." As he starts opening up mostly empty cupboards, he looks completely exhausted. He looks *lost*. He's probably not ready to confront the reality of his situation, so I offer up an easy intro to the topic.

"Sure you do. You've been off since your interview with Tamlin Park."

He frowns. "Roundy said the same thing." Then his hand strays back to his shoulder. He used to do that a lot, massaging the muscle before and after games, but this is different. This looks like he's trying to hold his arm together.

He needs to talk about this. "How bad is it?" I ask.

Though he doesn't say a word, he meets my eye with the most heartbreaking expression. Since the day I met him, Houston has only ever wanted to play baseball. He's one of the few who make it to the professional level, and he has exceeded all expectations. He's the best player the Red-tails have seen in decades, and if his arm is gone, that means he'll be losing the only thing he can really call his own.

We knew this day was coming—a man can only play hard for so long—but Houston has always wanted to go out on his terms.

"I'm sorry, man." I know that's not going to do him any good, but it's the best I've got. "So, what now?"

That sparks something in him. He stands up straighter, releasing his shoulder and breathing in deeply. "Got any jobs today?"

"Ha!" I shake my head. "You know full well I don't. And if I lose any business because you decided to cancel—"

"Okay, hey, give me some credit. I rescheduled. There's a difference."

"Why?"

"Because I need your help."

It's a good thing I love Houston like a brother, because he doesn't need help. He needs an entire reno team. Apparently he has new renters moving in this weekend to the other half of the duplex but hasn't had time to clean it up after the last renters, who were either slasher film fanatics or actual serial killers because the amount of red paint splashed across the walls is astounding.

We've been cleaning up for hours, and we've hardly made a dent.

"Seriously, just hire a cleaning company," I beg him. I've lost track of how many times I've said this over the last few hours, and I should really be going through my potential new client list.

Houston rolls his eyes and pulls yet another murder painting out of the crawl space under the stairs. It's the fifth one, just as gruesome as the first four, and it will be going straight into the dumpster I rented this morning. Who knew there could be so many different naked death scenes to paint?

I fold my arms, refusing to touch the painting. The blood looks way too real for me to be comfortable. "Dude, I know you like doing things yourself, but this is borderline ridiculous. You have money. You can pay other people to do this for you and stop stressing yourself out."

"Ha, that's funny."

"Why is that funny?"

Grabbing a sixth painting and stacking it with the others—why didn't they take any of these with them?—Houston straightens up and then folds his arms. "Do you know why I canceled all of your appointments today?"

"So I could help you with this nightmare. I'd better get paid, by the way."

He shakes his head. "No. I mean sure, I'll pay you, but I didn't find out about the renters until this morning."

Well, now he's not making any sense. "What are you talking about?"

"I'm talking about the fact that you haven't texted me since Saturday."

I pull my eyebrows together. We've literally gone months without texting before, so I'm not sure why he's making such a big deal out of this. It's not like we have to have nightly chats to share hot gossip and talk about girls. Anymore. "I don't know what you're getting at, but—"

"I know you, Jordan. And I know how you can get when you're overwhelmed with work."

Ah.

Stuffing my hands into my pockets, I duck my head so I don't have to feel his piercing gaze. I don't know what it is about the Briggs blue eyes they all have, but they're intense. All of them.

"Rick told me about Wednesday," Houston continues. "And I'm sorry. I knew you were wanting more business, but I didn't think about how much attention I would draw. You can pay someone to—"

"I can't." Wincing, I settle myself on the paint-splattered couch that is definitely going to go into the dumpster before the weekend is over. "The profit margins are too tight right now."

Houston rolls his eyes. "They're not. Besides, if you hire someone to do the scheduling, that will free you up to do the actual consults and lock in new clients. You have to spend money to earn money."

I raise an eyebrow. "Do they teach business classes during spring training or something?"

"You forget I lived with Lloyd for half my life. My stepdad is the king of business, and I swear every dinner conversation involved him spouting off business advice like he was Gandhi."

"That makes no sense."

"I know. I'm exhausted. *Someone* woke me up after I had a five A.M. flight."

Chuckling, I give his arm a gentle punch. He really is the best friend a guy could ask for. "Just be glad Tamlin Park isn't seeing you like this."

He shudders. "Let's pray I never have to face that woman again. She's even more terrifying in person."

"I'm sure she's lovely."

"She's a shark who smells blood and is waiting to close in for the kill."

The conversation wanders to highlights of the final Series game as we jump back into our cleanup, and we don't talk much the rest of the day. I want to bring up the idea of me dating Brooklyn, but Houston is way too tired and stressed for that right now. I'll let him settle in, and then I'll gauge his ability to handle a shift like that. His arm isn't going to help anything, but I'm feeling hopeful.

I just have to hope Brooklyn is as invested in this as I am. If she's not willing to put in the work to overcome her fears and the obstacles her past relationships have put in her way, I don't know if this is going to work. I can only tell her so many times how unbelievably amazing she is, and if she can't learn to love herself the way I love her...

I can't be her only support, as much as I want to. I've clearly got my own issues to work through—Houston knew I was working too hard when he wasn't even in the state—and I'm terrified of what would happen if I slipped and wasn't there for Brooklyn when she needed me. Another Natalie situation would kill me, and Brooklyn as she is now isn't strong enough to handle my problems.

She shouldn't have to be, but I won't risk hurting her more than she's already been hurt.

We've both got work to do.

Chapter Twenty-Seven

Brooklyn

I START SMALL. WHILE I have some pretty intriguing ideas, there's still the lingering fear that I'll fall apart if I run into Mark, so I have to do things that won't risk me running into him until I know for sure I can handle seeing his smug face.

I wait in my car Friday morning until he pulls into the parking lot and heads inside, and then I work quickly, untwisting Oreos and sticking them to the outside of his car, just on the backside so I can avoid the cameras and so he probably won't notice until he gets home. It's an inconvenience for him but nothing damaging, and my only regret is how much delicious Oreo I just wasted on the man who probably doesn't eat refined sugar because he's too cool for processed foods.

At lunch, I order him a pizza that has nothing but beef on one side. No sauce, no cheese, just a handful of beef chunks that probably don't taste like real meat.

During eighth period, I convince my class to sing Christmas songs while they work on their labs, knowing Mark has his prep period that hour and will absolutely hear my students as they sing their hearts out. (I once overheard Mark telling another teacher that he abhors Christmas music before Thanksgiving because the songs get stuck in his head too easily.)

None of the things I do will really make any sort of impact on the man who tried—and hopefully failed—to break my heart, so I head home with a clear conscience.

I haven't heard from Jordan, but Houston mentioned Jordan has been helping him get his rental ready for new tenants, so I tell myself that Jordan will reach out when he's not so busy. I can be patient while he's still frustrated with me.

I don't manage that quite as easily as I managed my pranks, but I'm trying.

Friday night, I get a call from Chad.

"Hi, Blondie."

I'm instantly alert. He sounds stressed, and Chad never gets stressed. "What's wrong?"

"Uh, it's snowing. That's not..." He groans. "Sorry. Micah just called me. She's trapped at the Greenwood Lodge in the storm and doesn't have power, and I'm kinda freaking out."

The Greenwood Lodge? That's where our mom married Micah's dad. "What is she doing there?"

"Her company is planning an event, so they were scoping out the venue."

"She's not up there by herself?" I breathe a little easier. "Is she okay?"

"I hope so. Listen, I called because I'm probably not going to be able to get out of here for a couple of days. With the lodge at a lower elevation, I'm hoping she can get back to Sun City sooner. Can you check on her when she gets back? Her boss put her in charge, and you know how she is."

My heart aches for my little sister. She's a literal ball of sunshine no matter what the situation, but as soon as someone puts her in charge of something, she panics unless she has good support behind her. I hope she's not having to handle everything by herself. "Yeah, of course. Are you okay? Do you have power?"

He sighs, but he sounds calmer now that he knows I can look after Micah. He definitely has a soft spot for her, which I love. "No, we don't have power either, but we're pretty well set up to last a few days."

"We?"

"Don't read into it. I've got both my neighbors here, and I doubt Hank is in any danger of me falling in love with him."

I laugh. "Wait, is he that mystery writer who never leaves his house?"

"Yep. Nice guy."

I've never met Hank, but Chad did when he bought his Laketown house, and he sounds as fascinating as his plotlines. He's too young to be a hermit and always fills his books with romance. I feel like there's a story there, though I'll probably never hear it.

"Do you need anything, Chad?"

He sighs again, and I know he hates feeling useless while Micah is in need. It's a good thing he never felt inclined to buy a snowmobile or he would probably be flying across the mountain right now to get to Micah. "No, I'll be fine. Thanks, Blondie."

When I hang up, there's a text waiting from Jordan. My heart speeds up way too much to be healthy, but I don't care.

Jordan:

How's the search for the real Brooklyn coming, Queens?

I want to tell him about the pranks I pulled today, but something tells me he won't be as proud of my accomplishments as I am. Pulling these pranks was still a way for me to get back at Mark, and I have a feeling Jordan wouldn't like that.

Back in the day, though I never admitted it back then, the pranks I pulled were more fun than they were vindictive, and Jordan and I often ended up laughing together after all was said and done.

Somehow, I forgot that part.

That was the best part.

Maybe that's what Jordan is talking about. I've forgotten to have fun and enjoy life. I've been so focused on being whatever my boyfriends wanted me to be that I've stopped living for myself.

And I'm miserable.

The text I send back is vague, but it's the best I can do until I figure out how to let go of all the trauma I've been carrying over the years.

Me:

I'm working on it.

Jordan doesn't respond, but he doesn't need to. I have to do this for myself as much as I do it for him, or it's never going to stick.

October 19

I wake to the sound of the lawn mower, which sends my heart racing. I don't want to seem overeager, so I take my time getting ready, putting on a pair of leggings and one of my favorite old band t-shirts, one I know Jordan likes as much as I do. Though I go minimal on my makeup so I don't look like I'm trying, I make sure my hair isn't a mess and spritz some body spray.

It might be overkill, but I don't care.

By the time I make it outside, Jordan is tossing the last of his tools into his trailer and looks like he was planning to leave without saying hi. As soon as he sees me, though, he freezes, his eyes tracing over me and leaving a trail of heat as he goes.

"How's Houston?" I ask. Apparently I'm too afraid to address any topics directly related to the two of us, even if my brother is still relevant to whatever is happening between us.

Jordan folds his arms and leans against the trailer. He looks way too good, glistening in the sun in his tank top. "He's fine. He's expecting too much of himself, as always."

"So, he has new tenants coming?"

"Yep. A brother and sister, apparently."

"That should be fun. Maybe she's cute and Houston can start dating someone normal for once."

He laughs, shaking his head. "I doubt Houston would know what to do with someone normal. I'm still rooting for him and Tamlin, no matter how unlikely it is he'll see her again. Stranger things have happened." He says that last part with a smolder in his eyes, like he's trying to tell me so much more.

I think I understand. I never could have predicted that I would connect with Jordan Torres as easily as I did last weekend. After all the nonsense we threw at each other, we were destined to be enemies. Not whatever this is.

I take a step closer, noticing the way Jordan stands up straight as soon as I do. "Did you talk to him?"

He shakes his head, watching each of my steps. "I didn't get a chance. He wasn't in the right mood, anyway."

"But you will?"

His arms drop to his sides as soon as I get close enough to be within touching distance. He seems to be struggling to keep his eyes on mine. "Yes, I'll talk to him. What are you doing?"

I grin. "Just coming closer so I don't have to shout across the yard."

"Brooklyn. I'm still frustrated with you."

I touch the hem of his tank top as if curious what it's made out of. And maybe my fingers accidentally brush against his stomach at the same time. "I'm frustrated with myself," I admit, laughing inwardly at the way he grimaces as soon as my fingers make contact with his warm skin.

"My mom grounded Mateo, and I'm lucky he's still talking to me. I feel like I'm one wrong move away from sending him running." Jordan keeps his eyes on my hands, like he's afraid I'm going to touch him again.

He's right to be afraid. This time, I reach up and brush nonexistent dirt from his shoulder, enjoying the feel of his smooth muscle.

"I'm sorry," I tell him. "About Mateo. Maybe I can talk to him? At the very least, I would like to apologize for getting him into trouble. That really wasn't my goal, but I wasn't thinking straight." I drop my hands, and when my fingers run down his torso, this time it really is an accident, and I blush. Hard.

To my surprise, Jordan reaches up and touches my cheek as if he wants to feel the heat there. "This is going to be harder than I thought," he murmurs to himself.

I don't know why he thinks he needs to keep his distance. "We can still be friends while we figure all of this out," I say quietly.

Something burns in his eyes when he meets my gaze. "Friends." He chuckles. "You are seriously overestimating my level of control." His hand stretches to my neck, his thumb pressed against my cheek by my ear, and he leans in.

His watch buzzes against my shoulder, making us both jump.

Groaning, he takes a wide step to the side and looks down at the message he got. "I've got a consult in a few minutes, and one of my guys is out today so I need to step in and cover for him," he says without looking at me. "If I stop by later today, will you be here?"

Micah will probably show up at some point today, but until she does, I am totally free. "I'll be here," I tell him. And I mean that more than just today. I hope he understands that. "Jordan?"

He stops halfway to this truck, his eyes hopeful as he looks at me.

I smile. "We're going to figure this out. *I'm* going to figure this out."

The grin he gives me seems to outshine the sun, which is saying something when we live in a place called Sun City. "I know you will, Queens."

Chapter Twenty-Eight
Jordan

Leave it to Houston to look up the schedule and beg me to come back and help him with the duplex as soon as I finish up with work. After our quick interaction this morning, I'm desperate to see Brooklyn again, but I can't ignore her brother when he is quickly becoming our biggest obstacle.

He may not know he's an obstacle, but he is. In more ways than one.

Telling him I'll be over soon, I head to Brooklyn's first, my heart picking up speed the closer I get. After this morning, I've come to the conclusion that she needs to know more about Natalie. I'm going to hate this conversation, but it needs to happen if I want Brooklyn to know what she's getting into.

She's waiting for me outside, curled up in a chair on the front porch with a notebook and pen. I've never seen anything more beautiful, and it almost hurts to look at her knowing there's a chance she'll reject me after I explain why I've been hesitant.

She looks up when I close the door of my truck, her eyes sparkling. "Hey."

I stop a few feet away from her. "Hi."

She has to feel the awkwardness between us that came with my decision, but she hasn't stopped smiling. "How was landscaping?"

Honestly, I probably had too much time to myself while trimming hedges because the last several hours have been full of thoughts of her. "You look different," I say.

She tucks her hair behind her ear. "It's been a really good day. I've been doing a lot of thinking."

"You're about to do some more." Of course that confuses her, and I groan as I run a hand over my hair. "Sorry. It's been a long week, you know?"

Chuckling, she closes her notebook and stands up. "Yeah, I know."

With every step forward she takes, I take one step back. After three steps she stops and frowns, making me feel terrible. I'm not doing this right.

"Brooklyn, I..." I sigh. "I need to tell you something. About my marriage."

That catches her attention, dimming all of her features as she folds her arms in a protective stance. "Okay."

This already sucks, and I haven't even started talking yet. "I don't have a lot of time, but do you want to sit?" I gesture to the porch and the two chairs sitting there. Whoever lives in the top half of the house must own them, but I'm glad Brooklyn can use them so she isn't stuck in the basement all the time.

I only spent a weekend down there, but I hated it. Someone needs to find this girl a better place to live, but I'm going to hazard a guess that she's too stubborn to let anyone help her pay a more expensive rent.

"Okay," she says again and leads the way to the porch, returning to the chair she was in when I got here.

I settle in the other chair, unsure how to begin. With the things I've learned about Brooklyn in the last few days, I need to be careful.

"First of all," I say, "this has nothing to do with you. I'm telling you this so you can understand why I've been distant the last couple of days."

"Okay."

Is that the only word she knows now? Taking a deep breath, I push forward and hope I get more of a response from her as I get into it. "Natalie and I were good together. We met through a mutual acquaintance, and things progressed easily. Our marriage was solid."

I can see her chewing her lip, which probably means I'm going about this all wrong.

I shift to the edge of my seat so I'm closer to her. "Things at work were really good too, and I moved up the ranks quickly. I loved my job, and I felt like I had really found my calling. I got promotions, started earning more, and I was on track to become a partner at the firm. I was really building something for us, and I loved that feeling of success. I was on top of the world."

I shake my head, dropping my gaze to my shoes. "But the problem with being on top of the world is all the stuff that gets left at the bottom.

The higher I rose, the busier I got. The more time I spent at the office. Late afternoons turned into late nights, weekends became two more days of work I could pack in each week, and my career was exploding. But not in a good way.

"Natalie was the one paying for my rise to riches, and I had no idea. That's the worst part—I didn't even know it. I never saw my wife because I was always either at the office or off on business dinners, and there were times I even slept on the couch in my office because I was there so late that there was no point in going home. Nat and I…"

This is the part I hate the most, but it's the most important part. "We were roommates at best. Not even that after a while because she started spending her weekends with her friend an hour away. And me? I didn't care. She could do what she wanted, and it didn't change my ability to work, so I. Didn't. Care. Natalie rightfully made the decision to leave because I couldn't see how much of an idiot I was being."

I sigh, wishing I was brave enough to look at Brooklyn and gauge her thoughts. They'll be written on her face, as always, and that's terrifying. She's got to think the worst of me—who wouldn't?—but I keep talking anyway.

"It wasn't until she asked for a divorce that it all hit me. It was like I'd been thrown out of a plane without a parachute, and if I had just opened my eyes, I would have seen the chute sitting right there, waiting for me to grab it. I didn't even try to argue Nat's decision; I agreed to the divorce without hesitation and put in my notice at my job the next day. It was the wakeup call I needed but never should have had. As soon as everything was final, I came back to Sun City and have been trying my hardest to focus on the most important parts of life."

And now that I've said all that, I jump into the important part of this conversation. The one that relates to her and will hopefully explain why I've been such a jerk the last few days. Explain, but not excuse. I'll make sure she knows that part.

"Clearly I'm a work in progress," I say, running my hand through my hair. "Houston gave a shout-out to No Mow Problems in an interview this week, which is awesome, but I fell right back into old habits. I could have been hanging out with you, but instead I was sitting on a sticky diner seat answering emails that didn't need to be answered. Houston literally canceled an entire day's worth of work so I would take a break because I am so prone to only focusing on one thing at a time, even if it's the wrong thing. I went an entire day without talking to you, and I hate that. I'm a mess."

And at this point I won't be surprised if she decides she's better off without me. She has her own things to work through.

"I thought you should know," I finish quietly. "Before, you know… Before you decide you might want to see if we can be something."

Then I hold my breath. Waiting. I'll wait here all night if I have to, but I need to know what she'll say.

"Jordan?" She doesn't say anything else until I look up, and for once, she's impossible to read. I can't tell if she's worried, angry, amused… Nothing. "Thank you. For telling me all of that. I know that can't have been easy."

While I appreciate her sympathy, it does nothing to ease my tension. "You and Houston have always been my rock," I admit. No sense in stopping my oversharing now that I've started.

Brooklyn's careful mask finally cracks, her eyebrows pulling low as she cocks her head. "Why? I mean, why did you stay over so often?"

I shrug. "I never felt like I had to be or do anything specific when I was at your house. It was so much easier to forget I had stuff to do, and it was like any expectations were gone and the pressure was off."

A smile plays on her lips. "Is that because I thought so poorly of you?"

"Maybe." I chuckle.

"Or maybe we set the bar so low that—"

I grab her hand, cutting her off. "No. You have always been leagues above me. And literally no one but you can compare to Houston. The two of you are cut from the same overachieving cloth."

She scoffs, and I know exactly what she's going to say. "You're comparing my award-winning, million-dollar salary, professional pitcher brother to *me*? An underpaid high school teacher who thought sticking Oreos to a man's car would make him rethink his life?"

I choke on my ready response, thrown by her last comment. "Wait, you did what?"

Blushing, she shrugs and turns her focus to our connected hands. "You know that thing high schoolers used to do when they wanted to be edgy but were too afraid of actual vandalism?"

"You Oreo'd Mark's car?"

"And ordered him a lame pizza for lunch. And sang Christmas carols because he hates them."

My laugh bursts out of me, breaking through my post-confession anxiety for the first time. "Okay, when I said you should get in touch with the old Brooklyn, I didn't think you would go that far into the past. It's like when we drove your stepsister crazy by getting the songs stuck in her head all summer."

She grins, her hand tightening around mine. "That's where I got the idea. I was trying to think of things I used to do to get after you and Houston."

"We were a united front on the Christmas songs," I remind her.

"That was one of my favorites."

"*That's* why I spent so much time at your house," I say, pointing at her smile. "You've always made life better, Queens."

I love the way she blushes but says nothing.

Okay, well, how am I not supposed to read into that comment? She enjoyed being with me rather than against me, and the fact that she's smiling at me right now has to mean she's not completely scared off by my faults.

"By the way," I say, wishing I wasn't already on the edge of my chair because I don't feel close enough. "Just because you're not a professional athlete, it doesn't mean you're not important. Yeah, Houston makes a ridiculous amount of money and has his face on a cereal box, but he also sets impossible standards for himself because he doesn't think he's good enough. We all have something, Queens. And whether in a lab or a classroom, you're going to change the world."

Though tears fill her eyes, she keeps her smile firmly in place. "Thanks, Torres."

I brush her hair away from her face. "I don't know why I love you calling me that, but I do."

We sit there for what feels like ages but is probably only thirty seconds or so. I'm pretty sure we're on the edge of a cliff, waiting for the right moment to fall, and I'm so tempted to take that leap right here and now.

But I can't do that. Not yet. Besides, that doesn't fit with Rick's bridge metaphor. Groaning, I drop my head and curse my sense of duty. "I should go. Your brother needs my help."

"You could ignore him."

"Ha! Houston Briggs is not a man who is used to being ignored." It's a miracle he hasn't called me yet, so I force myself to vacate the porch before I run the risk of moving too quickly. This thing with Brooklyn feels more like a rope bridge than the massive brick version in New York, so I need to move slowly. Take my time. "Besides, I need to fix myself before I'm anywhere close to being worthy of you. I'm working on it." I use her own words, hoping that helps her believe me.

Brooklyn stands too, her eyes bright. That's a good sign. "Can I take you and Mateo to breakfast tomorrow? I know it's a little...questionable...but I want to try to help things between you."

I didn't expect that, but her request makes me smile. "That depends. Are you going to order a salmon omelet?"

She pinks, but her warm smile gives me hope that I haven't completely turned her away. "I guess that depends on what you're ordering and if I want to switch with you."

Chuckling, I stuff my hands into my pockets and slowly back away toward my truck. "I don't know if I'll be able to get Mateo to come with me, but I'll try."

"Trying is all I need. And if he doesn't come?"

"Then it'll be a date. You and me."

I love the way she turns a bright scarlet at that, and though I would love to walk back up to her and show her how I really feel, I force myself to climb into the truck and drive away. Before I lose myself in my feelings for Brooklyn—before I cross that bridge—I have to make sure my best friend won't be stuck on the other side by himself.

Chapter Twenty-Nine

Brooklyn

I'm usually asleep before ten, but Micah is an endless ball of energy, even if she just spent twenty-four hours stuck in a powerless lodge with a couple dozen people to look after and a coworker to crush on. She doesn't fall asleep until after midnight, so I'm ready to crash as soon as I know she's settled and in no danger of reliving the panic attack she had at the lodge.

She always bounces back so quickly, and I wish I had her fortitude. She'll be out the rest of the night, thankfully. Once she's asleep, she's asleep.

My brother, on the other hand... His text comes in right as I crawl back into my bed next to Micah after using the bathroom so I don't jostle her in the middle of the night.

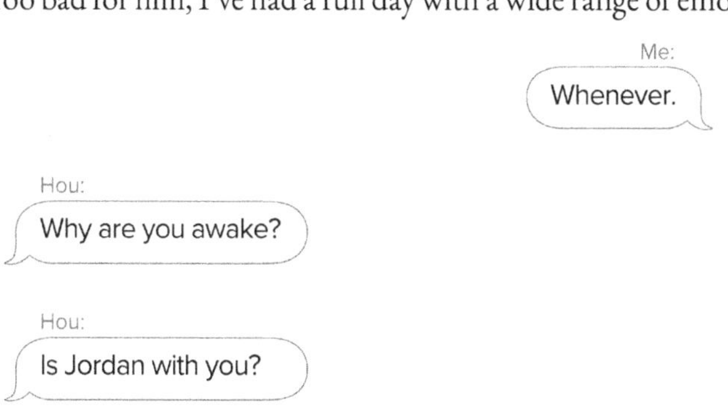

I sigh. He probably thinks I'm asleep and is hoping to catch me in the morning, when I'm less filtered and more likely to give him a straight answer. Too bad for him, I've had a full day with a wide range of emotions.

I frown. What does that mean? Did Jordan talk to him and tell him that there's mutual attraction between us? I'd better play it safe, just in case.

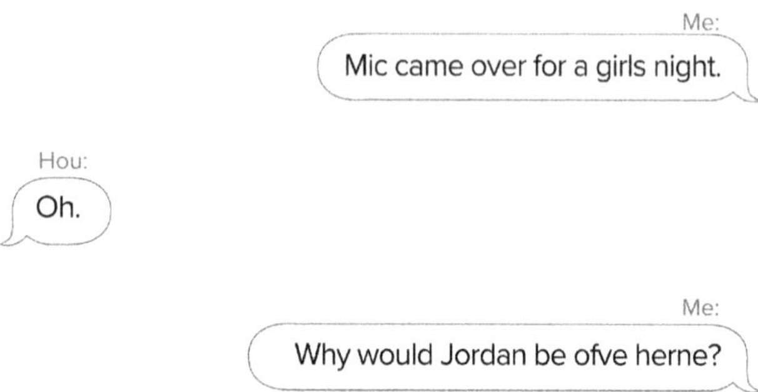

I don't even bother correcting that. Houston is smart enough to interpret and know I meant *over here*.

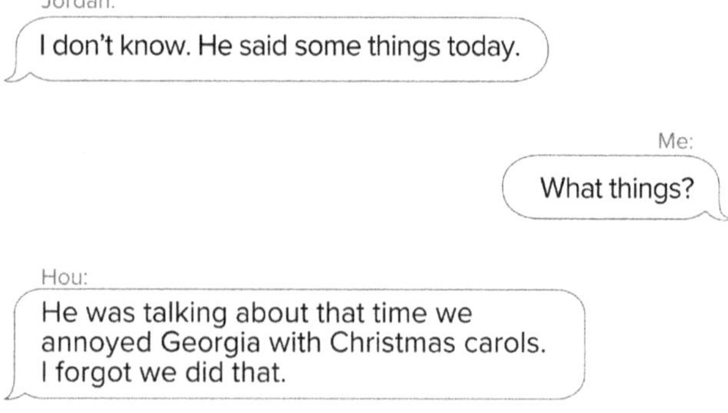

There's no *we* in this situation. Houston rolled his eyes at us and spent most of the summer making out with his girlfriend. I don't know how I forgot, but Jordan still hung around the house a lot, even when Houston was occupied. He drove me crazy, as always, but in hindsight I had more fun that summer than I'd had in years.

That was right before I started dating Garrett, my itchy sweater of a cheating boyfriend. *Huh*. Jordan's insults really do make it easier to be honest about my opinions of people. Anyway, I saw a lot less of Jordan once I started dating Garrett, and now I'm starting to wonder if I know the reason why.

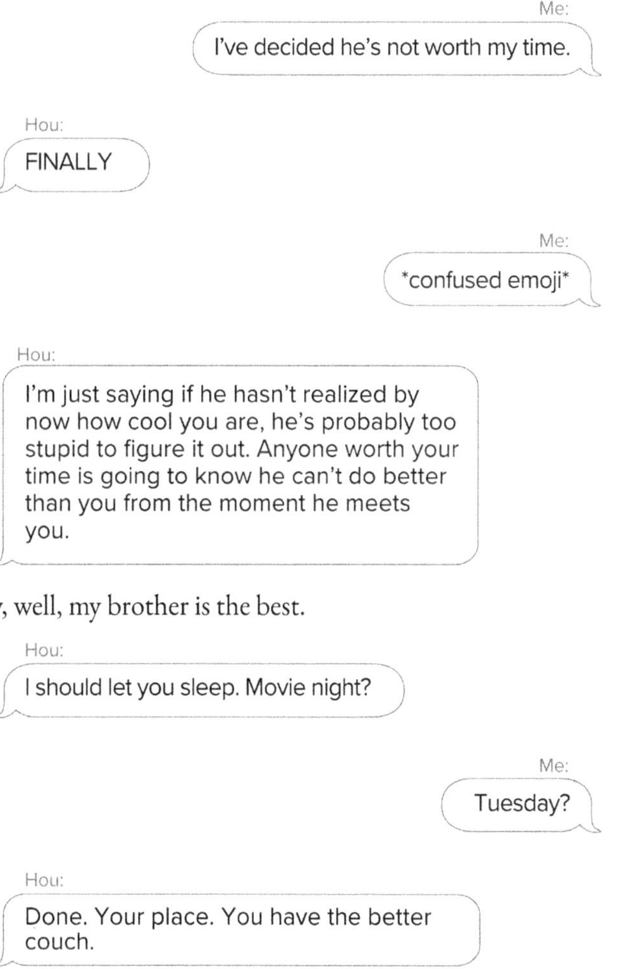

This feels like the sort of conversation we usually have during our movie nights, so I think he's secretly fishing for info about Jordan. I should really go to bed, but if this gets me closer to being able to be open about my growing feelings for Jordan, I can sacrifice a few minutes.

Okay, well, my brother is the best.

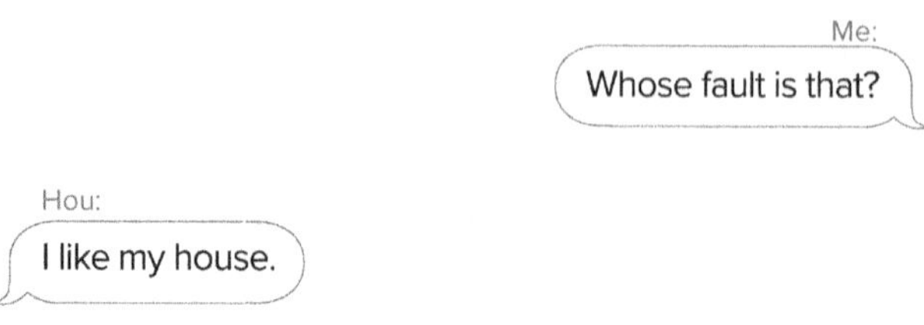

His house is a picture-perfect model home with no sense of life about
it. Granted, it's mainly above ground, so it's better than my rented basement, but he could afford a mansion in the hills. I've never understood
why he sticks to the suburbs on the outskirts of town.

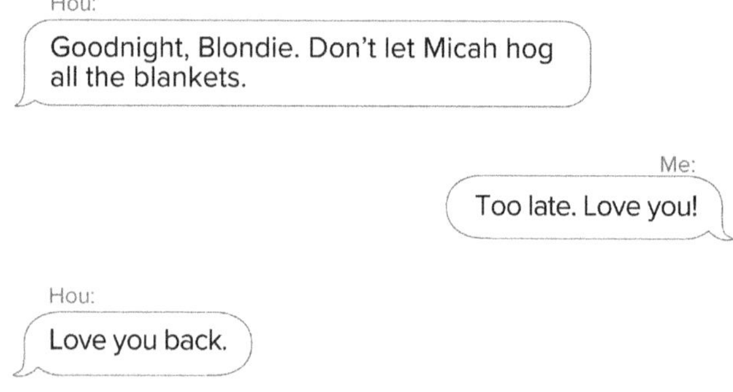

Right before I lock my screen so I can finally go to sleep, another text
comes in. This one makes me smile and take a second to hug my phone
as if it might bring the words closer to my heart.

I don't know how he knows, but I swear Jordan knows exactly what
I have planned for Monday. With all my thinking time today, I decided

I can't cower behind my comfort zones anymore. Mostly because my comfort zones aren't even that comfortable right now. Maybe I'll get Teacher of the Year, and maybe I won't. But I'm tired of being miserable.

Me:

I have the perfect plan. But I might need some help.

Jordan:

Anything you need, I'm there.

Micah moans and reaches out for me, wanting to cuddle even in her sleep. I'm pretty sure her coworker Fischer would love to fill in for me—when he dropped her off, he looked at her like she was the only light in his life. But until Micah figures that out, I'll be her person. It might be the only way I get cuddles too until Jordan realizes he doesn't need to be perfect to be perfect for me.

With that thought—both comforting and terrifying—I slowly drift off to sleep.

Chapter Thirty

Jordan

October 20

I'm PRETTY SURE THE only reason Mateo is giving me the time of day this morning is because I promised him food, though he looks like he's regretting his decision as he sits in the passenger seat of my truck and stares out the window. Well, food and Mom convinced him. As soon as she found out I was trying to take Mateo out to get breakfast, she begged him to go with me.

And no one can say no to my mom.

"Did Friday go okay at school?" I ask, desperate to fill the silence as I drive. I could turn on some music, but with my luck, it will be something he hates.

Mateo barely reacts to my question. "Sure."

"What classes are you taking outside of math from that annoying teacher?" It's my pathetic attempt at camaraderie.

He may not be facing me, but I *know* he rolls his eyes. "We don't have to make small talk, Jordan. I know this was Mom's idea to get us to bond or whatever."

"It wasn't her idea." It also wasn't mine, but I'm not about to tell him that his teacher wants to meet up on a Sunday morning. If I thought it was hard to get him to come already, that would put a nail in the coffin of our brotherly relationship. I'm nervous about how he's going to react, but Brooklyn deserves a chance to apologize for the whole Mark thing.

"How long is this going to take, anyway?" Mateo asks when I pull into the restaurant parking lot.

Brooklyn said she would get here early and grab us a table, which will make it easier to keep Mateo from trying to skip out. Hopefully.

"Why?" I ask. "Got somewhere to be?"

"Maybe." He says that without looking at me. Not at all suspicious...

After a quick glance at my watch to make sure we're not early, I lead the way out of the truck and into the restaurant. Thankfully, I spot Brooklyn in a booth right away, so I throw my arm around Mateo's shoulders and steer him in that direction.

To no surprise, he fights to wriggle free all the way up to the point when his eyes lock on Brooklyn in her t-shirt and jeans. Then he goes still as a statue, mouth gaping open like a fish as if he's having a hard time comprehending the idea that a teacher could exist outside of a school. Especially dressed so casually. While she looked incredible for her date with Mark, I like the dressed down version of her so much more. It feels more like her.

"Something wrong?" I ask, still holding Mateo tight.

Brooklyn, who clearly hears my amused question, throws a glare at me and then stands up. "Hi, Mateo. I know this is weird."

"Weird," he parrots.

"Jordan, why didn't you tell him I'd be here?"

Mateo turns to me. "You *know* Miss Briggs?"

Oh, I know her. Right now, I feel like she knows me better than anyone in the world. Even Houston. "Give her an hour, okay?"

"Fifteen minutes."

"This isn't a negotiation."

Brooklyn clears her throat. "How about I tell you why I asked Jordan to bring you, and then you can decide if you want to stay?"

Though he glances around the restaurant, as if making sure no one will recognize him, Mateo slowly makes his way to the booth and slides in.

Brooklyn returns to her seat across from him, and suddenly I'm faced with a decision. I can join Mateo on his side so he doesn't feel like we're teaming up against him, but he might see that as being trapped. If I sit with Brooklyn, there's no way I'll be able to stay focused with her so close, but at the same time I'll have an easy excuse to accidentally touch her as often as I want. Pros and cons to both.

Brooklyn clears her throat again and glances at the bench beside her. Decision made for me.

As I slide into the booth, I immediately become aware of just how small this booth really is. I'm not especially large, but my shoulders are broad enough that I can't sit comfortably without being pressed up against her. *Oh no. I'm so bummed.*

Brooklyn elbows me in the ribs as if she can hear my thoughts. "I'm glad you came, Mateo, and I want you to know that this has nothing to do with Jordan. This is all me."

I glance at her, lifting an eyebrow and smiling at her. She ignores me, which is probably a good idea.

"When I heard what happened with Mr. DeNiro, I felt so bad about what I told you. I shouldn't have encouraged you to point out his mistakes, and I never wanted you to get into trouble. I am sincerely sorry about all of it."

Mateo listens with plenty of wariness in his eyes, but he doesn't seem quite as eager to run as he did before she started talking. And when she finishes, he purses his lips and looks down.

Alejandro does the same thing when he's feeling awkward or unsure, and I can't help but smile at the similarities between my two brothers despite the nine years between them. I don't remember the last time we were all together; Alex has been deployed for the last year, and I spent most holidays with Natalie's parents in California after we got married.

The three of us probably haven't been in the same place since my wedding four years ago, and even then I was a little preoccupied. Have I *ever* spent a lot of time with Mateo?

"Thanks," Mateo says eventually, shoulders hunched as he studies the menu in front of him.

Brooklyn bites her lip and looks at me with worry in her eyes, like she's afraid she didn't say enough.

I shouldn't, but I grab her hand under the table anyway. Really, it just makes sitting in this small space more comfortable, and she could use the reassurance. "Hey Brook, did you hear about what happened to Mr. DeNiro's car?"

Her eyes immediately light up. "You mean when someone covered it in halves of Oreos?"

"Really?" Mateo says, clearly forgetting the fact that he was feeling awkward. "Someone did that?"

Brooklyn grins. "On Friday before school. Looks like you're not the only one who thinks Mr. DeNiro is a little too serious sometimes."

Mateo risks a smile, and his hands appear on top of the table now to unwrap his silverware onto the table. Was that really all it took to get him to stay? "I wasn't trying to make him feel stupid when I called him out. I just want to make sure everyone learns the formulas right so they can do well on their tests."

"Is that why you've been tutoring?"

Mateo drops his hand in shock, landing it directly on his fork. It goes flying, crossing the restaurant until it lands in an old lady's high hairdo.

She doesn't even notice.

"How did you know about that?" Mateo asks, voice cracking.

"Uh, yeah, I want to know that too," I say. "You've been tutoring?"

Though Mateo looks terrified—I'm not thrilled by that reaction to something that should be a good thing—Brooklyn smiles gently. "I asked around about you on Friday," she says. "I'm surprised you have enough time to do it all on top of your college classes."

"What college classes?" I ask, feeling entirely too ignorant at the moment.

Mateo throws me a glance but speaks only to Brooklyn. "I do my homework while in class so I can tutor people after school. I'm just auditing the college classes."

None of this is making sense to me. "How can you afford to audit college classes?"

"He charges for tutoring," Brooklyn says, as if it should be obvious. "You're still working with kids from your old school?"

Nodding, Mateo seems to be slowly relaxing again. "That's why I got into those fights. One kid didn't get a good enough score on his test, and he blamed me. Convinced his friends to jump me after school."

Brooklyn yelps, and I realize I'm squeezing her hand too tightly. "Sorry," I say with a wince and then turn back to my brother. "Why didn't you tell us?"

He rolls his eyes, back to a surly teenager in an instant. "Tell who? Dad's never home, you're always working, and I didn't want to make Mom worry."

"She was worried anyway! You could have explained—"

This time Brooklyn squeezes my hand. "I know how it feels to want to avoid being a burden," she says softly, "but you should never be afraid to tell the people who love you what you're going through."

"I didn't want to make things worse," Mateo mumbles. "And now I've already been sent to the principal's office. Mom thinks I'm a failure."

"She doesn't." I don't hesitate with my response. "Trust me. Mom thinks way more highly of us boys than she should, and you lucked out as the baby of the family."

"Accidental baby."

Boy, am I glad the service in this restaurant is terrible and there hasn't been a single sign of a waitress to interrupt this delightful conversation.

"You weren't an accident," I argue, though I've dropped my voice so the family a couple of tables down won't hear.

Mateo scoffs, twirling his knife on the table. "There's nine years between Alex and me. Pretty sure I wasn't part of the family plan."

"Mom cried the day she found out she was pregnant with you."

"Because she didn't want me."

"Because she'd been waiting almost a decade for you! They tried for years and thought they'd be stuck with just Alex and me for the rest of their lives." Groaning, I run my free hand through my hair and shake my head. "Clearly our family needs to work on our communication skills. I thought you knew."

Mateo finally looks up, enough emotion in his face that I think he might actually start crying. I don't blame him. Did he really think all his life that he wasn't desperately wanted? "I didn't know," he croaks.

"See? This is why you should have come to lunch with me instead of glowering at me. Ow!" I glare at Brooklyn, who threw her elbow into my ribs again. "I'm just saying this conversation might have happened sooner if we'd—"

"When?" she asks. "With all your free time that your job gives you?"

Her comment is a bit of a gut punch, but it doesn't land as hard as I would have expected. She's not wrong. "Low blow, Queens. I respect that."

She wrinkles her nose in a combination smile and sneer that drives me crazy. I simultaneously want to challenge her to a prank war and kiss the sneer right off her face. I could probably do both and come out the victor either way.

"Can you two wait until we eat before you start making out?" Based on the disgusted look on Mateo's face as he looks between us, he's not joking. "School is about to get all sorts of awkward."

"I hope so," I murmur, which sends crimson rushing into Brooklyn's face until she's beet red. She doesn't look away from me, like I expect, which makes her even more tempting. Despite our reluctant audience, it couldn't hurt to test the waters and give her one quick kiss, right?

"Hi! Welcome to Rita's Family Restaurant!" An all-too energetic waiter appears with a beaming smile and a bounce in his step, speaking with full enthusiasm even though I'm scowling at his interruption. "My name is Charlie, and I'll be your server today. Here are some waters for you guys. Is there anything else I can get you to drink before I take your order?"

"Maybe a sippy cup for the kid," I grumble.

Brooklyn and Mateo kick me at the same time, but they're both smiling. "He's paying," Mateo says, "so I'll have a coffee and a Coke."

I raise an eyebrow. "Both?"

He shrugs. "My level of genius runs on caffeine. Deal with it."

Honestly, he probably is a genius if he's tutoring his own classmates *and* auditing college classes for the fun of it. Why doesn't he try to get the college credit, though? That would be a way better use of his money.

"And for you, miss?"

"Hot chocolate," Brooklyn says sweetly.

"I'm good with water," I mumble, taking a sip as if I need to demonstrate. Charlie leaves to get the drinks, and we're left in silence. I drink a little deeper, searching for a topic of conversation.

"Mateo, did Jordan ever tell you about the time he got sent to the principal's office for proposing to his favorite teacher?"

I choke, water going everywhere as Brooklyn's words hit me. I can't breathe as I try to cough the water out of my lungs, but Brooklyn only smirks at me.

Mateo's eyes are wide. "When he did *what*?"

"Proposed. Got down on one knee with a ring and a flower." Brooklyn sounds serious, but the mischief in her eyes is unmistakable.

Mateo frowns as he looks between us. "You're joking, aren't you?"

"I wish she was," I mumble after one final cough to clear my lungs. "I can't believe you just brought that up."

Tossing her napkin at me, Brooklyn shrugs. "I thought it would make Mateo feel closer to you."

"It makes me feel something, for sure," Mateo says with a chuckle. "Why would you propose to a teacher?"

I fix my eyes on Brooklyn. "Because teachers are pretty awesome."

I didn't think she could go redder than she did before, but she does. Hopefully that means she understood my meaning, though it's not like I'm planning on proposing to her. She would be worth it if I did.

"But you were in high school?" Mateo clearly wants to hear the full story.

Sighing, I nod and stretch my arm along the back of the booth behind Brooklyn, letting my fingers dangle almost within reach of her shoulder. "In my defense, I wasn't really proposing."

Brooklyn nudges into me, which ends up tucking her under my arm. If she notices, she doesn't react. Or maybe she's too red for me to tell. "I'm pretty sure the words 'will you marry me' came out of your mouth, and you had some pretty specific details you claimed to love about her."

I narrow my eyes at her. "I *thought* I was helping her boyfriend with his proposal. From my understanding, there were going to be a bunch of us performing similar proposals until she got to the real thing."

"That doesn't make any sense," Mateo says.

"It really doesn't," Brooklyn agrees, far too innocently. "Why would any man hire a bunch of high schoolers to propose for him?"

"He wouldn't," I answer. My hand slips down of its own volition, fingers brushing the bare skin of her arm. *Stay focused, Jordan.* "Because Miss Henderson wasn't even dating anyone at the time."

"What do you mean?" Mateo says.

"*Someone* convinced me it was real so she could take a video to use as leverage someday, only she didn't count on Miss Henderson freaking out and calling the school cop."

Brooklyn cringes. "Did I ever tell you I was sorry for that? In my defense, that was after you announced my birthday to the whole school during school announcements, so I was feeling vindictive."

"I announced *Houston's* birthday. Not yours."

"We're twins, doofus. People naturally connected the dots."

"I got detention for commandeering the microphone," I remind her, "so I really didn't need payback."

"You really did. Three different freshmen tried to buy me lunch that day and ended up blocking the lunch line for ten minutes while they argued and trapped me there."

"Oh no! Free lunch! The horror."

"Says the guy who wouldn't ever let Houston pay for his food."

"I could afford my own lunch, thank you very much."

"So could I."

"Ahem."

We both turn to face Mateo, who is now standing next to a wide-eyed Charlie by the booth.

"I'm going to get my food to go," Mateo says, looking between the two of us as if he thinks we're a lost cause. I don't know what the cause is, but it's most assuredly lost. "Miss Briggs, you're pretty cool."

"Wait!" She tries to stand up, but there's the minor problem of the bolted-down table and my arm fully around her shoulders now, which means her stilted movement makes her lose her balance and throw her hands out to catch herself. One slams into the wall, and the other slams right into my lap. Specifically the crotch area.

I go down, folding in half like an ironing board as the pain momentarily overwhelms my senses. I'm vaguely aware of water spilling over the table edge and into my lap—blessed, cool relief—while laughter rings out above me. Honestly, I'm not sure if it's Mateo or Charlie. Maybe both.

"OhmygoshIamsosorry." Brooklyn scrambles for napkins and starts throwing them at me.

I slowly sit back up, though I keep my hands in my lap to safeguard my assets from further damage as she flails her hands around. "Does this mean I'm going to get you as my nurse for the rest of the weekend?" My voice may be higher in pitch than normal, but I don't care. I'm going to tease her about this for the rest of her life.

Bright scarlet again, Brooklyn seems to debate something as she gazes at me with a handful of crumpled napkins. "I suppose that's only fair," she says. "But I'm not massaging anything. Oh!"

I snort into laughter at the same time as Mateo, while Brooklyn looks like she wants the world to swallow her up after her accidental innuendo. She drops her face into her hands with a groan. This has been the strangest breakfast of my life, but I don't remember the last time I laughed this hard.

"I was going to ask for your help with something, Mateo," Brooklyn says through her hands. "With Mr. DeNiro. I think he could use some cheering up after everything last week."

With laughter still in his eyes, Mateo returns to his seat and accepts the coffee Charlie has been holding for who knows how long. "What did you have in mind?"

For the next hour, we enjoy a thankfully pain-free breakfast while Brooklyn lays out her plan. It is absolutely a prank, but it's the kind of prank where no one gets hurt. In fact, it'll practically be doing Mark a favor unless his pretentious self decides to take it too seriously, in which case that's on him.

When we're done, I satisfy myself with a kiss to Brooklyn's forehead and a promise to see her tonight, after I finish helping Houston get his house ready before his tenant shows up this evening. She smiles and tells me she can't wait, and even Mateo's relentless teasing as I drive him home can't dampen my mood.

Chapter Thirty-One
Brooklyn

"Houston is in so much trouble." Jordan greets me with those words when I open my door Sunday night, and he's got the sort of grin that would have me worried if it wasn't in relation to my brother.

I step aside so he can come in. "What does that mean?"

"It means his new renters showed up early this afternoon, and he's already smitten with Darcy."

"Darcy?"

"The sister. Houston couldn't keep his eyes off of her."

Before I can say anything, Jordan wraps me up in a hug so tight that I can't breathe for a second as he pulls me into his chest. Not that I'm complaining. While he held me the other night after Mark was...Mark, it wasn't anything like this. On Tuesday, he was holding me together. Tonight, he's holding me close. There's a huge difference, and I feel every bit of that difference in the pounding of my heart while I tuck my head under his chin.

I've got a noseful of his amazing scent and nowhere pressing to be, which makes this moment so nice.

"Thank you," he says after a while.

"For what?"

"Everything. Especially for Mateo. It's like he finally understands me."

Emotion sprouts in my chest, annoyingly pricking at my eyes at the same time. As if I did anything this morning. Jordan is the one who made sure his brother knew he was always wanted. He's the one who let us laugh at him because it would help Mateo see him as an equal.

"Maybe you finally understand *him*," I suggest. "I see it all the time with my students. They're doing everything they can to be the best they can be, and they just need someone to acknowledge that they're trying. Someone to tell them that who they are is enough."

"You saw that right away. He was already different after that first class with you."

I wrap my arms more securely around his back, noticing each muscle as he moves while adjusting his hold to me so it's less of a crush and more of a hug. "Thank you."

He chuckles. "For what?"

"For being that person for me. It's been so long since anyone..." I wasn't going to do this. We've had a rough few days, so I was going to do everything I could to make tonight drama-free. But the words seem to be crawling up my throat, desperate to get free.

I hug Jordan tighter. "There's something I didn't tell you about James and the job at the lab."

Just as I expected, he tenses, muscles flexing around me. "Are you sure you want to tell me? You don't have to."

"You don't really mean that."

One of his hands finds my hair and starts stroking from root to tip. "I really do. I want to know everything about your life, Queens, but if you're not ready to—"

"He's the reason I got fired." I flinch, unsure how he's going to respond to that.

His next word comes out in a growl. "Explain."

I take a deep breath. I've kept this to myself for years, but it's time I let someone else help me figure out how to get past it. "When he found out that the promotion I was up for was the same one he wanted, he told his boss that I had been holding back the research with my incompetence and was the reason our project stalled. He told *me* that he had just been praising me to make me feel better but that I was holding him back. I would only damage his career if he kept up a relationship because I had clearly been lying about my credentials. He didn't want my bad reputation to sully his. Up until recently, I believed him when he said I was incapable of working in research without someone to hold my hand."

I bury my face into Jordan's shoulder, glad that he can't see my face right now. I can feel his reaction, though. Every inch of him is rigid and solid, like his anger is pulsing through his body with each heartbeat and making him stronger.

"That's not all," I whisper, tears sprouting in my eyes. "I don't know how, but he managed to convince every lab in Sun City that I am undesirable. I applied to every position possible, and I never even got a phone call. The one person I managed to get in contact with over email told me that my employment history called up some red flags and they were unwilling to consider me at the time. Unless I want to leave Sun City—leave my family—I can never get a job doing what I love. Thanks to James. That's why this fellowship is my only chance. Why I'm so desperate to be Teacher of the Year, even if it's a long shot."

I don't know how long we stand there before Jordan finally speaks. "Brooklyn Briggs," he murmurs, far gentler than I expect. "You are the strongest person I know."

"I'm not. I'm miserable."

"You're still standing, no matter how many men have tried to knock you down because of their own insecurities." He pulls away, though he keeps his hands on my shoulders as his eyes lock on mine. "I am honored to know you, Queens. Every part of you."

I don't think anyone has ever said anything more beautiful than that. Even his nickname for me sounded like the highest of praise. "Jordan." I don't know what else I can say.

His hand shifts until his palm cups my cheek, thumb brushing away my tears. Something sparks to life in his eyes as he gazes at me, and he clenches his jaw. There's a chemical reaction happening inside him, like potassium in water, burning hot and fast. And when he speaks, his voice is raw. "Brook, I really want to kiss you."

My breath catches. "I really want you to kiss me too."

He doesn't waste that invitation, closing the space between us and pressing his mouth to mine. His lips are warm and firm as he takes his time with this kiss, exploring each curve of my mouth like an archaeologist unearthing a fragile bone.

I've kissed a lot of guys. It's not necessarily something I'm proud of, but it's fact. And I know when a man is holding back. So I wrap my arms around his neck and take charge, diving in deeper. We're past the point of subtlety—I want a kiss, and I want it now. This is not the time for carefully dusting away the sand around the treasure; give me a crowbar and I'll get us to the prize.

Jordan groans, hands sliding around my waist as he pulls me closer and matches my enthusiasm with his own. He backs me up until my hips hit the back of the couch, and then his hands are in my hair, at the small of my back, around my waist again. It's like he can't decide where to hold, and each touch feels like fire against my skin.

I've never been kissed the way Jordan kisses me. It's not a simple desire fueling our embrace but something deeper. Stronger. Jordan kisses me with intention, telling me with each touch of his lips that he's here by choice and wants to stay.

When we finally break apart, I don't remember the last time I took a breath, and I drop my head against his chest as I struggle to inhale. Jordan seems just as breathless as he uses one hand to brace himself on the couch, the other holding me in place.

"Queens," he rasps.

"Yeah," I reply. I don't actually know what he was going to say, but I agree.

One of my hands has ended up pressed against his abdomen, which means my fingers are getting an up close ab experience through his shirt, and I'm not mad about it. I run my fingers from his ribcage down to the hem of his jeans, counting as I go.

Jordan laughs and grabs my hand before I can do any more exploring. "Are you trying to get me into trouble?"

Though his words are a joke, there's truth to them, and my stomach clenches as I lift my head to meet his gaze. "Houston."

He nods, but then he captures my mouth with another kiss as if he can't help himself now that he has made visual contact with my lips again. He keeps this kiss far tamer than I would like, but that's probably for the best.

"He's going through something right now," he says eventually, running his fingers through my hair to smooth it. "I'm worried he's going to think he's losing everything."

I frown. "Everything? What about baseball?"

Jordan sighs. "That's not my secret to tell."

I don't like the sound of that. Why would Houston be losing baseball if he still has a year on his contract? "Maybe this Darcy girl will be able to help him get through things, if he really is interested."

"Maybe." He doesn't look convinced, though.

Reaching up, I trace the length of his jawline as he closes his eyes, like he wants to truly feel my touch. He's always been so handsome, but I've never given myself the time to really look. He has a scar on his chin, just a small one on the right side, but the rest of his face is so perfect, like he was sculpted from clay. Stubble lines his jaw, though it will be gone in the morning because Jordan has always been clean-shaven, but the rest of his skin is so smooth and flawless. I'm almost tempted to ask him for his skincare routine.

As if reading my thoughts, Jordan smiles and opens his eyes. "I know it's hard to believe I am this handsome, but I don't want to keep you up too late when you have a big day planned tomorrow. We were supposed to watch a movie tonight."

Who needs a movie when I've got my own romance blossoming right in front of me? I put on my best flirty smile and hook my fingers on his belt loops so he can't get far. "I seem to remember you saying something about having a hard time sitting still during movies."

He chuckles. "Don't worry, Queens. I'm happy to massage your feet."

I shake my head and lean up on my toes so my mouth is level with his. "I had other ideas in mind."

Fire ignites in his eyes again as he leans forward and accepts my invitation with a slow, delicious kiss. Though I never thought I would say it, this is way better than the Mr. Darcy hand flex.

By far.

Chapter Thirty-Two

Brooklyn

October 21

OBSERVATION: I AM EXHAUSTED but way happier about being at work than I usually am.

Hypothesis: Jordan Torres makes everything in life better.

Prediction: The more time I spend with Jordan, the better off I'll be.

Ideas for experiments run through my head as I walk into school Monday morning, things like going bowling and watching the BBC version of *Pride and Prejudice* and letting Jordan teach me to cook even though his techniques make no sense. Though he stayed way too late last night—not entirely his fault—I've had a bounce in my step since the moment my alarm went off this morning.

He sends me a text right before my first period starts, and I have never been so excited to get a text before.

Jordan:

> Sorry for cutting into your sleep time, Queens. Hopefully you can stay awake long enough to complete your mission with Mr. Math.

Though my class is filing in and settling at their lab tables, I hang out in my office long enough to reply, taking my time with each word so nothing comes out wrong.

Me:

> I'll survive. As late nights go, last night was the best. :)

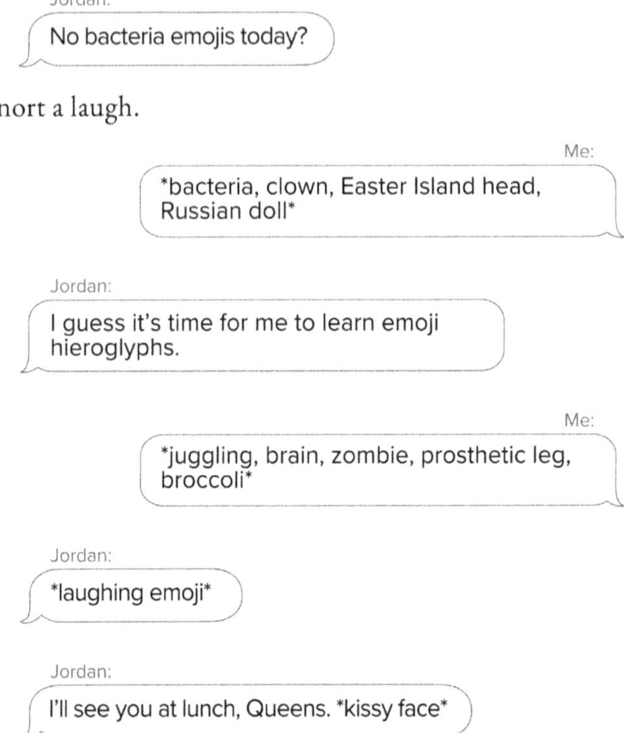

I snort a laugh.

Well, concentrating today might be harder than I thought, and I might need to amend my hypothesis. Jordan makes a lot of things better, but he's not exactly making me want to teach when I could be with him. At least he'll be here at lunch to help me with my last prank against Mark, but I'm not sure I'll be able to easily wait that long.

My first two classes drag on, even though this lab is one of my favorites. Jordan doesn't send any more texts—I try not to check, but I can't help it—and I tell myself multiple times that he has a job too and we can't spend all day texting each other.

Doesn't mean I don't wish we could.

By the time the bell signals the end of second period, I'm practically brimming with pent up energy, and I'm more than happy to see Mateo when he appears at my door after everyone else clears out.

"Are you sure I won't get in trouble?" he says as I grab my bag of supplies.

Jordan will be bringing the rest, and I sure hope he's here or this will be the lamest prank ever.

I give Mateo a wide smile. "How could you get in trouble for wanting to celebrate your teacher's birthday? Besides, he won't know it's you. He always takes lunch in the teacher's lounge."

"I have a delivery for Brooklyn Bridge?"

I'm pretty sure that's Jordan changing his voice to be deeper, though it's hard to tell because he's blocked by the ridiculous number of balloons he's holding just outside my classroom door.

I roll my eyes. "Thanks, *Daniel.*"

He pokes his head through the many strings, giving me a mock scowl. "I can't believe you would call me that, Queens. What did I do to deserve that? Hey, Matty."

Mateo glances between us—me with what I'm sure is tomato-red cheeks and Jordan with a dumb grin forming on his lips. "Gross," he mutters and then grabs half the balloons from his brother. "Can we get this over with?"

We spend the next twenty minutes tying balloons to each of the chairs in Mark's classroom. Jordan and Mateo hang a huge birthday banner on the back wall, and I place a unicorn-themed birthday hat on Mark's podium up front. The cake is my favorite part. It's just as colorful as the rest of the decor and in bright green letters says, "Happy 34th birthday, Mr. DeNiro!" so there's no confusion as to who is celebrating today.

I even got a bunch of plates and forks so his students can enjoy the cake while he teaches.

"It's perfect," I declare, grinning at the absurd amount of color we just added to Mark's otherwise dull classroom.

"Almost," Jordan corrects. He picks up a fork and scoops a bite out of the middle of the cake, stuffing it in his mouth before I can stop him.

Honestly, I don't care, even though a week ago that would have driven me crazy. Clearly Jordan has been a bad influence on me. Or maybe a really good one.

"We should leave before he gets back," Mateo says, already heading for the door. He has my class next, but since he missed lunch because of this, I told him he can sit in my office and eat the food I brought for him. He seems determined to follow through with that.

Jordan follows me back to my classroom, though we stop just inside the open door, out of sight of the hallway. We have a couple of minutes before lunch ends, which means we have a couple of minutes to test my hypothesis.

Jordan laughs as soon as he gets a look at my face. "I'm not going to kiss you in your school, Queens."

"Then your text was incredibly misleading."

He shakes his head. "No. I've gotten in trouble too many times for kissing on school property."

"And whose fault is that?"

"Yours, mainly."

I huff in frustration, but he's not wrong. I definitely ratted him out a time or two. Or several. "Okay, well, if you had been kissing *me*, you wouldn't have gotten caught."

He cocks his head, a smirk pulling up the corners of his mouth. "I was under the impression you hated me in high school."

It's hard to imagine hating this man with the way his hands snake around my waist, pulling me closer. Besides, the more I think back on the years we knew each other before, the more good stuff I've remembered. Maybe it wasn't all that bad. "Hate may be too strong a word," I say breathlessly.

He brushes a kiss against my jaw. "Mm, I can think of other strong words that I like so much better." He kisses the delicate skin below my ear. "If I had tried to kiss you in high school, would you have let me?" He kisses my eyelid.

I can barely get the words out. "Probably not. But I was also pretty young and stupid in high school."

"You did date Garrett Butler, so that's true." He finally brushes a kiss against my lips, sending a shiver through me. "I'm glad we ended up here eventually."

Me too. Instead of saying that, I hook my finger on the collar of his t-shirt and drag him closer, kissing him like I've wanted to do since he left my house last night. He doesn't complain, diving into the kiss right along with me.

"Oh," someone says.

We break apart, and though I try to distance myself, Jordan keeps an arm around my waist and holds me close. "Mark," I gasp.

He scowls, eyes jumping between the two of us. "I was going to ask if you saw who trashed my classroom, but I have a pretty good guess."

Jordan's arm tightens around me. I put my hand on his chest, hoping to keep him calm before he says something he shouldn't. "Someone trashed your room?" I ask. "I didn't see anything. Jordan was just dropping something off for his brother." It's sort of true.

Mark scoffs and folds his arms. "His brother. Sure. Now I see why you've been avoiding me all week, Briggs."

While that's true, it's not like he's made an effort to see me either.

"Do you need help cleaning up your room?" I ask. "I've got a lab today, so I could probably step away for a minute if you have a lot of mess."

His eyebrows drop. "It's not a mess, necessarily. My mom must have done it for my birthday."

"It's your birthday?" My loud question is genuine, which makes Jordan cough a poorly covered laugh. Talk about coincidence! "Happy birthday!"

The bell rings overhead, making me jump.

Chuckling, Jordan presses a kiss to my cheek and gives me a squeeze. "I'll see you tonight?"

I nod, glad that I picked Tuesday for my movie night with Houston. It will give me one more day to figure out how to break the news to him that Jordan and I are together.

Though he seems reluctant to leave, Jordan pauses next to Mark and sizes him up, even though they've met twice now. They're similar in height, but Jordan looks so much better in every way.

"You must feel pretty good about yourself," he says, making me tense. I do not need him to start a fight or make Mark angry. But then he adds, "Anyone who is at the same level as Brooklyn must be exceptionally smart. Good luck with the whole Teacher of the Year thing." He winks at me, and then he disappears through the door right as my first students start to show up.

Mark looks like he can't decide what to make of Jordan, which is pretty standard when it comes to Jordan Torres. He steps closer, lowering his voice. "Guess this means I'm not getting a second date?"

You didn't want one anyway, I want to tell him, but with the way he's looking at me, that might not be true. Maybe there *is* some real interest there.

"Sorry," I tell him. "Things with Jordan happened pretty quickly."

"Clearly."

Well, this is awkward. And he should really get back to his classroom. Who knows what the kids might be doing with that cake?

"Uh, happy birthday again," I say, tucking my hair behind my ear.

That seems to confuse him. "You really didn't put all that stuff in my classroom?"

"I didn't know it was your birthday."

"Huh. Okay. Well, thanks."

With his hands in his pockets, he shuffles off with a lot less swagger in his step than he usually has. Is that my fault?

"He'll be fine," Mateo says as he pokes his head out of my office. He must have been listening, which is slightly mortifying. "Hey, do you want me to pair up with anyone specific today?"

He sounds so eager, even though he could easily take half of the class period for his lunch like I offered. Something tells me he likes feeling useful, and an idea starts to form. TAs aren't really a thing in public high schools, at least not when it comes to the teaching part, but I could probably make an argument for it with how well Mateo already knows the material. It would help me out, and it would give him a challenge. He likely doesn't get many of those.

That's for another day, though.

"Do you think you could join Pedro and Weston today?" I point to their table, grinning when Mateo heads right over and starts chatting with the two boys.

This could definitely work.

The laughter starts up in the middle of fourth period. I don't have a class this period, so I've been working through the finished lab reports from today in the blessed quiet of my prep period.

When I hear a class laughing every couple of minutes from the direction of Mark's classroom, I can't help but investigate.

Jaydin appears at her door at the same time I do, even though she has a class this period, and together we creep toward Mark's room. I'm afraid of what I might find, but Mark isn't yelling or anything, and the laughter is sporadic. Hopefully it's nothing problematic.

To my surprise, when I peek my head through the open door, Mark is at his smart board, teaching like normal, and all of the kids are paying rapt attention.

"How do we figure out the slope of a curved line?" Mark asks calmly. Several hands go up, and he points to a girl in front.

Before she speaks, she lifts a balloon to her mouth and takes a deep breath. "We need to find the limit," she says, her voice high pitched and warped from the helium.

The class busts up, but only for a second. They quickly quiet back down, giving Mark a chance to continue his teaching. The next time he asks a question, a kid in the back gives his answer on helium as well, sparking more laughter.

"Mr. DeNiro?" a kid asks, sounding like a chipmunk. "Can you explain that last part again?"

I've watched Mark teach more times than I would care to admit, but I've never seen his students this engaged before. I've also never seen him smile like this, like he's having almost as much fun as his students are as they all try to get a chance to answer a question with a helium-affected voice.

"Where did the balloons come from?" Jaydin whispers. She seems just as fascinated as I am, though she pays more attention to the kids than to Mark. "Also, don't you sneak away after school without talking to me, girly. I saw Mr. Bronze Abs leaving your classroom today."

Heat flushes my face, and I press my hands to my cheeks. "Apparently it's Mark's birthday today."

"You're going to give me all the juicy details about Hot Landscaper no matter how much you deflect." Giving me a narrow-eyed stare, she scurries back to her own class, leaving me alone in the hallway.

I watch for a few more minutes, until Mark tells his students to try the problem he put on the board. He encourages them to work together, which prompts several inhalations of helium as they jump into discussions. Then he wanders over to the door where I've failed to remain hidden.

"Interesting technique," I say with a smile.

He blushes. Blushes! "Torres started it," he mutters, hands back in his pockets. "Nearly sent him to Cheng again when he convinced the rest of them to try it, but some of these kids usually never say a word in class." His eyebrows pull low as he looks over the students as they work out the problem with smiles on their faces.

"Sometimes you have to make things fun for it to stick," I tell him, even if he's been teaching way longer than I have. "It's nice to see my noble gasses lesson from a couple of weeks ago sank in." Though, they really shouldn't breathe in too much of the helium unless they want to pass out from oxygen deficiency. This is what I get for demonstrating the hilarious effects of helium on the vocal cords.

"Mr. DeNiro?"

As Mark heads over to help his student, I catch Mateo's eye. Though he's not working on the problem with the others, he seems incredibly pleased about the direction the class has gone. He grins at me with a look that seems to say, "I told you he would be fine."

I head back to my classroom with a huge smile on my face. My prank turned out better than I could have planned, and I feel more like myself than I have in years.

Conclusion: Jordan absolutely makes everything better.

Chapter Thirty-Three

Jordan

How did I go from overworking myself to barely doing anything with my company at all? Houston. That's how. For some reason, he thinks he needs to step into my life and take control because I'm not living it well enough, which means Monday afternoon I'm knocking on his neighbor's door because I really don't know how to say no to the guy.

Darcy opens the door slowly, like she's unsure what she wants to find on the other side, but she relaxes as soon as she sees me. "It's you."

I offer a crooked smile and a shrug, glad that she answered the door instead of her brother, who is huge and terrifying. "It's me. I brought some light bulbs for the basement and a router and modem for the internet. Mind if I come in?"

Her smile grows as she steps aside and opens the door wider. "I was just starting to get used to the red lights in the murder basement, but I'll take regular cool white as well."

I laugh. Darcy has an easygoing personality that fits well with her girl-next-door vibe. In terms of appearance, she's like a mix between Micah and Brooklyn, blonde and short and solidly built, so she probably has an athletic background. I can see why Houston is interested, even if he denies it.

I'm pretty sure he's convinced Darcy's first impression of him negated any chance of a connection. Considering she thought he was going to murder her—long story—he might be right. But maybe I can change that. Houston needs someone like Darcy, who can hold her own against a bigshot like him.

"So, where's your friend?" Darcy hops onto the kitchen counter as I set up the router in the corner by the toaster. According to Houston, it's the only place with an internet connection, which is a little ridiculous.

I glance at her. "You mean Houston?"

She shrugs, but pink sprouts on her cheeks beneath her freckles. "I'm just curious why he's not the one setting this up when he owns the house."

I'm curious about that too. He's right next door, probably pacing while he waits for me to come back and give a report. Darcy seems to scare him for some reason. "He's a busy guy."

"And you're not? You own your own company, right?"

We talked a bit while I helped her and her brother move her stuff in yesterday, but I'm surprised she remembered. She seemed just as fascinated by Houston as he was by her.

"Yeah," I tell her. "But I have a pretty good team, so I can step away every now and then."

All things considered, I've barely worked the last week, and it's all Brooklyn's fault. Well, Brooklyn and her brother, who for some reason decided to stage an intervention where I'm concerned. The more time he tries to spend with me to keep me from working, the sooner he's going to find out how I feel about his sister. I'd rather have a conversation with her first—really lay out my intentions—but Houston isn't a dummy. He already suspects something is happening, and I know he doesn't like it.

That's going to make things more complicated than I would like.

"And Houston plays baseball for work?" Darcy asks.

Everything seems to be working with the router, so I tell her how to connect so she can test it before I answer her question. "Yes, he plays baseball." And I have a feeling she knows that better than she's letting on. Or maybe she's just curious by nature and really doesn't know that she's living next to a literal celebrity. "He does some other stuff too," I add, though I don't want to elaborate because Houston is a weirdo who doesn't like people to know how insanely generous and business-minded he is.

I should probably finish up my tasks and get out of here before I get sucked into some kind of drama that will keep me away from Brooklyn.

"I can change the bulbs downstairs," Darcy says when I pick up the bag from the counter. "Thanks for bringing them over, but you don't have to do all this when you clearly want to be talking to someone else." She winks, and I laugh.

"Do you know something I don't?"

"I know you and Houston's sister aren't just friends."

I fold my arms, as if that might protect the truth from her. "Why do you think that?"

"I said I know. Not that I think." She tilts her head side to side with a little shrug. "And you called her *delicious* last night."

Ah, right. I did that. I was joking around and called her hot to gauge Houston's reaction, and he wasn't a fan. So I found some other words to describe Brooklyn, and *delicious* was in the mix along with *bodacious* and *enchanting*. There aren't enough words in the English language to properly describe Brooklyn.

Sighing, I shift my hands to my pockets. "It's a new thing," I tell Darcy, though why I trust a stranger with this secret, I couldn't tell you. "And we don't know how Houston is going to take it."

She gives me a warm, sympathetic smile. "And you're never going to know if you don't tell him. He can't react to what he doesn't know."

I raise my eyebrows. "Are you a therapist or something?"

"Psych major during my undergrad. But I also have eyes, and you clearly feel more for Brook than you're letting yourself admit. Your relationship might be new, but it isn't fragile. Not on your side, anyway, though I doubt Brook is any less involved with the way Houston seemed to do everything he could not to think about the two of you together."

I'm back to folding my arms. It's like I'm afraid she'll see too much if I don't protect myself, though I feel ridiculous being intimidated by a woman nearly a foot shorter than me. Maybe that's why Houston is scared of her? She sees a lot, and Houston has plenty to hide.

"I hope you're right about how Brooklyn feels," I tell her. "And I hope Houston can get over the idea of the two of us dating."

"That's not really up to him."

"No, but he's my best friend. I don't want to ruin that if things go south with Brooklyn."

"Do you think they'll go south?"

"I hope not." In fact, I'm hoping this thing I have with Brooklyn turns into a forever kind of thing. I've always enjoyed being around her, and she knows all my deepest darkest secrets now.

Okay, that's not true. There are a lot of things I did in high school and college that she doesn't know about, but I want to tell her all of them. That has to count for something.

Darcy grins at me, a knowing look in her eyes. "Hopefully Houston doesn't put up a fight when he learns you are in love with Brooklyn. I literally just met him, so I can't say if he's a rational adult, but I like to see the good in people."

"That's a great way to live."

"I think so too. Thanks for the light bulbs, Jordan."

It's a clear dismissal, which is fine by me. I can tell Houston that I did what he asked, and I can tell him that Darcy is way cooler than any of the supermodels he's dated in the past.

"By the way," Darcy says as she follows me to the door, "word on the street is you're the only person who can make those famous waffles of yours."

"Why is that the word on the street?"

"Houston and I had a bit of a breakfast kerfuffle this morning. He mentioned something about almost burning his house down when he tried to make your waffles."

Ah, so that's why he texted me for the recipe this morning. Unfortunately for him, I had to guestimate some of the ingredients because I always go by texture, and Houston has never been much of a cook. He failed enough times in college that he decided to leave the cooking to me, and he's been able to afford to order in ever since.

"What, exactly, is a breakfast kerfuffle?" I ask as I step onto the porch and turn around to face her.

She grins. "Eh, it's nothing important. It was good to see you again, Jordan."

"You too. Don't let Houston intimidate you if he's being cocky. He likes to think he's a bigger deal than he is."

Something sparks to life in her eyes, like a bit of mischief that tells me Darcy can hold her own against my famous friend. She may be small, but she seems fierce. "Don't worry. I've seen his old man slippers. And I don't put a lot of stock into fame. He's just as human as the rest of us."

I can't help but laugh as I cross the shared porch to Houston's side of the duplex and let myself in.

"What?" Houston says immediately. Just as I suspected, he's standing in the middle of his living room, which means he's been pacing. His eyes dart to the wall he shares with Darcy. "What did she say?"

I shake my head. "You are in way over your head, Houston Briggs."

"What is that supposed to mean?"

"You'll understand when you're older. What's this I hear about a breakfast kerfuffle?"

Houston gives the wall another glance and then sighs, weariness settling in his shoulders again. "Nothing." He's quiet for a moment. "Practice was interesting today."

Okay, either he is finally hitting a point in life where he willingly jumps into vulnerable topics, or he's trying to change the subject away from Darcy. Or maybe it's both.

I glance at his left arm, which he holds stiffly at his side. He hasn't played a game in a week, so this can't be post-game stiffness. "You're injured more than what you've told me," I guess.

His jaw tightens. "Solano won't let me throw for at least a week, maybe more. The guys are going to start to talk."

He hasn't even told his team about his arm going out? I take a step closer. "Houston."

He sinks onto his couch, dropping his face into his hands and looking like his world is crashing down around him. "I don't know what I'm going to do, Jordan."

When I hear the pain in his voice, my stomach twists until I feel sick. Now is not the time to shake up his life even more, when he's already in danger of losing the one thing in his life he loves more than anything. I have every intention of building something with Brooklyn, but it might have to wait.

I hate that. I don't know if Brooklyn will agree with me, but what else can we do?

"Whatever happens," I tell Houston, "I've got your back. You know I do."

He gives me a strained smile that holds so much emotion. He's barely holding it together, and he's going to need a solid support system over the next couple of weeks as he figures out his future. I hope that future includes Brooklyn and me together, but we're going to have to take this one day at a time and hope for the best.

For tonight, I need to be there for my best friend.

Chapter Thirty-Four

Brooklyn

October 22

JORDAN DOESN'T COME OVER Monday night. He texts to tell me something came up, but when I ask if he needs anything, he doesn't respond. He's probably busy with work or his family, so I tell myself not to think too hard about it.

I don't do a very good job.

Tuesday I wake with the beginnings of a migraine. I take some meds to ease the sting and hope it doesn't get worse, and then I head to school.

Students bring their own balloons today, filling the school with helium voices until Principal Cheng announces that any balloons will be confiscated upon entering a classroom. I tell my kids that if they can accurately tell me why helium affects the vocal cords, they're allowed to answer with a helium voice, and I'm impressed by how many of them remember our gas lesson.

By the time I get home on Tuesday, I'm tempted to ask Houston if he's willing to reschedule our movie night. But it's been so long since I've seen my brother, and I've already had to wait all weekend. Granted, it was a pretty great weekend, but that doesn't make me miss Houston any less. Especially because Jordan has been able to spend so much time with him while I haven't even seen him.

After a dinner of cereal and soda, I curl up on the couch and search for something to watch while I wait. Before I can settle on anything, my phone starts ringing. Apparently I managed to take it off of vibrate because it blares "Immigrant Song" at full volume and scares the willies out of me.

Scrambling to grab it from underneath me, I immediately relax when I see that it's Jordan calling. I hadn't even noticed how tense I was.

"Hi," I breathe into the phone. "How are you?" And could I sound more breathless? Probably not. When did my ringtone even change?

Jordan is quiet for a second. "Did I scare you?"

I can hear the laughter in his voice, which sparks a blush. "No! Yes." I almost add, *I miss you,* but I don't want to seem too clingy. It's only been a day and a half since he came to help set up Mark's birthday surprise, and I don't want to come across as needy.

Jordan, on the other hand... "Man, I've missed you, Queens. Twenty-four hours is too long to go without you."

My heart settles in my chest, beating far more steadily now that I know he wasn't ignoring me on purpose. "I've missed you too. And it was twenty-eight hours."

He chuckles. "Not that you're counting or anything."

"Is everything okay?" I ask, though I feel a little silly asking it when I have no idea what actually came up last night. "I mean, with the stuff you had to do yesterday?"

"That's why I called. I know you're hanging out with Houston tonight, which he really needs, by the way, but I didn't want you to think I forgot you. Well, I did forget you, but..." He groans, and I do everything I can not to let my heart sink into my stomach. "That's not what I meant. I meant I got stuck on a single-minded track again. There was a whole thing with Houston last night, and then I had several consultations today with prospective clients, and I didn't realize what time it was."

He lets out a heavy sigh. "I'm sorry. I'm not making excuses, and it's killing me that I've already let you down."

"You didn't let me down."

"Please don't lie to me, Queens. I never want to hurt you, but I need to know when I do. You are more important to me than anything." He groans again. "And this is the kind of conversation we should have in person, not over the phone. I'm worried your technology curse will somehow interfere with what I'm trying to say."

He doesn't have to worry about technology making it difficult to understand him; my tears are doing that just fine on their own. I sniffle, wishing I hadn't forgotten to replace my tissues when they ran out the other day. I keep a box by the couch because I have a bad habit of crying during emotional movies.

"Brooklyn?" Worry colors Jordan's voice.

"I'm fine."

"You don't sound fine."

"No one has ever told me I'm important before." I almost laugh at how pathetic that sounds. "You just caught me off guard."

"Now I really wish I was there instead of on the phone. You *are* important, Queens." He says this with utter sincerity in his voice, and I clutch my blanket tighter around me as he keeps talking. "You've always been important to me, from the day you smiled at me when Houston introduced us. I didn't know it then, but I needed you in my life. My track record the last few days hasn't been great, and I know you deserve better. Will you give me some time to work on it? I don't want to let you go just because my idiot brain overtakes my heart. You're too special to give up."

Who needs a blanket when they've got Jordan Torres to surround them with the most meaningful compliments I've ever heard. *Important, needed, special.* Things no guy has ever tied to me and meant it as deeply as Jordan seems to mean it.

I'm probably grinning like an idiot as I press my phone harder against my ear, as if that might make Jordan feel closer. "Remind me again why I'm hanging out with Houston instead of you tonight?"

Jordan laughs. "Because you love your brother."

"Yeah, well, I love you more." I drop my phone as soon as those words register in my mind, and in the process of trying to catch it, I accidentally end the call, leaving my home screen staring up at me and my heart pounding an erratic rhythm that is sure to end my life because no one can survive this kind of arrhythmia.

"Did I just tell Jordan that I love him?" I ask my empty basement, as if someone might be there to respond. "Over the *phone*?"

I wait in horror for Jordan to call back, but the call doesn't come. What does that mean? There are too many scenarios, most of which involve him being too stunned to react, which could be good or bad. I should probably call him and explain, but I don't feel confident in his side of things to know what to say, so I'll wait for him to make the first move.

But he doesn't do it. Maybe he doesn't feel the same way. Maybe he *does*. Maybe he doesn't think I meant it. Maybe he is in his truck, driving over here even though Houston is showing up any second because he can't go another minute without telling me that he loves me too and he's the type of guy who would want to say that in person so he can say it with a kiss.

I get so caught up in that last fantasy that when I open the door after someone knocks, I am genuinely disappointed to see Houston standing on the other side.

He, on the other hand, grins wide and wraps me in a huge bear hug. "Blondie!"

I can't help but laugh at his enthusiasm, instantly feeling guilty about my disappointment. I can go one night without seeing Jordan—okay, two—when I haven't seen my twin in over a month. "Nice of you to finally stop by," I tell him.

"Uh, you know exactly where I live, you dork. And you're the one who picked tonight."

I can't argue that. "Did you eat yet?" I'm already hungry again despite eating a giant bowl of cereal, which is something I will never tell Jordan or he'll gloat about being right. Or maybe I *should* tell him so he'll cook me dinner more often.

Houston laughs and heads for the couch. "I already have Mexican on the way. I wasn't about to risk my dinner on the hopes that your technology curse is taking the night off." He flops into his usual spot, which happens to be the side of the couch Jordan has spent a lot of time on recently. My stomach churns a little. Do I tell him that I might be in love with his best friend?

There's no *might*. My admission to Jordan may have caught me off guard, but I meant it. I love him. Outside of my family, he knows me better than anyone, and there are even things he knows that my family doesn't. I trust him more than I've ever trusted anyone in my life, especially after his phone call today.

We both have things to work through, like his workaholic tendencies and my insecurities, but we can deal with those together and be stronger.

As I head to the fridge to grab a couple bottles of water, my phone buzzes in my hand.

Is that because he doesn't see this going anywhere? I shake my head as soon as that thought hits me. At what point will I stop immediately thinking the worst in every situation?

"Are you coming, Blondie?" Houston asks, looking over at me with an eyebrow raised.

I hold up my phone, glad he's too far away to see who I'm texting. "Sorry, I just need to finish this conversation."

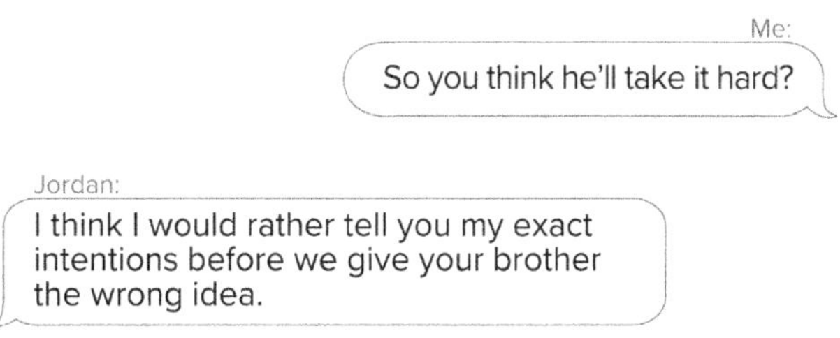

My stomach does a flip, making me dizzy. That could mean any number of things, and my mind wants to go straight to the bad stuff. He wants to keep things casual. (Possible, with his dating history.) He sees me as just a friend. (That one is ridiculous, with the way he kissed me.) He is ready to drop to one knee and ask for forever. (As laughable as it is improbable.)

He texts again before I can fall into a downward spiral.

Jordan:

I'm in this, Queens. You and me. I want to make sure you know that beyond a doubt before we flip Houston's world on its head. Okay?

I smile, feeling the weight of his words. It's not *I love you,* but it's so much better than anything a man has ever said to me.

Me:

Okay. Will I see you tomorrow?

Jordan:

I have a lot of organizing to do with work, but I'll text you as often as I can and hopefully get enough done by the time you're done with school.

Jordan:

And if you don't hear from me, please text me. I want to think you'll never be far from my mind, but I told you the other day. I'm a mess.

Me:

We can be a mess together.

Is that a weird thing for me to say? It should bother me that Jordan knows he'll slip again, but I have also been on my own long enough that I don't need constant communication. Maybe a little too used to it... We just have to find a balance and help each other out as we figure out this relationship.

Jordan sends a GIF of someone making a heart with his hands, and I fight against my grin. I don't need Houston demanding to see what I'm smiling about, as I know he will.

By the time I make it back to the couch, Houston looks like he's fallen asleep with his head tilted on the back of the couch. His initial exuberance has made way for exhaustion, which has me thinking more deeply about what Jordan said about last night. Whatever came up that kept him away, it had to do with Houston.

"Rough day?" I ask.

He opens his eyes with a groan. "You have no idea. How are the kids this year?"

As I settle on the couch, I narrow my eyes at him to tell him I won't let him get away with changing the subject.

He squirms.

"You want to talk about it?" I push.

He clearly doesn't, but Houston knows me too well to think I'll drop the subject. "There's a journalist who won't get off my back."

If it's that brunette one who did the interview after the game, the one he ran away from, I'm going to be way more intrigued by this problem than Houston will like. When I ask if it is, he gets an odd look in his eyes, and I have a feeling Houston is going to be distracted by more than just his pretty neighbor, Darcy.

Looks like there may be a story brewing with Tamlin Park as well.

Chapter Thirty-Five

Brooklyn

October 23

"Hey Briggs, do you have a second?"

I've just finished inputting some grades during my prep period, though I need to head to the auditorium for a school-wide assembly. Hard to do when Mark is standing in my office doorway. He must have just sent his class down the hall, though I have no idea why he's here. We haven't even made eye contact since Monday.

"Sure," I tell him anyway, though I stand up and gesture that we should start walking.

Thankfully, he follows me out to the hall, talking in low tones as we go. "Cheng is announcing the Teacher of the Year."

I nearly trip over my own feet. "Is she?"

He nods, eyes on the ground. "And I just wanted to say, no matter which of us gets it, I'm sorry for what I said on our date. I shouldn't have asked you to take your name out of consideration. That was...awful."

I wince. He's not wrong, but I'll feel mean if I agree with him. "You want to become a professor, right?"

He shrugs. "Not really. It's more of the...the *more*, I guess. My mom is always telling me that I need to move up in the world if I want a woman to stick around, you know?"

I don't know, but I can understand the pressure of living up to someone else's standards. "You should do whatever makes you happy, Mark. *With* whoever makes you happy. You're single now, but you won't stay single for long."

"You didn't." He nudges my shoulder with his.

Aaaand I'm done with this conversation. I'm still annoyed with him for leading me on and for the way he reacted to Mateo pointing out his mistakes, so I'm not about to talk about dating or Jordan or anything, really. Plus, I've still got that underlying migraine from yesterday, and it seems to throb with more *oomph* the longer this conversation goes.

"Well, Jaydin is saving me a seat," I tell him and step to the side so a few students fill the space between us as everyone piles into the auditorium. "Good luck."

Though he frowns, as if he doesn't understand why the conversation ended, he gives me a single nod. "You as well, Briggs."

I get a text right as I sit down next to Jaydin. Though she's looking between me and Mark, who found a seat a few rows ahead and to the side of us, she thankfully doesn't ask any questions. I know she wants to.

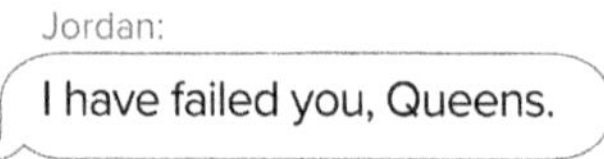

It's the first text he's sent me all day, something I am all too aware of, though I've tried to keep myself distracted. With this assembly, we've had shorter classes today, so that helped me stay focused on teaching. Micah called me at lunch, though she kept bringing up Jordan and reminding me that he hadn't reached out yet. She keeps trying to convince me to bring Jordan to the trivia night we're going to with our stepsister and her husband tomorrow, even though Houston will be there. Micah has her own love life to worry about with her coworker, Fischer, but instead she keeps trying to butt into mine.

Assuming I have a love life. At the moment, it doesn't feel like I do. Yes, I could have sent Jordan a text to remind him of my existence, but should I really have to do that?

Last night during the movie, Houston was completely distracted and kept thinking about his neighbor, Darcy. They've barely spoken to each other and have known each other for less than three days, but he couldn't get her out of his mind. What does that say about Jordan that he can't remember to send me a good morning text or ask me how my day is going?

He texts again as if in answer to my question.

> **Jordan:**
> In my defense, I thought about you in the shower this morning.

> **Jordan:**
> Not in a creepy way!

> **Jordan:**
> It was more of an "I wonder if Queens still steals secret sniffs of my body wash" kind of way.

"Um, what?" Jaydin says, grabbing my phone out of my hand. "I wasn't actively trying to read your texts, but girl! What is this?"

The texts keep coming, and we read them together because this is easier than trying to tell her all of the details while Principal Cheng starts up the assembly, telling the students about all of the different teacher awards they will be giving out. Based on the low murmur of conversation around us, the students don't care in the slightest. It's too early in the year for them to have any preference on who gets what.

> **Jordan:**
> I thought about you when my mom asked how Houston's sister was doing while I was on my way out the door. She likes you, by the way. I like you too.

> **Jordan:**
> I thought about you while I was mowing a lawn because I remembered you haven't changed your phone background to my abs yet. I can do that for you if you want. I would hate for you to accidentally delete my picture, though I'm happy to provide another one if you do.

> **Jordan:**
> I thought about you while I ate lunch with my coworker Rick while we scoped out some new hires. He thinks you're too good for me. (He's right.)

"Why did you fail to tell me hottie landscaper has mad game?" Jaydin asks in a whisper. "I'm sweaty just reading his texts!"

I throw my elbow into her ribs. "Would you stop?" She's not wrong, though. My face is burning, and I can only imagine how much worse my blush would be if he was saying this to me in person.

"Hey, I'm living my love life through you right now!"

"And for our Humanities, we present the Teacher of the Year award to Mr. Brunner!"

I look up as Cheng applauds along with the half of the school who are actually paying attention. She hands the history teacher a plaque when he arrives on the stage, and they take a picture before he returns to his seat.

"Does anyone else find it weird that they are doing this two months into the school year?" Jaydin says as she claps politely.

"Very weird," I agree, though I'm not going to question it. If it means I can work the fellowship at the university next summer, I'll take it.

"For Science, Technology, Engineering, and Mathematics," Cheng says, and my heart skips a beat while all of my senses go into overdrive. Mark looks like he's holding his breath. This is it. "We present the Teacher of the Year award to Mrs. Kim!"

What? A buzzing fills my ears as Sonya Kim hobbles up to the stage with her cane. She teaches Physics, but I had no idea she was even a candidate.

"Did you know she home-tutored, like, six different kids last year?" Jaydin says to me as she claps. "*And* she helped that Meyer kid set up a fundraiser so he could pay for college. I want to be Sonya when I grow up."

Mark glances over at me, his brow furrowed, and I'm probably matching his expression. I can't even be mad about Sonya winning because she's an incredible teacher and an even better human being.

That doesn't mean I'm not disappointed.

The assembly continues until all of the awards have been given out, and then Cheng drones on about something. I don't even know what. I'm too numb to care.

This was my one chance. My one chance to move back into research where my passion lies. And now I don't know what to do. Will I have to move out of state? I don't think I would be brave enough to leave my family. Everything I've ever known is here. My brothers and sister, my mom's grave, even my dad, though it's been a few years since I last visited him in prison. He's due to be released any day now, and weirdly I want to see him. I want to tell him that I turned out okay despite his inability to be a father.

What I don't want to tell him is that I've failed in the one promise I made to my mom. It was years after she died, but I promised her that I would find a way to save others from the heartbreak of terminal cancer.

That's never going to happen now.

Jaydin still has my phone, and I am vaguely aware of her typing out a text and glancing at me every couple of seconds. When she hands it back, I look down and read what she sent.

Me:

> Hey Hot Landscaper Man, this is Jay, Brooklyn's friend. She just found out she didn't get teacher of the year and she needs you.

Jordan texts back immediately.

Jordan:

> Tell me where to be and I'm there.

Chapter Thirty-Six

Jordan

I GENERALLY LIKE TO drive fast, but I hit new records as I make my way to the Sun City Cemetery, even though I know Brooklyn still has to finish out the school day. I got that text from her friend and immediately panicked, knowing how much Brooklyn wanted that award. She didn't even talk about it that much, but I saw it in her eyes.

To my surprise, Brooklyn's car is already parked at the cemetery when I pull up, even though it's only been twenty minutes since I got the text telling me to meet her here. I don't know who sent it, Brooklyn or Jay, but I wasn't about to ignore it.

She's not in her car, so I start making my way into the span of graves, toward the field of sunflowers that rests behind the cemetery. Houston has mentioned that field before, so I have to guess that their mom is back in that direction. Though there aren't many flowers left, it's enough to guide me.

To my relief, I find her quickly, sitting in the grass and hugging her knees as she stares at her mother's headstone. I pick up my pace, and when she turns at the sound of my footsteps, my heart breaks. She looks completely miserable.

"Brooklyn," I say and drop to my knees at her side.

She immediately falls into my arms. She isn't crying, but I can feel it ready to break loose as she trembles against me. "You came," she whispers.

I hate that she wasn't sure if I would. "I will always come when you need me. And when you don't. I may come even when you don't want me to."

She lets out a single, miserable laugh. "I don't know why I'm so disappointed. It's not like I thought I had a chance."

"You had every chance, Brooklyn. And you would have deserved it."

"I don't know what to do now. I'm never going to get a job in research."

I wonder if she really tried every lab in Sun City. We're a decently sized city, but I have no idea how many research facilities there are, particularly centered around cancer treatments. With how hard Brooklyn took this loss, I would imagine she really has tried every avenue.

If her stupid ex-boyfriend hadn't gotten jealous and blacklisted her, maybe she wouldn't be in this mess. There has to be someone who can take another look at her resume. Someone who might be willing to overlook the questionable circumstances from when she got fired. If I could get in touch with the right person...

But why would anyone listen to me? I'm personable, but charisma only goes so far in this kind of situation. What Brooklyn needs is someone with *influence*.

I curse under my breath. I know exactly the man who has that kind of influence, and he's even in the right field. But that's not a conversation I am eager to have. Still, for Brooklyn, the awkwardness would be worth it.

Brooklyn shifts in my arms, pulling my focus back to her as she sits back. "I was ten when my dad went to prison."

I blink. Not only do I know this information from Houston, but I also have no idea how it is relevant to Teacher of the Year.

Sighing, she starts pulling up handfuls of grass and setting them in a pile between us. "When we went back to live with Lloyd, I was so afraid of him. I mean, you've met my stepdad. He's intimidating, and gruff, and he doesn't do well with emotional things."

I grab one of her hands, allowing her use of the other one to keep building her grass pile. I have met Lloyd, and I actually really like the guy. He's the reason Houston got a scholarship to USCB, and he always chatted baseball with us. Even let us throw parties at his ridiculously nice house. But that isn't what Brooklyn is trying to get at, so I keep silent, letting her take her time.

"It took me years before I asked him about my mom. Trying to remember what she was like, you know? I was only seven when she died, and there was so much I forgot. Lloyd...he had a hard time talking about her, but he sat down with me for hours and told me all his favorite stories. We talked about when she got sick and all the things she went through.

And I made a promise to myself that I would do whatever I could to make sure no one else had to go through that. I made a promise to *her*."

She turns and looks at the headstone, which has an old pot of daffodils that have seen better days. "Chad," she says, nodding to the flowers. "He comes all the time because he misses Mom more than anyone. How am I supposed to tell him that I can never work in research again? He doesn't even know why I left in the first place."

Honestly, Chad could probably fix her problem for her by digging into the company she was working for, but I know she'll never ask. Besides, she wouldn't want anything bad to happen to anyone. Not even James, her smelly sock of an ex. My way might not work, but I hope it does. Everyone would win.

This time I take up Brooklyn's other hand as well, scooting myself forward until my knees touch her legs. "I know not getting that award sucks, and that you're hurting. I know you're frustrated and feeling lost. I know there's nothing I can do or say that will make you feel better right now. But please don't give up hope. If anyone can change the world or make a difference, you can, and you never know what doors might open if you allow yourself a little patience."

Though her eyes are still watery—I don't know how she hasn't started crying yet—she offers up a tiny smile. "Sometimes when you say things, I want to believe you."

I grin, even though I don't feel like smiling when she's hurting this bad. "Only sometimes?"

One shoulder lifts in a half shrug. "All the time. When you say something, I can't help but think it's true."

"Hold on to that, then, and believe me. Please. Everything will be okay, even if it doesn't look the way you thought it would."

"You sound like Micah."

"Good. More people should see the world the way she does." I open up my arms, inviting her to fall into my hold again. She does, and we sit there for a long time in silence. Brooklyn is probably trying to figure out how to see light in her future, but I'm trying to figure out what I'm going to say to Jeff when I talk to him. Assuming he'll want to talk to me. We didn't exactly part on good terms, and I have a feeling I'm going to have to take a more cautious, indirect approach.

I like that even less than talking to Jeff directly.

After an hour or so, Brooklyn shivers as the sun sinks lower. A breeze has picked up, so a storm must be blowing in. "I should get home," she says.

"Let me make you dinner."

Thankfully, she smiles when I hop up and hold my hand out to her to help her up. "You do know the way to a girl's heart."

"Only yours," I argue. "I'm going to pick up some ingredients to make you dinner, and then we're going to watch whatever you want. I'll even read something to you if you want to close your eyes."

She cocks her head. "Why would I want to close my eyes?"

I thought that would be obvious. "Because you have a migraine."

"I do? I mean, how did you know?"

I tuck some of her hair behind her ear, relishing each touch of her soft skin. "Because I know you, Queens. I can see it in your face, even though you're trying to hide it. You don't have to hide when you're in pain."

Next thing I know, her arms are around my neck and she's kissing me, her lips frantically tugging at mine like she might find something if she searches deep enough. My brain short-circuits for a second, letting my instinct take over. I dive into the kiss like it's been days since I last touched her because it has. I need her mouth on mine like I need air to breathe.

Logic kicks back in a few seconds later, reminding me that what Brooklyn needs right now is hope. Kissing me might distract her for a little while, but that's a temporary solution. And while I would love to employ this tactic continuously, it's not a feasible option.

She needs a reason to see something bright in her future so she doesn't give up on her own brilliance.

I gently break away from her, regretting the loss of her kiss immediately. "I'll happily do that as much as you want tonight," I tell her, kissing her forehead because I want to kiss *something*, but her mouth will be too hard to give up again. "But first, you need waffles."

Her eyes go wide. "Your famous waffles? The ones no one can make as well as you?"

"Only my mother is better," I confirm. "Go put on some pajamas, and I'll follow you home once I have what I need."

Her eyes fill with tears again, though I don't think she's going to start crying. There's something shining in her eyes that looks a lot like love. "Home," she repeats.

I told myself I wouldn't tell her how I feel tonight, not while she's feeling so vulnerable. But I can't stop myself from smiling as I tell her, "Home is anywhere you are, Queens."

I walk her to her car, giving her one last kiss, and then promise to be at her house within the hour. It will probably be sooner, but I can't guarantee how my impending conversation is going to go, so I want to give myself enough time to present my arguments. I wait until Brooklyn drives away, and then I pull up the number I thought I would never call again.

She answers quickly. "Hello?"

"Hey, Natalie."

"Jordan. It's been a long time."

Considering we were married for several years, this last year has felt like a lifetime. "It has. Listen, I know I don't have any right to ask anything of you, but I need a favor."

She's quiet for a long time, and I don't blame her for being wary. I owe her so much already for what I did to our marriage, and I'm genuinely amazed that she answered my call in the first place. "What do you need?" she asks eventually.

I breathe a sigh of relief. It doesn't mean she'll help me, but her willingness to listen is more than what I deserve. "Is your dad still working with the Department of Health? I was wondering if he could talk to someone for me."

Chapter Thirty-Seven

Brooklyn

TRUE TO HIS WORD, Jordan arrives at my house about an hour after I leave the cemetery, laden with all sorts of fresh fruit, whipped cream, and other ingredients. There's a certain bounce in his step as he comes inside, and I wish I could share his optimism. Then again, he didn't lose his dream job today—his business is thriving—so he has a right to be peppier than I am.

Or maybe I have a right to be moody.

"You need all this to make waffles?" I eye the loaded grocery bags with skepticism. I've heard about these famous waffles of his, but I've never tried them. Houston swears they're made of something magical, though.

Jordan winks at me as he starts pulling ingredients out onto the counter. "Don't knock the process, Queens. After tonight, you'll be begging me to make these waffles for you every day."

"Would you?" The question comes out of me without my permission, but I absolutely want to know the answer.

Pausing, Jordan looks up at me with a veritable twinkle in his eyes. It's like he's remembering what he texted me earlier today and trying to decide if now is the time he wants to give me a response to what I said to him on the phone yesterday.

I don't know why I can read him so easily right now, but I'm not mad about it. I would love to understand him this well all the time.

He glances down at the carton of eggs in his hand, a debate clearly running through his mind. "How hungry are you?" he asks.

My stomach rumbles at the question. "I'm hungry for a lot of things." I obviously still need to work on my flirting skills, but I think he understands me because he sets the eggs on the counter and steps toward me with measured movements.

But he stops halfway across the kitchen, still several feet from me as he grimaces. "Nope," he says, almost to himself. "If I don't stay focused on these waffles, they're never going to get made." He turns back around and continues working.

A thrill runs through me, my heart beating with a little more enthusiasm. "Are you saying I'm distracting?"

He laughs without looking up from the eggs he has begun separating into a couple of bowls. "Brooklyn Briggs, you have no idea how distracting you are. I almost disemboweled a dinosaur last week because of you."

I"I have no idea what that means, but I like the way it sounds. Did you really think about me when you were in the shower?"

He snorts, again without looking at me. "Maybe."

I swear he blushes. It's so hard to tell with him, with his darker skin, but I definitely see some color in his face.

Considering I told him I love him yesterday and haven't really gotten his response, I'm feeling far braver than normal. I move slowly, inching my way into the kitchen until he finally notices me. He immediately freezes, eyes darting in my direction before they jump back to the eggshells in his hands.

"You're in dangerous territory," he says, his voice low and rumbly.

"Yeah, well, you interrupted our last kiss."

"You were feeling desperate."

I shake my head. Okay, maybe I *was* feeling desperate, but I'm not desperate now. I'm no longer wallowing in misery or stuck imagining my unfulfilled future, and that's all thanks to him. "Jordan Torres, you are the best thing to ever come into my life." I grab hold of his bicep and brush a kiss against his cheek. "And I meant it when I said I love you."

Dropping the eggshells into the carton, he grabs a towel to dry his hands and then takes hold of my head to pull me in for a kiss. If anyone feels desperate, *he* does as he kisses me with an earnest enthusiasm that steals my breath. If I thought our kisses were good before, I was deluding myself because this kiss is beyond delicious.

"I love you, Queens," he says against my mouth.

A little squeak escapes out of me. It's not at all flattering, but Jordan doesn't seem to mind. Doesn't stop my face from turning bright red, though. "You do?"

He chuckles, brushing his thumb across the heat of my cheek. "Yeah. But I wasn't about to say it in a text. And I was going to use the waffles to solidify my feelings, but I've clearly taught you too well. You are…" He presses a long and slow kiss against my mouth. "Temptation at its finest."

I am more than content to kiss this man all night long, but my stomach has other ideas. With his hand on my waist, Jordan feels every rumble, and eventually he is laughing too hard to keep kissing me properly.

"Okay," he says, holding his hands in the air and taking a step back. "I hear you." He says this directly to my stomach, though his eyes stray from my belly to other areas, as if he's cataloging all of my curves.

I press my hands to my burning cheeks. "What are you looking at?"

"You." He returns his gaze to my face, eyes locked on mine. "I love every part of you, Queens. Inside and out." He gives me a gentle smile. "Especially inside. Your soul is my favorite part."

I shake my head, trying to understand why all of this feels so unfamiliar and yet so comfortable at the same time. "How are you this good at flirting?"

He laughs. "Way too much practice. I had to distract myself from you somehow back in the day." But then his smile falls, and he takes a step back. "I love you," he repeats, but it almost sounds like a question. "How am I supposed to tell Houston?"

Oh. Right. "You're asking the wrong person." Then I remember what Micah told me earlier today, something I've been doing my best to ignore ever since we set it up on Saturday. "We're all going out to dinner tomorrow," I say slowly. "My stepsister Skyler is coming into town with her husband, Kit. Micah is bringing her coworker, Fischer." Assuming he ever responds to her… Apparently he's gone radio silent. "Maybe you should come and we can tell Houston there."

He seems to consider that. "You want to tell Houston that we're dating in front of his whole family?"

"Chad won't be there."

"That's a relief."

I smack his arm. "Chad will be fine with you and me. He already knows you. I just think… Kit—Skyler's husband—is really good with people, and Houston looks up to him a lot. If anyone can convince Houston that you and I aren't a bad thing, he can."

He nods, a smile slowly growing on his lips as he wraps his arm around my waist. "You think we're good together?"

"I think we're great together." I lean back before he can claim my mouth with a kiss. "But I really am hungry. Do I need to help you focus on these waffles?"

His laugh rumbles through his chest. "I don't think anyone has ever had to *make* me focus before. What are you doing to me, Queens?"

"Good things, I hope."

"Very good things."

He steals a quick kiss and then turns to his cooking, the biggest smile on his face.

I'm pretty sure I have one to match.

Chapter Thirty-Eight

Jordan

October 24

RAIN FALLS IN BUCKETS for most of Thursday, which means my team can't do their jobs. The boys seem glad for the break, which probably means I need to hire a couple more sooner than later, so I spend the morning sitting at the desk in my bedroom and calling up the guys Rick and I agreed would make good additions to the team.

They're both eager to join No Mow Problems and plan to meet me Monday morning to get started.

The afternoon involves another conversation with my ex-father-in-law. When we talked yesterday after Natalie told me she was having dinner with her parents and handed the phone over to Jeff, he seemed skeptical about my request but told me he would look into some things.

Today is a different story.

"I managed to get a copy of her resume," Jeff tells me. "If all of this is accurate, Miss Briggs is more than qualified to work in any lab she chooses. I want to hire her myself."

I grin, though he'd better not offer her a job because I don't want the risk of her moving to California. Then again, if she chose to go somewhere else, I would absolutely go with her. Rick would probably love being promoted to president of my company.

"I told you she was special."

"And you say she had a supervisor who has prevented her from finding a new position?"

"That's what she said, and Brooklyn is not the sort of person who would spread slander. I'm honestly surprised she told me about her supervisor in the first place. If anyone were to ask her about her termination, she would probably blame it on a problem with the research or something." I didn't mention anything about Brooklyn's romantic relationship with James, though I'm tempted to bring it up in case it makes a difference. But Brooklyn trusted me with that information, and I won't share it lightly.

Jeff hums, papers rustling in the background. "I didn't want to dig into the company who let her go, but I may need more information if I want to get to the bottom of this. If she was fired under false pretenses, I think—"

"I just want her to get a chance," I interrupt. "She won't want justice, no matter how much she deserves it."

"So, what do you want me to do?"

I wish I knew exactly what would work. "I want you to convince someone to look beyond the termination. To give her a chance no matter what they've heard about her. If she can get an interview, she'll blow them away as soon as she opens her mouth."

"I can do that."

"Thank you."

We're both quiet for a moment, but I know he has more to say. I spent enough time with Natalie's family to know when Jeff has thoughts on his mind.

"Natalie told me she's going to stop accepting alimony," he says.

She told me that too. Right after she told me she is engaged to a plastic surgeon in Los Angeles. They met through her father, and he absolutely dotes on her. She said she wants me to use that money on the woman who truly captured my heart. I don't know how she knew how deeply I'm coming to feel for Brooklyn, but she did.

"I never wanted to hurt her," I say quietly. It's the apology I should have given this man a year ago but was too much of a coward. "I loved your daughter so much, but I couldn't... I've had to do a lot of work on myself this year."

Jeff grunts. "Nat didn't inspire you like this one does. You're a good man, Jordan, and I'm glad you were smart enough to leave without a fuss. Natalie is happy now."

"I'm so glad she is."

"Hopefully you don't hurt Brooklyn too."

His caution sits heavy on my shoulders, adding to the weight of the fears I already carry. "I have every intention of giving her the life she deserves and more. Starting with this."

"It took courage for you to ask this of me, and I commend that. But I hope you know that I will personally see to it that you pay for your mistakes if you mess up again. I'll be watching you."

Jeff isn't a frightening man by any means. He is in his sixties, five foot eight on a good day, a grandfather to six, and laughs more than he frowns. But I feel his warning in every inch of me. I definitely don't deserve this kindness he's showing me.

"Yes, sir," I say, letting my voice wobble so he knows that I understand. "Thank you."

"Hopefully we can get Brooklyn in a lab where she belongs. I'll keep you updated."

"Can you..." I pause, debating this. "Keep my name out of all of this. Brooklyn needs to know that she's getting this chance through her own merits, not because I know important people."

He chuckles. "Trying to pull a Mr. Darcy? I will do my best, but you know she's going to figure it out at some point."

I can't help but laugh at his reference, given that this is Brooklyn we're talking about. She would love to compare me to Mr. Darcy. "Probably, but for now, I had nothing to do with this."

"Done. Take care of yourself, Jordan. And tell your mom that I'm rooting for her."

"Thank you, Jeff. For everything."

Once we hang up, I sit in my chair and think about how Brooklyn might respond if she ends up getting a call from a lab. Will she doubt herself? I hope not. She has seemed more sure of herself the last little bit, but who's to say how she's really feeling after her disappointment yesterday?

I send her a text, even though she hasn't responded to any of my texts yet today. She's at school, so I don't blame her for focusing on her classes.

Me:

I noticed you took the leftover waffles for lunch today. I guess you liked them. ;)

To my surprise, she texts back immediately.

Then suddenly she's calling me.

I grin and answer, curious to see if she meant to do that. "Hey, Queens."

"Oh! I didn't mean to hit the call button."

Knew it.

"I don't mind," I tell her. "I'll listen to your voice any day."

"I have my last class starting in a minute, so I can't talk long."

"That's okay. Any minute I get with you is a good minute."

I need to figure out a way to get an accidental video call to be more of a possibility so I can see her blush. I'm sure there are some messaging apps that have a video call button in an inconvenient place.

"What have you been doing today?" she asks. "This rain has been crazy."

"Thinking about you, mostly." While that's true, I've managed to get a lot done, all things considered. Today has been a good demonstration of my ability to do my job while still constantly thinking of the moment I get to kiss Brooklyn again. I want to do my work faster so I can see her sooner, and that's a feeling I'm going to hold on to and never let go.

Brooklyn giggles. "You're full of it, Torres."

"I'm really not. I'm counting down the minutes until you're home from school and I can show you just how not full of it I am." I glance at the clock on my nightstand, grimacing when I realize it's barely after one. What am I supposed to do for the next two hours? Houston has a team thing this afternoon, and I basically have no other friends. I haven't minded before now because it was easy to get sucked into work.

"Hey, Queens?"

"Yeah?"

"Have I told you that I love you?"

She lets out a deep sigh. That had better be a *happy* sigh. "Not today you haven't."

"I love you."

"I love you too, Torres."

I shake my head, tempted to laugh. "I *really* like when you call me that."

She does laugh. "It's a good name."

I'm glad she thinks so, because someday I'm going to offer it to her. We can share it.

"I should go," Brooklyn says, though she sounds reluctant enough that I do a fist pump. Not that I don't want her to do her job, but I want to be wanted.

"Remember, I'm counting down the minutes."

"So am I."

"See you soon, Queens."

"Not soon enough."

I hang up with a contented sigh. We're still planning on talking to Houston tonight, so we can't stay in this bubble forever, but I'm not mad about where things are going. Brooklyn Briggs loves me, and I've never felt so happy.

"Have you had lunch yet, Danny?"

I yelp, flailing my limbs in the worst fight or flight response I've ever experienced. My chair tips, sending me toppling backward, and I crash to the floor in a heap. It's only when the proverbial dust settles that I see my mom standing in the doorway. She took the kids to the aquarium today, but apparently they've returned. I didn't even hear them, but I hear them now, playing some sort of screaming game downstairs.

Mom smirks at me, leaning on the door frame. "What has you so on edge?"

As I slowly get to my feet and right my chair, I try to find the best answer to give her. "I'm not on edge."

She narrows her eyes.

"Okay, maybe a little. I need to have a conversation with Houston tonight, and I don't know how it will go."

"Telling him that you're in love with his sister?"

My stomach drops like I'm on a roller coaster. "How long have you been standing there?"

Chuckling, she comes into my room and sits on the edge of my bed, gesturing for me to sit next to her. "Long enough to know you're happier than you've been in years."

I match her laugh. "Is it written all over my face?"

"It's written all over your soul." She places a hand on my chest, over my heart. "You weren't like this when you married Natalie. I know you loved her, but she didn't know you. And you didn't know her. You have a history with Brooklyn that can't be built with anything but time, and she's special."

My mom has only met Brooklyn a handful of times, but clearly that's enough for her to see everything I saw in the beginning.

"I wish I had realized what she meant to me years ago," I say, grabbing my mom's hand and giving it a gentle squeeze. "I feel like I wasted so much time not being with Brooklyn."

"Oh, Danny, you can't choose when you love. Just like you can't choose when you go through hard times."

I wrap her up in a hug when a tear slips from her eye. She's been so strong through all of her treatments, and I don't know how she does it. "I'm sorry I can't be home more often to help you through this, Mama."

She drops her head onto my shoulder. "You don't need to be sorry, Danny. Your father will be home soon enough."

"I don't just mean today. I mean all the time."

"So do I," she says with a laugh. "He's retiring."

The shock of that announcement hits me harder than it should have. Obviously I knew my dad would retire at some point, but in my head he would always be working because that's how I've always known him.

"Retiring," I repeat. "But he's only fifty-four."

She laughs softly. "We've saved up enough to last us until we can access our retirement fund. We'll be fine."

"But—"

"He wanted to spend as much time with me as he could, in case..." She doesn't finish that sentence, for which I'm grateful. None of us want to think about her losing this battle she's in.

I don't know why I'm having such a hard time processing this when it sounds like good news. *Great* news. Why did I think they were struggling financially? Why does it suddenly feel like I have a lot of money, what with Natalie no longer requiring alimony and my parents not needing any help? Why does this make me feel so untethered?

Mom gets to her feet and pats my cheek. "I told you, Danny. I don't need you to take care of me. Your dad and I will get through this together, like we've done everything else, and you will go build a life with Brooklyn." She heads for the door but pauses, looking back. "Houston will be fine. You've been friends for years, and you became brothers the moment you collided with each other on the field in tryouts and gave each other black eyes."

I snort a laugh. We'd both been going for the same fly ball and weren't looking where we were going. The collision hurt, but slamming into Houston meant I gained not only a new best friend but a friend in his sister as well. "You think he'll be okay with Brooklyn and me?"

"I think he doesn't get a say in what makes you happy. But how could he be anything but okay with it? You're the best of men, Danny, and you'll treat her right."

"Have *you* eaten lunch yet?" I ask before she gets very far. "I could make us something."

She smiles. "I would love that."

Maybe I don't need to take care of her, but I'm going to soak up every minute I can get with my mom before my dad claims all of her attention.

Chapter Thirty-Nine

Brooklyn

WHEN I HEAR THE knock at my door, I practically leap over my couch to get to it, speaking before I've even opened the door. "You're finally—Houston!"

Houston frowns and glances behind me, as if he's expecting to see someone else in my basement. "I'm finally what? Are you okay? You seem breathless."

I let out a nervous laugh. "I'm just excited about tonight." Excited and terrified, though it seems like our big conversation with Houston is going to happen sooner than later; Jordan will be here any second.

Houston flashes a grim smile as he steps inside and sits on the back of the couch. "Yeah, it's been a while since Kit and Skyler have been in Sun City. Think they'll actually want to do trivia night?"

"I didn't think we were going to give them a choice."

He laughs, but there's no real amusement in it. Something is wrong. My always sunny brother looks miserable.

"Hou? Are you okay?"

"Huh?" He looks up at me, eyebrows pulled low. "Yeah, I'm fine. Not sure how I feel about Micah bringing a boy, but..."

That can't be what's bothering him, but I'll play along. "I've actually met Fischer." And he is absolutely not a boy. Micah's coworker is a certifiable man who is deeply interested in our sister, whether she knows it or not. "He seems nice," I add. Maybe a bit gruff, but so is Chad. I only interacted with him for a minute or two when he dropped Micah off after the storm, but I think he would fit right in with our family.

Houston nods. "That's good. Too bad Chad isn't here to intimidate him, huh? It'll be weird doing trivia without him, but he seems to be doing well in Laketown. Think he'll ever come home?"

Okay, now I know something is wrong. Houston and Chad get along fine, but I don't know if I've ever heard Houston say anything about missing our brother.

I grab a pillow, holding it cocked and ready. "Tell me what's wrong, or I swing."

His eyes go wide and dart to the pillow. "What?"

"You heard me."

"I asked Darcy out and she said no." He says it quickly, all of the words smashed together like he's afraid of them. "And I am way more disappointed than I should be. Happy?"

I frown. "No, of course not. I'm sorry, Hou."

"I thought maybe there was something there, but when she said she had to work tonight, I—"

I swing the pillow right into his head, nearly knocking him back onto the couch

"Ow! What was—"

"Having to work is not the same as a rejection, you wingnut!" And here I was feeling sorry for him. "Have you never had someone tell you they're busy before?"

I'm concerned that Houston doesn't have a response to that, though I shouldn't be surprised. From the day he was drafted, he rose quickly to stardom, and I don't want to imagine the number of women who canceled plans or missed important events because Houston Briggs asked them on a date.

My door opens before I can explain to him how the real world works, and Jordan pokes his head into the basement. "I thought I saw your piece of junk truck out there," he says to Houston, though his eyes jump to me.

I shrug.

Houston sighs. "Apparently I'm overreacting, even though it feels like I'm going to be alone forever." He's definitely just being dramatic now. "What are you doing here?"

Jordan shrugs as he comes inside, keeping some distance between us. "I was in the area and thought I would give Queens a ride. I know how much she hates driving in the rain."

My jaw drops. How does he remember that? There was a single day in high school where I nearly got into a wreck when my car hydroplaned, and I've hated driving in the rain ever since. But it's not like I constantly talked about it. I don't even know if I ever told Jordan about that day. Why would I?

Jordan must see my question because he grabs his phone and types something out. My phone buzzes a second later. "Why are you going to be alone forever?" he asks Houston.

While Houston bemoans Darcy's job, I open Jordan's text.

> Jordan:
> You always made Houston drive places whenever it rained. I connected the dots.

With my heart swelling and threatening to spill out through my eyes—that's a metaphor that doesn't make a lot of sense, despite the accuracy of the feeling—I type back my own text, taking care that every word is right.

> Me:
> I don't know how you see me so well, but I love you for it.

Jordan glances at the message on his watch and smiles wide. "Houston," he says, though he throws a glance at me, "I hate to break it to you, but most people have real jobs. And rent at your place isn't cheap. I'm sure she would have come if she could. Besides, I thought you had a thing going with that reporter, Tamlin."

Houston's eyes nearly bug out of his head. "Are you kidding me? I hope I never have to see that nightmare of a woman ever again."

Tamlin Park is at the bar.

Houston is the first to see her after we settle in at a table at Grey Bird Tavern after dinner. In the middle of our conversation, he chokes on his drink when he catches sight of her sitting at the bar and chatting up a man who looks like he wants to eat her. That doesn't stop my brother from marching right up to her and starting a conversation.

"Okay, what am I missing?" Kit asks, eyes locked on Houston's glower. He may be new to the family—he got together with Skyler last summer—but he tends to pick up on the little things. That makes him dangerous.

Jordan and I silently decided Houston is in no frame of mind tonight to deal with our new relationship, which means we've been trying to stay away from each other since showing up at the restaurant. It isn't easy, and we keep accidentally bumping into each other or brushing hands, and it's driving me crazy. Jordan's temptation lesson keeps popping into my head, and at some point I need to tell him that he was totally right. Every time he touches me, my whole body yearns to lean into that touch.

But that's not what Kit is asking about. My stepsister's husband is perceptive, but I hope he's not *that* perceptive.

"He did an interview with Tamlin the night of the final game," Jordan says with a chuckle. His knee shifts, bumping into mine.

I bump his knee right back, mostly to remind him to keep it to himself. I'm glad Fischer got showered with Houston's soda when he choked and went to clean up with Micah; those two have been doing nothing but giving each other eyes all night. Dinner was a nightmare, watching them shoot furtive glances at each other while Kit and Skyler have never been shy about their affection for each other. Houston's the only one on his own, and it's for that reason Jordan and I are stuck pretending we wouldn't rather be making out on my couch instead of pushing each other away.

"What's wrong with an interview?" Skyler asks. "Also, she is gorgeous."

"She's known for taking down athletes," Kit says with a shrug. "Though, I doubt Houston has anything to hide from her, so he should be safe."

Jordan tenses up, failing to hide his scrunched up grimace.

Kit sees it too. "Does he have something to hide, Jordan?"

Jordan grabs his soda and starts chugging. *Subtle.*

"Are you and Houston going to make a bet on the trivia game?" I ask Kit, changing the subject even if I want to know the answer to his question just as much as he does.

Kit laughs as Skyler rolls her eyes. "Think he would go for it? He seems a bit distracted."

Distracted is an understatement. I've never seen Houston this focused on another person before. Though they're too far away to hear what they're saying, the conversation looks intense.

"Does he want to kill her or kiss her?" Jordan asks, tilting his head. "I genuinely can't tell."

"Could be both," Kit says with a laugh. He turns back to me. "What kind of bet would really get to him but not hurt you? It needs to be a team thing." He looks at Tamlin again, mischief in his eyes.

Jordan catches on quickly. "We're short a player, aren't we? I want the quick-thinking reporter on my team. Queens?"

I usually don't care for Houston's antics with Kit, but this sounds like a great way to bring my brother down a peg or two. He's never going to settle down if he doesn't have to work at a relationship, so it would be nice if something didn't come easy for him.

"Loser has to wear a Halloween costume of the winner's choice," I suggest as Jordan hops up and heads straight for Houston and Tamlin. "But don't make it too terrible."

Kit hums thoughtfully. "What will Jordan think of that one? Or will he not care because he loves you too much to say no?"

I shake my head. "You are creepy sometimes, Kit Morgan."

"No, you're just not subtle," Skyler says. "Even I can see the way you two look at each other."

"Houston doesn't know," Kit guesses.

"Not yet."

And that's as far as the conversation goes because Jordan and Houston are returning, Tamlin Park right behind them. I have a feeling it's going to be a long night.

Chapter Forty

Jordan

I'm a flirt. I'm not ashamed of that fact, and I will probably never change. (The only difference being I will only flirt with Brooklyn from here on out.) But as I sit next to Brooklyn during the most intense trivia game I've ever seen, I have to wonder if I've been doing it all wrong.

Houston and Tamlin haven't looked away from each other the entire night. I brought her into the game because I thought it would be entertaining to watch Houston squirm, but this isn't squirming. This is the most sexual tension I've ever seen, and I can barely concentrate on the trivia game as I watch the two of them go head-to-head.

It's a miracle they haven't started going mouth-to-mouth.

"There's almost no point in trying to answer any questions, is there?" Brooklyn whispers to me. She leans in close to say it, which means her breath brushes my neck and makes me shiver.

She's the other reason I haven't been able to concentrate on the questions tonight. We're trying to play it cool, but we're both incredibly bad at keeping our hands to ourselves. Take now, for example. Brooklyn doesn't need to touch my arm to talk to me, but she does, her cool fingers wrapping around my forearm and leaving a scorch mark behind.

And I have to lean close to her to respond so Tamlin, who's sitting next to me, doesn't hear me, which means my shoulder brushes Brooklyn's. "No one would guess he was pining over his neighbor two hours ago," I mutter.

"It's not Victoria Falls," Houston says sharply, eyes narrowed at Tamlin.

She folds her arms, gaze just as fiery. "You're saying I'm lying?"

"I'm saying you're wrong."

"Do you want to win this game or not?"

Before Houston can respond, the quiz master reveals the answer as Victoria Falls, and we lose the point because Houston wouldn't let Tamlin write it down.

"I know there's a bet riding on this game," I mutter to Brooklyn, "but I can't decide if I want to win or lose at this point."

"Tell me about it." She suddenly grabs my hand, though she's so focused on her brother that I'm not entirely sure she realizes she does it.

We're pretty well hidden under the table, and Houston is far too occupied with the stunningly beautiful reporter that I doubt he remembers we're even sitting here. That makes it easy to lace my fingers between Brooklyn's and hold her a little tighter.

With Houston so caught up in his supposed hatred of Tamlin—it looks more like attraction from where I'm sitting—I don't think we'll be talking to him tonight. I'll need to take every moment with Brooklyn that I can get.

Houston answers a question right, gaining us a point, but we're still behind Micah's team. None of the other teams in the bar are anywhere close to us in score, so it's down to the two of us, but I have no idea who's going to actually win. Houston and Tamlin seem determined to prove they're the smarter person, but Kit has a winning look in his eyes. This could go either way.

Brooklyn leans in again, this time resting her head on my shoulder until she's done speaking. "I don't know about you, but I think they just need to kiss already."

I snort a laugh that's loud enough to draw Tamlin's attention my way. Thankfully, the quiz master announces a ten minute break before the lightning round.

"I'm going to go to the ladies' room," Tamlin says, though her eyes linger on Brooklyn and me.

Houston breathes a sigh of relief as soon as she's gone. "Finally."

"You okay there, Texas?" I ask with a laugh, using the nickname his siblings gave him long before I met him.

He rolls his eyes and steps over to talk to Kit, who looks like he's having the time of his life tonight.

"Enjoying yourself?" Kit asks him brightly.

"Not as much as I want to be," I murmur to Brooklyn so only she can hear me. Houston seems pretty focused on his conversation, so I pull her hand into my lap and start massaging her palm. "What about you?"

She turns a delicious shade of pink, her eyes on Houston. "The night could be better, but that doesn't mean I'm miserable. It's hard to be miserable with you around."

I can't help myself; I press a kiss to her temple, breathing in the smell of her shampoo. It's something floral. Jasmine, maybe? "Have I told you yet that I love you?" I whisper.

Her eyes dart to Houston, who is now focused on his phone and oblivious to the world, and then she captures my mouth with a quick kiss that leaves me reeling. I don't know if it's the forbidden flavor of it or the fact that Brooklyn was the daring one instead of me, but I'm left completely speechless.

"It's probably his neighbor," Brooklyn says over my head, speaking to Micah's table. How in the world was she paying attention to their conversation when I'm over here ready to throw caution to the wind and kiss her again? Let Houston see.

"His neighbor?" Micah says. "Isn't his neighbor married? And, like, fifty?"

Ah, they're talking about Houston, who can never pay attention to anything but his phone. Multitasking is not his forte. He's grinning at the screen, clearly enjoying himself. He must be texting Darcy. "New tenant moved in this week," I explain. "Her name is Darcy."

And while Houston is obviously interested in Darcy, that doesn't change his burning attraction to Tamlin tonight. He'd better be careful.

If he really is texting his new neighbor, he needs to stop looking at Tamlin so intently as she returns from the restroom and gracefully slides into her seat. That will only get him into trouble, with or without Darcy in the picture.

There's something oddly familiar about Tamlin, though I can't figure out what it is. Maybe I've just seen her on TV often enough to have her in my head. Regardless, I don't exactly have the mental bandwidth tonight to contemplate the reporter and her unexplained presence. That will have to be all Houston.

"Are you in this, Briggs?" she says when Houston takes his seat. "I can't keep carrying the team forever."

I can't stop the laugh that bursts out of me, and I'm glad to hear Brooklyn laugh as well so I feel like less of a jerk. Houston really has met his match, though I didn't think anyone could so easily ignore his fame.

Houston doesn't appreciate our amusement, throwing us glares before returning his full attention to Tamlin. "Oh, I'm in this."

"And now for our lightning round!" the quiz master says. "Sports."

Houston and Tamlin both go on high alert. Houston has lived and breathed sports for the last decade and a half, but Tamlin's entire job is based around knowing sports facts. They're like two fighters in the corners, ready for the bell to tell them they can start throwing punches.

Brooklyn lets out a little sigh and takes my hand again. "At least we're going to win, right?"

"Speak for yourself," Kit says, though he's glancing between Houston and his nemesis with doubt in his eyes.

"Who has won more grand slam titles?" the quiz master says into his microphone. "Venus or—"

"Serena!" Tamlin looks a little too proud of herself as she shoots Houston a smirk.

"Next question. Who was the first US president to throw the ceremonial pitch in—"

"Taft," Houston says before the question is even finished.

"Okay," I mutter, "this is getting ridiculous."

The two of them answer question after question, rarely letting any other teams get a word in. And while tonight has been entertaining, I'm starting to worry about Houston. Tamlin looks like she just wants to stick it to Houston, but he seems to think beating her has some sort of significance. This is more than just a professional dislike.

When I glance at Brooklyn, her eyebrows are furrowed as she watches them go back and forth with no sign of slowing. If she's feeling nervous too, then it means I'm not making things up. She knows Houston better than anyone, and she has always been empathetic toward her brother, which means she'll be feeling his confusion all night.

On the final question, both Houston and Tamlin remain silent, staring at each other. Kit calls the answer, earning his team the winning point, but they don't seem to notice. They're too focused on each other.

"Didn't know that one?" Houston says gruffly. He sounds a lot like Chad right now, which isn't like him. He's usually such a carefree guy.

Tamlin tilts her head like she's studying him. "Hate to disappoint, but I don't know everything. I should go."

Houston follows her to the door, leaving me alone with Brooklyn for the first time all day. *Alone* being a relative term, considering the rest of her family sitting at the table next to ours. But Fischer and Micah seem fully occupied with each other—their relationship must be a new one—and Skyler and Kit get up to claim their trophy and take a picture for the Wall of Winners. Soon enough, Fischer and Micah head to the door to follow Houston.

My arm immediately wraps around Brooklyn and pulls her against me. "Much better." I nuzzle my nose into her neck, loving the way her pulse picks up speed.

"Houston is probably still outside," she warns.

"I don't care." I press a kiss below her ear. "I'm talking to him tomorrow. First thing in the morning. I need him to know that I am head over heels for you, Queens, and that is never going to change."

She gasps, and I don't think it's because of the kiss I place on her jaw. "Never?" she repeats shakily. "Do you really mean that?"

I know this relationship of ours is so new. I also know she's been burned so many times by bad relationships and sad excuses for men who didn't deserve her. As someone starts up a song on the karaoke machine in the back—an old familiar song from our high school days—I take both her hands and lift her to her feet.

"Dance with me, Queens."

She looks around. "What? Here?"

No one else is dancing—it's hard to dance to a drunken rendition of "All of Me" by John Legend—but I pull her into my arms anyway. This particular song feels like fate, and I can't let it go to waste.

It doesn't take her long to relax into me, dropping her head onto my shoulder and letting me sway with her to the music.

"I probably would have gone with the original if given the choice," I say quietly, "but this song is important. Do you remember why?"

She shakes her head. "No, why?"

"Because this is the song we danced to at prom when we were royalty together."

Her body stiffens in my arms, but only for a second. Then she leans into me more heavily, like she'll never be close enough.

I keep talking, hoping I can get the words out right. They're too important to mess up. "I lied to you the other day. When I told you I didn't cheat to get voted in as king? I knew you were going to be voted queen, and I couldn't stand the thought of someone else standing up next to you. Especially not your bumblebee of a boyfriend."

"Bumblebee?"

"Going from flower to flower. It's not my best work."

She hums into my chest. "I like it. I don't like that you lied to me."

"I know. I'm sorry. And I'm sorry I was too stupid to realize what you meant to me back then. I could have saved you from so much heartbreak because I never would have let you go once I had you."

I don't know if we would have made a good couple back then or what our lives would look like now if we hadn't spent so much time apart. What I do know is how little I want to waste any more time.

"I'll tell Houston everything, whether or not he's ready to hear it. I'm not letting you go now." I tip my head back, waiting until she looks up at me with watery eyes. "You'll always be my queen, Queens. Can I be your king?"

She snorts a laugh, her face turning red as she fights to control her expression.

I wrinkle my nose. "That's not the response I was expecting."

Covering her mouth with her hand, she shakes her head and takes a step away from me. "That was the cheesiest thing I've ever heard. Queen Queens! And you're no king, Torres."

"I'm not sure I like that I brought the old Brooklyn back," I mumble. "The quiet, people-pleasing you was much nicer."

She cups my cheek with her hand. "I don't need a king. Just promise to love me. That's all I need."

"Always."

I kiss her, silently promising that she will always be the first thing on my mind no matter what life throws at me.

Chapter Forty-One

Brooklyn

October 25

I'M PRETTY SURE I'M hallucinating. It's the only thing that explains why I have an email from the top research lab in Sun City asking if I'm available for an interview today because they had a spot open up on their cancer treatment team. Like, it is way too specific to be anything but a dream, and yet several pinches have yet to wake me up.

So I call Jordan, hoping he can jolt me into reality.

"Good morning, love."

"Is this real?"

I can practically hear him trying to make sense of that question. "Is what real? Me wishing the most incredible woman I know a good morning?"

Okay, I'm not mad about hearing him say that, but that doesn't make this moment feel any more real. I should really be getting ready for work, but on the slim chance that this email is not a fever dream, I need to respond as soon as possible.

"I just got an email from Hepburn Labs asking if I can come in for an interview today."

"Wait, really? Today?" He mutters something under his breath that I don't quite catch. "That sounds amazing, Queens."

"It doesn't make any sense. They told me years ago that I didn't have the resume they were looking for. They didn't even bother calling. Just sent a generic email."

"But they emailed you again this morning? Something must have opened up."

"That's what they said in the email…" I frown at my phone. Okay, yes, that's a generic job phrase, but Jordan doesn't sound nearly as surprised as he should. "Jordan."

"Queens."

I glare at my phone as if he can see me. "Did you get me a job interview?"

He laughs. *Hard.* "Brooklyn Briggs, I know you think highly of me, but how in the world would I set up an interview for you? I've never even heard of Whatever Labs. Are they here in Sun City?"

"Yeah."

He's right. How would a landscaper convince a prestigious lab to reach out to a nobody like me? He is charming, but that can only go so far.

"So, this *is* real?" I am too breathless to get the words out properly.

"Sounds like it. When do they want you to come in?"

I glance at the email again. "Eleven."

"Are you going to do it?"

How does he know I'm waffling? Not only is this a research job, which I'm desperate to get back to, but this is my *dream* job. This lab is the one I've wanted to work in since the moment I discovered its existence. They've had more breakthroughs in cancer treatments in the last decade than all the other Sun City labs combined. If I can work at Hepburn… I might actually be able to fulfill my promise to my mom.

"I want to," I say, my voice wavering.

"But?"

"But I'm in the middle of the school year. Middle of the first semester!"

"Maybe they'll be willing to wait or work you part time until your contract is up."

"I would have to get a sub today."

"I'll file that under lamest excuses ever. You probably already have sub plans ready to go in case you ever get a migraine because you plan for everything."

I groan. "I hate that you know me this well."

"You love that I know you. And I know you're going to take this chance because you're not the sort of person who backs down from a challenge."

He's right. How is Jordan always right? Though I feel pathetic admitting this while lying in bed, knowing Jordan is the only one listening makes it easier to say what I need to. "I'm scared, Jordan. What if they made a mistake?"

"They didn't."

"What if they decide they don't want me?"

"Then they're idiots. But even if they don't want you, it doesn't make you less of a person. It just means you'll have to wait a little longer for the next opportunity. But it will come, just like this one did."

Peace settles in my heart because—yet again—he's right. Maybe this position won't be the one for me, but that shouldn't stop me from trying. I will be guaranteeing failure if I don't show up.

"How did I get so lucky to have you in my life?" I ask, wishing he were here to hold me in his strong arms and shut out the world for a while.

Jordan chuckles. "You can thank your brother and his refusal to listen when I clearly shouted, 'I've got it!'."

I laugh.

We're both quiet for a moment, and I wouldn't be surprised if Jordan was thinking the same thing as me. "Do you think Houston will be okay?" I ask.

"We'll find out in about an hour. I'm planning to catch him before he heads to practice. And Brooklyn?"

I love when he uses my real name. It happens so rarely that I know there's always going to be something important with it. "Yeah?"

"Even if I show up at your house later with a black eye courtesy of your brother, it's not going to change anything. I love you regardless of his opinion of me. Hopefully he doesn't make me choose, but if he does, I'll choose you."

"If he makes you choose, he's going to have to deal with me," I reply. "I can come at him with a pillow if I need to."

The laughter that bursts out of him feels like it builds up my already bountiful hope. Neither of us is going to lose Houston today. We can't. We'll both do everything we can to help my brother accept this new reality.

"You two and your pillow fights," Jordan mutters. "I am so glad I never got involved in those because you are brutal."

"I had to stay ahead somehow."

"I'll keep you posted, okay? Promise me you'll do the same. I'll have my phone on full volume all day, waiting for your call."

If only he could come with me and hold my hand the whole time so I don't panic. Still, knowing he's just a phone call away will help. "I love you."

"I love you more. You're going to do great, Queens."

And because it's Jordan who says that, I believe him.

Chapter Forty-Two

Jordan

I DON'T KNOW IF I've ever been more nervous in my life, and that includes the day I proposed to Natalie, not knowing if she would say yes because we never talked about it. (That probably should have been a sign that we weren't meant to be, but I digress.) Standing on Houston's porch is a million times worse than that.

I know I'm being dramatic, but this conversation could end our friendship. He won't be rid of me, even if he wants to be, but I really don't want Houston to go from a friend who's practically a brother to a brother who's barely a friend. It's not like I set out to cause problems when I literally dropped into Brooklyn's life.

"You're delaying the inevitable," I tell myself, raising my hand to knock.

Before my knuckles make contact, I turn around and walk back down the porch steps.

My phone pings with a text before I reach my truck.

Queens:

Got my interview outfit all ready to go.

A picture quickly follows, one she took in her bathroom mirror. She's wearing a bright yellow blouse and navy slacks that hug her curves in a way that makes me tempted to drive over there and tell her how dang good she looks. It's not just the clothes. She looks *confident*, like nothing could go wrong with this interview.

I type out a text with shaking fingers.

Me:

You are the most beautiful, fierce, intelligent woman I've ever known. Knock 'em dread.

I hit send right before I notice the typo on that last word, and I bust up laughing, my tension dissipating with each breath.

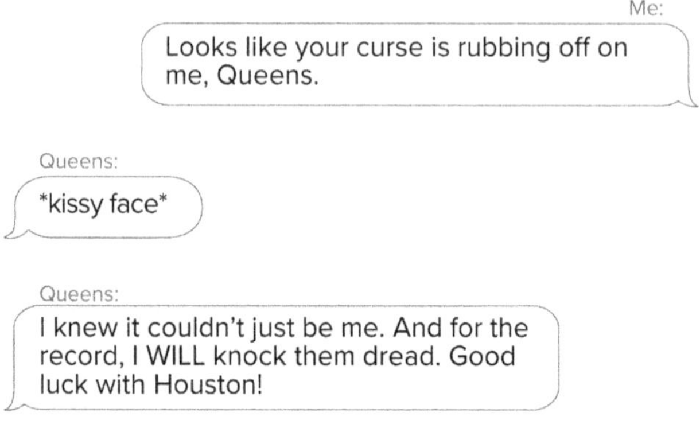

Though I groan, dreading this conversation as much as Brooklyn will be knocking dread into her interviewers, I can't be such a coward when she is facing a huge fear. Before I can talk myself out of this again, I march back up to Houston's door and unlock it, letting myself in.

"Honey, I'm home!"

There's a bang upstairs, followed by a loud curse and a string of muttered expletives that tell me I might have just woken Houston up with my shout.

I glance at my watch. It's almost eight, and Houston rarely sleeps past four or five. I've had enough four A.M. text conversations with the man to know he's as bad at sleeping as I am. Maybe worse.

Sure enough, he stumbles down the stairs a minute later in a pair of basketball shorts and a t-shirt that is both backwards and inside out.

Sleep lines crisscross along his face, while his blond hair—which is too long, in my opinion—sticks up in several different directions. He looks like a toddler who just woke up from the deepest nap of his life as he stares at me with one bleary eye.

I grin. "Good morning, sunshine."

Dragging a hand down his face, he looks around his living room as if that might explain why I'm here. "Jordan," he croaks.

"Late night?"

"Not really." But then his eyes land on a mostly empty to-go container of what I'm pretty sure is nachos from the tavern where we did trivia night, and he turns bright red, eyes wide. For a second, I think he might try grabbing it from the coffee table and hiding it behind his back, but he's not quite *that* asleep. "Um."

I nod toward the container. "Nachos? I *know* you didn't eat those because you ate half a plate by yourself at the tavern and were probably feeling that all night." He never eats junk food during the season, which means he can't tolerate much when it comes to the good stuff.

"Um."

My smile grows. "So who were the nachos for, I wonder? Could it be you had a late night rendezvous with your spunky neighbor?"

He opens his mouth, clearly about to argue, but then he sinks onto the couch with a heavy sigh. "I like Darcy."

I fake a gasp. "What? You? Like *Darcy*?" I don't dodge his foot quickly enough when he kicks, which means he gets it hooked around my leg and tugs me right off my feet. I land with a crash and a groan because that's twice in two weeks I've gone from standing to lying flat on my back. He and Rick would get along.

"Sorry," Houston says. He doesn't look sorry. In fact, he looks downright angry.

He's always so good-natured, which has made our friendship easy. This doesn't feel easy. Still on the floor, I frown at him. "Hey, sorry, I didn't mean—"

"When were you going to tell me you're dating Brook?"

I freeze. Literally, my whole body goes stiff and it feels like my heart stops pumping, sending a chill through me. "What?"

Houston clenches his jaw. "You. And Brooklyn."

"How did—"

"I saw you last night. When I went back into Grey Bird to get the nachos for Darcy."

I curse and slowly sit up. "I was going to tell you last night."

"Clearly you didn't."

"There was that whole thing with Tamlin."

"What does she have to do with you making the moves on my sister? My *twin* sister!"

I don't like having this conversation from the floor, so I stand up. So does he. "I didn't *make any moves*," I growl. "Stop making this sound like it's some sort of game."

"Isn't it?"

"No!"

Houston groans and runs his hand through his hair. "It's *always* a game with you, Jordan. Even your marriage only lasted a few years, so how long before you break Brook's heart like you've broken everyone else's?"

Were he anyone else, I would probably punch him in the face for that one. But this is Houston. My best friend, my brother, the only person in the world I care about as much as I care about my family. He's second only to Brooklyn, and I hate that this has turned into a fight. We're not the kind of friends who fight.

Ducking my head, I fold my arms and breathe until I'm calm again. "I am deeply, madly in love with Brooklyn," I say without looking at him. "I've always admired her, and I've spent the last two weeks relearning who she is and why she's the most amazing person I've ever known. The only reason—and I mean the *only* reason—we agreed not to tell you before now was because we didn't want you to think either one of us was going to abandon you. And I wanted to be sure I could be the man she deserves so I could promise you I will never hurt your sister. She's everything to me, Houston. She's my reason to look beyond my job and actually live again."

When I finally look up, Houston has fallen back onto the couch. He looks almost lost as he stares at me with his mouth hanging open. "You and Brook," he says eventually, as if testing the idea. "You're in love with her? How does she..."

I sit on the edge of the coffee table so I'm not towering over him. "She says she loves me. Heaven knows why."

"It's because you're a good guy, Jordan." He manages a fleeting half-smile. "You're way better than any of the jack—uh, jerks she usually dates."

"I appreciate that. But you have to admit, the bar was pretty low."

He chuckles. "Insanely low."

"Are we good?" I hold out my hand.

Houston eyes my hand for longer than I'm comfortable with, but then he slides his fingers along mine and turns it into a fist bump. "We're good. I'm still mad at you for not telling me."

"That's literally why I'm here this morning, Houston."

"Oh."

And I guess that's it? Honestly, it went better than I expected, though it wasn't easy, and it doesn't look like I'll be losing my best friend today.

I glance at the to-go container next to me. "So... You brought Darcy nachos last night?"

He's on his feet in a flash, grabbing the container and taking it to the kitchen garbage. "I'm not talking about it with you. You're going to read too much into things, and I need to get to practice."

"You're the one who said you like her," I remind him.

He pauses with one foot on the stairs to go up to his room. "I *really* like her." With the way his shoulders sag, that admission seems to cost him a lot. Darcy is so unlike the women he usually dates—women like Tamlin—that I would imagine he has no idea what to do with her. That could be good or bad, depending on where things go.

"You sure you don't want to talk about it?"

He glances back. "Not today."

I don't blame him. With my admission about Brooklyn on top of his shoulder stuff, he's dealing with enough this morning as it is. "I should go to work," I say. "Let me know if you need help with the Darcy situation."

He nods once.

"Thanks for not punching me for kissing your sister."

He shudders. "Don't expect me to get used to it anytime soon."

"Wasn't planning on it. And I meant it, by the way. When I said I'm not going to hurt her."

"Good."

I let myself out so Houston can process in peace, glancing at my watch as I head back to my truck. It's not even eight thirty, which means I could stop by Brooklyn's place and really wish her luck.

But something holds me back. While I know she would love the company and the reassurance that everything will work out, I think she needs to do this one herself. Jeff got her foot in the door—I need to send him a gift basket or something for making it happen so quickly—but Brooklyn will be the one to prove she's incredible.

Still, she could probably use an extra boost of serotonin to get her through the morning until her interview arrives.

Me:

Houston, we have liftoff. *GIF of a rocket launching*

Queens:

PLEASE TELL ME THAT'S A GOOD THING

Me:

All systems are go.

Queens:

I'm already freaking out about this interview, Torres. Don't make me interpret NASA references.

Me:

Houston is fine. We're fine. Everything is fine. And you're going to do great in your interview. I'll be rooting for you, Queens.

Chapter Forty-Three
Brooklyn

I GENUINELY DON'T KNOW how to feel right now. After several hours of building anticipation and nerves, all of this feels...anticlimactic? It's like putting baking soda and vinegar in a fake volcano to make it erupt but not realizing you actually grabbed flour instead of soda until it forms nothing but a goopy paste. Or maybe dropping Mentos in your soda can, only to realize you have lemonade, not Coke, so the big chemical-like reaction you were expecting just looks like a waste of food.

That's not accurate either. There's no waste, just...confusion.

That's probably the reason I'm sitting on a bench just outside Hepburn Labs instead of...literally anything else I could be doing right now.

He said you would say that. That sentence is stuck in my brain on repeat, and at the moment it's the only takeaway I've got from the interview. Well, that and a job offer because apparently Hepburn has been desperate for a biochemist for over a year.

I pull up the video chat app that I didn't know was on my phone until I was trying to waste time in the parking lot because I got here over an hour early. Playing around on my phone was a dangerous pastime, but it did lead me to finding this app.

I have a feeling Jordan installed it for me at some point.

As I call Jordan, I stare at my face on the screen. I look shell shocked, which feels pretty accurate.

The call connects, and Jordan's face fills the screen. "Hey, Queens! How did it go?" His smile is wide but not as bright as usual, and his eyebrows are pulled low. It's getting easier to read him, and I love that he's nervous for me.

"They offered me the job."

His jaw drops. "That's amazing! But...why don't you look excited? Do you not want it?"

"I accepted the offer. I'll work every other Saturday and during school holidays until June, and then I'll be full-time. It's my dream job."

He grimaces, shifting his hold on the phone. I can't tell where he is, just that he's leaning against a tree with the sun making his brown eyes glow amber. "I know I'm more outgoing than you, Queens, but you really don't look like you just got your dream job."

"Did you lie to me?"

"When?"

"When you told me you didn't talk to someone at Hepburn about giving me an interview."

Though his eyebrows shoot up, he looks more hurt than guilty. "You think I would lie to you like that?"

I deflate, my confusion only growing. I know he's right and I should be more excited, but I can't shake the feeling that there's something he's not telling me. "No, you're right. Always right. You would never lie to me."

"I've only ever lied to you once, Brooklyn, and I don't plan on doing it again. But I *might* know someone who works for the Department of Health and Human Resources," he says slowly. "Before you go over-thinking everything, even he doesn't have the kind of power to force anyone into emailing you." He winces as he looks at me. "Do you hate me? I just asked him to get someone to look past your termination and really look at your resume for what it is. That's it."

My stomach starts to fizz, bubbles in my chest making me sit up straighter. "That's it? They asked me about my job at the lab where James worked. They wanted to know why I was let go, and I told them things didn't work out with the research. Then one of them said, 'He said you would say that,' but I don't think I was supposed to hear that."

Jordan wrinkles his nose. "I guess Jeff must have passed on something I said to him. I told him you were too good a person to want to get revenge on James or anything like that."

There's definitely something happening inside me. Maybe my volcano isn't as dormant as I thought. My flour might have some baking soda after all. "So, I didn't get the job because you feel bad for me?"

His smile shifts, like he can see the change happening inside me. "I've never felt bad for you, Queens. You've always been leagues ahead of me in every way."

"And whoever this Jeff guy is, he didn't use intimidation to scare Doctor Anderson into hiring me?"

He snorts a laugh. "Jeff's my ex-father-in-law, and he's about as intimidating as Houston's old man slippers. But he's smart enough to recognize a fellow genius when he sees her resume. He said he wanted to hire you himself, but it wouldn't be in a lab, so…"

Yep, my vinegar has definitely reached baking soda, which means I'm ready to blow. Unfortunately for me, that apparently means bursting into tears and sending Jordan into a panic.

"Brooklyn! What's wrong? What did I say? What can I do?"

Answering him is going to be pretty much impossible with the way I've suddenly become a blubbering mess. My whole body is shaking from my sudden eruption of so much pent up emotion that I'll probably be lucky to be alive when it's over.

"Brook, baby, tell me how to get to you and I'll be there in ten minutes."

"Do *not* call me baby!"

"Wait, are you *laughing*?"

I try to take a breath but end up snorting. I drop my phone as another bout of laughter overcomes me, though it lands screen side up on the bench next to me so Jordan can still see me. Yes, I'm laughing and crying at the same time. That's where I'm at when it comes to emotional stability.

"Sorry," I gasp. "That's just the worst pet name. Anything but that."

He lets out his breath all at once and falls back against the tree, knocking a few dead leaves onto his head. "You're okay," he says, more to himself than to me. "Seriously, though, where are you?"

"Just outside the lab. But let me come to you. You're always the one chasing me, and I want to repay the favor."

"I don't mind chasing you, Queens. I can come—"

"Jordan."

He sighs. "I'll send you the address. Don't let your phone send you in the wrong direction, okay? I'll be on the line the whole time, until you're safe in my arms."

Twenty-one minutes later, I throw myself into Jordan's embrace outside of a huge house with a giant dinosaur-shaped bush, while his team cheers him on. He holds me like he's afraid to let go.

"I got my dream job," I say into his shoulder. It finally sank in on the drive over, after I got over the initial shock of it all, and I haven't stopped grinning ever since. One of the interviewers told me he'd wanted to hire me years ago but was overruled, and he was glad to finally get the chance to see what I can do.

Jordan holds me tighter. "I knew you would."

"Did you really talk to Natalie's dad to help me?"

He laughs. "It was awful. But yes."

"Because you love me?"

"Have I told you that yet today?"

Goodness, I didn't know anyone could feel this completely happy. I'm crying again, but it's still good tears. "You have," I say with a sniffle, "but you could tell me again."

He loosens his hold, glances at his team who are still watching us instead of trimming rose bushes, and then takes me by the hand and tugs me around a large hedge until we're out of sight of everything except a skeptical-looking garden gnome.

"One," Jordan says, gripping both my hands but taking a step back so he can get a good look at my outfit. "You are positively stunning, as always. Two." He moves in close and touches his forehead to mine. "I am so proud of you. You've earned this job. And three..."

He brushes his lips against mine with agonizing care, like he's savoring each taste. "I will tell you how much I love you every day for the rest of my life if you're okay with that."

My heart skips a beat. "Are you saying...?"

He smiles against my mouth. "I'm not proposing, Queens. Not yet."

"Yet?" I squeak back. Why doesn't that word scare me like it should? Probably because Jordan's kisses are incredibly distracting and his employees are hooting and hollering on the other side of the hedge and making this moment far less intimate than it could be. It feels oddly right. Plus, if he did ask me, I would probably say yes. I have no reason to panic.

Jordan finally picks up on the ruckus behind the hedge, and he groans. "This is why I wanted to come to you."

I wrap my arms around his neck. "You could have warned me they were here."

"Maybe I wanted to get chased."

"As long as you let me catch you, Torres, I'll chase you any day."

The smile that lights up his face is so much brighter than the sun overhead, though he looks a little bewildered. "You've already caught me, Queens. You caught me years ago. I'm sorry it took me so long to come back."

"I'm sorry it took me so long to let you in."

He catches my mouth with a kiss that makes me forget everything around me but him. This, right here, is perfection.

Chapter Forty-Four

Brooklyn

October 31

"This may never come out of my hair." I tug at the pumpkin string that's halfway plastered to my forehead, the rest of it tangled up in my locks. Using the microwave as a mirror isn't really helping me get it all out, but I guess that's what happens when you get in a food fight with a bunch of grown adults.

Chad's poor kitchen looks like a war zone.

"Need I remind you, dearest sister of mine?" Houston says behind me. "*You* started the food fight."

I gasp, spinning to face him. But since the kitchen floor is covered in spinach dip and pumpkin guts after we sort of massacred the place, I practically spin off my feet, tumbling right into Houston's arms. He grunts at the impact, and I struggle to right myself.

"Sorry," I say. "Thanks. And I did *not* start the fight! *You* threw the first seeds!"

Houston smirks, way too proud of himself for that. "I sure did. But only because you cheated."

I am not going to get into the details of jack-o'-lantern judging with my brother right now, mostly because I've barely talked to him since Jordan came clean about us last weekend. I don't want to spend what little time I get with him arguing, and we still have a lot to clean up to get Chad's kitchen back to its pristine state.

Glancing at Jordan, who is helping Houston's date, Darcy, pack up any edible food left on the table, I tug Houston into the living room. Chad is out on the porch with the woman he has supposedly fallen in love with, though none of us have seen her for more than a few seconds after she showed up out of the blue after dinner. And I'm pretty sure Micah and Fischer are busy making out in the bathroom instead of cleaning themselves up like they said they were doing. That means we're alone, at least for now.

"Hou, I'm sorry."

He frowns. "For starting the food fight?"

If only this conversation could be that easy. "Of course not for that. I'll start a fight with you any day, and I'll win. I mean for everything with Jordan. I wasn't trying to keep it from you, I swear."

His hands ball into fists at his sides as he keeps his gaze locked on a point on the wall behind me, right above my head. "I know you weren't." He's lost pretty much all of the expression on his face, which isn't going to help me judge his feelings on the matter. He's good at hiding when he wants to be. "We really don't have to talk about this, Blondie. You can love whoever you want."

I know this is a serious conversation—one we need to have—but I make the mistake of glancing down and seeing the sheer amount of food caught in Houston's tutu. The poor thing is torn in several places and barely hanging on, and there is nothing dignified about the way my twin looks right now.

I take a step back, giving myself a better view of him. "I wish I had my phone right now," I mutter, picturing the look on Kit's face if he caught sight of Houston smothered in barbecue sauce and whipped cream. Kit was already overjoyed to see how thoroughly Houston followed through on the bet from trivia night, but this mess is so much more hilarious. I'm sure my own tutu and leotard are equally trashed, but I genuinely don't care what I look like.

Houston wrinkles his nose. "Knowing you, you'd probably end up accidentally putting that picture on the internet and making me a global laughingstock," he grumbles.

He's not wrong. "Are we okay?" I ask once the distraction of his outfit has worn off. "I hate thinking I hurt you with this whole thing."

"You didn't hurt me." Tilting his head, Houston looks over into the kitchen right as Jordan bursts into laughter with Darcy. "You promise he's not annoying you?" He looks almost pained despite what he said, but at the same time I think he's come to terms with the idea of me being with Jordan. It's been almost a week, after all. "I mean, you're happy with the way things are going?"

"Of course I am. I've never met a guy who makes me feel as loved as he does." I shrug and pick at some dried pumpkin on my arm. "He helped me get my dream job."

Houston's eyes snap back to me. "Jordan didn't tell me much about the job, but you in a lab makes so much more sense than teaching. I always wondered why you left." He narrows his gaze. "Why *did* you leave the lab back then?"

I know he knows there's more to the story that I gave him years ago—he thinks I left willingly—but I'm not sure I'm ready to open up about James. So I ask my own question. "Why does Jordan keep hinting you might be done with baseball?"

That cracks his mask, his eyebrows pulling together. I expect him to argue, but his mouth stays shut. Is he really leaving the sport that has been his life for so many years?

"We don't keep secrets from each other." The way he says it almost sounds like a question.

He's one to talk. I'm more convinced than ever that he's keeping a huge decision a secret, not just from me but from himself too. He rarely hesitates—probably why he's so good at baseball—so I don't know what's holding him back with whatever this is. Doesn't he know that I can help him get through it? (I know, I know. Hypocrisy.)

"No, we don't," I say and give him as intense a stare as I can muster.

It turns into a staring contest, neither one of us willing to be the first one to spill. Something tells me Houston isn't going to crack unless I do, and we both can be a little too stubborn for our own good.

"Hey Queens, can you help me find the kitchen towels?" Jordan pokes his head into the living room right as Micah and Fischer return from the bathroom looking more disheveled than they did when they went down the hall.

I give Houston one more chance to start talking, but he keeps quiet. I turn to face Jordan. "They're in the pantry."

Jordan shakes his head. "I'm pretty sure I need your help. To *search* the pantry." He raises an eyebrow, and Houston groans.

"Darcy," he says, voice cracking as he heads toward the kitchen. "Want to help me get the cabinets clean?"

I touch Houston's arm before he passes, bringing his attention back to me. "You seem happy with Darcy," I tell him.

I expect him to smile, and he does, but there's something hidden beneath that smile. A hesitation of sorts. Maybe I can't read most people, but I can definitely read my twin, and I don't think he's as sure of his choice of Darcy as he's pretending to be. I think there's still a part of him that can't get Tamlin the reporter out of his head.

"I took Tamlin out to lunch today," he says, echoing my thoughts.

I frown. "And now you're on a date with Darcy?"

Groaning, he runs a hand through his hair and then grimaces at the food left behind on his fingers. "I'm trying to figure stuff out, but they're both..." He shakes his head, turning so he's facing me again instead of Darcy and Jordan. "I don't know what to do, Brook. It's like half of me is falling for one and the other half is drawn to the other. I told Tamlin we're just friends, but she's... I don't want to be that guy."

I wish I knew how to help him. After meeting Darcy tonight, I can tell she's really good for my brother, but I also saw the way he looked at Tamlin at trivia night last week. I don't think there's an easy answer.

"Then don't be that guy," I tell him with a shrug. "You're here with Darcy, and it's obvious she really likes you. Maybe you shouldn't mess that up for someone who's not here for the long run. I just hope no one gets hurt." I'm not sure who's in more danger—him or the women he's pursuing.

Houston nods before heading into the kitchen and scooping Darcy onto his shoulders to help her reach the top of the cabinets.

As soon as I'm alone, Jordan grabs my hand. "Everything good?"

Oh, what a question. "I hope so." And, since there's nothing I can do for Houston tonight, I decide to lighten the mood. "What were you saying about towels?"

He grins, zero hesitation as he tugs me into the kitchen and closes the pantry door behind us, leaving us in the dark in Chad's large walk-in pantry. "See any towels, Queens?" he asks, leaning in until he has me pressed against the wall. "I'd like to get to the end of this party, but if Micah and Fischer are allowed to sneak off and make out, I want my chance too."

We've been doing well all night, keeping our displays of affection to a minimum, but I'm with Jordan on this one. It has been way too long since I last kissed this man, and it's going to take forever before we get Chad's kitchen clean so we can leave.

I'll talk to Houston. Really talk to him and tell him everything. Just maybe not tonight.

"Not seeing any towels," I say breathily. I search the darkness until my hands find his torso, and then I grip his tutu and pull him closer. I'm a little bit angry that of the three of us, he's pulling off the ballerina look the best. At the same time, I'm not mad about the way the pink fabric hugs his body and gives me a great view. "But I'm thinking we should try to be thorough."

His laugh rumbles deep in his chest. "Oh, I can be thorough. Have I told you yet today that I love you, Brooklyn Briggs?"

I grin. "You have. But feel free to tell me again."

He does so with a kiss that far surpasses my wildest dreams because that's what Jordan is. He's everything I could want and more, and I can't wait to see what our future has in store.

Epilogue
Jordan

February 22

THIS MIGHT HAVE BEEN a bad idea.

"Are you sure we won't light anything on fire?" I ask for the third time.

Mateo gives me a deadpan stare at the same time he clicks on the lighter he brought. He doesn't say a word, but his expression is saying so, so much.

I fold my arms. "Well, *excuse me* for trying to be the safe one, but I'm not the one who figured out how to graduate high school next year with an associate degree. I'm sorry I don't understand basic chemistry."

He scoffs. "That's why you should stop asking questions."

Someone whistles a bird-like tune on the other side of the gate, to which Mateo responds with a lower-pitched whistle, like a secret code.

I roll my eyes as I unlatch the gate and pull it open. "Was that really necessary?"

Alejandro scrunches up his face at me as he comes into the backyard where we've set everything up. "And you used to be the fun one. Now you're just old."

Maybe it's immature of me, but I wrap my arm around his neck and drag him down toward the ground anyway, hoping to get him in a headlock. Unfortunately for me, I somehow managed to forget the fact that my little brother is a decorated Marine and way stronger than me, which means my attack ends with me on the ground in a heap. I need to stop letting this happen.

I groan. "When are you going back overseas again?"

"Hopefully never. Where's this girlfriend of yours, anyway?" He grabs me by the wrist and lifts me back to my feet. "I need to make sure she's strong enough to put up with you."

Alejandro has only been home for a few days, spending most of that time with his wife and kids (perfectly understandable). He hasn't met Brooklyn in person yet, and I'm dying for them to connect because he's the last piece to this puzzle that is my life.

But to do that, I need Brooklyn. "She's coming," I tell him. "I hope." I put Houston in charge of getting her here, and while he's been fine with the two of us dating, this might be more than he's bargained for. After all, it's only February, and a lot of people have already told me it's too soon to take this step.

But I knew back in October that I wanted to marry Brooklyn. It's honestly a miracle that I've made it this long without putting an engagement ring on her finger. For the sake of Houston's sanity—not that he has any room to talk with the way he acts with his girlfriend—and maybe out of slight fear of Brooklyn's older brother, Chad, I've been patient.

That patience is at an end.

Alejandro whistles again, this time as he takes in the yard. I left a grassy section on the side where we're standing, big enough for some lawn games if we wanted to have family or friends over. A stone patio sits behind it, leading to a built-in gas grill and dining area next to a raised firepit. Eventually, when I can afford a hot tub, it'll go over by the house, and I've fenced off a little section for a vegetable garden in the east corner. When I was searching for a house, I wanted one with mature trees, and several large sycamores run along the fence line providing shade and perfect branches for hanging a hammock or two. Once spring comes, flowers will be popping up all over the place, and I'm planning on filling the western edge with daisies once it gets a little warmer. Brooklyn's favorite.

"Okay," Alejandro says, "you might actually be good at your job."

I punch him in the arm. "What do you mean by *actually*? Why is this always such a surprise?"

Mateo chooses to answer my rhetorical question with a roll of his eyes. "You've never been a very serious person so it makes sense that you wouldn't take your business seriously either."

"Ouch." I put a hand over my heart. "Just because I'm not some genius, it doesn't mean I'm incapable of running a successful business. You should have seen me when I was in California."

"I'm glad I didn't."

I'm glad too. It's hard enough getting Mateo to look up to me as it is when he is way smarter than I ever will be, and if he thought I was too busy for him a few months ago, he would have hated me during my PR days. Over the last few months, I've dedicated time for us to get to know each other, and he's a really good kid. He could probably stand to work a few hours in the sun, though. Get his hands dirty.

Okay, maybe I'm just jealous that he gets to spend a lot of time with Brooklyn after school working the tutoring gig they set up together. When she's at the lab every other weekend, I want to claim every second of her time that I can.

Hopefully I won't have to fight for her time for much longer. I bought this house—with Houston's help—so we can have a place of our own and neither of us has to leave at the end of the night. I just have to hope Brooklyn likes it.

I pat my pocket, making sure the ring is still there. "Why is this so terrifying? Alex, were you this nervous when you proposed to Paige?"

Alejandro laughs. "Yeah. You'll get over it."

"It's not like this is your first time," Mateo reminds me, rolling his eyes again. It's his favorite thing to do with me. "You've done this twice before."

"Twice?" Alejandro asks.

I groan. "The high school prank *does not* count."

"Uh, I'm going to have to hear this story immediately."

"Later," I grumble. *Or never.* "Right now, I need to make sure every-thing is set up."

My watch buzzes, and my heart rate kicks into overdrive as soon as I read the text from Houston.

So much for double checking everything. "Mateo?"

"Locked and loaded," he says with a smirk. I really don't like the way he's playing with the lighter right now.

Can't focus on that. "Alex?"

He bows. "I'm ready to introduce myself even though I've only met this girl through video chats. Then I'll bring her back here, where you'll be waiting."

My parents are inside the house and will absolutely be watching through the window, ready to bring out sparkling cider in celebration. Assuming she says yes, anyway, though I'm not too worried. Now that Mom is in full remission and has way more energy, she and Brooklyn have become fast friends, and Mom has been hinting that Brooklyn wants this as much as I do. Hard to say if that's wishful thinking on Mom's part or not, but she is incredibly excited about this proposal.

I have to hope Houston did his job right and brought the whole Briggs crew, though I've been coordinating everything with him over text and video call because the guy is rarely in town. When he is here, he spends most of his time with Brooklyn and me, and it feels like old times but so much better.

I shake out my arms, hating this nervous energy inside me. "She'll be okay with getting engaged this quickly, right?" That's only the stupidest question I could ask my brothers when I am minutes away from asking the biggest question of my life. I already know the answer, but there's still a part of me that knows she's too good for me.

Alejandro laughs. "And here I thought you were the unbothered one. I'm going to get into position; good luck dealing with this mess, Matty."

As soon as Alejandro closes the gate behind him, Mateo wraps his arm around my shoulders. Somehow he got taller than me over the last few months, which officially makes me the smallest of my brothers. I don't like it. "You seriously need to calm down. You're making *me* nervous." Considering he's the one with the fire, that's a bad thing. "Brooklyn picked you for some reason, and she's not the kind of person who changes her mind. You don't have to worry that she won't want to marry you."

"You're right. I guess I'm..." I frown when I catch the amusement in Mateo's eyes. "That wasn't exactly what I was saying."

He shrugs, stepping away from me. "Am I not allowed to paraphrase?"

"Paraphrase all you want. That was something else."

He is definitely trying not to smile now as he ducks his head and starts fixing my display.

"Mateo, is there something I *should* be worried about?"

"Like what?"

"You tell me."

Alejandro does his low whistle again, and Mateo clicks his lighter and holds it to the large sheet of paper we prepped with potassium nitrate last night. The one I'm using to ask Brooklyn to marry me.

"Wait!" I shout, but it's too late. The message is already burning into the paper, following the path of the invisible words I painted. Only, it doesn't say "marry me" like it's supposed to.

I stare at the sheet and the words left in the holes that burned away. "Turn around?" I read out loud.

Before I can turn to question Mateo, a bag is pulled over my head at the same time someone grabs my arms behind my back and loops a rope around my wrists. My heart rate spikes as adrenaline shoots through me, and for half a second I think I am actually in danger.

But then Alejandro speaks in my ear. "I wanted to use chloroform, but Mom wouldn't let me."

"What?"

He shoves me forward, holding me up as I stumble across the lawn. We hit the sidewalk, and then two pairs of hands grab me, lifting me up despite my struggling. Wherever they're taking me, I don't want to go. Once I land in what I'm pretty sure is the trunk of a car and I'm no longer being manhandled, I start trying to free myself.

"Relax, Torres."

I freeze. "Houston?"

"This will all be over soon."

"That's not as reassuring as you think it is!" I snarl, but the closing trunk cuts me off, leaving me in silence.

I guess now I get to contemplate my life and consider finding new brothers?

As the car starts moving, I work to free my hands, though it isn't easy. Alejandro was always good at knots, and we spent plenty of hours of our childhood tying each other up and/or locking each other in small spaces. Maybe that's a strange way to bond, but it helped us get closer. Thankfully, it also helped me learn how to get free from my younger brother's knot skills, and my hands eventually come loose.

I sigh with relief and tug the bag from my head, only to find the trunk lit with a lantern. There's a duffel near my feet with a paper taped to the front that says, "Get dressed."

Swearing, I search my pockets for my phone, but of course one of my brothers took it. I would think maybe they were trying to sabotage my proposal if not for Houston being a part of this, though now I'm wondering if he's not as cool with the idea as he pretended. But why would Alejandro have anything against Brooklyn? He hasn't even met her. And I know Mateo likes her. He's the one who came up with the potassium proposal.

What in the world is going on?

"Are you changed yet?" a static-laced voice asks near my head.

I flinch, scrambling to grab the walkie talkie just behind me. "Chad? What's going on?"

"I'll keep driving until you're dressed."

I curse again. If Brooklyn's terrifying older brother is involved, I'm not getting out of whatever this is.

I don't have a lot of space in this trunk, so when I grab the duffel and open it to find a tux, I consider my options. I could struggle through changing and hope that gets me out of this cramped space, or I could refuse to comply and see if that messes with whatever plans they've made.

I click the walkie talkie to open the channel to talk again. "Where's Brooklyn?"

Chad doesn't answer, instead pushing the car a little faster. He's barely made any turns, which means we're getting progressively farther from the house. I don't like that.

I spend a few more minutes weighing my options and even consider unlatching the back seat so I can crawl into the cab of the car, though I'm not sure I want to go head-to-head with Chad. He likes me for the most part, but he's never been afraid to tell me to keep my guard up. Any missteps, and he won't hold back.

"Dressed yet?" Chad asks in his rough and gruff voice.

I sigh. I'm not going to have a choice in this. Grumbling, I kick off my shoes and start working my way into the tux, which is extremely difficult in this cramped space. I'm definitely going to come out of this looking like a rumpled mess, but at least I'll be able to leave the trunk.

I hope.

When I'm as presentable as I can be, I grab the walkie talkie again. It's not easy; at some point, I accidentally kicked it down by my feet, so I have to use my foot to shove it back up toward my hands until I can reach it.

"I'm wearing the stupid tux. Happy now?"

"Took you long enough." Chad slows the car down until he comes to a stop, and then I'm pretty sure he does a U-turn and starts driving back the way we came.

"Were you on the highway?" I ask in alarm. It's the only road he could have taken for that long, which means we're probably outside of Sun City now.

"You took forever. I told you I would keep driving." He sounds far too amused by the fact.

"Can I at least get out of the trunk for the drive back?"

"Nope."

I know better than to argue, which means I get to spend the next twentyish minutes asking myself if I really want to become a part of this family. It's a stupid question because the answer is always going to be yes, but it's fun to pretend I have a choice in the matter.

Houston has told me more than once that if I ever break Brooklyn's heart, he'll break my body. Chad told me he has enough dirt on me that he can make my life a living hell if I give him a reason. Even Micah has tossed out her own threats, which by themselves aren't all that frightening but when backed by a glaring Fischer are downright terrifying. He is Micah's opposite in every way and would probably burn the world down for her if she asked him to. Throw in Brooklyn's stepdad and extended family, and she has a whole army behind her in case I slip up.

She wouldn't need them, of course. Over the last few months, I have fallen victim to plenty of Brooklyn's pranks because the old Brooklyn has come back with a vengeance. And the crazy thing is each prank has always made my life better somehow. Like when she convinced my team to mess up the schedule one day, which meant every job I tried to do was already done before I got there, so I ended up with a down day to spend with my mom. Or when she hired a mariachi band to follow me around one day and the attention brought in some new clients because they loved my energy.

The longer I'm in this trunk, the more I'm thinking this has Brooklyn written all over it.

The problem is she would have to know I was going to propose if she wanted to get everyone in on it. Everything was supposed to be a surprise, so someone blabbed, and I can't figure out why Brooklyn would hijack my proposal and force me into a tux.

Unless...

"Nearly there," Chad says into the walkie talkie, and the car starts to slow. He takes a few turns, including three lefts in a row, and then pulls the car to a blessed stop. "Still alive back there, Torres?"

"Open the trunk and find out," I growl back.

I hear him laughing as he comes around to the trunk and opens it up, blinding me with sunshine from the setting sun. "No hard feelings?"

I take his offered hand and scramble out of the trunk, only to discover we're right back where we started, parked in front of the house where I set up my proposal. Maybe Brooklyn isn't actually involved in this? She doesn't know anything about this house.

Houston comes through the gate with a huge smile on his face, and I'm pretty sure he's trying not to laugh as he takes in the sight of me. "What, did you get dressed in the trunk of a car or something?"

The only reason I don't tackle him is because he's only a week off of his surgery to fix his shoulder, which means his arm is bound up in a sling. That, and he's wearing a tux to match mine.

I frown. "What...?"

Chad starts fixing my tux, tugging and smoothing and adjusting until he's satisfied I'm presentable. He's also dressed to the nines, though he's in a regular suit instead of a tuxedo.

"That's better," Houston agrees when Chad steps back. Then he looks at me. "Ready for this?"

I feel like I'm about to fall apart. "Ready for what?"

I don't have to wait long to find out. The Briggs boys lead me through the gate and into the backyard that has completely been transformed. In place of my little chemistry experiment is a lattice arch full of daisies. Lights are strung along the fence and overhead, giving the evening a warm glow. A table sits at the back of the yard, laden with all sorts of food and treats.

It's the chairs in the middle that steal my breath. They're full of friends and family, all of them facing the arch where my brothers wait with huge smiles.

"Is this what I think it is?" I gasp as Houston grabs my arm and tugs me into position in front of the arch. Then he stands next to Alejandro and Mateo while Chad disappears into the house.

My dad comes up to me, looking dapper in his Army Dress Blues. "Breathe, son," he says gently, straightening my tie just like Chad did. "Your mother and I are proud of the man you've become, and Brooklyn is lucky to have you."

Oh. Those are words I didn't know I needed to hear, but I can't find a reply before he takes his seat next to Mom, who's already crying. Even Brooklyn's dad is here, sitting in the far corner and avoiding eye contact with everyone. But he's *here*. That's a big step for him.

When the music starts up and everyone stands, looking back toward the house, my heart nearly stops. This is really happening.

Micah comes out first, looking radiant in a deep blue dress that reminds me of the prom dress Brooklyn wore our senior year. Jaydin follows her, wearing something so similar to the dress I picked out for Brooklyn for her date with Mark that I almost wonder if it's the same one.

Then I see her.

With her arm tucked in Chad's, Brooklyn steps out of the house dressed all in white. Her full-length dress is simple, draping loosely over her curves, with a high neckline and lace overlay with sleeves that go all the way to her wrists. Her hair is done up in elegant curls with a daisy chain crown across her head to match the bouquet she carries. She's the most beautiful thing I've ever seen in my life, and I can barely breathe at the sight of her.

She and Chad are both in tears, and I'm right there with them, though I brush mine aside so I don't miss any second of the moment as she walks toward me. Houston puts a steadying hand on my shoulder, but he's emotional too.

When they reach me, Chad kisses Brooklyn's cheek and then moves to stand on our other side, apparently to officiate.

My hands are shaking when I take Brooklyn's in my own.

"Surprise," she says with a sheepish smile.

I can barely speak. "How did you...?"

She bites her lip, cheeks blossoming with pink. "I was trying to look something up on your phone, and I accidentally pulled up your email.

It automatically opened up the confirmation for the ring, so I asked Houston if he knew what the plan was."

We both glance at Houston, who shrugs his good shoulder. "I didn't want to lie to my sister," he says.

Brooklyn laughs, still with tears in her eyes. "I couldn't resist turning it into a prank, though I'm sure your proposal was going to be really great. Micah did all the planning, and her team set it all up while you were with Chad. Are you mad?"

I can't help myself. I lean in, pressing my forehead to hers. "This is the world's best prank, Queens."

"So, you want to get married?"

"Stupidest question I've ever heard."

Chad clears his throat. "Should we proceed, then?"

I don't bother looking at him, keeping my focus on the woman I am desperately in love with. "As long as none of the ceremony involves me getting stuffed into a trunk again, I'm all for moving forward." Bring on a life with Brooklyn Briggs. Brooklyn *Torres*.

She beams. "I am so ready to move forward with you. Wait." Brooklyn glances between me and Chad. "What do you mean, *again*?"

The End

Also by Dana LeCheminant

Love in Sun City
Kiss Me if You Can (a novella)
She Likes It, Hey Micah
The Chad Next Door
Crossing the Brooklyn Briggs
Houston, We Have a Problem

The Wonder Boys
Love on Camera
Love in Writing
Love on Display
Love in Disguise

Simple Love Stories (Sweet Love Stories)
Simplicity
Growing Young
Bittersweet Brews
In Front of Me
As Long as You Love Me
Dear Dalia
Let Go

Terms of Inheritance (Sweet Romance)
Forever You and Me
Holding On to Everything
A World without You
Love, Strictly Speaking

Historical Romances
The Thief and the Noble
A Twist of Christmas (part of The Holly and the Ivy anthology)
What Dreams May Come
This Above All

About the Author

Dana LeCheminant has been telling stories since she was old enough to know what stories were. After spending most of her childhood reading everything she could get her hands on, she eventually realized she could write her own books too, and since then she always has plots brewing and characters clamoring to be next to have their stories told. A lover of all things outdoors, she finds inspiration while hiking the remote Utah backcountry and cruising down rivers. Until her endless imagination runs dry, she will always have another story to tell.